# PRAISE FOR THE NOVELS OF G

### THE BELLINGHAM BLOODBATH

"A terrific story . . . both storylines come together in perfect symmetry, making for an incredibly pleasing mystery. The author nails it yet again!"

—*Suspense Magazine*

### THE ARNIFOUR AFFAIR

"Co⋯⋯⋯⋯⋯⋯⋯⋯⋯⋯ng,

Books by Gregory Harris

THE ARNIFOUR AFFAIR

THE BELLINGHAM BLOODBATH

THE CONNICLE CURSE

THE DALWICH DESECRATION

Published by Kensington Publishing Corporation

# THE
# DALWICH
# DESECRATION

*A Colin Pendragon Mystery*

# GREGORY HARRIS

KENSINGTON BOOKS
www.kensingtonbooks.com

KENSINGTON BOOKS are published by

Kensington Publishing Corp.
119 West 40th Street
New York, NY 10018

All Kensington titles, imprints, and distributed lines are available at special quantity discounts for bulk purchases for sales promotion, premiums, fund-raising, educational, or institutional use.

Special book excerpts or customized printings can also be created to fit specific needs. For details, write or phone the office of the Kensington Sales Manager: Kensington Publishing Corp., 119 West 40th Street, New York, NY 10018. Attn. Sales Department. Phone: 1-800-221-2647.

Kensington and the K logo Reg. U.S. Pat. & TM Off.

eISBN-13: 978-1-61773-888-3
eISBN-10: 1-61773-888-3
First Kensington Electronic Edition: April 2016

ISBN-13: 978-1-61773-887-6
ISBN-10: 1-61773-887-5
First Kensington Trade Paperback Printing: April 2016

10 9 8 7 6 5 4 3 2 1

Printed in the United States of America

*For Diane Salzberg—for so very much*

# CHAPTER 1

Even with my head buried deep inside the large armoire in the second bedroom of our flat, I could still manage to hear Colin railing at poor Maurice Evans. The good man had only just received the nod from Scotland Yard that morning informing him that he had been chosen to transitionally replace his former superior, the late Inspector Emmett Varcoe. This meant that, for the time being, Mr. Evans had earned the wholly convoluted title of "Acting Inspector." It had apparently been determined that, while he might not yet be good enough to actually *be* the inspector, it was perfectly appropriate to have him carry all the duties and responsibilities therein. Which is what had brought him to our Kensington flat to suffer Colin's diatribes mere hours after the announcement of his novel sort of non-promotion. I only hoped that his paycheck had been adjusted to properly reflect the newly won hazards he now faced.

"...careless misstep..." I heard Colin scolding in between the sound of discordantly clanking metal, alerting me to the fact that he was hefting his dumbbells about even as he upbraided poor Mr. Evans. I knew it to be less an attempt to improve his physique than to assuage his own frustrations at having allowed

Charlotte Hutton to slip away before he could prove her complicity in our last case. For though she had appeared to remain above reproach throughout our investigation, she had, in the end, proved to be the mastermind behind the murder of five men and her own young son in a cruel plot to appropriate extraordinary sums for herself. And one of those men killed was Maurice Evans's superior, Inspector Varcoe.

Seizing the pair of boots I had been fumbling for, I stood up and tossed them on the bed next to the nearly filled trunk just in time to hear Acting Inspector Evans say something about *cooperation*. The word made me cringe as it was our uncharacteristic cooperation with the Yard that had led to the shooting death of Inspector Varcoe. It also levied the first black mark on Colin's otherwise unblemished record for resolving cases. So I was not the least surprised when I heard Colin rapidly fire back something about "incompetence," "foolhardy," and "bloody disgraceful." What I did not know was whether he was referring to the unfortunate Inspector Varcoe, Maurice Evans himself, or the whole of Scotland Yard.

I eyed the trunk, taunting me from atop the bed, and knew I would have to come back to it. Never mind that we had been summoned without delay to the small Sussex town of Dalwich to investigate the mutilation and murder of the abbot there. I could tell that if I didn't quickly intervene between Colin and Mr. Evans, we were bound to end up at cross-purposes with the Yard again. Giving the trunk a final guilty look, I headed out to our parlor at the front of the flat.

"... utmost respect for you and Inspector Varcoe ..." Colin was carrying on without a great deal of conviction. "But the two of you, in fact, the whole of your blasted Yard, failed to fulfill the expectations placed upon you by your constituency."

"My constituency ... ?!" Acting Inspector Evans sallied back as I came into the room, the poor man appearing as perturbed as I knew Colin to be. "It isn't as if we are elected officials. We aren't the Parliament, you know. Most of us are just trying to earn our way to a decent pension before our knees give out."

"And *that*," Colin groused, "is the first honest thing you have said this morning." He was sitting on my hard-backed desk chair curling his dumbbells as though trying to fan a fire. The poor seat shuddered and groaned as he raised and lowered the metal plates with smooth fluidity, his muscles bulging against his damp undershirt in an obvious attempt to cow Mr. Evans.

"You will forgive our informality," I muttered even though I was properly clothed. "And if you break my chair," I said to Colin, "I shall be quite bloody well peeved." I glanced back at Mr. Evans and was pleased to find him biting back a grin as I sat down across from him. "Has he even offered you any tea?"

"Stop being nice to him when I'm trying to make a point," Colin protested as he began swinging the dumbbells behind his head in a further display of his irrefutable upper-body strength.

"I'm certain your point is already well made. I heard most of it myself from the back room. Besides, I don't know why you think he deserves your grief, it's not like he was in charge of the Connicle investigation. Even now he's only managed to boost himself into some transitory sort of hinterland. *Acting* Inspector, isn't it . . . ?" I ribbed.

"Well, I'll not take the blame for Charlotte Hutton's disappearance." Colin continued to carry on as he dropped his dumbbells onto the floor and popped out of the chair. "Can we please get some fresh tea up here, Mrs. Behmoth?" he called down the stairs as he toweled his face and arms and stalked over to the fireplace. "Your Yard lost track of her, which allowed her to siphon those funds into Swiss accounts that we can't get a bloody read on. And *that* has left a stain on *my* reputation." Just saying those words caused his brow to cave in, his annoyance as fresh as if the event had just happened a moment before. "So, now I am left to set this Hutton business to rights when Ethan and I must leave in two hours' time to investigate this ghastly slaying of an abbot. A case, I might add, that my *father* has personally asked me to undertake." He turned away and stared into the fire, shaking his head from side to side.

"I'm sorry, Mr. Pendragon. I only came because I thought we could work together against Mrs. Hutton. To set that case to rights. Perhaps I was being foolish."

I was stunned by Maurice Evans's smoothness as he stared at Colin's back with grave earnestness, and wondered where he had learned to be so polished. "Work together . . . ?" Colin scoffed as he turned back around and glared at Mr. Evans, though I could see that he was enticed by the man's diffident words. "Your Yard has already dragged me into its mire, and given that we have to leave town I don't see as I have much choice." He swept one of his pistols off the mantel and began quickly disassembling it. "So, tell me, what in the ruddy hell is your Yard doing to locate Mrs. Hutton?"

"Well, ain't that a fine way a speakin' ta comp'ny," Mrs. Behmoth blurted as she reached the landing with a fresh pot of hot water and a plate of biscuits. "'E sure as shite ain't got the silver tongue of 'is father," she added as she moved to the table and re-filled the teapot with the water from her tray before setting the plate of biscuits down.

Mr. Evans snickered and I found I could barely stop myself from doing the same. "I like to think that every man has his own good qualities," he managed to say after a moment.

"The only good qualities they got is the ones the women who bring 'em up give 'em." She turned and headed back to the stairs.

"Such insight," Colin snapped at her, the pieces of the pistol he'd been working on spread out on the mantel beside him. "Thank you so much."

Mrs. Behmoth stared back from the landing, the tea tray hanging from one hand and the empty water pot in her other, her eyes fixed on Colin. "Yer welcome," she fired back before trundling off down the stairs.

Colin's expression soured as he quickly reassembled the pistol and came over to his chair to sit down. "I feel like she just took credit for the whole of my upbringing. Not that there isn't a fair amount of truth to it," he grumbled as he shoved the pistol beneath his seat cushion and leaned forward to pour us all more tea, fixing his gaze on Mr. Evans. "Ethan and I will indeed help you solve the disappearance of Mrs. Hutton and bring that ghastly woman to justice, but we will expect your lot to do your part."

A lopsided smile swept across Mr. Evans's face. "It will be an honor to have your aid," he answered at once, and I knew he meant it. "I shall propose the arrangement to my superiors at once. I am certain they will be as grateful as I am."

"And just how do you propose that we begin to hunt for this woman?"

Mr. Evans appeared to ponder the question a moment, but as he did so I caught the glimpse of a thought already well formed and knew he had come here with a specific idea in mind. "Well . . . ," he started to say, his tone a touch too solemn, "we are going to need someone to speak with the Swiss authorities. The only way I can conceive of flushing Mrs. Hutton out is to allow the Yard some latitude in accessing her accounts at Credit Suisse, which is the last place her financial maneuverings led us."

"But that will require a trip to Geneva," I spoke up. "We can't possibly do that now."

"Zurich, actually," Mr. Evans corrected, tossing me a pointed look that momentarily confused me. "Credit Suisse is headquartered in Zurich. It is easier to get to than Geneva, but perhaps a visit would not be required at all. . . ." He let his voice trail off and that was when I realized what he was up to. It wasn't Colin's help he was seeking, it was that of his father.

"I haven't the time to go to Zurich now," Colin reiterated with a frown, and I rather pitied Mr. Evans in that moment because I knew Colin would never arrive at the conclusion he was seeking. "Really, Mr. Evans, isn't that a task better handled by the Yard?"

"I'm afraid you give the Yard too much credit, Mr. Pendragon."

"Oh . . . I hardly think you can accuse me of that," Colin shot back.

"What you are *really* looking for," I cut in, anxious to lead Colin to the heart of the request, "is something of a more . . . diplomatic assist. Isn't that it?"

"Precisely." Mr. Evans practically crowed his relief. "A point of entrée with the Swiss authorities to get us started. And after that"—he smiled with an eagerness that I found disconcerting—"the two of you would be like a part of the Scotland Yard team itself."

"I don't fancy being an actual part of your team." Colin dismissed the idea as he went back to sipping his tea.

"It's just a turn of phrase," Mr. Evans delicately backtracked, waving a hand through the air, his gray eyes alive with equal parts desperation and determination. "I meant more like an adjunct of the Yard. A critical one. Like the head. You'd be like the head of Scotland Yard with access to all of the Yard's resources and information, but you wouldn't actually *be* part of the Yard. You'd be *above* it. Like . . . the head . . ." Poor Mr. Evans finally ran out of steam with a look that bordered on embarrassment.

"Do you hear yourself?" Colin asked, one eyebrow arcing skyward.

Mr. Evans shook his head and rubbed his brow before looking back at us. "I don't need to. I've been practicing this folly for two days."

It was enough to get Colin to crack a smile. "You are a cheeky one, Maurice Evans," he muttered. "Better that you should just come right out and say what you mean. That works best for me."

"Oh . . ." I cut in with a chuckle, "I'm afraid there is an endless parade of victims of your unabashed forthrightness who would disagree." I turned back to Mr. Evans. "Better you should continue your folly."

Colin slid a look of mock offense to me as he set his teacup down before settling his gaze on the acting inspector. "I suppose Mr. Pruitt is not wrong. I am hardly the man to convince a government, a corporate institution, or even a canine to alter its ways. I simply haven't the patience for it. As Mrs. Behmoth so willingly pointed out, I may be a diplomat's son, but I am not a diplomat. Which leads us to the true purpose of your visit here this morning. . . ."

"I was trying so hard to be discreet," Maurice Evans lamented.

"A sorry waste," Colin repeated. "Mr. Pruitt and I will stop by my father's estate on our way to Victoria Station. He is bound to know at least one or two of the Swiss Federal Council members. I shall ask him to lend us a hand in getting some information about Mrs. Hutton's accounts at the bank. If anyone can do it . . ." He did not need to finish the sentiment as he polished off his tea. "But as I said before, I will insist that you and your Yard do your own diligence while we are away. I find it impossible to believe that there are not some channels of diplomacy already open between your lot and the Swiss Department of Justice and Police. I shall expect you to needle the appropriate conduits to get whatever you can. Don't expect me to settle this Hutton affair and share the accolades with you Yarders unless they are well earned."

"I would not accept it any other way," Maurice Evans answered at once. "You have my word that I will be doing whatever I can to help prod the Swiss authorities while the two of you are gone. It is the least of what I owe Inspector Varcoe."

Colin flinched slightly, but I don't believe Mr. Evans caught sight of it. "Of course," was all he said.

"And just what is this case you're off to investigate?" Mr. Evans asked.

"The abbot of a small monastery was found stabbed to death in his room two mornings ago. An extraordinarily blood-soaked scene from what little we have heard. But most disturbingly we are told that his tongue was cut right out of his head. It has never been found."

"How awful," Mr. Evans gasped. "That's a hell of a way to silence a man."

"Indeed."

"But who the bloody hell would kill a monk?" He looked from Colin to me, the very thought of the repugnant deed wholly evident on his face.

"Who," Colin repeated, "and why . . . ?" He yanked out his pocket watch and gave it a quick glance. "I'm afraid we haven't the time to deliberate it as we really must be going if we are to stop by my father's on our way to the station."

"I just need a minute. . . ." I bolted up, abruptly reminded of the yawing trunk still waiting for me to finish with it. I did not miss Colin's cocked eyebrow as I hurried past him, nor his last directions to Mr. Evans as he led him downstairs.

"You will send me a telegram if you should learn or hear *anything* while we are away," he was instructing Mr. Evans, "and you will not make a move on Mrs. Hutton unless I am right beside you. I shall have your word on both things."

I did not hear Maurice Evans's reply. But then I didn't need to.

# CHAPTER 2

The cell—for that was how the priest had referred to it—was small, sparse, windowless, and scrupulously clean. The very sight of it was both astonishing and disheartening. I could not believe how austere a place it was—though I could not now recollect what else I had expected to find in a monastery—and as I scanned my eyes around the pristine little space I appreciated Colin's distress at discovering that the monks had taken it upon themselves to obliterate all signs of the horrendous murder that had taken place here only sixty hours before. The harsh tang of lemon and lye was the sole remnant of something gone awry, though for all I knew this was the standard by which this monastery maintained itself, assuming the brotherhood believed the old adage of cleanliness and godliness.

"The only crime that I can see," Colin said, his voice taut with displeasure as the three of us stared into the cell, "is that you have allowed the scene of this assassination to be so completely eradicated. And this when you say you have kept the room locked since the morning of the murder. I am . . ." He shook his head and did not bother to finish his thought, which seemed the best course of action given that we were speaking to a cleric.

"Oh no, Mr. Pendragon." Father Nolan Demetris quickly spoke up. "It was not me. I wasn't here on Tuesday. I live in Chichester and serve under Bishop Fencourt at the cathedral there. I only arrived myself this morning once we had gotten word that you and Mr. Pruitt were coming. The bishop sent me to ensure that the two of you get acclimated and access to everything you require." He hesitated before clearing his throat. "Most of the brothers here are not used to dealing with people from outside, you understand."

Colin turned to the dark-haired priest with a scowl. "Then who was it who purged this cell, and whyever was it done?"

"It had to have been one of the senior monks. Probably either Brother Clayworth, Brother Morrison, or Brother Silsbury." Father Demetris scrunched up his doughy face with evident embarrassment. He looked to be a man in his later middle years who was cursed with soft, rounded features. His frame appeared to be lithe from what I could detect of the way his black cassock hung from his curved shoulders, and he moved with a hesitancy that made me suspect he had lived the bulk of his life in deference to others. This was clearly not the type of man who aspired to anything more than he had long ago achieved. "As to why it was done . . . ?" He tilted his head sideways like a pup listening for the sound of its master's voice. "I'm afraid you will need to ask those senior-most monks at supper. I can only surmise that such a scene left unattended was too much for their sensibilities. The only reason you will have the opportunity to view the abbot's remains tomorrow is because Bishop Fencourt forbade the brothers from laying the poor man to rest. He knew an examination of the body . . ." Father Demetris left the rest of his statement unsaid, making it clear how uncomfortable he felt at the thought of Colin and me examining the remains.

"An examination of the corpse is crucial if there is no autopsy performed," Colin bothered to explain, though neither of us relished the thought of having to do such a thing.

"An autopsy . . . ?" The priest paled with a stern shake of his head. "Oh no, an autopsy would never be allowed."

"So I was informed," Colin muttered flatly as he turned back and gazed into the cell.

The diminutive space was lit solely by two oil sconces hanging one on each side wall and a single oil lamp on a small, square table shoved into the far corner of the room. The room stretched back no more than twelve feet at the very most and looked only half again as wide. Other than the little table and the homemade-looking wooden chair pushed up beneath it, there was only a single-sized bed—really nothing more than a wood-sided cot—a tall, round stand across from it upon which sat a white porcelain bowl, though its matching pitcher was conspicuously absent, and a square cutout bit of plain rug made of some sort of reed or fiber at the bedside. There were no windows, no adornments of any kind, and nothing to suggest any but the most rudimentary levels of comfort.

"This is where Abbot Tufton slept for the last ten years of his life," Father Demetris said with obvious pride.

The very thought of it astounded me. There were years I lived in meager surroundings myself, but they had been transitory at best and nothing that matched the severity of what I was now looking at. Still, to Colin's point, other than the curious absence of the pitcher atop the stand, it was impossible to tell that anything untoward had ever taken place here.

"The asceticism of these monks is startling," Colin muttered as he slowly entered the space.

"These men are Benedictine monks," Father Demetris explained. "Their devotion to God is absolute."

"So it would appear," Colin said as he gently ran a hand across the tabletop, his eyes continuously roving throughout the room.

"Once a novitiate accepts the Benedictine vows, he enters his community and, for the greater part, leaves the outside world behind. It is a profound and admirable dedication."

Colin knelt down and began studying the plank flooring in an ever-expanding arc, curling the small prayer rug back as he did so. "It is certainly bleak," he mumbled.

Father Demetris looked momentarily taken aback before finally letting a thin smile touch his lips. "This way of life is not for everyone. Even a man of faith can have his doubts now and then." He released a small sigh. "I suppose that's a part of the human condition."

"A condition, is it?" Colin said as he stood up and glanced around one last time, his eyes raking across every inch of the space as though determined to find the one speck that had been overlooked upon which the entirety of this case might turn.

"More of a curse, I sometimes think," Father Demetris responded solemnly.

His grim answer surprised me, but I kept quiet as I watched Colin snuff out the three lights before backing out of the cell, his gaze remaining intensely focused inside despite the immediate and utter blackness. The priest pulled the door shut, oblivious to Colin's vacant stare, yanking out his key and swiftly re-bolting it.

"You say this door has been locked since the morning of the murder?" Colin asked again, his brow well furrowed and his deep blue eyes marred with obvious displeasure.

"Yes," the priest answered, turning and leading us back through the stark, narrow hallway with its low ceiling pressing down upon my head. "As soon as the bishop received word of what had happened he ordered the room locked and the abbot's body preserved." He flicked his gaze sideways at Colin. "I believe his second wire was to your father."

"I only wish he had ordered the cell left untouched," Colin grumbled. "An investigation is infinitely more difficult when all signs of it have been so thoroughly wiped away."

"I am sorry for that." Father Demetris cringed ever so slightly. "You can imagine we have no protocol for such a thing. Even a locked door is entirely out of character for a monastery." He tipped a small shrug. "It feels enough that these men have not been allowed to bury their abbot. . . ."

"It is not enough when it comes to the solving of their abbot's murder," Colin fired back impolitely. I tossed him a scowl and he clamped his mouth shut even as he returned my harsh gaze.

We remained silent as we followed the priest back toward the front of the monastery. Each hallway we traversed was punctuated by only the minimum amount of light from smoke-stained glass sconces interspersed too infrequently along the way. Their thick, oily scent permeated the claustrophobic passageways and stifled the air, putting me in mind of the opium clubs I had spent too much of my youth inside. I wondered why they had yet to convert the monastery to gas. It was eminently safer than these oil lamps that continuously needed their wicks trimmed and oil pots refilled, and all I could surmise was that perhaps it had to do with their austere way of life.

We passed a small door off a side entry and, though it was closed, I could hear the low, sonorous cadence of male voices chanting some indecipherable litany from behind it. It was clear we had come abreast of the chapel. I found the tone mystical, almost other-worldly, and yet it also seemed to contain an edge of something darker, something vaguely foreboding.

"Here we are, then," Father Demetris announced in his quiet manner as we rounded the end of the hallway, turning into a slightly wider passage where the brooding ceiling thankfully lifted several feet above my head. "We shall talk here in Abbot Tufton's office until called for supper."

He swung the door wide onto the first vaguely pleasant-looking space I had seen since our arrival almost an hour before. The room was a suitable size, big enough to hold a large desk of dark, almost black wood ornately carved in a bacchanalian fashion with cherubic faces, a tendril of vines, and small bunches of grapes. A huge, overstuffed chair sat behind it covered in a deep burgundy fabric with a nap that appeared to be velvet. Facing the desk were two plain, straight-backed chairs that I was certain would be as uncomfortable as the abbot's looked inviting, and behind those sat a plaster-fronted fireplace painted dove gray that held the faces of eleven men in relief, five on one side, six on the other, that I decided must be meant to represent the apostles, sans Judas. The best feature of the office, however, were the two narrow leaded-glass cathedral windows that rose up along the opposite wall from where we stood, letting in a veritable ocean of colorful, prismatic light.

Father Demetris gestured us to the harsh-looking chairs as he settled himself behind the desk. "It doesn't seem right to be sitting here," Father Demetris said, and indeed, he did look ill at ease. "Abbot Tufton was only the second man to lead this pious brotherhood since Whitmore Abbey was consecrated thirteen years ago. His predecessor served just eight months before he was called home by the Heavenly Father, so it was Abbot Tufton who formed the community you see here today."

"Where did the abbot serve before coming to Whitmore Abbey?" Colin asked.

"Mostly Ireland. John Tufton spent time in several dioceses under several different bishops. He was highly regarded, even as a young man. He was invited to spend time in the Papal States studying under His Holiness Pius the Ninth right out of seminary. A remarkable feat for one as young as he was." A wistful sort of grin flitted across his lips. "He could have risen much higher in the church, but this was his calling. This is where he knew he belonged. Bishop Fencourt considered Abbot Tufton his monastic blessing." Father Demetris looked infinitely sad as he said the words.

"How many monks live here?" Colin pressed ahead, and I knew he had no intention of getting caught in such sentimentality.

"Thirty-three, not counting the abbot. It is a small order, but then the town of Dalwich cannot claim more than five thousand residents itself. I don't think the whole of Sussex County is even half a million."

"Still . . ." Colin gave a slight smile. "That's a fair amount of souls to save for such a small band of men."

Father Demetris shook his head. "I'm afraid you confuse these monks with missionaries, deacons, and vicars. The brothers of Whitmore Abbey do not conduct services for the public, nor do most of them have much contact with any laypeople beyond these walls. They are monks, Mr. Pendragon. They are here solely to dedicate themselves to prayer, divine contemplation, and devotion to God. They are a rare and august breed of acolyte, you see. Very few receive such a calling or are up to the challenge of accepting it if they do."

"Of course," Colin muttered with a note of irritation, and I suspected he was annoyed at having made such a fundamental error. "Have all the men who live here now been here from the beginning?"

"A good many, but not all. The church built an additional dormitory about three years ago. It can house ten additional monks, but for now there are only three brothers living there. As I said before, this is not a life for everyone."

"Quite so." Colin nodded curtly. "And are those three monks the last to join the monastery?"

"Precisely."

"How long did you know Abbot Tufton?"

"I knew John almost forty years. We spent quite a bit of time together in seminary back in Dublin. I considered him a dear friend." He released a labored sigh. "He will be sorely missed."

"Your fond memories do him fine honor." I spoke up even though I found the priest's sorrow keenly distressing. While I understood how he would miss his friend, I had thought he would be held fast by his surety of the afterlife.

"When did you and Bishop Fencourt learn of Abbot Tufton's murder?" Colin cast me an arched eyebrow as he prodded the conversation right back on point.

"We received a telegram on Tuesday, not an hour after the abbot's body was discovered. We were told that Abbot Tufton had failed to appear for morning prayers so one of the brothers had been sent to check on him." He shook his head and turned his gaze to the windows, the pained look on his face in marked contrast to the warm hues of the setting sun filtering back through. "They tell me it was a terrible scene."

"Who told you?" Colin pushed.

Father Demetris glanced back at him. "Brother Morrison and Brother Silsbury. And poor Brother Hollings, of course, the young monk who found him."

"Of course," Colin repeated perfunctorily before pressing the matter as I knew he would. "What exactly did Brother Hollings find?"

"They said the abbot was collapsed across the floor of his cell with one arm stretched out as though he were reaching for something while the very life force drained out of him. A horror," he tutted as his eyes drifted back to the leaded-glass windows. He remained transfixed for several moments before finally continuing. "There was no mistaking what had happened. Brother Hollings said the walls were so streaked with blood that he didn't even enter the cell to check on John but just turned and ran to fetch Brothers Morrison and Silsbury."

"Why them?"

"They're the senior members of the community along with Brother Clayworth. Brother Silsbury attends to the infirmary. He is not a doctor, but he is a man with some knowledge of health and healing."

"And what did they determine when they went back?" Colin asked as I hastily scribbled down the names of each monk and the information we were being given about them.

Father Demetris sucked in a rasping breath as he quickly crossed himself before answering. "Brother Silsbury noticed bloodstains across the back of Abbot Tufton's nightshirt and discovered slash marks all across it. So he and Brother Morrison rolled the blessed man over and . . ." His voice broke and he closed his eyes for a second time, his lips silently reciting something before he opened them and began again. "They said his face was covered with blood and that the front of his nightshirt was cut almost to shreds. There were wounds over his chest and neck . . ." He let his voice drift off as he shook his head and flicked his eyes back toward some distant place out the window. "I understand it took some time before Brother Silsbury realized that the abbot's tongue had been removed. Perhaps it was the amount of blood on his face; I have not asked." He abruptly looked back at Colin, his soft features heavy with his grief. "I will leave that to you, Mr. Pendragon. I simply haven't the stomach to hear anything more."

"There is no need for you to do so," Colin answered at once. "Do you know whether Brother Silsbury made any determination as to *when* the attack may have occurred?"

Father Demetris nodded slightly and wiped a quick hand across his brow. "Given that Abbot Tufton was still in his nightshirt with no covering upon his feet, it is likely he had not yet risen when the murderer entered his cell. I know John Tufton to have been a man who arose each morning at four to begin his personal devotions, so I presume that someone must have set upon him deep in the heart of the night."

"And what time do the brothers usually retire?"

"Most of them return to their cells shortly after supper. Some will pause to congregate for a brief time to discuss matters of the monastery or share evening prayers, but I believe every man has gone back to his cell shortly after nine at the latest. Matins . . . morning prayers . . . begin at five each day, so the men are up by four thirty to prepare. I am sure you are aware that idleness is the devil's tool."

"Most certainly," Colin agreed, and that was indeed a doctrine he had embraced as long as I had known him. Only sleep stilled him and even then there were times I had been clouted by a stray arm or leg. "Do the men ever gather in small groups in their cells?"

Father Demetris allowed a thin smile. "You have seen the size of Abbot Tufton's cell. Perhaps it would surprise you to learn that it is larger than the cells of the other monks. Most of the brothers have nothing more than a mat on the floor for sleeping and a woolen blanket in winter for warmth. There is no room for any such congregating in their cells."

"Then it would be uncharacteristic for one monk to go to another's cell under any circumstances?"

The priest nodded and I could tell he was puzzled by the question. "Only in the case of an emergency," he answered after a moment, "but I am not aware of any such occurrence that night."

Colin pursed his lips and nodded, and I was certain he was already weighing some possibility. "Can you tell me whether there has been any word back to the bishop about any dissension within the monastery of late? Disagreements or fractures that perhaps the abbot had sought the bishop's advice on?"

Father Demetris considered the question for only an instant before answering. "There is always the occasional harsh word or impassioned debate as with any community," he explained, "the monks here are but human. However, I know of nothing that was causing Abbot Tufton any undue concern. And I can assure you, had it been the case, word of it would not have reached Bishop Fencourt without first coming through me."

'"So you are a secretary to the bishop?"

"It is one of the duties I perform." Father Demetris nodded, and I could tell it was an obligation he was proud of.

"How familiar are you with the daily workings of Whitmore Abbey? Are you called here often?"

"Once or twice a year. But there are no mysteries to life here. As I have said before, these good monks lead a simple and pious existence."

"Yes, of course." Colin waved the priest off in a careless manner that made me wince, though I knew he was tired of being reminded of the devoutness of these men given that one of them had quite possibly committed murder. "Do any of the citizens of Dalwich have access to the monastery? Do they ever worship in your chapel or are any of them employed as cooks, service staff, or perhaps to attend the grounds?"

Father Demetris shook his head vehemently as though the very idea of it was anathema and, given the way they lived, I supposed it was. "The chapel at Whitmore Abbey is solely for the use of the brotherhood. They do not minister to the townspeople in any way nor does anyone from Dalwich work here. The brothers take care of themselves in all ways. Each monk is assigned tasks, whether that be preparing meals, scrubbing common areas, or tending the fields alongside the refectory. The care of their clothing and cells, however, is the responsibility of each individual. In fact, other than the local constable and the two men he brought with him on Tuesday, I would say that no more than a handful of the monks have ever even met anyone from Dalwich."

"I see . . ." Colin rubbed his jaw with the hint of a scowl. "And this constable, did he see the abbot's cell before the monks purified it?"

The priest shook his head. "I'm afraid not. Putting the abbot's cell in order was of paramount concern. Out of respect," he hastily added. "I trust you understand."

"I understand," Colin groused, "but it does not please me in the least. Has this constable been hanging about for the last two days?"

"I have not asked, though he did not come by today. I sent word to him upon my arrival this morning that the two of you were on your way to assist in the investigation at the bishop's request. He dispatched an immediate response that he would be by tomorrow to meet with both of you."

"How very fortunate," Colin muttered, a sarcastic smile darting across his lips. "Have there been any recent changes here?"

"Nothing at all for quite some time. It is this steadfastness of the church that is one of its most compelling attributes. God's way is neither random nor shifting. And so it has been from the moment of creation."

"I do believe I envy you the stoutness of your convictions."

"Faith is a mighty sword," Father Demetris said. "And available to all."

"Indeed . . ." Colin replied without any real fervor, and I imagined that he was feeling as out of place in this monastery as I was.

"Are you sure I cannot convince the two of you to stay here at the monastery?" Father Demetris pressed for the second time since our arrival, an idea that seemed a horror to me. "Our cells may be sparse, but they are dutifully clean and I can promise you beds rather than a mat on the floor."

Colin shook his head with what I presumed was meant to be an appreciative grin. "You mustn't trouble these good monks by having us constantly underfoot. Our presence here can only serve as a grim reminder of what has just taken place. We will be fine at the inn in Dalwich." He glanced at me. "What's the name of it?"

"The Pig and Pint," I reminded.

"Yes." Colin scrunched his face. "Not a very appealing name for an inn."

Father Demetris gave a low chuckle, the first I had heard since our arrival. "Well, it is the only place in Dalwich with rooms to let, so I suppose they can call it what they wish. Should you change your mind there is always room for you here."

"You're very kind," Colin said with the ghost of a grin that assured me we would do no such thing.

A tentative knock on the door interrupted us as a young, sandy-haired man stuck his head in and beckoned us to supper. Father Demetris thanked the young monk, who maintained a solemn façade as he pulled the door shut again. "There is one thing I would ask of you," the cleric said as the three of us got to our feet. "I would appreciate it if you would do your best to be sensitive to the routines the brothers follow in practicing their daily devotions. Those are the foundations of their lives here and the bishop is anxious for these men to return to some semblance of normalcy as quickly as possible."

"Of course." Colin gave an obligatory nod. "But you do understand that at some point these men, these monks, are going to be most grievously distressed."

The priest paused at the door and looked back at us, his hand holding the knob as though it were the most delicate fixture and liable to shatter. "Whatever do you mean?"

"Someone has slain your abbot in a most unspeakable way. You have said yourself that most of these monks have no association with the people of Dalwich. I am afraid that would tend to suggest that the perpetrator is a man who dwells here."

Father Demetris looked as though Colin had struck him, his

right hand bolting from the doorknob as he quickly crossed himself. "How can you say such a thing?" he gasped, his voice coming out harsh and ragged.

"How can I not?" Colin replied. And I knew he was right. We were about to sit amongst these righteous men, one of whom had almost assuredly ravaged one of the foremost covenants of their faith.

# CHAPTER 3

Half-a-dozen chipped porcelain platters were brimming with cut-up parts of roasted chicken, of which each monk took only a single piece. Tubs of white rice and bowls of shredded cabbage mixed with what tasted like vinegar and oil rounded out the repast, though there was also an apple alongside each monk's plate. I assumed the meager piece of fruit was to take the place of spice cake with clotted cream or fresh berry trifle, either of which I would have greatly preferred. The food was so rudimentary that I found myself pining for the slightly more exhilarating fare that Mrs. Behmoth would have rummaged up for us. While she was never going to earn herself a position in a royal kitchen, compared to the simplicity of what had been set before us this evening, our Mrs. Behmoth seemed like quite the culinary vanguard.

Colin, Father Demetris, and I were seated at the first of two long tables that looked to have room for fifty. The tables consisted of dark wood planks interlocked in an uneven pattern that stretched on for what had to be greater than twenty feet each. We were seated on benches rather than chairs, with the room's only true chair at the far end of the opposite table. While it carried no adornments or any cushion upon its seat, I was certain it had belonged to the abbot, which made the severity of its emptiness a stark and distressing reminder. It was, without doubt, contributing to the austerity of the monks' behavior this night beyond the usual solemnness we had already been encountering. For if this was truly the day's social occasion for these highly reserved gentlemen, I could see little sign of it. I had presumed at least a few of them would want to query Colin in some sort of fundamental way, but no one spoke to us and, in truth, they hardly said anything to one another, either.

Colin and I had been seated across from each other with the monks lined up to my right in their identical black tunics and cowls, free of any sort of embellishments on their clothing whatsoever. Only the differences in their hair initially set them apart until the variety of their ages and statures gradually became apparent. Still, upon first and even second glance, there was little to distinguish one from another, and it was clear this was the way it was intended to be.

Their differences became more apparent as the meal drew to a close and the monks who had finished began to stand up—plates, cups, utensils, and apples in hand—and filter out through a rear door after setting their dishes on a small table beside the exit. Though most of them left singly, those who did leave in pairs or small groups continued to maintain their silence, amplifying the oppressiveness of the meal and making me wonder if it was always thus.

When there were only five monks left at our table, Father Demetris leaned over and spoke to us in as gentle a tone as I would have expected had we been in the midst of a Sunday service. "I asked these brothers to stay behind," he explained. "I am quite certain they are the ones you will be most interested in speaking with tonight."

"Very good," Colin answered in an equally hushed tone, making me realize that he was clearly feeling as awkward in the place as I was. "Then I presume these are the senior-most men"—he turned and nodded toward a pale young monk with fiery hair sitting several places down the table from us—"and he must be the unfortunate lad who discovered the abbot's body."

"You are correct on both counts," one of the monks answered before Father Demetris could, an older man with broad shoulders and short, tightly cropped brown hair who I could tell would prove to be an unusually tall man when he stood up. "I am Brother Silsbury," he announced in a stolid tone. "I was one of the first beckoned to the scene Tuesday morning, as I run the infirmary, though that fact counted for naught, I'm afraid." He released a burdened sigh.

Father Demetris turned and acknowledged the man with a tip of his head. "You did what you could, Brother Silsbury," he said before nodding toward a rounder man with a full head of short silver hair and a pinched expression on his broad, well-lined face that either spoke of his discomfort with the topic or his dislike at Colin and me being here. I could not tell which. "Brother Morrison oversees the daily functioning of the monastery." Father Demetris next gestured toward the ginger-haired, lanky, young monk with an oval face who had to be somewhere near the middle of his twenties, though he looked quite mired in his teens. "Young Brother Hollings you have already spotted. He attends to the upkeep of our public areas and serves as an aide to Brothers Morrison and Silsbury." The priest gestured to the thin, older man to my immediate right with a shock of silvery-white hair atop a face that appeared ruddy from either too much sun or exertion. "Brother Clayworth runs the brewery. . . ."

"Brewery?" I blurted out without a second's thought.

"Oh yes," Brother Clayworth chirped right up. "We make a very fine ale that we sell to the owner of the Pig and Pint," he explained. "Mr. Chesterton carries it at his pub and distributes it to the neighboring villages on our behalf. It supplies us with what small income we require."

"Of course," Colin replied with a nod. "There are many monastic orders producing spirits for their livelihood."

"It's quite good," Father Demetris added quietly. "They call it Whitmore Ale." He pointed to the last monk sitting with us, a slender man with an angular face almost ashen in color and a thin covering of dark brown hair that was brushed back with the severity of a spinster's. "And this is Brother Wright, who tends to the gardens along the back of the monastery. Brothers"—Father Demetris spread his arms toward Colin and me—"this is Mr. Pendragon and Mr. Pruitt of London. They are the men I told you about who have been requested by Bishop Fencourt to assist in the investigation of Abbot Tufton's murder."

Colin winced slightly. "Assist . . ." he started to say until I caught his eye with a scowl. Now hardly seemed the time to quibble over his inevitable maltreatment of the local constable.

"What is the young Dalwich constable's name?" Father Demetris asked the assembled brothers.

"Lachlan Brendle," Brother Morrison answered, his craggy face shifting like stones caught in the tide's onrush. "A nice enough lad, though hardly the brightest sort."

"Now, Robert . . ." Brother Clayworth began to say, his words coming out slightly thick and leaden, making me wonder if the flush on his face might actually be the result of a touch too much of his vaunted ale.

"It is a statement of fact." The older man cut him off with the wave of a hand. "The Lord's children come in every shape and manner."

"I can certainly attest to that," Colin pronounced succinctly. "I understand this constable was muddling about the morning of the murder?"

"I suppose he was trying to do his job," Brother Silsbury answered.

"He hadn't a notion *what* to do," Brother Morrison grumbled.

"Now, Robert . . ." Brother Clayworth started to scold for the second time before Colin cut him off.

"That's as it ever is." Colin flashed a curt grin. "But tell me, when the constable showed up—a lad, did you say . . . ?—when he showed up, I am told he was unable to see the cell as it had been discovered by Brother Hollings. . . ."

"That's right," Brother Silsbury answered grimly. "I gave the order to move the abbot's body to the infirmary, and Brother Morrison instructed to have the cell cleaned at once. It was unseemly."

Colin released a tight sigh. "Murder tends to be. Unfortunately, your tidying will have obliterated vital clues."

"I really cannot say that I was much interested in such things with Abbot Tufton's dignity and legacy at stake. Do you not imagine that poor Brother Hollings here shall forever be marked by the sight that assaulted him that morning?"

"Without question," Brother Morrison agreed with a grumble. "I myself find it difficult to restrain such thoughts from the forefront of my mind. It is the reason Brother Silsbury and I forbade any of the others from coming near the abbot's cell that morning. It is the reason we set a lock upon it."

"You will find your release through prayer, Brother Hollings," Father Demetris said as he gazed down several places to where the young monk remained hunched forward, his eyes cast down.

Brother Hollings managed the slightest of nods, keeping his hands folded in front of himself and his eyes glued to his pale, interlaced fingers as though his very salvation might be found there.

"So, it was the three of you who obliterated all signs of what took place in the abbot's cell that morning?" Colin pressed much to my alarm, his gaze raking across those particular monks.

"It was Brother Hollings," Brother Morrison responded with what I was beginning to realize was his customary disapproval. "As you can see, I am an old man and hardly agile. I guarded the cell while Brothers Silsbury and Hollings moved the abbot's body to the infirmary. When Brother Hollings returned he immediately set himself to the task at hand and did a fine job." Brother Morrison glanced toward the young man. "You did a fine job, Rupert. The Lord is pleased."

Brother Hollings gave a grim sort of smile, his teeth gnashed together, before immediately dropping his eyes again, and I could not help but wonder if perhaps he hadn't been more ill-suited for such an undertaking than any of these men realized.

Colin, however, seemed to take no note of it as he continued to press the young monk. "Was there anything atop the small table in the abbot's cell when you discovered him? Paperwork . . . ? Books . . . ? A *Bible* . . . ?"

Brother Hollings twisted his face and shrugged uncomfortably. "I cannot remember," he answered with some hesitation, his voice thin and strained. "I saw him . . . I saw all the blood . . . and I ran to find Brother Morrison. I didn't even stop to see whether—" He abruptly halted and in that instant I realized the spectre that was gnawing at him.

"There was nothing you could have done for him." Brother Silsbury spoke up at once. "Abbot Tufton was deceased long before you stumbled upon his body. Your actions served you well, Brother Hollings. You must give your burden to God, for it is His to carry now."

"Yes, sir." But though his words were acquiescent, his tone remained burdened with regret.

"Must you continue to plague Brother Hollings tonight?" Brother Morrison turned to us, his great leaden face tight with his displeasure. "He has suffered unaccountably and I should think an evening of contemplative prayer will serve him best now."

Colin took a moment before he finally answered. "Yes, of course. But we shall need to trouble you tomorrow or the next day. You are a vital witness, Brother, and we would be remiss to not learn everything we can from you. There may be critical things you saw that you are not yet even aware of."

"You make it sound like witchery," Brother Morrison snapped, shifting a surly grin between his fellow monks and Father Demetris. "Go on, Brother Hollings, there is no reason for you to listen to this babble. You go and pray for your salvation. Your words will be heard."

"Thank you," the young monk mumbled as he quickly got up and left the room on ghostly silent feet.

"I should think I can answer most of the questions you have," Brother Silsbury said as he looked at us, his face grave but his hazel eyes not unkind. "I was involved in a great many of the decisions that were made when the abbot's body was discovered."

"Nevertheless," Colin insisted with a look that was more determined than accommodating, "because that young man discovered the body I *will* need to speak with him again. Especially given that he alone cleansed the abbot's cell after his body had been removed."

"It will be arranged," Father Demetris said at once, his soft voice carrying the weight of Bishop Fencourt's will.

"You are like a mongrel with a bone," Brother Morrison hissed. "We will *not* apologize for the decision to rectify the abbot's cell. We were not about to let that bloodied scene of carnage become a thing of gawking and gossip here. It demanded to be contained . . . controlled. We may be monks, but we are also mere men. So when Brother Hollings assured me that he was up to the task, I readily agreed. In fact, I believe it helped him to avoid dwelling on what he had seen by putting his distress into physical action. It pains me to see that now that a bit of time has passed, it has allowed the scourge of guilt to begin fouling his mind."

"He is young in his faith," Brother Wright put in, his voice as tight as the sharpness of his pallid face.

"It is not his faith I seek to question," Colin remarked crisply, and I felt Father Demetris stiffen beside me and knew I would need to remind Colin to tread more carefully amongst these men. "How much time do you suppose would have passed between Brother Hollings's discovery of the abbot's body and his beckoning of the two of you?"

"It would take a man of Brother Hollings's age no more than a minute or two to run from Abbot Tufton's cell to our chapel," Brother Silsbury answered.

"Did you and Brother Morrison go back straightaway?"

"Well, of course we did," Brother Morrison shot back, the scowl on his face thick with his offense.

"Forgive me"—Colin tossed him a curt nod, his lips forming a straight line—"I do not want to presume anything." He slid his eyes back over to Brother Silsbury, who appeared to have remained unperturbed. "Can you please describe for me what you saw when you arrived at the cell?"

Brother Silsbury blinked as though stung and quickly crossed himself. "There was blood on the walls and a great pool of it on the floor beneath the abbot's head. He was facedown and his right arm was stretched out as though he had been reaching for something, but there was nothing in his hand."

"Do *you* remember whether there was anything on the table in his cell?"

"I don't even remember looking at it."

"You might imagine that we were focused solely on Abbot Tufton," Brother Morrison added as though Colin was daft. "Why would we notice such a thing as that?"

Colin cast a glare at the elderly monk and I feared the extent of his flagging patience. "The pitcher from the stand in the abbot's cell is missing," Colin began again, sliding his attention back to Brother Silsbury once more. "Was it there that morning?"

"It was in pieces on the floor," Brother Silsbury said. "Brother Hollings cleared it away. We saw no reason to put another in its stead."

"Of course. And did you happen to notice whether there were any other signs of a struggle? Did it look like he had fought with his killer?"

"We are men of God, not combatants." Brother Morrison saw fit to speak his mind yet again.

The rigidity with which Colin was holding his body made me wish that I were sitting beside him rather than across the table. There was little I could do to settle him from where I sat, so I stuck my foot out and hoped it was his shin that I connected with. "Men of God . . ." Colin repeated flatly as his eyes shot to mine, assuring me that he had received my warning. "Just the same . . ." He spoke slowly and I could see he was avoiding looking at Brother Morrison at all. "It has been my experience that a person will fight when they believe their life to be threatened. That the pitcher was smashed would appear to suggest—"

"It looked to me as though it had been knocked to the floor rather than wielded for defense," Brother Silsbury cut in with noticeable delicacy. "It lay about the foot of the stand as I should think it would had it simply fallen."

"Curious," Colin mumbled, his brow furrowing a notch. "Was there nothing else? Bed linens askew . . . ? The chair overturned . . . ?"

"Nothing of the sort," Brother Morrison grumbled as though the abbot's having tried to protect himself would have been absurd.

"God save his soul," Brother Clayworth added, hastily crossing himself.

"Very well." Colin pushed himself to his feet and, with great relief, I did the same. "I think we have enough information for one evening. If you will arrange for us to view the body tomorrow morning, Brother Silsbury, you may attend yourselves to his burial in the afternoon."

"I suppose that will have to be all right," he responded bleakly.

"It isn't decent," Brother Morrison protested once more, his craggy face as grim as it was angry. "It should not be allowed." He swung an infuriated glare at Father Demetris.

The gentle priest responded with a resigned shrug. "I am afraid Bishop Fencourt has asked that we cooperate with Mr. Pendragon and Mr. Pruitt," he explained, though without the conviction I would have wished for.

"We shall be expeditious," Colin promised. "If we can meet you at nine tomorrow I am certain our examination can be completed within the hour."

"I shall expect you at nine then," Brother Silsbury agreed.

"You will need to excuse me tomorrow," Father Demetris said as he too stood up. "I must get back to Chichester first thing tomorrow, so I shall leave these two gentlemen to your care, brothers. You will look after them for the bishop?" It sounded less a question than a statement.

"Of course we will," Brother Clayworth answered for the lot of them.

"One last question before we depart." Colin hesitated at the refectory door. "Were all of the monks in services that morning? Was your abbot the only one missing?"

"Yes . . ." Brother Silsbury began to answer.

"No," Brother Wright instantly corrected, his birdlike face almost uncomfortably pinched, and I wondered if this very question was what was giving him such a bleak mien. "I was in my cell. I was taken with a migraine that morning. That is my burden to bear."

"I had forgotten." Brother Silsbury nodded, shifting his eyes back to Colin. "Brother Wright came to see me well before dawn and I gave him a tincture of laudanum, as I do whenever such spells overcome him." He turned back to Brother Wright. "You must have been quite asleep when everything happened."

Colin's forehead contracted and I knew what he was going to say as soon as he began to form the words, yet there was nothing I could do to stop him. "Did you actually *see* him take the laudanum?" he queried as though speaking to a roomful of incorrigibles.

"Well . . ." Brother Silsbury flicked his eyes to Brother Wright and it was all the answer needed.

"What do you mean to suggest?!" Brother Morrison growled like thunder, looking as if he might be about to call the Heavens down upon Colin.

"Suggest?" Colin maintained the façade of an innocent. "It was merely a question." He gave a quick nod of his head and exited the room before another word could be uttered.

# CHAPTER 4

Father Demetris took us into Dalwich in the monastery's well-worn buckboard, which was really nothing more than an open cart. Our conversation with the priest had been stilted during the first part of the journey, mostly monosyllabic and wholly uncomfortable, until Colin had finally assured the cleric that his inference regarding the possibility of one of the monks being involved in the abbot's murder was meant only to reassure the brotherhood. Whether it proved to be the case or not, he'd intended solely to let them all know that he would leave no stone unearthed in his quest for the truth. And after a few moments' rumination, the priest had seemed to settle into Colin's explanation, though I knew it had only been done to placate. What most intrigued me, however, was that this priest was one of the few men I had ever known Colin to bother placating.

The remainder of our two-mile ride proved far more pleasant, or as pleasant as anything could be given the present circumstances. Father Demetris promised to have one of the monks see us back to the inn each evening if we would make our own way out at the start of the day while they were in their morning prayers. We agreed, though I hoped this was a ritual we would not need to repeat too many times. Unfortunately, it felt very much like a lark given that we were only at the start of this case with little sense of what we were truly facing. The only things I was certain of were Colin's ability to rattle the monks and the inevitability that he would solve this case. I only hoped he would see to the end of the case long before he reached the end of the brotherhood's tolerance.

"If I don't see you in the morning before I head back to Chichester, please be sure to keep Bishop Fencourt apprised of your progress. Just send a telegram every couple days to my attention," Father Demetris instructed as he brought the cart to a stop in front of the rather woebegone-looking Pig and Pint Pub and Inn. "I will remain at your service should you need me and will return at the beginning of next week in any event."

"Very good," Colin muttered as he climbed down and pulled our trunk from the back of the wagon.

Father Demetris took a moment to gaze up at the flat, unadorned clapboard front of the Pig and Pint, its color a faded cornflower blue that had likely not seen fresh paint since my own boyhood, and sighed. "If you change your mind, you are always welcome to stay at Whitmore Abbey. You would be quite comfortable and will be left well alone unless you wish to speak with the brothers."

"We shall certainly keep that in mind." I spoke up as I reached into the back of the wagon and grabbed our valises. "But please know that we will see to the swift and precise resolution of this case just the same."

"Yes . . ." Father Demetris nodded wearily. "I just . . ." He paused again and then shook his head as though trying to dismiss an unpleasant thought. "Good evening then, gentlemen," he said, and without another word shook the reins and turned the wagon around, heading back for the monastery.

"Such strange lives those men lead," Colin said as we watched the wagon kick up small whirls of dust from the road.

"The priest or the monks?"

"The lot of them," he said as he turned toward the Pig and Pint and arched a single eyebrow. "Well . . . let's see if we can get a room here." He reached behind us and grabbed our trunk by the handle, dragging it through the open doorway of the Pig and Pint while I followed behind with a valise in each hand.

We approached a long, well-worn bar on the left side of the moderately sized pub. There was a smattering of scruffy tables and chairs dotting the central space filled with chattering people eating generous portions of common fare such as meat pies, bangers and mash, fish cakes, and pasties. Libations of all sorts were being dispensed by two young women, one dark haired and heavy with an infectious smile alighting her face and the other auburn headed and gangly with nary a smirk to be seen. The two of them were not only attending to the customers at the tables but also the flush of people huddled all along the bar.

"*My good man!*" Colin called out to the ruddy-faced, heavy-set man with a piping of white hair circling the sides and back of his head who was hovering behind the bar. He was wearing what appeared to be a permanent scowl as he carelessly swabbed out a glass with the soiled apron hanging around his waist. "I am hoping you can accommodate the two of us at your inn for an undetermined length of time."

The man set the glass he'd been smearing onto the bar before leveling a critical eye upon us. "Wot ya mean, undetermined?"

"I am Colin Pendragon and this is Ethan Pruitt," Colin answered as though that might mean something to a man in the small town of Dalwich.

The barkeep pursed his lips and crossed his meaty arms over his chest. "I didn't ask for yer bleedin' names."

Colin's smile stiffened as his eyes flared their umbrage. "Yes," he said flatly. "I am aware of that fact. But I am rather well-known in London for . . ."

"Ya ain't in London. This is Dalwich. We don't give a shite about them that's well-known in London. So wot's undetermined mean?"

"Are you givin' these two 'andsome gents a load a yer guff, Raleigh?" The thickly built woman with the perpetual smile and cascade of shoulder-length hair was standing right next to me holding a small tray with a couple of empty tankards clutched in her fists. "Ya gotta forgive 'is snarl," she said in a mock whisper, her broad face highlighted by the mischievous sparkle in her warm brown eyes. "'E ain't never learned the value a bein' nice ta people since 'e's the only one got rooms ta let."

"Ain't you got tables ta take care of," the barkeep growled, earning himself a hearty laugh from the vivacious young woman.

"Nobody ever complains about the job I do," she volleyed right back before turning her attentions fully on us. "What brings the two a you ta Dalwich? It sure can't be the people," she snickered.

"As a matter of fact"—Colin turned to the young woman with a fleeting smile that nevertheless managed to convey his appreciation for her intervention—"we are here at the behest of the monks at Whitmore Abbey. Perhaps you have heard about the bit of trouble out there?"

"*Bit a trouble?!*" the round-bellied barkeep repeated as though Colin were daft. "The ruddy abbot got himself killed. I'd call that a helluva lot more than a bloody bit a trouble."

"*Raleigh Chesterton!*" the woman shot back peevishly in spite of the obvious note of affection still evident in her tone. "Is that any way ta speak ta two men wot's come all the way from London?"

One corner of Colin's mouth twitched in amusement as he gave her a generous smile. "You are very kind, Miss . . ."

She stuck out a hand. "Maureen O'Dowd," she announced with girlish pride.

"Colin Pendragon and Ethan Pruitt."

"Spare me this rot," Raleigh Chesterton groused. "If ya want rooms, ya gotta pay a week in advance. Ya don't pay in advance and I'll give yer rooms away if I need 'em. I don't give a shite where in hell you're from."

"Yer bein' a wanker, Raleigh," Miss O'Dowd scolded again, "wot with them 'ere ta 'elp at the monastery."

Mr. Chesterton's face curdled. "I ain't runnin' a blasted workhouse. Same rule for anybody walks through that door even if it's Her Royal Missus."

Miss O'Dowd burst out in a great hoot. "Yer a right spiv, Raleigh, sayin' such a thing 'bout our Victoria. I'd like ta see the day she walks through that ratty door." She turned to us with a gleam in her eyes that was as sharp as it was full of mirth. " 'E'll give ya two rooms fer the price a one," she said with a wink.

"*Like bleedin' hell!*" Mr. Chesterton roared. "They don't pay fer their rooms and I'll take it outta yer wages."

Maureen O'Dowd released another howl of laughter. "Then you'll never get yer money with the shite wages you pay."

"Get back ta work," he growled. "Annabelle looks about set ta toss her biscuits out there by herself."

Miss O'Dowd barely looked back over her shoulder before stating, "She's doin' fine. It's *you* wot gets 'er in a state." She leaned across the bar and stuck a hand out. "Now gimme the keys fer these fine gentlemen and I'll show 'em to their rooms right quick. Ya won't 'ardly even know I'm gone," she added with finality as she slid her tray onto the bar top. "Any a these blokes get outta 'and fer Anna and you get yer arse out there and 'elp 'er. It'd do ya some good ta get out from behind there anyway. Yer gonna get yerself stuck back there one a these days," she chortled as she reached over and poked a finger at his bulging gut.

"*Hey!*" He swatted at her hand. "You got no room ta talk," he sneered as he tossed his chin toward her ample frame before settling his glare back on Colin and me. "You *still* gotta pay in advance or I *will* give yer rooms away if I need 'em."

"We will only need one room," Colin answered. "We are accustomed to sharing and that way you shall have plenty of extra space when all the impending travelers you seem so concerned about finally come flooding through your doors begging for a place to stay."

Miss O'Dowd clapped her hands with a screech of laughter, though it was evident that Mr. Chesterton was not likewise amused. "Rooms have only got *one* bed. So you'll be needin' two jest like I been sayin'," he snarled with the conviction of a man who knows he has the final word. "And you can pay fer 'em *both* in advance."

"It's fine," I hastily cut in, stepping forward and pulling some coins from my pocket. "A week in advance for two rooms then."

"Yer a right pip, Raleigh," Miss O'Dowd chuckled, shaking her head with that ever-present grin of hers.

"And yer a loudmouth," he huffed back as he swept the money out of my hand before sliding two slightly bent and pitted keys across the bar. "Welcome ta the Pig and Pint," he grumbled, shifting his scowl back to Maureen O'Dowd. "And don't you dally takin' them up 'cause I ain't waitin' on no feckin' tables."

Miss O'Dowd waved him off with a snort. "I'll be back before you can finish smearin' them glasses you're so busy foulin' up." She reached out and snatched the two keys off the bar. "Come on, gents," she said with the enthusiasm of someone on the verge of a whirlwind holiday, "let me show ya wot ya got yerselves into." She loosed another satisfied chuckle as she started for the back of the bar.

Mr. Chesterton frowned as he held the glass he'd been working on up to the light. "It's frightful," Colin spoke up, leaning in toward the man.

"I'll get it bloody clean," Mr. Chesterton snapped back.

Colin raised a single eyebrow. "I was referring to the abbot's murder."

Mr. Chesterton glared back at Colin. "Wot's it ta do with me? Long as I get their ale every month, I don't give a good piss wot that lot does. Maybe they oughta keep at each other 'cause it's already got me two rooms booked." He gave a harsh snicker, pleased with his own joke, before ambling off to the far end of the bar.

"Ya mustn't mind Raleigh," Miss O'Dowd said when we caught up with her in a hallway just off the back of the bar. Colin had our trunk balanced on one shoulder while I trundled along with the two valises. "'E's jest sore 'cause 'is wife went off ta visit 'er sister in Cornwall 'bout a year and a 'alf ago and ain't never come back."

"That's terrible," I agreed.

"Thing is . . ." She didn't seem able to hide the snicker that was rippling up from her ample bosom. "'Is wife ain't *got* a sister in Cornwall." And now a laugh burbled out of her, but even so it managed to sound neither mean nor derisive. " 'E'll warm up ta ya. You'll see."

"We shall live for the moment," Colin groused from behind me.

"Yer funny." She tossed back a beaming grin as she started up a dark, narrow staircase off the short hallway we'd been navigating. "It must be so excitin' livin' in London. All them fancy people toddlin' everywhere and always somethin' wonderful ta do. I've dreamt me 'ole life a goin' there." She cast another grin back at us. "Me betrothed is gonna take me ta live there as soon as we're married." She pressed a single finger to her lips. "Ya can't tell no one. We ain't told Raleigh yet and 'e's gonna burst a bollock when we do."

"When are you to be married?" I asked.

"Soon . . ." she answered vaguely, though I would swear I caught something of a gleam behind her eyes. "One a yer rooms is at the back a the building and the other looks out onto the street in front. There's only one WC, but with you two bein' the only ones 'ere right now you won't 'ave any problem gettin' ta use it. It's right across from the room at the back if that makes any difference 'bout 'oo stays where."

"Which one is closer?" Colin huffed against the compounding weight of the trunk.

"The one up front." She reached the top of the stairs and veered off to the right.

"Let me help you," I said, scuttling back behind him as soon as he stepped onto the landing.

"Just get this blasted thing off my back!" he groused.

I grabbed the strap on top and we lowered it slowly to the wooden floor, its heft catching me by surprise. "Why didn't you ask for my help?"

"You were too busy carrying on about getting married and moving to London . . ." he grumbled, rolling his shoulders backward and forward. "But I'm sure as hell not carrying that damn thing back down. When it's time to leave I'll pitch it out the bloody front window first."

I started to laugh, but as he began dragging it the short distance to the open doorway Miss O'Dowd was standing in front of, I rather believed him.

"It may not be The Cavendish," Maureen O'Dowd said with a grin, "but it's clean."

I gave her a smile as I stared into the room that looked nearly the same size as the monks' cells. "Thank you . . ." I mumbled, hearing the surprise coloring my voice.

The bed it contained defined its size. There was a single side table wedged between the side of the bed and the wall that held a ceramic pitcher and bowl, both of which looked well used based on the number of chips on their respective rims. The only other piece of furniture was a slim wood chair stationed at the foot of the bed that undoubtedly belonged to some long-defunct dining set. The room was so diminutive that it was physically impossible for someone to sit on that lone chair unless it was turned sideways to provide room for a person's knees between the chair, the bed, and the wall. Two gas sconces hung above the bed, one listing toward the room's only window on the far wall and the other badly scorched across its face.

"Yer other room is about four doors down on the other side a the stairs. Right by the WC. Ya can't miss it." She gave a sideways smirk and I wasn't at all sure whether her comment was relevant to finding our other room or if it was some veiled warning about the WC.

"Might we trouble you at some future point with a few questions about the monks at Whitmore Abbey?" Colin asked.

"Whenever it pleases ya." She gave another of the hearty smiles that illuminated her entire face. "But I really don't know much about 'em. I don't think they like women, ya know? The ones I seen don't 'ardly look at me, let alone talk ta me, and I just ain't that scary." She laughed. "Why don't ya come down and try a pint a their ale. I'll clear a table for ya, don'tcha worry 'bout that." She gave us a wink. "Will ya come back down?"

"How could we say no to an offer like that?" Colin grinned.

"I'll keep an eye out for ya," she said with more enthusiasm than I thought we deserved, and was gone before either of us could say anything more.

"I'm not at all sure this is one whit better than the monastery," I muttered from my spot just inside the door.

"I'd say Miss O'Dowd herself is a vast improvement. She almost makes that Mr. Chesterfield palatable," he said as he kicked the door shut so he could slide the trunk into the corner behind it.

"Chesterton," I corrected.

He waved me off indifferently. "We shall leave the trunk here for the duration." He unlocked it and shoved it wide and I was amazed to see that there was just enough space to maneuver past it as long as one turned sideways first.

An abrupt knock on the door made me swivel around in the compact space. "Is that you, Miss O'Dowd?" I asked as I opened the door to a pretty, young woman in a gray smock with black hair tied up tightly at the back of her head.

"I'm yer chambermaid, Dora," she answered with a ready blush, and I suddenly felt as though I had been caught doing something untoward. "Mo . . . Miss O'Dowd . . . asked me ta bring some water up fer ya." Sure enough she was cradling a large pitcher of water in her hands and sloshed it tenuously, but without spilling a drop, as she gave me a quick curtsy.

"Very good," Colin spoke up from somewhere behind me.

"Oh!" She looked surprised and I realized she had not noticed him.

"Why don't we get out of your way then," Colin said as he squeezed past the open trunk. "Please get some water up to Mr. Pruitt's room as well, won't you?"

"Yes, sir." She curtsied even deeper this time, once again managing to do so without splattering so much as a drop of water.

I was happy to scuttle past the bashful young woman and get back downstairs to the exuberance of the tavern crowd. Pints of honey-colored ale were being raised and drained as quickly as the ever-beaming Miss O'Dowd and her auburn-haired companion could hand them out. Nevertheless, the instant Colin and I stepped out of the back hallway I heard Miss O'Dowd holler to us from the table where she was passing out a half-dozen ales to a tableful of rowdy blokes.

"*Mr. Pruitt! . . . Mr. Snapdragon!*" she called with a wave of her free arm. "*Over 'ere!*" She turned in a single fluid motion to a small nearby table where two scruffy young men were seated next to a door that I suspected must lead out to the kitchen. As we headed toward her she smacked one of the men on the shoulder and shoved them both out of their seats. "Go on 'ome, ya buggers. We got a couple a fine gents come all the way from London. I ain't 'avin' 'em stand around."

To my surprise the two men moved off without a word, minding Miss O'Dowd as though she were their headmistress.

"You really needn't have done that," I said when we reached her.

She grabbed their used glasses and wiped the table with a singular swipe that spoke of too many years of practice. "Don't trouble yerselves over them. They don't need a table and chairs ta get pissed. Besides, their wives'll thank me if they get 'ome early fer once. Or maybe they won't." She let out a raucous laugh. "Two Whitmore Ales?"

"If you please," Colin answered with a smile. "And it's Pendragon."

She tossed him a curious look. "Wot?"

"My name. It's Pendragon, not Snapdragon."

"Ah . . ." She laughed. "I ain't good with names." Her smile widened as she got a pixie's twinkle in her eye. "And do ya remember *my* name?"

Colin's grin widened as he stared back at her. "However could I forget the delightful Maureen O'Dowd?"

Miss O'Dowd beamed her amusement at being thusly dubbed. "I'll jest bet ya got a swirl a ladies back in London waitin' in line for you ta pay 'em a bit of attention like that."

"Oh"—Colin lifted his eyebrows and gave her a mischievous grin—"you *would* be surprised."

She let loose another hearty laugh. "I'll fetch yer ales," she said, leaning in suddenly and giving a conspiratorial wink. "And the first one's on the 'ouse." She lowered her voice. "Don't tell

Raleigh." And with a merry chortle she was off, swallowed up by the crowd in a flash.

"I like her," Colin chuckled.

"And it would seem she is equally enamored of you, the poor girl."

He laughed outright. "How you cut me."

"Never mind that. What do you make of those monks?"

"Ah . . ." He leaned back in his chair, his eyes clouding. "I appreciate that they have suffered a terrible and shocking loss, but they really do seem like such a grim lot."

"They're monks," I reminded, "not circus chimps."

Colin rolled his eyes just as Miss O'Dowd swept back and slid two pints onto the table. "Here ya are. Some a the Lord's better ale," she said, giving us an impish grin before charging back off with her tray full of pints artfully balanced in one hand.

Colin immediately snatched up his mug and downed a healthy swallow. "Wheat," he announced as he licked his upper lip.

"Pardon?"

"The brewing. They use wheat, not hops. It's rather like a German Hefeweizen. Brother Clem . . ." He hesitated.

"Clayworth," I supplied.

"Yes, he has much to be proud of." He toasted my glass and took another sip.

"I'm glad you're pleased with their ale-making talents, but I would much rather hear what you're thinking after our discussion at the monastery tonight."

"Thinking . . . ?" he said before he tipped his pint back and took another swallow. "We have spent all of about three hours with them thus far. What should I be thinking?"

"Surely someone has caught your attention," I pressed, not believing him for a minute.

He gave a small shrug as he drained his pint.

"Very well," I grumbled, shoving my unfinished pint away from myself with a frown. "I think I've had enough for one night. Are you ready to retire?" I dropped a generous handful of coins onto the table for Miss O'Dowd.

"I am." He stood up and stretched before following me through the doorway at the back of the pub.

"I hope it won't be too noisy," I carped as we trudged upstairs.

"We'll stay in the room at the back. That should be quieter," he yawned.

"What?"

"The room at the back," he repeated as we reached the landing. "We'll stay there. It's bound to be quieter than facing the street."

"What are you talking about?" I continued as he followed me to the room at the rear of the building.

"Am I speaking a foreign language?" he queried impatiently as we went into the miniscule room and he slipped off his jacket and vest.

"You can't stay here." I bothered to state the obvious as I too began to undress before washing my face and hands in the bowl the young chambermaid had brought up earlier. I dried my face on the folded towel set nearby and turned to find Colin stripped to his undergarments.

"Whyever not?"

"This is a small town, Colin. Mr. Chesterton already said—"

"That man's an old sot." Colin yawned again as he stripped off his undershirt and began to wash up. "I'm not sleeping alone because of him. You're worrying about nothing."

"It's not just him," I reminded. "It's the law. We could end up in jail. Look what they did to Oscar Wilde this winter."

"We're not aesthetics!" he snapped with finality as he dried himself before peeling the rest of his underthings off. "They have no reason to view us with suspicion. We'll simply wake up with the first light, and before that silly chambermaid comes scampering about we'll go and muddle the bed linens in the other room. She'll believe I've spent the night there because she has no reason to suspect otherwise. Now stop fussing." As if to prove his point he threw the covers back and climbed into the bed. "Get in here. I'm cold."

I wanted to continue to protest. Somehow it seemed as though that was the right thing to do. Yet as I glanced at him, his eyes shut and one arm stretched across the bed waiting for me, I began to lose my will. After all, he was right, the two of us were nothing like Mr. Wilde and his young fop, Lord Douglas. For discretion marked our every move outside of our home. We did not flaunt our bond as Mr. Wilde had so brazenly done. To do so was not only unseemly, but risked courting the very sort of censure that had garnered Mr. Wilde two years of hard labor. The poor man would be lucky to live through such a sentence.

It was folly to disregard the tenets of decorum, which is why Colin and I so closely guarded the true nature of our partnership. And because of that fact I realized that he was right. If we took care to disassemble the other room each morning there would be no reason for anyone here to imagine anything untoward. And so, after a brief final consideration, I finally released my internal debate, turned down the gas lamp, removed the last of my clothing, and crawled into bed beside him.

# CHAPTER 5

⟐

The cloying scent struck me with a familiarity that I could not at first place.

Colin and I were standing just inside the Whitmore Abbey infirmary, a compact building set a short distance behind the main monastery at the edge of the wheat and barley fields that stretched out beyond it. The infirmary was painted the same dusky white as the main structure and also had a roof of thick, deep, yellow thatch that sagged in spots and appeared thinner in others than would truly seem needed to effectively banish the outdoors from within. Only the monastery's small chapel had an actual tile roof, clearly defining that which the monks, indeed the church itself, believed most valuable.

Our morning had progressed exactly as Colin had said it would. We dressed, I disheveled the bed in the other room, breakfast was dispensed with all due haste, and we managed to complete the trek to Whitmore Abbey in a brisk twenty minutes. The last feat was as much the result of Colin's relentless pace as the mostly flat terrain. All of it, I understood without Colin's having to say it, had been undertaken to ensure we got as much accomplished as possible before the local constable showed up.

Carbolic acid, I suddenly realized. The sweet, tarry smell underpinning the small infirmary was the disinfectant carbolic acid, though there was also a twinge of alcohol beneath it. But what took another moment for my nose to discern was a sort of tainted sting that seemed to hover just along the periphery with a familiarity I could not yet name.

Three empty beds were lined up along the wall to our right, all made as crisp and concise as if by a military troop. A tall side table stood beside each of the beds atop which sat a single oil lamp and a white ceramic pitcher and bowl. Once again I found it curious that while the decision had been made to sequester this building, they still had not bothered to equip it with gas. I wondered if they would ever adopt the new electricity.

"*Hello . . .*" Colin called out. There were several doors on the wall to our left and opposite us, making it seem that Brother Silsbury could be anywhere.

Before either of us moved farther into the main room the door on our immediate left swung wide to reveal Brother Silsbury's towering form as he stepped out of a small office. "Gentlemen . . ." He gave a polite bob of his head as he pulled the door shut behind himself. "I will be glad to have this regrettable task swiftly concluded. I am ill equipped to store human remains, which has left our beloved abbot unsuitably treated." He quickly crossed himself.

"I understand," Colin answered in a rather perfunctory way, and I suspected it was because these monks seemed more concerned about the protocol of the situation than in ascertaining who had left the poor man thus.

"Very well," Brother Silsbury responded in a tone that did not hide his distaste for what we were there to do. With a stifled sigh he turned and headed for one of the doors along the back wall. "I have had hundreds of pounds of ice brought in to try and contain—" He waved a hand beneath his nose but did not finish his sentence.

As he did so I finally recognized the cause of the sticky tang permeating the air. Walking through this infirmary was no different than being in Denton Ross's deplorable morgue. I was surprised that I had not identified the cloying scent at once, but as we neared the specific door, the growing stench of putrefaction mixing with the prick of alcohol and carbolic acid, I felt my stomach starting to roll.

"I appreciate the sacrifice you and the other brothers have made," Colin allowed. "There is an extraordinary amount to be learned from both the murder scene and the victim's body."

"You misunderstand, Mr. Pendragon," the monk clarified, his tone grim. "This was not a sacrifice but an order."

He swept the door open and led us into a small, windowless room about half the width of the building and no more than a dozen feet deep. A single rectangular table stood in the center of the room that appeared to be an old dining table that had been mounted on outsized legs to bring it to a more comfortable height for working on whatever was placed upon it. In this instance it was clearly the body of their abbot; the telltale protrusions of the forehead, nose, chin, shoulders, belly, knees, and feet unmistakable beneath the covering sheet. There was a patchwork of deep umber streaks littered across the front from the neck to the midsection with only the lowest part of the abdomen and legs appearing to be thusly unadorned. Yet it was the area around the lower part of the face that had clearly borne the most severe damage, a great swath of dried blood having saturated the thin fabric there.

"Be careful," Brother Silsbury muttered from his position at the door. "His body is resting on ice and, as you can see, it is melting faster than I can get more fetched. All manner of fluids have drained to the floor and made quite a disagreeable slurry."

"We shall make quick work here," Colin reassured again, and I knew quick work was all that either of us could tolerate given the sharp air.

"Thank you," Brother Silsbury murmured. "Then I will leave you to it. Call me if you require anything." He took an unsteady step backward and pulled the door shut, making me only too aware that the only fresh air leaking into the room had now been shuttered out.

"Shall we?" Colin spoke low and taut, his face appearing every bit as dour as Brother Silsbury's had been.

I did not bother to answer as I watched him move toward the

body with a determination I simply could not match. There was little more I could even convince myself to do beyond continuing to stare at the covered form while desperately trying to conceive of any way to delay the inevitable. Yet such is the very definition of the word *inevitable* that I finally forced myself forward even as I considered why this aspect of an investigation never got easier.

Colin slowly peeled the sheet back from the abbot's face and did not stop until the body lay fully revealed. Abbot Tufton had been a plump man of late middle years, with a full head of silvery hair. His eyes, thankfully, had been drawn closed and his skin was pallid and chalky. But where normally I would have expected to see a demarcation of bruising along the lowest portion of his body lying against the table—a product of his blood pooling as his heart ceased to function—there was almost no sign of it.

"What a sight this must have been for Brother Hollings," Colin said under his breath. "The abbot clearly lost an immense amount of blood during the attack given how little is left to accumulate along the back of his body. No wonder that young monk remains so aggrieved." He leaned in over the abbot's face, peering closely, and then quite suddenly reached forward and pried open the man's jaw. "Oh . . ." He drew the word out even as he pulled back with a slight jerk.

"What?"

"His mouth . . ." he started to say as he gestured toward the abbot's mouth. "I cannot recollect what I expected it might look like to have his tongue removed, but I must admit it is rather worse than I imagined. . . ."

While I did not relish seeing the sight, neither could I stop myself from leaning over and glimpsing inside. The mouth was caked with blackened blood and it was obvious at once that something was dreadfully wrong. Still, it took a moment to realize that the tongue was not nestled against the bottom jaw where it belonged, leaving a gap that was as shocking as it was unexpected. Even so, it took another moment to spot the nub of flesh that had dropped far back into the throat that, in spite of an angry red incision, looked as though it had been carefully filleted.

I stumbled back a half step before catching myself and forcing a deep intake of breath. "It's awful," I heard myself say.

"That it is," Colin mumbled agreement. He had moved across from me and was bent over the abbot's neck and shoulders, running his fingers over the areas, both of which were covered with a veritable jumble of slash marks. The monk's chest, arms, upper abdomen, and right side were equally marred, and while I assumed the left side would be as well, I did not immediately advance to see. "Here"—Colin waved to me as he continued to peer at several of the neck wounds from a distance of mere inches—"count these wounds. I want to know how many there are."

The thought of it made me blanch, but I was glad Colin had not noticed. It wouldn't have altered his request anyway. I quickly swiped at my nose and then wished I hadn't as a fresh wave of stink assaulted me. It was enough to make my head go light and I had to flick my eyes up to the ceiling for a moment until I could gather my wits again. I could do this, I scolded myself.

The slicing wounds started just below the jawline with most of them occurring on the sides of the neck. There was only one, in fact, that was on the throat itself, coming very close to the Adam's apple without actually touching it. I started to count the wounds, trying to convince myself that the thin black lines had been drawn on with charcoal.

Working slowly, I progressed down the right arm and side, counting to twenty-three, before having to step around Colin, who was now studying the right hand so intently that someone unaware might have thought he was pondering whether the abbot might have held the knife himself and delivered the blows. I moved back around to the other side of his chest, adding up the marks across the abdomen before beginning to inspect the left arm and side. Curiously there was far less damage there, yet even so, I had nearly reached fifty by the time I leaned back and stepped away from the body.

"What do you have so far?" Colin asked as he released the abbot's right hand, his brow tightly knit.

"Forty-eight."

He shook his head. "Help me roll him up so we can see his back."

"His back?!" I blurted without thinking. Of course he would want to see the monk's back.

Colin did not respond, nor did I expect him to, as I went over and stood beside him. Stealing a quick intake of breath, we rolled the body away from us and I was glad to find that it moved more easily than I had expected. Without having to be told again, I leaned forward and resumed counting the hash marks across the back, neck, and shoulders of Abbot Tufton. Colin was poking around the upended right side, but as I was too focused on my own work I could not tell what had caught his attention this time. It was only after I heard the hushed swing of the door behind us, followed by an abrupt gasp, that I stopped my counting.

"*What in the name of the Holy Father are you doing?!*"

"Examining the body," Colin replied flatly as he nevertheless signaled me to lower the abbot back down. "It may not appear to be a reputable duty, but I can assure you it is quite critical."

"Nevertheless, it *is* unseemly." Brother Silsbury reiterated the charge from the night before. He quickly came forward and snatched up the sheet that Colin had carelessly bunched up at the abbot's feet. "Abbot Tufton was a highly regarded man in this monastery," he explained, his voice taut and brittle. "I cannot condone this sort of pawing about his remains. I'm sorry, but I cannot." He tossed the sheet over the midsection of his abbot's body. "He would not want it."

"We mean no disrespect," I said before Colin could reply.

Brother Silsbury's face was ashen and very much distressed. "Please tell me you are finished here."

"We are." Colin spoke up, his tone as smooth as ever. "We have learned a great deal. Thank you."

"Good." The relief was immediate on Brother Silsbury's face. "Then perhaps all of this"—he waved a rigid hand toward the abbot's body on the table—"will have served some purpose."

Colin nodded grimly. "Rest assured that we are already drawing nearer to the perpetrator of this horrendous murder. I believe we shall see a resolution within the week."

Brother Silsbury looked stunned. "Then I owe you an apology, sir," he said stiffly, "for I confess I did not think such a thing possible."

"You must have faith," Colin answered wryly. "And you may be certain that I will not fail the brothers of this monastery, no matter the outcome." He gave a curt nod and exited the room before Brother Silsbury or I could respond in any way.

# CHAPTER 6

A fair-haired monk who looked to be in his late twenties with a trim shape, compact features, and an expression about as welcoming as any we had yet seen sat across from us in the well-stocked library. Brother Morrison had brought us here to introduce us to the monastery's librarian, Brother Bursnell.

"I am hoping you might be able to give us some information," Colin was saying. "Is this an appropriate place for us to speak . . . ?" he asked, sliding his gaze around the otherwise unoccupied space.

"As you can see," Brother Bursnell answered with a congenial nod, "you won't disturb anyone here today. I seldom get many visitors. Sometimes I think I do my job more for posterity than any daily usefulness," he added wistfully.

Though that may have been the case, this was the largest single room we had yet visited in the monastery with the exception of the refectory. Bookcases hugged the four walls from the floor right up to the low-slung ceiling, and there were half-a-dozen rows of shorter bookcases that rose to a height of some five feet arrayed all around the large, rectangular oak table that we were sitting at in the room's center. The table had a dozen chairs pulled up around it and, given its well-worn appearance, I presumed that many a gathering had taken place here in spite of Brother Bursnell's contention.

"I shall leave the three of you to it," Brother Morrison muttered in his usual way. He started to leave and I noticed that he limped slightly, causing him to favor his right side. When he reached the door he turned back and added, "I was much heartened by your intention to conclude your investigation within the week." But I did not think the gruff, elderly man sounded in the least bit heartened. "It is important for the lot of us to return our attentions back to God's work. It is who we are. It is why we are here. Our abbot would wish it so."

Colin's expression remained steady, though I caught a flicker of displeasure charge across his eyes. "Of course."

"After all, you would be wise to remember that justice belongs to God alone."

"Ah"—Colin flashed a tight grin—"I thought God attended to those who attend to themselves."

"That is not Scripture, Mr. Pendragon," Brother Morrison grumbled. "It is moralistic tripe used to exonerate otherwise inappropriate behavior. Please do not misconstrue my great affection for Abbot Tufton with my commitment to God and this brotherhood. For I can assure you that I do not confuse the two." And having said his piece, he pushed out into the hallway, letting the door snap shut firmly in his wake.

Colin pursed his lips and glanced back at the young monk, whose pale complexion had flushed noticeably during the exchange. "I do seem to rile that man," Colin noted casually, "and without even meaning to."

I wanted to laugh but managed to hold my tongue as Brother Bursnell spoke up. "You must forgive Brother Morrison his resoluteness. He has been in service to the church since boyhood, and I believe this dreadful murder has left him more adrift than any of us."

"Since boyhood?!" Colin repeated with astonishment as he plunged a hand into his coat pocket and extracted a silver crown. He immediately began flipping the coin back and forth across the back of his right hand with the dexterity of a juggler. "Are you telling me he became a Benedictine monk while just a lad?"

Brother Bursnell's eyes followed the twirling coin with some measure of shock before he looked up at Colin. "What are you doing?"

Colin stared right back at him, failing to register the monk's reference for a moment before suddenly glancing down and quickly sweeping the coin into his palm. "This?" He held the shiny coin up between thumb and forefinger, a crooked grin alighting his face. "It's just a silly habit I picked up in school. I suppose it helps me concentrate. I can't say I'm even aware that I'm doing it half the time."

"Money is the devil's tool," Brother Bursnell stated solemnly. "We do not permit its use here in the monastery. What little we earn through the production of our ale is kept in the abbot's office. It is only dispersed if one of us is going into Dalwich to purchase necessities we cannot otherwise provide on our own. To see you tossing it so casually about . . ." He shook his head with an awkward grimace.

Colin's expression congealed as he quietly slid the coin back into his pocket. "Forgive me. . . ."

"You couldn't have known," the young man said with a brief smile. "I know we are not the easiest to understand. And those who have been devout the longest—Brothers Morrison and Clayworth and Silsbury—are often the least tolerant. I only hope you will forgive us our zealotry."

"I would be a fool to begrudge you your convictions," Colin answered briskly, allowing a thin smile. "And I must also admit to being surprised by the volume of books and manuscripts you have here. Surely it must be a great deal more than strictly theological."

Brother Bursnell nodded and I thought he was pleased by the question. "You are spot-on, Mr. Pendragon. We keep all manner of writings here. Educational, fine art, historical, scientific, some literature, and, most certainly, theological. We expect the brotherhood to be well-learned and mean to keep them that way. After all, a devotion to God does not preclude a quick and erudite mind."

"I commend you for such insight. Now, what were you telling us about Brother Morrison? That he has been with the church since he was a boy . . . ?"

Brother Bursnell nodded again, his youthful face belying a maturity and intelligence that was evident in his eyes. "He began his training at thirteen and became a novitiate four years later when he moved to Derry. I believe that's where he met Abbot Tufton. They attended seminary school together. Father Demetris was there as well. The three of them go back quite a long way."

"And Brother Silsbury? Is he likewise as extensively embedded?"

Brother Bursnell gave a soft chuckle. "You make it sound as though we are affixed in a setting like the colorful shards of glass in the chapel windows."

"Well, it *would* seem you are all permanently placed, though the perpetrator of this murder will undoubtedly find himself excised at the end of this."

The young man winced. "I have been praying that you will *not* find the hand of one of my brethren in this travesty."

"Nevertheless . . ." Colin's lips pulled taut and I knew what he was going to say. "You must prepare yourself for the possibility. We have been told the monastery is self-sufficient with only Mr. Chesterton allowed to make regular visits for the procuring of your ale."

"There is also Mr. Honeycutt." Brother Bursnell spoke without thinking, his face instantly going ashen. "Of course, I don't mean to imply that he had anything to do with the abbot's murder. . . ."

"Who is Mr. Honeycutt?"

"George Honeycutt. He's a local farmer who brings us deliveries of milk and eggs several times a week. He, and sometimes one of his sons, drops them off near the kitchen while we are at matins. I've met him a time or two. He's been coming as long as I have lived here. I believe his farm is just over the ridge to the north of Dalwich."

I jotted down the man's name and directions to his farm on the pad of paper I always carried for just this reason.

"You mentioned his sons . . . ?" Colin pressed.

"Yes, he has three or four of them. I'm not certain. I met his eldest once. I think he called the lad Edmond or Edward, but you'd be best off speaking with Brother Green, as he's the one who attends to our kitchen. I"—he gestured at the room around us—"spend most of my time here."

"Yes." Colin gave a swift smile before standing up and meandering over to a shelf of books. He casually ran a finger along the spines of several volumes and it looked like a gesture borne of excess energy. I suspected he was lamenting being unable to fidget with his coin. "Is there anyone else who makes visits to your monastery?"

"No, if there is anything else needed, one of us will go into Dalwich to fetch it, but that doesn't happen more than once every six or eight weeks."

"Has there been any dissension amongst the brothers of late?" Colin asked with a feigned innocence that I knew Brother Bursnell caught as his face flushed slightly, the paleness of his skin revealing his mood with a persistence I was certain he must dislike.

"Dissension?" he repeated anyway, his answer as cheeky as Colin's question had been.

"You know . . ." Colin prodded offhandedly as he continued to brush a finger across countless books, ". . . disagreements about the way things are run, perhaps? Anything that might have caused a bit of tension amongst your brotherhood?"

"The principles governing our monastery do not change," Brother Bursnell responded firmly. "Our standards and faith are dictated by the word of God, not the whims of man or time."

Colin dropped his hand and finally turned to look back at us, his expression pleasant, though I could see the rustlings of impatience within his eyes. "I do not mean to question the tenets by which you live, Brother, but as Father Demetris pointed out, monks are also men. And as men living in a tight community I would suspect it to be within the realm of possibility that there might be conflicts now and again."

The towheaded monk nodded ever so slightly, his youthful

face keeping the frown that he seemed determined to adopt from appearing on his forehead as he pinched his eyebrows. "And so there are," he allowed. "But not to any end that you might be seeking to imply."

Colin came back over to us, his gaze holding steady on Brother Bursnell. "You are defensive of your brothers and I wonder if I have made you so. Please be assured that I am as prepared to find the killer of your abbot outside these walls as within. I mean only to review all possibilities."

"Yes, of course," Brother Bursnell muttered, his face flushing yet again as he slid his eyes away from Colin. "You must understand, Mr. Pendragon, that life here at Whitmore is uncomplicated. Sometimes there can be a bit of griping if the crops are not producing properly, or the ale production is too high or too low, or there is too much fish served and not enough chicken, or any number of other petty trifles, but they are no different than those solved every day by thousands of people everywhere."

"And so it is," Colin answered curtly. "Tell me, was your abbot a writer?"

Brother Bursnell looked surprised. "He was. He set many doctrines and ideas onto paper. I have a small section along the back wall where all of his writings are kept. But whatever would make you ask such a question?"

"There is a desk in his cell but not a scrap of paper found upon it. So, you were tasked with keeping his writings?"

"I was. Whenever he completed something I logged it and placed it on his shelf. Everything we have is available to all of the brothers. There is no secret in that."

"Indeed. And when was the last time your abbot gave you something to include here?"

The young monk gave a small, uncomfortable shrug. "I really don't remember. A few weeks perhaps. I can check my records if you'd like."

"That won't be necessary just now. For the moment I think we shall go and find your Brother Green. I assume he is likely to be in the kitchen?"

"Yes, just across the hall and to the left."

"Perhaps this afternoon we might get a look at whatever your abbot gave you most recently. Would that be possible?" Colin asked as I followed him to the door.

"Certainly," Brother Bursnell replied.

And offering the thinnest of smiles Colin pushed out into the hallway with me on his heels. "You are forever riling these poor monks with your insinuation that one of their own could be culpable of this deed," I whispered.

"Don't be naïve, Ethan. These men are individuals first and monks second." And before I could press him on his sardonic reply, he shoved his way through the first door on the opposite side of the corridor.

As I hurried in after him I found myself standing in a medium-sized kitchen, certainly smaller than I had expected considering that three meals a day were prepared here. A large butcher-block table stood at the center of the room upon which was spread a rabbit's fantasy of fresh greens and vegetables. Two sinks were aligned against the back wall, and two ovens stood just down from those. Long, well-beaten wooden counters stretched along the other two walls and were piled high with pots and pans of varying shapes and sizes. It was a cluttered mess that I knew would drive our Mrs. Behmoth well out of her wits.

It took me a moment to notice the small monk, easily less than five feet, of middle years with straight black hair nearly down to his ears and the round face of a cherub who was staring at us from the far side of the vegetable-laden table. He proved to be a striking dichotomy when a second monk burst out of a small pantry at the rear of the room with a beatific smile upon his face. This was a towering bulk of a man with a large, round belly that looked as though he had swallowed a melon whole. Yet it was his beaming visage, like a child on Christmas morning, that held my eye.

"We have visitors!" the second monk enthused. "Come and sit down, gentlemen. We are delighted that you've come to see us."

"Colin Pendragon . . ." Colin said as he stepped forward and shook the big man's hand, looking uncustomarily diminutive. "And this is my partner, Ethan Pruitt."

"But, of course. You joined us for dinner last night." The monk swept two chairs over to us. "Our little abbey doesn't get many visitors, so you can be sure we know who you are," he beamed. The sincerity of his glee was infectious until he quite abruptly lost his smile. "We only wish you were visiting us under better circumstances," he added unnecessarily.

"As do we," Colin assured as we sat down.

The giant man pulled over another chair and waved to the small monk still gaping mutely by the central table. "This is Brother Rodney. He helps me here and I thank God for him every day. I would be lost without him." The little monk nodded but did not smile or speak, reminding me yet again how distinctly opposed these two men were. "And I'm sure you will have guessed that I am Brother Green. I make sure everyone has food enough to stay healthy." He chuckled as he cast a guilty glance down at his belly. "Some of us are perhaps a bit more healthy than others, but I have a rule never to serve anything unless I have tasted it first myself. Isn't that right, Brother Rodney?"

The little monk gave a quick nod, his countenance otherwise remaining resolutely stoic.

"You both do a fine job given what we ate here last night." Colin smiled. "Is it true that everything is grown right here on the monastery's grounds?"

"God prefers that we take care of ourselves," Brother Green explained simply. "Our lives are dedicated to the service of the Lord. There is no greater calling than that." He quickly leaned forward, and added, "Of course, it isn't for everyone. But it isn't meant to be, you know."

"We'd be a finite species if it were." Colin flashed a brief smile, earning an unabashed chuckle from Brother Green. "But what can you tell us about Mr. Honeycutt? We understand he's a farmer who makes deliveries of eggs and such several times a week?"

"That he does. He's a wonderful man. We are very blessed to have him as a friend to us here."

"He *and* his sons?" Colin prodded. "Brother Bursnell tells us he will sometimes bring one of them with him."

"Not his youngest boy, Benjamin. He's only just turned

eight. But the older boys—Edward, Daniel, and David—have all been here."

"Four sons . . ." I noted as I scribbled down their names.

"And five daughters: Clare, Francine, Margaret, Louise, and little Josephine," Brother Green grinned. "The missus bore him five sons as well, but God called one back home, bless his little heart. Fevers took him a couple of summers ago. But George Honeycutt's faith is strong and he did not question God's will."

"And what is the regularity of their visits?" Colin asked.

"Every Monday, Wednesday, Friday, and Saturday," he answered. "They have never let us down."

"Does Mr. Honeycutt ever send one of the boys alone?"

Brother Green shook his head thoughtfully. "Not very often. Mostly it's George and one of his lads, but there've been a few times when Edward came by himself. He's the oldest one." He turned to his slight compatriot. "Wouldn't you agree, Brother Rodney?"

The little monk nodded his assent once again. I decided he was either painfully shy, which seemed ideal for the life of a monk, or else overshadowed by the grandiosity of Brother Green.

Colin opened his mouth to say something when the sound of the kitchen door swinging open behind us interrupted him. I craned around to find Brother Morrison in the doorway with a handsome young man who didn't look yet out of his twenties by his side. It was immediately evident that the younger man was not a monk, as he wore a black suit with a white shirt and rust-hued vest, a perfect complement to his dark ginger hair. He clutched a black bowler in both hands and his strong, symmetrical features, while turned down in what appeared to be displeasure, still could not spoil his striking face.

"Here you are . . ." Brother Morrison grumbled with obvious irritation.

"Mr. Pendragon . . . ?" the young man interrupted.

Colin stood up with a wary smile and a single eyebrow arched skyward. "Might you be the constable of Dalwich we've been hearing about?"

"I am," came his answer. "Lachlan Brendle." If the man was surprised to be so easily marked he did not show it in the least as he stepped forward and shook our hands.

"We had heard you would be joining us today," Colin continued with noticeably greater charity than he usually dispensed on the local constabulary, and I knew he was charmed by this handsome young man.

"I had every intention of doing so," Constable Brendle replied in a quick, stiff voice, "but something has happened." He hesitated, shuffling his feet and clearing his voice, which suddenly made him seem every bit as young as I thought him to be. "Mr. Chesterton told me I would find you here," he continued, his voice remaining firm and steady, though I could now detect a thin hitch in his tone that made me suspect that whatever had happened, this young man was in over his head.

"What is it?" Colin asked.

"Maureen O'Dowd . . . the dark-haired barmaid who works for Mr. Chesterton . . . ?"

Colin nodded, a smile coming easily to his face. "Miss O'Dowd is a charming young woman with a devilish sense of humor."

Constable Brendle's shoulders sagged almost imperceptibly as he struggled to hold Colin's gaze. "She has been murdered, Mr. Pendragon. Either sometime late last night or very early this morning. I need your help. I very much need your help."

# CHAPTER 7

The woods that surround Dalwich are neither thick nor dense, which was why Maureen O'Dowd's body had been discovered with the first light of the new day. As the carriage that bore Colin, Constable Brendle, and me pulled up near a patch of tall grass just off the road on the outskirts of Dalwich's west side, it looked almost as though the effervescent young woman had simply overindulged and passed out with her oversized coat yanked up over her face to protect her from the morning sun. But as we came to a stop, the taller of the two men standing near the body reached over and swept the coat from atop her to reveal that her repose was, in fact, quite unnatural. Her legs and arms were akimbo, and her dress was hiked to an improper height, her bodice ripped nearly fully open, making the intention of this attack woefully obvious.

"*What have you done?!*" Colin shouted as he leapt from the carriage.

"What . . . ?!" The other man guarding Miss O'Dowd's body recoiled as though he and his partner had been accused of the deed itself. The second gentleman was stockier and easily the older of the two, with the swarthy coloring of someone from the Middle East.

"Whose coat is that?" Colin seethed. "Who told you to touch it?"

"It's mine." The first man winced when he answered. He was exceedingly tall and uncomfortably thin, and no matter what he said next, and I already suspected what it would be, I knew he was going to be condemned for it. "I was only trying to cover her indecency."

"*Indecency . . . ?!*" Colin bellowed the very answer I had presumed. "She is not *indecent,* you damned fool, she is bloody well *dead.* And now you have most assuredly destroyed this crime scene by tossing your blasted bollocky coat over her."

"I . . ." But the man had no defense and simply stopped speaking.

I almost found myself feeling sorry for him given that he had acted out of propriety rather than any sort of malfeasance, yet Colin was right. The damage was irrevocably done. In spite of Constable Brendle's expedient summons, this site would now prove to be as contaminated as most every other scene we were beckoned to.

"You must forgive his error." Constable Brendle spoke up, his own mortification visible in the flush of his face. "I'm afraid we are all well beyond our means here. . . ."

Colin shook his head without uttering a word, choosing instead to move off toward Maureen O'Dowd's remains.

"I'm Ethan Pruitt," I said to the constable's two men, attempting to defuse the situation even only slightly.

"Forgive me," Constable Brendle responded at once as though the breach in etiquette had been his. "These are my men, Ahmet Masri," he said, gesturing to the olive-skinned man, "and Graham Whitsett. They both serve as assistant constables and are invaluable to me."

"I'm sure they are," I allowed as I shook their hands, assuming this was the best a small town such as Dalwich could come up with. "And my partner is Colin Pendragon of London. A man who undertakes investigating with unfailing seriousness." I gave a meager grin as I said it, though I had no intention of exonerating their foolishness just yet.

"As do we." The constable spoke up again. "I do try to keep

the three of us abreast of the latest techniques, but as we are a small town that suffers from little more than the occasional drunken escapade or a clipped item here and there..." He allowed a small, uncomfortable shrug. "Nothing like this..." He pursed his lips as he slid his gaze back to Miss O'Dowd's body. "It is unimaginable to have two such incidents." He dragged his eyes back to me. "Which is why I am so grateful that Bishop Fencourt sent for the two of you to assist with the murder of Abbot Tufton. We..." He did not bother to finish his thought. Given what had already transpired at this scene there was little more that needed to be said.

"Helping to solve the abbot's murder is one thing," I said to the three men, "but Mr. Pendragon and I had the pleasure of conversing with Miss O'Dowd last night. We both found her to be a delight, which makes this current turn of events especially upsetting."

"Everybody loved Maureen," Mr. Masri said in a soft, hesitant voice. "This cannot be..." He swiped the heel of a hand against his eyes and looked off toward the horizon as though trying to spy something there when, in truth, I knew he was only attempting to compose himself.

"If I have done anything to impede this investigation..." Mr. Whitsett started to say, his own voice tremulous at best.

"Mr. Pendragon will solve this," I assured them when Colin did not bother to answer from where he was kneeling over the body.

"Did anyone come by or try to interfere in any way while you were waiting for me to come back?" Constable Brendle asked his men with a stern authority that belied his age as he was easily the youngest amongst the five of us. It made me wonder how he had managed to achieve his status at so youthful an age.

"A few folks went by on their way into town," Mr. Whitsett answered first, "but we kept them moving along."

"No one tarried or touched anything," Mr. Masri hastily added, though it made little difference now.

"Why don't the two of you get back to town and direct the

coroner out here when he arrives," the constable instructed. "We have no need for our own coroner in Dalwich," he explained to me, "so we share a man from Arundel with several nearby towns. He may already be here and waiting at my office." We looked around and watched the constable's two associates waste no time in barreling off on their horses. "I must apologize again for the carelessness of my men. We have discussed maintaining the integrity of a crime scene, but there remains a great chasm between theory and practice," he said loud enough for Colin to hear.

"What's done cannot be undone..." Colin muttered from where he remained crouched over Miss O'Dowd. His proximity to her body was enough to clutch my belly. It felt unfathomable that this cheerful, amusing young woman had been slain and so brutally discarded. No one deserved such an end, but Maureen O'Dowd, with her clever smile and caustic wit, was a character above the rest.

"Do you see anything of note, Mr. Pendragon?" Constable Brendle asked, and it was not lost on me that the young man had yet to move forward, either.

"There is much to see," Colin answered gruffly as he leaned even closer over Miss O'Dowd's neck and décolletage. "Perhaps the two of you wouldn't mind pawing around a bit"—he abruptly lifted his head and looked back at us—"you know ... from back there." He flicked the ghost of a grin before immediately bending back to whatever he was studying.

"Are we looking for anything in particular?" the constable asked.

"Anything out of the ordinary," Colin tossed back, just as I had expected.

I glanced over at Constable Brendle and found him already crouched amongst the grass along the side of the road, running his fingers through the bent weeds with great intent. He was, I decided, positively relieved at having finally been told what to do. "May I ask your age, Constable?" I simply could not resist as I too bent to fumble through the brush a short distance from the body.

"Twenty-eight," he answered without diverting his attention from the task at hand.

"Impressive. And have you ever assisted on a murder investigation before?"

This time he did look over at me and I noticed his face bloom pink. "No, is it obvious?"

"Quite the opposite."

"I read any textbook I can find and will even resort to fiction if I think its ideas worthy of consideration. It seems to me some of the most creative thinking comes from men like H. G. Wells and Jules Verne. Imagine if even a trifle of their whimsy should ever come true."

Before I could fashion a response to such a flight of fancy, Colin spoke up. "The both of you should come here," he said, leaning back and pointing to the path he had blazed when he'd approached the body. "Follow my tracks if you will."

The young constable seemed almost rejuvenated by his foraging along the road's edge as he circled to where Colin was pointing before I could even fully regain my feet. "What is it, Mr. Pendragon? Have you found something?" he asked as he began to carefully pick his way toward him.

"Everything is something," Colin muttered blithely, which I thought a maddening response. "Who found Miss O'Dowd's body?" he asked as I came up behind Constable Brendle, now likewise crouched down beside Colin.

"A local farmer was on his way to begin his deliveries in town," Constable Brendle said. "He was on his way to the monastery, actually, with one of his sons. When they found Miss O'Dowd he sent the boy to fetch me."

"George Honeycutt?" I asked.

The constable turned and stared at me. "How could you know that?"

"Mr. Pruitt is good with names and, as I am sure you are aware, they don't get many visitors at Whitmore Abbey."

"Of course." He nodded.

"Which son was he with?" I asked for no better reason than

to see if I could remember which order the lad was in the Honeycutt family.

"Thankfully it was his boy David."

"Thankfully?" Colin repeated.

"His oldest son, Edward, and Miss O'Dowd were known to have grown quite close over the last year. It would have been a terrible thing if he had been with his father this morning." He let his eyes fall onto the desecrated body.

"A bit of good fortune then," Colin stated grimly, but I knew he didn't believe any such thing. We'd never found fortune or chance as random as most people alleged. "Tell me what you see here," he said to the constable, his words striking me oddly since they were usually meant for me.

Constable Brendle closed his eyes and shook his head. "The poor girl . . ."

I looked down at Miss O'Dowd and noticed two things at once: a startling redness in her slightly protuberant eyes, and a smear of pinkish fluid along her cheeks and jawline. The two symptoms seemed distinctly unique, yet I wondered whether Colin had found some correlation therein that I had not considered. There were signs of inflammation around her neck and her skin appeared pallid, making me suspect that she had been strangled. A quick glance along her body revealed neither bloodstains nor other points of damage, including a curious lack of scratches where her bodice had been torn asunder. I found myself sympathizing with Mr. Whitsett's determination to cover this poor woman, as the tableau was an offense to the grace and dignity of the vigorous person she had been. Yet I also knew there was a distinct tale being told in her having been left like this—most specifically about the man who had done it.

"Her face is so white," the constable said in a whispered tone, "and yet there seems to be a pink hue around her jaw. And her eyes . . ." He looked up at Colin. "What has happened to her eyes?"

"She has been strangled," he answered softly. "Such an action bursts the blood vessels in the eyes and almost always causes the fragile hyoid bone in the neck to break."

"I believe I have heard of that . . ."

"It's a thin, U-shaped bone at the top of the larynx that serves as the host for a series of neck muscles. If you feel here"—Colin ran his fingers gingerly up along the underside of Miss O'Dowd's jaw—"you will be able to tell that it has been broken." But Constable Brendle did not reach forward, instead choosing to simply nod his understanding. "I also don't believe she was murdered here," Colin continued. "Miss O'Dowd was a woman of some substance and would not have been strangled without a struggle. You can see the evidence of that by the dishevelment and tearing of her clothing. Had she been garroted from behind it might have been possible to subdue her without as great a struggle, but the broken hyoid bone suggests an attack from the front. I'm quite certain the coroner will be able to lift at least one handprint from her throat. And if you look around the area"—he scanned his eyes across the underbrush and I found myself doing the same—"you will notice by the pristine state of the scrub and grasses nearby that no such struggle could have taken place here."

"I've found countless horse prints and wheel ruts along the roadway." Constable Brendle spoke up as he slid a hand through his wavy, dark ginger hair. "But I can't tell if any of them were made today or a month ago."

"And you, Ethan?" Colin glanced over at me.

"I saw some newer horse tracks coming from the direction of the woods, but I can't be certain when they were made, either," I answered, dissatisfied with my own response.

"More than one horse?"

"No."

Colin's face remained bleak as he turned back to Miss O'Dowd's body. "I shall look then," he mumbled. "Your other observation, Constable, is well-made. There is indeed a pinkish tone across the bottom of her face." To my shock, he abruptly leaned forward and pried her mouth open. "If you will look you will see that her tongue has been rather badly removed."

I felt the constable recoil beside me even as I felt compelled to lean slightly forward and gaze into the dark cavern of her mouth. A deeper rose color was smeared across her teeth and I could see the ravaged nub of her tongue lolled up against the back of her throat.

"Just like the abbot . . ." Constable Brendle blanched.

"Yes," Colin said as he stood up. "So it would seem." He glanced at me from over the top of the constable's head as I straightened up, and I could see that there was something exceedingly troubled within his gaze.

# CHAPTER 8

Raleigh Chesterton, the portly, ill-tempered owner of the Pig and Pint, quite suddenly became a wholly other man in light of the travesty that had been wrought against his barmaid, Maureen O'Dowd. So profound was the change in the man that he had immediately volunteered to take Colin and me out to the Honeycutt farm to interview George Honeycutt. Since Constable Brendle had already spoken with both George and his son David, Mr. Chesterton's magnanimity had allowed the two of us to go out and speak to the Honeycutts on our own.

"She were a pip, that one," he said as he brushed a thumb across his eyes for the second time since we'd climbed aboard his wagon. "I knew her since she were a toddler. She started workin' for me at about twelve or thirteen . . . I don't remember which . . ." He let his voice trail off as he shook his head and stared out across the gently rolling hillside that surrounded us, reminding me of the lush, emerald Ring of Kerry near where Maureen O'Dowd had been born.

"What about her parents or siblings?" Colin asked.

"Her pop died in a mining accident when she were jest a little shite. She didn't even remember him. That's when her mum brought the two kids here ta Dalwich. Her mum worked for me fer a while, but that woman could be a holy pain in the arse, so I had ta let 'er go."

"You severed her mother's employment because she had a bad attitude?!" I fired back with disbelief. It was, after all, less than twenty-four hours since Mr. Chesterton had accorded us an appalling greeting upon our arrival at his lackluster establishment.

Raleigh Chesterton tossed a sour frown my direction. "Her attitude came from too much time spent in a bottle," he shot back defensively. "What of it?"

"Nothing at all . . ." Colin said as he waved a dismissive hand at the same time he clapped my ankle bone with his nearest boot. "Mr. Pruitt didn't mean anything. We all know a man has to protect his livelihood."

" 'At's right." Mr. Chesterton bothered to send a satisfied scowl my direction. "So while Maureen's mum drank herself ta death, I gave Mo a job. 'At's a kind a man I am."

"And this was when she was about twelve?" I repeated, determined to keep the sarcasm from my voice.

"Near about. Her mum died when Mo was fourteen, so she mighta been eleven or so. Who the hell remembers," he sniffed, clearly daring me to counter his declared generosity.

"You mentioned there were two children?" Colin pressed.

"She has a brother . . ." he started to say before shaking his head with a protracted sigh. "Doyle's gonna be nobbed off when the constable gets word ta him about what's happened ta Mo. They was close even though he lives over in Mountfield. He's been workin' the Mountfield gypsum mine since he were fifteen. A scrawny lad, but I guess he does all right fer himself."

"Is he older or younger than Miss O'Dowd?" Colin asked.

"Couple years older."

"Do you know when they last saw each other?"

" 'Bout a month ago. Doyle came here. The two a them took turns goin' back and forth. This was Doyle's turn. I know 'cause he always spends a lot a time sittin' in me pub glarin' at anyone who gives his sister the slightest bit a grief or a randy smack on the arse." He chuckled at the memory. "Like she couldn't take care a herself." His laughter abruptly caught in his throat with the obvious flaw in his statement. "Shite." He spat the word out as though it tasted rotten.

"And what does her brother think of the boy she's been courting?"

"Courtin'?" Mr. Chesterton snorted with amusement. "Mo wasn't courtin' nobody. You make her sound like one a them upper-crust snoots wot hangs off her gentleman's arm swoonin' every time he looks at her while she waits ta shove a litter out for him. That weren't Mo. Ya bloody well met her. I'd a think you'd a seen that." He eyed us critically. "She were the type who could have what she wanted and weren't shy about takin' it. Ain't too many women know their own minds like that," he pronounced.

"I rather think the true art of a woman is in letting the man believe he's in charge when all the while she is bending him to her will," Colin replied.

"That was Mo," Mr. Chesterton snorted. "She could make me starkers. You'd a thought I was workin' for her half the bloody time." He shook his head again, this time with a wistful hint of a smile tugging at the corners of his mouth.

"And you say she wasn't seeing anyone in particular then?" Colin pushed back to the topic at hand.

"She'd been gettin' close to a fine lad the last bunch a months, but they wasn't doin' any high-flyin' courtin'."

"Are you talking about the Honeycutt boy?"

" 'At's him. Edward Honeycutt."

"A fine lad you say?" Colin repeated, casually leaning back in the wagon and glancing about the bucolic scenery as though he were only enquiring in passing, which, most certainly, I knew he was not.

Raleigh Chesterton nodded without a second's thought. "He's a smart, reliable sort, which is sayin' a lot given he's not yet quite twenty. He helps me out at the pub gettin' me books ta tally. I ain't never had much of a head for numbers," he scoffed. "And I let him putter about the kitchen and tend to the bar once in a while. Those are the skills he'll really be able ta use."

"I'd say he's taking a uniquely divergent path from his father's occupation," Colin remarked.

" 'At's the truth. Edward's always readin' and studyin' so he don't have ta muck about in cow and chicken shite like his father does. That'll be left for his brother David ta do. That boy can't tie his ruddy shoes without an extra hand."

"Miss O'Dowd told us she was going to move to London as soon as she got married. Did you know she and young Mr. Honeycutt were harboring those plans?"

"Those two didn't have a feckin' farthin' between 'em. They weren't goin' nowhere. And after all I did for 'em. Ungrateful little shites," he snarled.

Colin's closest eyebrow arced up before a benign smile tickled the corners of his lips. "And what about Miss O'Dowd's brother? What did he make of his sister's relationship with Edward Honeycutt?"

Mr. Chesterton gave a shrug that seemed to border on annoyance. "I already told ya he's in the mines. Doyle ain't got nothin' ta do with anything."

"I understand that," Colin shot right back as we turned onto a long, muddy drive that led to a large, well-used farmhouse. "But he must have had some opinion if he was as close to his sister as you've said."

Raleigh Chesterton tossed a foul look at Colin and I could tell he was displeased at being goaded by him. "Yer about ta meet Edward yerself, so why the hell don't ya ask him?!"

"Indeed," Colin muttered under his breath and, to my relief, left the subject alone.

I turned back to study the farmhouse as we drew nearer and noted that while it was indeed weary looking, it still showed the signs of being cared for. It was a two-story, plaster-coated structure of a grayish hue, though whether it had once been white, I could not be sure. There were dark green shutters astride each of the half-dozen windows across the face of the house, and while the shingles on the roof were a similar tone they had settled into more of a mossy green while the shutters had deepened to something closer to a greenish black. A small porch was attached to the center of the house's face by the door, and someone had planted a row of sunflowers across its front in an effort, I presumed, to make it look more cheerful. The remainder of the yard was more scrub and dirt than grass, with a litter of children's toys about, including a handmade child-sized tractor constructed of wood that spoke to the craftsmanship of either George Honeycutt or one of his sons.

Three small children, a boy and two girls, had been playing in the side yard between the house and a sorrowful-looking barn, but they now stood mutely watching us as Mr. Chesterton guided the wagon to a stop nearby. "Hullo, Benny, Louise, and dear little Josey," he called with a chuckle. "They're the Honeycutts' youngest," he muttered to us. "They got nine. Bless 'em."

The littlest one instantly raced for the house and flew through the front door as though her skirts were aflame, but the other two stood their ground as we climbed from the wagon and headed toward them.

"These gents have come all the way from London ta talk ta yer pop," Raleigh Chesterton explained with uncharacteristic softness. "Is he about?"

"He's out back with the chickens," the boy, who looked about eight, answered at once. "He says they're layin' like shite."

"Hush," his sister scolded.

" 'At's all right," Mr. Chesterton chuckled. "He's only tellin' the truth, Louise. And there ain't nothin' wrong with tellin' the truth."

"*Mr. Chesterton?!*" a strong female voice bellowed from one of the upstairs windows of the house. "*There somethin' I can do for ya?*"

"Hullo, Mrs. Honeycutt." He brushed a hand across the top of his bare skull as though to be sure he looked his best. "I've brought these two gentlemen wot want ta speak ta yer mister about Miss O'Dowd."

"Oh," her tone dropped. "That poor girl."

"It's a terrible thing," Mr. Chesterton agreed. "But these men are here ta help our constable. They're gonna make it right." He glanced at us with an expectant nod as though our job were as easy as driving his wagon.

Colin ignored him, turning a smile toward the woman of the house. "Perhaps we could speak with you as well, Mrs. Honeycutt?" he called up to her.

There was a momentary silence before her answer drifted back. "I wasn't with 'em when they found 'er, ya know."

"Yes, I know. But sometimes a woman's thoughts are a powerful tool. You might be able to help us more than you know."

Once again there was a protracted silence before Mrs. Honeycutt responded. "All right then. I'll meet ya by the chickens. That's where you'll find George."

"Thank you," Colin said with a wave, though neither of us had even seen the woman nor could we be sure from which upstairs window she had called.

"Ya want me ta take ya round back?" young Benjamin asked.

"If it wouldn't trouble you," Colin replied with an easy smile before glancing at Mr. Chesterton. "You'll wait here for us then?"

"Course." He climbed back onto the wagon and stretched his legs out. "Ya do what ya need. I ain't goin' nowhere."

Benjamin seemed quite pleased to escort us, skipping excitedly around the side of the house with us and his sister in his wake. He chattered incessantly about the chickens before pointing to a nearby hillside where a herd of slender cattle were idly grazing, which, he proudly informed us, also belonged to his father.

My first glimpse of George Honeycutt found him in the midst of an area no more than twenty feet by twenty feet that was surrounded by a small, tightly constructed wooden fence no higher than my thighs. There was a tatty coop at the back of the fenced section that looked like it might house as many as fifty chickens, all of whom seemed to currently be in the open area pecking around the feet of the thin, weathered man with a harsh nose and strong, square jaw. His brown hair was sparse, giving him the appearance of being well into his middle years, though I suspected him likely younger given that his eldest, Edward, was only nineteen.

Mr. Honeycutt was grumbling at the birds as he flicked seed

about, not taking any heed of us until little Benjamin finally called out in a singsong voice. "Da, Mr. Chesterton brought these men from London ta talk to ya."

Only then did George Honeycutt turn his dark eyes toward us with an expression that was as uninviting as it was wary. "London . . . ?" he repeated in a graveled voice.

"We are in Dalwich at the behest of Bishop Fencourt of Chichester," Colin explained patiently, clearly having also noted the man's unease. "He has asked that we investigate the murder that took place up at the monastery."

"Wot's 'at ta do wit' me?"

"Nothing, I would hope." Colin gave a stiff grin that was not returned. "We would actually like to speak with you about Miss O'Dowd," he went on with a renewed sense of gravitas. "I understand that you and one of your sons were the first to happen upon her body this morning."

Mr. Honeycutt glanced back behind us, glaring at his young son and daughter. "Go on . . ." He shooed the children as he crossed to a short gate, which he unlatched to let himself out of the pen. "I already talked ta the constable," he informed us as Louise and Benjamin dutifully raced off. "I don't know nothin' else but wot I already said. Yer wastin' me time." He re-latched the little gate and wiped his hands on his grimy gray trousers as he headed toward the barn with a loping gait. "Go talk ta 'im."

"It is Constable Brendle's suggestion that brings us here to speak with you," Colin answered as we tagged along behind Mr. Honeycutt. "He has asked for our assistance in Miss O'Dowd's murder."

George Honeycutt reached a split-rail fencepost near the great run-down doors of his barn and stopped, snatching up a pipe and box of matches from atop the stanchion. He stuck the pipe between his teeth and lit the already-burnt tobacco stuffed inside, taking a generous inhalation that he immediately blew out through his nose. "Who the 'ell are you 'at ever'body wants yer 'elp?"

Colin forced a smile to his lips that did little to hide his annoyance. "Colin Pendragon," he answered before gesturing toward me, "and Ethan Pruitt."

Mr. Honeycutt eyed Colin closely as he took another puff on his pipe and shifted his gaze to me. "Well, I ain't never 'eard a either of ya."

"George . . . ?"

A familiar female voice piped up from behind me and I turned to face a short, heavyset woman in a long, straw-colored skirt with a white apron covering a fair amount of it as well as the faded blue blouse she was wearing. Her dark brown hair was pulled beneath a similarly hued blue scarf, and her broad face was pinched in a look of worry as she stared at the three of us.

"Wot are you doin' out 'ere?" Mr. Honeycutt mumbled as he took another match to his pipe and pulled in another drag before setting it down on top of the fencepost again.

"These men said they wanna talk ta me."

George Honeycutt flicked his eyes at us and twisted his face with displeasure. "Why you botherin' 'er? She weren't even out there with me this mornin'. She don't know nothin'."

"I was hoping to get some information about Miss O'Dowd from your wife," Colin answered, speaking slowly and carefully as though talking to simpletons. I only hoped the Honeycutts would not realize the tone of his voice. "A critical part of figuring out who might have wanted to hurt her is to discover something of who she was."

"She were a slag," Mr. Honeycutt barked as he shot a glob of yellowed phlegm to the ground.

"*George Honeycutt!*" his wife gasped, her hazel eyes telegraphing her embarrassment, though I noticed she did not correct him.

"I heard she'd been spending particular time with your eldest son," Colin pressed ahead.

"Edward's an arse," Mr. Honeycutt grumbled.

"Now, you stop," his wife scolded, taking a step forward even though she still remained some distance from her husband. Nevertheless, George Honeycutt reached back for his pipe and set himself to smoking it rather than speaking further. "Our Edward is a good lad," she continued. "Ask anybody. But when he started seein' Miss O'Dowd . . ." Her eyes shifted away as she said the name. "Well, she weren't who we was thinkin' would be 'avin' our grandbabies. She were nice enough and all, but she never struck me as the type who'd be 'appy settlin' down." Her husband grunted caustically and it earned him another scowl from his wife. "But ain't none of us ever wished that poor girl any 'arm."

"Of course." Colin shook his head, the wisp of an edge seeping into his tone just the same. "And we appreciate your honesty. Does your son know how you felt about Miss O'Dowd?"

"Me 'usband tends ta speak 'is mind," Mrs. Honeycutt responded with a flush as her husband banged his pipe against the fencepost, knocking the spent tobacco to the ground. It did not appear to me that he cared in the least what his wife was saying about him.

"What time was it when you found Miss O'Dowd's body this morning?" Colin looked back at him.

He gave a slight shrug. " 'Bout five thirty, I guess. We was just gettin' started."

"Which son was with you?"

Mr. Honeycutt glanced at his wife with a look that seemed almost defiant. "Me second oldest. David. The 'elpful one."

"You stop that, George," his wife admonished once again.

"Ach . . ." He waved her off. "You mollycoddle Eddie. It's yer fault 'e's soft."

" 'E ain't soft," she shot back defensively as she tossed a quick look at Colin and me, embarrassment and a hint of anguish evident behind her eyes. " 'E's jest mad 'cause Edward don't wanna work on this farm 'is 'ole life. 'E 'elps Mr. Chesterton out at the Pig and Pint. That man's been right good ta our boy."

"I got work ta do," Mr. Honeycutt groused as he turned and started for the barn.

"One last question," Colin called after him. "Did you or your son approach or touch Miss O'Dowd's body before you sent for the constable?"

Mr. Honeycutt turned and stared back at us with disdain. "Now why in 'ell would we do that?" He shook his head and spit again before continuing into his barn.

Colin allowed a thin sigh to escape as he turned to Mrs. Honeycutt. "Is Edward at home? Might we have a word with him?"

She shook her head. " 'E's gone ta town ta do some marketin' with one a 'is sisters." Her face looked drawn and pained. " 'E's a good boy. George gets 'isself outta sorts, but our Edward is a good boy."

Colin gave her a smile that held no subterfuge. "I'm sure he is. You mustn't trouble yourself. These are only questions."

"I jest want ya to know that wotever 'appened ta that poor Miss O'Dowd ain't got nothin' ta do with any of us. We're a good family. A God-fearin' family."

"Please . . ." Colin tried again to reassure her as he began to sidle back toward the front of the house. "I am not trying to accuse anyone in your family of anything. I am only seeking information to make certain that the right person pays for this most egregious crime."

"Yes . . . of course . . ." she mumbled, her expression solemn as she broke from our side and headed back toward the house. "Thank you," she added with little conviction. She disappeared inside as we continued to the wagon where Mr. Chesterton remained stretched out in the afternoon sun.

"That was curious," Colin said softly before we reached the wagon. "I couldn't tell whether she was actually trying to convince us or herself."

# CHAPTER 9

The three of us were silent on our ride back to Dalwich, which I found odd as I knew Colin had to be anxious to pepper Raleigh Chesterton with further questions. The sun had begun to stretch past the treetops and the shadows on the ground were lengthening, all of which served to make my stomach start clamoring for supper as it reminded me that we had never stopped for any sort of lunch. Only when we started clattering down Dalwich's one cobbled main road did Colin finally stretch his legs out and ask, in the most perfunctory way, "Mr. Honeycutt seems rather sour on his son Edward."

"George don't give 'alf a shite about that boy a 'is. It's 'cause Edward's so smart. How on me dead mum's arse George Honeycutt ever managed ta produce a son like that I'll never bloody know." Mr. Chesterton shook his head. "He favors his boy David 'cause the two a them ain't got the sense of the chickens they're always mucking with."

I caught a grin tugging at the corner of Colin's lips before he quickly collected himself and pushed on. "Mr. Honeycutt also showed little kindness when speaking about Miss O'Dowd. . . ."

"Feck George Honeycutt," Raleigh Chesterton snapped as he guided the wagon around behind the inn to a small stable shared by several of the nearby establishments. "He's a right sorry cur. If you're gonna listen ta everything that pox says, you can go stay at his house instead a here." He hopped down and began untethering his horse.

"My apologies . . ." Colin held up his hands with a smirk as we both climbed out and headed for the back of the inn. "I'm only trying to learn as much as I can about Miss O'Dowd. To see who might have wanted to cause her harm."

"Then you oughta take a ruddy look at George Honeycutt. And he has the temper ta do somethin' stupid when he's got a bellyful a ale in him. I've tossed his potted arse outta me pub plenty a times." And having so slandered the reputation of the man he had just taken us to see, Raleigh Chesterton yanked his horse into the stable and disappeared from view.

"I rather like that a person always knows where he stands with Mr. Chesterton," Colin muttered as I followed him in through the Pig and Pint's rear entrance.

"Of course *you* would like that," I taunted with a laugh.

He peered back over his shoulder as we passed through the hallway and into the main part of the pub, where young Constable Brendle was to meet us at half past the hour. "And what is that supposed to mean?"

"Well, it hardly seems to me that you could be accused of filtering your opinions."

"What would be the point in it?" he answered back as he sat at a table near where we'd been the night before.

"And this from the son of a diplomat," I chuckled.

Colin shot me a surly glance with one eyebrow cocked toward the ceiling. "I do wish we'd had the opportunity to speak with Edward Honeycutt," he sniffed, letting me know he was quite done with my jibing. "The young man is bound to be our primary suspect at this point."

"Primary suspect?!" I repeated with surprise. "How can you possibly have determined Edward Honeycutt to be the primary suspect if we haven't even met him yet?"

"Because," he answered slowly, continuing to stare at me, "when there are lovers involved, it can be nearly impossible for one not to assault the other when there are quarrelsome personal judgments bandied about." He leaned back with a self-satisfied smile and waved at the auburn-haired barmaid, Annabelle White.

"Oh, fine . . ." I grumbled as the young woman approached us carrying a tray full of empty mugs.

"Gentlemen." She spoke softly and her face was understandably somber with a pain behind her eyes that looked ready to erupt in an instant.

"Miss White . . ." I spoke up first, assuming Colin would have no memory of her name. "You have our deepest condolences on the death of your friend Miss O'Dowd."

" 'Tis a tragedy," she said with the swipe of a hand against her eyes. "She never 'urt no one and I'll never understand 'ow someone could do such a thing. I 'ope ya 'ang the bastard by 'is bits when ya catch 'im."

"Were you and Miss O'Dowd very close?" Colin asked.

"We was like sisters. She were always lookin' out fer me. I don't know 'ow I'm gonna get along without 'er." She dropped her head into her free hand and began to sob, so I gently removed the tray from her other hand to give her a moment to collect herself.

"Here now . . ." Raleigh Chesterton's voice bellowed as he came stalking over from the back of the pub. "Yer gonna drive me customers out if ya start slobberin' all over the bloody place." He turned the young woman about and shooed her from our table. "Git yerself right or go home. I ain't payin' ya to make everybody feel worse than they already do." He took the tray out of my hands and glared at us. "Ya want somethin' ta drink?"

Colin flashed a tight grin. "Could we just have some tea?"

Mr. Chesterton screwed up his face. "Suits me fine, but ya ain't gettin' any a that tiny shite food ta go with it. Ya want somethin' ta eat, ya gotta order dinner."

"That'll be all we need until after we finish speaking with the constable," Colin informed him.

"What are you serving tonight?" I asked, unable to help myself since my stomach had already begun to rumble its displeasure at the very thought of having to wait longer.

"Hell if I know," he shot back before heading off with Annabelle White's tray in one hand.

"This day . . ." Colin heaved a sigh and settled back in his chair. "Those blasted monks continue to exasperate me."

"Colin . . ." I scolded, fearful that someone at a neighboring table might hear him.

"It's true." His eyes flashed his annoyance. "I feel like I have to watch every word I say and now I'm forbidden to even flip my coin to settle my thoughts." He seized a crown from his coat pocket and held it up like a talisman. "Who knew this ridiculous metal disc could cause such a ruddy furor with those blasted—"

"*Colin!*" I hissed again. "Mind yourself or we're liable to be run from Dalwich like a pair of heretics."

"They wouldn't dare," he groused as he ran a hand through his tawny hair while continuing to finger his coin with the other. Colin looked as though he was about to say something else when he suddenly seized the coin and leaned toward me. "Be discreet," he whispered under his breath, "but turn around and see who we are about to get an unexpected visit from."

It was all I could do not to spin my head around, but I convinced myself I was the very definition of discretion as I feigned a yawn, stretching my arms out, and casually glanced back over my shoulder. While my actions earned me a snicker from Colin I still caught a glimpse of round, craggy Raleigh Chesterton standing by the kitchen door pointing toward the two of us as he spoke into the ear of a tall, handsome young man with a build nearly as solid as Colin's. I could not discern his exact age given that he had a close-cropped brown beard covering his steely jawline, but I guessed he had likely not yet reached his thirties.

"Am I supposed to know who that is?" I asked as I straightened up again.

"That was quite a performance," he chuckled.

"You aren't funny."

"Here he comes," he announced under his breath, his enthusiasm contagious. "Now see if you can't spot his mother's coloring and the angularity of his father's face."

Not a moment later a strong male voice asked, "Mr. Pendragon . . . ?"

I studied the young man's face as casually as I could, and as I did so, I could see exactly what Colin had meant about the similarity of this young lad to his parents.

"Edward Honeycutt." Colin stood and shook his hand.

"Yes, sir," he answered as I also stood to introduce myself. While he was an exceptionally handsome young man, there was not the least hint of joy or mischief upon his face. Rather, this was a person whose profound sorrow was as obvious as the color of his hazel eyes.

"Please sit down, Mr. Honeycutt," Colin urged, nearly foisting him into a chair to avoid any possibility he might decline. "I cannot tell you how aggrieved we are by the murder of Miss O'Dowd. Please be assured that your willingness to present yourself to us now is a testament to your great affection for her and will only help Mr. Pruitt and me to make a hasty end to this horrendous event."

"I did not come here to accommodate you, Mr. Pendragon," Edward said, his voice every bit as lost as the expression on his face, "but rather to keep myself busy and away from my family."

"And why exactly would that be?" Colin asked, though we both knew the answer.

"My da did not like Mo. Even now he chides me for my sorrow and I find that I would rather be here, working for Mr. Chesterton, than staying at home around him."

"It is a terrible thing that your father's manner has contributed to your grief," Colin remarked darkly. "For what it is worth, I do believe most parents mean well. . . ."

"That may be true of the Pendragons," Edward answered at once, "but it is not so of the Honeycutts."

"Your mother feels likewise, does she?"

"My mum has five children under thirteen and four above. She does not have time to consider anything my da has not told her."

"Of course," Colin nodded as though he too had suffered anything like the same sort of umbrage in his youth. "And to what did your father claim to object?"

Edward dropped his gaze and his brow furrowed slightly, though no lines could crease his youthful forehead. "I have attended more school than anyone else in my family ever has," he explained with neither pride nor boastfulness. "He would have you believe that I should be betrothed to one of the royals. Never mind that he wishes me to take over that stupid bloody farm of his. . . ." His eyes flashed hotly as he stared up at us, a mixture of fury and heartache battling for ascendance. "But I *loved* her. We were going to be married and go to London so I could get a proper job. Make something of myself . . ." He dropped his chin and I could tell by the shaking of his shoulders that he had begun to cry.

Colin gripped my nearest thigh and when I glanced over at him I saw that he had paled, his lips stretched into a line so thin that it looked like he might lose them completely. Without a word I slid out of my chair and moved behind Edward Honeycutt, dropping a hand onto his shoulder and squeezing it in hopes that he might understand that I knew what he was feeling. To my surprise, he quite suddenly turned in his seat and flung his arms about my waist, burying his face in my abdomen with a pitiful moan. I dropped my hand onto his back as a lump grew in my throat and the sting of tears bristled in my own eyes. "Edward . . ." I forced myself to say even though his name crackled in my throat. "Come with me."

He untangled himself at once and stood up, allowing me to clutch his elbow lightly as I led him to the rear of the pub. I did not permit myself to glance back at Colin as Edward and I made our way amidst the hooded gazes of the other patrons, fearing that I might fail to maintain my own restraint if I did not get us both out of there at once. I walked him down the short corridor, past the narrow staircase that led to the rooms on the second floor, and out the back. The cool evening air struck me as soon as we stepped outside, caressing my face, recharging my resolve, and settling the flux of emotions that had threatened to undo me a moment ago. To my relief, it seemed to have the same effect on Edward.

"I'm so sorry," he mumbled as he pulled out a handkerchief

and rubbed it across his face before blowing his nose. "I have made a spectacle of myself."

"You have done no such thing," I said and meant it. "You are fortunate enough to have loved someone well and been loved in return. There is no shame in that. It is we who owe you an apology. We should have been more sensitive to what you have been through this day. Sometimes Mr. Pendragon and I think only of the outcome with no thought to the journey along the way. I hope you will forgive *us*."

"Your efforts are only to solve this godforsaken crime and I can find no fault in that." He wiped at his eyes again before managing the thinnest of grins. "You will forgive me if I do not return to your table with you tonight?"

"I would not have it," I answered at once. "Go back to your work. Go for a walk if you will, but we will not pester you for anything more today."

"You're very kind, Mr. Pruitt," he said, stuffing his handkerchief back into his pocket and sticking out his hand. "I do apologize again if I have embarrassed you."

I looked into his handsome, young face with those grief-stricken eyes, his torment as palpable as the breeze rustling through my hair, and reached out and took his arm. "If I am ever embarrassed by the suffering of another, then I will know I have lived too long." I stepped back from him. "Good evening, Edward," I added, and withdrew to the door.

The pub smelled of stew and ale and lamb as I exited the little hallway for the second time that evening and started back toward the table where Colin had remained. I noted at once that things had changed in my brief absence. Not only were there two overflowing mugs of ale at our table, but Constable Brendle had finally arrived.

"Here . . ." Colin said as he pushed one of the ales toward me once I had settled in again. "I thought you could use this."

"I won't turn it away," I said with what I could muster of a grin before taking a sip and enjoying the bitter tang of it as it crossed my lips and burbled down my throat. It seemed to lessen the mantle of distress that had descended upon me and I felt my shoulders and head begin to relax. No wonder I had found such indulgences, both liquid and inhaled, so compelling in my youth.

"Did you have a difficult time at the Honeycutt farm?" the constable asked as Miss White delivered an ale to him.

"Mr. Chesterton just sent young Edward to see us," Colin answered after taking a healthy slug of his own.

"Edward . . . ?! He's here . . . ?"

"He confessed he could not sit idly by at his parents' house and chose to come to work instead. I, for one, heartily applaud such an action," Colin added before tipping his mug back again.

"That poor boy," Constable Brendle remarked, which struck me as being rather incongruous as he hardly looked older than Edward himself. "I knew he was well infatuated with her. Anyone could see it."

"He said they were to be married."

"Married . . . ?!" And once again the constable looked wholly surprised. "I had not heard that."

"Miss O'Dowd told us the same thing. And they both said they were planning to move to London thereafter."

"I'd not heard any of that," he said, more into his mug than to either of us.

"Edward also told us that his father did not think very highly of Miss O'Dowd."

The constable shook his head with a grimace. "As though George Honeycutt has room to look down on anyone."

"A troublesome man, is he?"

"He is an unschooled farmer who subsists on the generosity of the Crown and Parliament."

Colin leaned back with a taut grin, shifting his eyes to me.

"We are an urbanizing society," I felt compelled to say, "who would be in a sorry state were it not for people like George Honeycutt who are willing to work our lands and raise our livestock. I believe our government prescient in recognizing this change while there is still time to do something about it."

Colin's grin softened as he lifted his mug and saluted me before gulping down another mouthful. "Tell me, Constable, would it startle you to learn that Mr. Honeycutt viewed Miss O'Dowd as something of a fallen woman?"

Constable Brendle pursed his lips and leveled a scowl at the tabletop. "Maureen . . . Miss O'Dowd had a rough go of it in Dalwich. She was forced to look after herself from a young age, and I am sure she would admit to having made several youthful indiscretions while trying to take care of herself. You met her. She was a vibrant young woman with a ready smile and a randy wit. I should think you would be hard-pressed to find anyone, other than George Honeycutt, who did not like her."

"Do you suspect Mr. Honeycutt of more than just dislike, Constable?"

He sagged in his chair with a sigh, though whether aimed at himself or Colin I could not tell. "No," he said with modest conviction. "I didn't mean to give you such an impression."

"No matter. I am sure Miss O'Dowd would be pleased to hear you defend her with such passion." Colin pushed his emptied mug away from himself. "Can you be counted amongst her indiscretions, Constable?"

The young man blanched, giving Colin his answer before he could even speak it. "I did spend some time with her. . . ."

"Some time," Colin repeated, seeming to consider precisely what that meant as the bones of a wry grin flitted about his face. "Would that constitute *more* than a single evening, or *less?*"

"It isn't what you think." The young constable started to protest before snatching up his beer and swallowing the remainder of it. He slapped his mug onto the table and brushed a hand across his mouth. "We provided companionship for each other from time to time over the last few years. She was a comely woman and knew it. I don't see as there is anything wrong in that."

Colin's eyebrows lifted precipitously. "Did I say there was?"

Constable Brendle pushed himself from the table and stood up. "Miss O'Dowd was a rare bird and will be sorely missed. Now, if you don't mind, I have a commitment this evening and must be off. Shall I stop by tomorrow to fetch you both? I should prefer your continued assistance on both of these murders. If we could work together . . . ?" He let his voice trail off and I suspected he was testing Colin's opinion in light of his admission.

"An admirable idea." Colin gave a smile and stood to shake the man's hand. "We shall be ready by eight."

" 'Till tomorrow then."

As Constable Brendle crossed to the door I turned to Colin with a look I know was more suspicious than confused. "What are you up to? An admirable idea to work with some small-town constable? What sort of trifle is that?"

"Exactly the sort we need. There is something dreadful going on here, Ethan, and a man like that, who was personally involved with one of the victims, can only prove to facilitate our investigations . . . whether he means to or not," he added cryptically.

# CHAPTER 10

W e awoke the next morning, as was rapidly becoming our cus-
tom, with the waxing of the sun. The room at the back that we
had chosen to share faced east, which meant its single window
permitted unobstructed access to the first fiery tendrils of the
sun as they stretched up over the distant horizon. So by the time
the sun had finally raised its luminous head there was no further
consideration that one might continue to sleep. It was just as well
as it got us up and moving about at a respectable time; Colin to
wash and dress while I crept to our other room to tussle the bed
linens before pulling clothes from the trunk and getting myself
ready. We met downstairs for soft-boiled eggs, sausages, toast, and
the ever-soothing Earl Grey tea, and by eight o'clock we were
standing outside the tatty inn—for it did look so much more for-
giving under the glow of the moon and the hiss of gaslight—waiting for Constable Brendle to collect us.

The three of us rode out to the monastery in relative silence,
and while I knew Colin was ruminating these two disparate yet
similar murders, I wondered what the constable was making of it
all. Most especially because of his previous association with Miss
O'Dowd.

As we pulled onto the rutted driveway of Whitmore Abbey I caught sight of a rail-thin young man with ginger hair dashing into a side entrance. Though I did not get a decent look at him, I suspected it had to be Brother Hollings, the poor bloke who had discovered the abbot's body. Not a minute later, just as the constable was bringing the carriage to an easy stop, tall, doughy Brother Green burst out the front door with his ever-generous grin alighting his face, wiping his hands on a well-used kitchen towel.

"Gentlemen!" he called genuinely. "And how is the Lord's new day treating you?"

"As well as can be expected," Constable Brendle answered with a polite nod. "I only wish our business here was of a better nature." Brother Green's smile waned as he quickly crossed himself, and it made me appreciate just how polished this young constable was.

"Were you able to see to your abbot's proper burial yesterday?" I asked.

Brother Green's face changed yet again as a warm grin returned to his face. "Indeed, we did, and I thank you both for allowing us to do so with such haste. Our blessed abbot was dear to all of us, and it troubled our souls greatly to be unable to pay our final respects and return his body to the earth from whence it came." His eyes radiated the warmth of his words as he took a step back and gestured to us. "Come inside now and tell me how we can assist your investigation."

"If I may? . . ." Colin was, of course, the first to speak as soon as we were inside. "We should like to meet with Brother Hollings right off. Is he about?"

"Is he about?!" Brother Green gave a delighted chuckle. "Well, of course he is about. Where else would he be?"

The constable and I both smiled, but Colin did not flinch. He allowed only a stiff sort of grin to breeze across his face before Brother Green led us back to the refectory, where we had eaten dinner two nights before. "You gentlemen settle in here and I'll have Brother Hollings come and see you. I can offer you some tea, but I'm afraid we haven't much else to accompany it."

"You mustn't trouble yourself," Colin said. "You attend to your business and we shall do our best to be as unobtrusive as possible."

"It's no trouble," Brother Green assured at once. "We may be monks, but we are not without our manners." He chuckled as he swept out of the room.

"That monk has the most generous way about himself," Constable Brendle noted as he sat down across from Colin and me. "His calling seems to bring him a great deal of satisfaction and pleasure."

"So he would have us believe. . . ." Colin muttered, though I caught a hint of mischief behind his eyes. "It seems to me he acts as though his abbot has only stubbed a toe or overslept. I find it all rather curious."

Constable Brendle frowned and appeared to be considering Colin's observation, which made me feel rather bad for the young officer, though not enough to speak up on his behalf. After several moments pondering, he apparently grew weary of the prospect and settled on changing the subject. "And what do you hope to learn from Brother Hollings?"

"The truth of course," Colin answered.

Before the conversation could hobble any further, the young monk we had come to see presented himself in the doorway, gangly, reticent, and cursed with the paleness of a true redhead.

"Brother Hollings." Colin stood up and gave him the first honest smile I had seen him produce since our arrival. "Thank you for joining us. Please do come in and sit down."

The young man nodded, his wavy red hair continuing to bob for a moment after his head had stopped moving. He crept forward on silent feet, managing to keep even his cassock from rustling, before seating himself on the same side of the bench as the constable. Rather than slide in beside Constable Brendle, however, he left a gap between the two of them that only seemed to further demonstrate his ubiquitous discomfort.

"I know this has been a terrible time for everyone here at the monastery," Colin began, "and I appreciate how that must be especially true for you."

Brother Hollings nodded and dropped his gaze, appearing to concentrate on his folded hands resting on the table as though there might be some solace to be found there. I wondered how old this young man was, with his soft blue eyes and skin so pale and clear that it looked as though the sun had never had occasion to alight upon it. But most of all I wondered what had led him here, hiding away from the world in the single-minded pursuit of spiritual devotion. Had something fearful driven him to right-eousness just as it had driven me to opiates and pilferage? Or perhaps he had found himself dispossessed? Or maybe he truly had been called to something profound? Something that some-one like me could never understand. Whichever the case, I could not shake the feeling that save for the shading of degrees, this young man and I were not that different when the spectre of our futures had forced us to respond.

"How long have you been at Whitmore?" Colin asked.

The young man's lips pursed and it looked almost as though he was in pain. "About two years," he finally answered in a voice as soft as it was hesitant.

"Are you the last monk to join?"

"No, Brother Nathan is."

"Brother Nathan . . . ?" Colin glanced at me, and I knew he was checking to see whether we had heard the name before.

"I'm not familiar with him," I said for Colin's benefit. "Where does he work?"

The young monk slid his gaze up, though his chin remained resolutely pointed toward his lap. That he was shy and ill at ease was irrefutable, but there was something else about him that I simply could not reconcile. "Out in the fields with Brother Dun-can," he said after a moment.

"And you . . . ?" Colin took up the thread of the conversation again, such as it was. "You worked for the abbot?"

"Sometimes. Mostly Brothers Morrison and Silsbury."

Colin nodded with interest, his eyebrows knitting as though he found the whole thing quite fascinating, which I was certain he did not. "And what exactly do you do for them?"

"Whatever is needed," came the taciturn reply. "And I attend to the upkeep of our common areas."

"Very noble," Colin allowed with the ghost of a smile that the young brother did not see. "Now, I know this is difficult for you, Brother Hollings, but I need to ask you some questions about the morning you discovered your abbot's body."

Brother Hollings nodded grimly and I could almost physically feel him steeling himself. I felt sorry for the young man. He clearly felt close to the late abbot, which made the fact that he had not only discovered the poor monk's body but subsequently scoured his cell of its carnage that much more horrific. Even so, Brother Hollings appeared resigned to the fact of assisting us in spite of the melancholia that appeared ready to swamp him at any moment.

"How is it that *you* ended up going to the abbot's cell after he failed to show up for morning prayers?" Colin asked with his usual fervor, the details of another person's mood inconsequential when he was ferreting about on a case.

"I often did odd jobs for him," he answered in his reticent voice. "It was appropriate for me to go."

"Now, I know this is difficult for you, Brother, but I need you to describe for us exactly what happened and what you saw when you arrived at the abbot's cell."

The young monk released a laden sigh that seemed to have the effect of folding his body even further into itself, giving him an appearance of such insignificance that a fleeting glimpse would seem to reveal him more a shadow than a man. "His door was closed . . ." He spoke quietly and with a notch of hesitation in his voice. "I knocked twice, but there was no answer . . . no sound from inside. I figured he must have gone somewhere, but I opened the door anyway. I don't even know why . . ." He sat there for a moment, his shoulders hunched forward and his gaze boring into the tabletop as though it might keep the apparition so evidently struggling within his mind from surfacing. "He was lying on the floor," he started again, this time his words coming in a barely audible whisper, "he was facedown. There was blood . . ."

He blinked twice. "It was everywhere. I . . . I backed away. I didn't know what had happened. It was . . ." He dropped his face into his hands. "I ran to get Brother Silsbury. I didn't even check on him . . . I just ran . . ." His voice broke as he sank behind his pale fingers.

Constable Brendle was the first to speak up after he slid the short distance down the bench until he was beside the monk, where he rested a hand upon the younger man's shoulder. "You mustn't, Brother Hollings," he soothed. "You were trying to get him help. It was the right thing to do."

"I didn't even go to him. . . ."

"It wouldn't have made any difference," Colin cut in. "I can assure you most certainly that he was dead some time before you came upon him. Seeking aid in that moment was the best thing you could have done."

The monk drew in a slow, protracted breath. "I pray to God every day that I did the right thing."

"Of course you did," the constable reassured as he dropped his hand and gave a wincing sort of grin. "Even Mr. Pendragon here says so."

"It must have been a difficult thing to return to the cell," Colin pressed, and though his words were bound with compassion, I knew he expected an answer.

"They needed me to help move his body. Brother Silsbury is strong, but Brother Morrison is elderly and does not walk well."

"And then you went back again to clean it?" Colin prodded.

"I was grateful to set my mind to a task," Brother Hollings mumbled. "I didn't know what else I should do."

"Sensible," Colin stated in a curious sort of way. "Did you notice anything unusual when you were cleaning the cell?"

Brother Hollings shook his head once as his eyes drifted back to the table, demonstrating his relief at having been able to set himself to the ghastly chore. "I did not let myself think," he said. "I only worked at the task before me."

Colin's face remained impassive as he nodded, pursing his lips as though he were deep in thought, which seemed unlikely as I was certain he had laid out every question on our journey here this morning. "Did you pick up the pottery pieces from the bowl that was knocked to the floor?"

"It was the pitcher," Brother Hollings corrected. "The bowl landed safely on the bed. I set it back on the stand."

Colin nodded solicitously, but I knew he had only been testing the young monk. "When you discovered the abbot's body, did you notice whether he was holding anything in either of his hands?"

Brother Hollings looked to be considering the question before pinching his lips and shaking his head again.

"You've already told us you don't remember seeing anything on the abbot's table, is that right?"

"Yes, sir."

"Are you certain?"

"I cleaned the entirety of his cell. I couldn't have missed such a thing."

"Did you know whether he kept a Bible in his cell?"

The young man opened his mouth to answer and then shut it, appearing to be reconsidering. "I . . ." He stopped again and frowned before looking up at us from below his lowered brow.

"But you didn't see one that morning?"

He shook his head.

"Was anyone else missing from prayers that morning other than Brother . . ." Colin hesitated before flicking his eyes at me.

"Wright," I reminded.

"Yes." He gave a slight smile. "Brother Wright was in his cell with a migraine, I believe. Was anyone else missing?"

"No, sir," Brother Hollings answered after a moment.

"Very well then." Colin nodded succinctly. "I think we have asked enough of you for now."

Brother Hollings bobbed his head once and stood up, his face as forlorn as when we had started. His eyes remained downcast as though we were too daunting to look at, and as was true of his entrance, he was able to glide back to the door with nary a rustle of fabric. For a fleeting moment I wondered whether such restraint could actually be a part of novitiate training.

"Sirs . . ." the young man said from the doorway, his voice as tentative as ever. "Never avenge yourselves, but leave it to the wrath of God, for it is written, '*Vengeance is mine, I will repay, sayeth the Lord.*'" He dipped his head in a stiff sort of nod, as though his words should reveal something to us, and then he was gone.

"What in heaven's name was that?" I asked.

Colin chuckled. "Well said. It was a quote from the Bible."

"I gathered that. But what does he mean by it?"

This time Constable Brendle spoke up before Colin could. "I believe it's from the book of Romans, but I wouldn't swear to it." His pale cheeks flushed pink as a small grin tugged at his lips. "I suppose I shouldn't be swearing to anything in a monastery."

I allowed myself a grin both at the constable's words and at his embarrassment of them, but when I turned to Colin I found no such similar smirk on his face and decided my question was not so easily answered.

"I am less concerned about that lad's scriptural ramblings," Colin said concisely, "than I am about speaking with that monk who was missing the morning of the murder. Wright, you said?" He glanced at me, but I could tell he had the man's name well learned now that he was intrigued by him.

Before I could respond, a deep voice rumbled from the doorway behind the three of us. "I see you have come back." Brother Morrison stood just inside the refectory, his craggy, round face as cheerless as ever.

"Now, don't make a fuss . . ." Colin said as the three of us rose. "You will only embarrass us." He gave a fleeting smile that the monk did not return.

"I must profess," he said dourly, "that I am disappointed in your persistent need to badger Brother Hollings. He is a fragile young spirit who has suffered greatly these past few days. I should think that might earn him a modicum of grace on your part. If you can be so inclined to be thusly moved."

"Mr. Pendragon has been the very model of compassion with Brother Hollings." I spoke up at once, bristling at the elder monk's censure of Colin. "I am sure you realize that we could not conduct a successful investigation without speaking to all of the parties concerned. And I know you wish us to be thorough and expeditious," I added, even though I suspected he only truly wanted us gone.

Brother Morrison studied me for a moment before shifting his eyes back to Colin and asking, "And it is Brother Wright you wish to speak with now?" And in that instant I felt utterly dismissed.

"You have sound hearing," Colin answered with a tight nod.

"My innumerable years on this earth have not yet dulled me completely," he remarked with what I took to be a trace of mirth. "Come then. Brother Wright is tending to the gardens. I will show you where he is."

The three of us followed Brother Morrison through a door between the abbot's office and the library that let out onto the side of the monastery's main building. There was a good-sized vegetable garden planted just beyond, stretching a dozen rows deep and looking to cover some twenty yards across. It held a proliferation of lettuces, beans, pea pods, broccoli, carrots, and several different ground-creeping vines that I decided were either squashes or potatoes, though I didn't know which. Four monks were working in the abundant plot, their black cowls abolished on this sunny day, leaving them toiling solely in their full-length black tunics, which I decided could only be marginally cooler. None of them paid us even a moment's heed until Brother Morrison called out to Brother Wright, recognizable with his thinning brown hair and the neatly trimmed beard outlining his jawline. Only as Brother Wright began to make his way toward us did the other monks bother to slow their tending and give us a glance. They certainly had to know why we were here, especially as we were accompanied by Constable Brendle, yet there appeared to be little curiosity on their faces, which, as with so much about Whitmore Abbey, I could only find peculiar.

"Good day, Brother Morrison...gentlemen..." Brother Wright said as he joined us.

"These men tell me it is necessary to question you again," Brother Morrison grumbled, "though we have already made it clear that you were in your cell the morning our abbot was struck down."

Brother Wright gave the senior cleric a patient nod. "I have no issue with their desire to do so. If I can be of any help—"

"Then I shall leave you to it," Brother Morrison clipped him off, not bothering to let him finish his sentiment. He gave a stiff nod back to Brother Wright before turning and heading back the way we had come.

"Please come and sit over here," Brother Wright said, not giving the least indication that he was perturbed by Brother Morrison's manner. He led us to a row of well-worn wooden chairs on one side of the porch that abutted the back garden. "Make yourselves comfortable . . ." he said as he sat down and bade us do the same. "These old seats may not be much to look at, but they do offer some comfort at the end of a long day."

"We are sorry to be troubling you in the midst of your daily labors," Colin began as we rearranged the chairs into a loose circle, "but I do believe it imperative that we not dawdle so we can bring your abbot's killer to the swiftest possible justice."

"You have nothing to apologize for." The monk shook his head gravely. "You may count on any of the brothers here to give you whatever time you require to assist in the resolution of this heinous tragedy."

"Thank you," Colin said, fidgeting slightly as he spoke and making me suspect that he was sorely missing the feeling of a coin spinning between his fingers just now. "May I ask how long you have suffered from your vexing headaches?"

Brother Wright gave a tight sort of grimace as he stared back at Colin. "They have tormented me from the time of my middle teens." He scowled and shook his head just once. "That would be some thirty years now. I have always believed them to be my penance from God"—a soft smile fluttered across his lips—"though I cannot claim to know for sure, but when they strike me I am of little use to anyone, especially myself. Brother Silsbury will give me a draught of laudanum, but I can do little more than retreat back to my cell and attempt to seek a bit of solace in sleep. That is where I was the whole of Tuesday morning. I did not even hear about"—he hesitated an instant—"Abbot Tufton's murder until later that afternoon."

"Do you have any idea what time you were awoken by the pain that morning? Or what time you went to see Brother Silsbury to fetch the laudanum?"

The monk tilted his head back and stared up at the patches of cerulean blue poking out from between the frilly white tufts of clouds dotting the sky. "I wear no timepiece and the night is as dark at midnight as it is at four in the morning, so I'm afraid I really could not say. All I know is that it was silent and I did not see anyone else about." He gave the thinnest chuckle. "But then I suppose there is no surprise in that."

"Was Brother Silsbury awake when you arrived at his cell?"

"Oh no. I could tell that I had awoken him just as I ever do. He keeps the laudanum on his bed stand for the nights I have need of it. I cannot imagine how trying it would be if the two of us had to stumble all the way out to the infirmary."

"Do you pass the abbot's cell on your way to Brother Silsbury?"

"No, Abbot Tufton is two doors farther down the hall, and when I am in such a state I do not take one more step than is absolutely necessary."

"I can only imagine," Colin replied with a fleeting grin. "I . . ." But he got no further when a horse came careening around from the front of the monastery with Constable Brendle's man, Mr. Masri, astride.

"*Constable!*" The swarthy man huffed as though he had been the one doing the running. "Doyle O'Dowd arrived not thirty minutes ago and is tearing up one place after another looking for you. Mr. Whitsett and I have both tried to calm him down, but he's not having any of it. You'd better come at once."

"Bloody hell . . ." The constable cursed before catching himself and looking back at Brother Wright with mortification. "Forgive me. . . ."

Brother Wright returned a sympathetic smile as he stood up. "You get on with your other business, Constable. We shall be here when you need us."

Colin practically leapt to his feet before Constable Brendle could utter a response. "We shall go back with you as well, Constable," he announced. "I should very much like to meet this rebellious young man. He just might be able to provide the key to his sister's murder, and there is seldom a better time to question a man than when he is at his most unfavorable." He struck off toward Mr. Masri with unbridled enthusiasm, leaving Constable Brendle and me to hurry after him even as I tried to imagine where he had ever come up with that philosophy.

# CHAPTER 11

━━━━━━◆◆◆━━━━━━

Colin and I rode back to town with Constable Brendle, the three of us once again sitting as quietly as we had been on our journey out to the monastery, with Mr. Masri riding up ahead. This time, however, I noticed the constable's mounting discomfort as we drew closer to Dalwich. Somewhere along the way a thin film of dampness had sprung up on his upper lip, and his hands had begun fidgeting with the reins as though the straps of leather had suddenly become inexplicably hot. It was clear to me that for whatever reason, Constable Brendle was unsettled by this Doyle O'Dowd.

The instant we swung onto Dalwich's cobbled main street a great barrage of shouting could be heard, though I could not yet decipher any specific words. "Sounds like he's over at the Pig and Pint," Mr. Masri called back to us.

The constable quickly steered the carriage onto the macadam path alongside the inn, and he and Colin hopped out at once, with me close on their heels. The noise grew exponentially as we rushed along the side of the building toward the front. As we drew up to the main door I recognized Raleigh Chesterton's bellowing voice, though I could not say the same about the harsh, infuriated growls of the second man, who I presumed to be Maureen O'Dowd's brother.

Constable Brendle shoved the double doors open and barreled inside, his gait strong and steady even though I knew him to be well unnerved, with Colin following closely behind, his curiosity and fearlessness fully on display. "*Doyle!*" the constable shouted, his voice cracking the thinnest notch.

A skinny young man with shaggy black hair and the face of a boy turned around and glared at us. His eyes were dark and full of fury, and his skin was oddly smudged with light gray patches across his face and neck as though someone had tried to whitewash him. I suspected these were the remnants of too many years spent deep within the earth. The constable's other assistant, rail-thin, towering Mr. Whitsett, had planted himself in front of the youthful Mr. O'Dowd, looking as anxious as he was physically awkward.

"*Ya feckin' shite!*" Doyle O'Dowd hollered as he rounded on Constable Brendle. "You been hidin' like a ruddy fay." He advanced toward us, the sneer on his lips almost feral. "Wot have ya ta say about me sister, huh?!" He continued pounding his way forward and I suddenly feared that he might actually try to do the constable some real harm. " 'Ave ya caught the poxy bastard wot killed 'er yet? 'Cause if you don't, I will. I'll find 'im and skin 'im alive and feed his guts to the ruddy pigs."

"Doyle . . ."

But that was as far as Constable Brendle got before Mr. O'Dowd seized him by the collar and leered directly into his face. "Listen 'ere, ya sorry sot," he seethed, showering the poor constable with spit. " 'Ow dare ya let somethin' like this 'appen ta me sister. You was sweet on 'er once. '*Ow bloody dare ya!*"

"Mr. O'Dowd . . . ?" It took a moment for me to realize that Colin had spoken up, his voice calm, soothing, and patient. "I must ask you to release the constable at once and settle yourself or I shall be forced to do it for you."

Doyle O'Dowd barely moved his head as his eyes shifted over to Colin in the span of an instant. His rage seemed to neither cease nor waver, yet as he studied the fixed expression on Colin's face and the solidity of his frame, he seemed to come to an appropriate decision. Letting loose an infuriated howl, he abruptly shoved the constable aside and spun on Colin, although I noticed he did not come any closer.

"And who the mighty 'ell are *you*?" he sneered.

"He is Colin Pendragon," Constable Brendle answered first, yanking his shirtfront back into proper alignment and smoothing his ruffled jacket lapels. "He has come from London to help solve your sister's murder," he added with remarkable tolerance.

A wary frown crowded onto Doyle O'Dowd's forehead. "Why do you give a fig about me sister?"

Colin maintained his even stare, which, for some reason, began to make me feel uneasy. "I had the pleasure of making your sister's acquaintance just the other night . . ." he started to say, but before he could get another word out Doyle O'Dowd rounded off and sent a fist blasting toward Colin's jaw. I was so startled by the abruptness of the swing that I couldn't even draw a breath before Colin's left hand shot out and seized that arcing wrist, his right hand curling up and barreling forward like a careening locomotive. In the span of an instant Colin's fist collided with Mr. O'Dowd's chin, sending the scrappy young man to the floor in the blink of an eye.

"Oh, for shite sake!" Raleigh Chesterton roared as he hurried over. "What the bloody hell is wrong with you, Doyle?" He turned, and called over toward the bar, "Somebody get me a wet towel."

As I looked in the direction Mr. Chesterton had shouted, I noticed for the first time that Edward Honeycutt was standing just inside the doorway to the kitchen. It was hard to see him clearly through the scores of people, but I'd have sworn he had something of a satisfied grin tugging at the corners of his mouth. The moment auburn-haired Annabelle White came scurrying over with a rag, I saw Edward take a half step backward and disappear into the kitchen, leaving only the swinging door in his wake.

"Sit him up," the constable ordered Mr. Masri and Mr. Whitsett. The two men obediently yanked poor, dazed Mr. O'Dowd onto his backside, leaning him against the legs of a chair. "There'll be no more of this, Doyle, or you'll be placed behind bars until you can calm yourself."

The young bloke looked dazed as he reached up and tenderly tugged his jaw back and forth, making sure that all was still where it belonged, which most certainly it was. I well knew that if Colin had intended to remove some of Mr. O'Dowd's teeth, he would have done so. "Bloody 'ell . . ." Doyle O'Dowd groused after a moment, fixing his gaze on Colin. "Yer a right wanker."

Colin's eyebrows lifted and then he quite unexpectedly let out a laugh. "I shall remind you that you swung on me first."

"I was jest gonna nick ya," he grumbled as he pulled himself back to his feet with the help of Mr. Masri and Mr. Whitsett. "You were bein' cheeky about me sister and I think ya 'ad that comin'."

"I gave her a compliment," Colin corrected. "I found your sister to be charming and witty, which is why I remain pleased to be able to help Constable Brendle set this tragedy straight."

"Well . . ." Doyle O'Dowd shook his head gently. ". . . all I 'eard was somethin' about pleasure and the other night . . ." He did not bother finishing his statement.

" 'Ere, Doyle," Annabelle White said as she held out the damp cloth for him.

"I'm fine." Young Mr. O'Dowd waved her off, sliding onto a barstool and holding his head in one hand. "Why don't ya jest get me a snort. That'll stop the achin' that's settlin' into me 'ead."

"I would suggest you not swing on men you do not know, Mr. O'Dowd," Colin advised as he took the barstool next to him.

"If you're gonna slug me ya might as well call me Doyle," he said with a grimace. " 'Oo the 'ell are you again?"

"Colin Pendragon," he answered, offering his hand. But Doyle did not shake it, instead reaching past him to pick up the shot of whiskey Mr. Chesterton had laid out for him and downing it in a single gulp. A trace of appreciation drifted across Colin's face. "I am a private investigator from London," he continued. "I have been sent to solve the murder of the abbot out at Whitmore

Abbey. While staying here at the Pig and Pint with my partner, Mr. Pruitt, I had the distinct pleasure of making your sister's acquaintance. So when she was found yesterday morning, Constable Brendle did not have to ask twice for our assistance."

"Me sister was a good girl," Doyle snarled as he banged the shot glass on the bar top to get Mr. Chesterton's attention.

"You'll get no argument from me," Colin nodded with a fleeting smile, and I suspected his patience was beginning to fracture.

Doyle O'Dowd pounded down his second shot before returning his glare on Colin. "Mo and I never 'ad an easy go a things," he mumbled as he shoved the little glass toward Mr. Chesterton again. "People was always talkin' shite about our family and I'm ruddy well sick of it." He wiped a sleeve across his forehead and stared at the shot glass as though it were the devil, and that's when I finally realized just how torn up this young man was, his anger an armor against a flood of emotions he was ill prepared to express.

"Doyle . . ." I spoke up, earning me a foul glare from him. "We only just met your sister two days ago. We had nothing but good will and admiration for her, which is what has made her loss all the more compelling for us. It is an unthinkable tragedy. But you can be sure that Mr. Pendragon will bring your sister's killer to justice. That is a comfort you may count on."

Doyle O'Dowd stared at me a moment, seeming to gauge the words I'd just spoken before glancing back around and pounding his shot glass on the bar again. "Ya suspect anybody yet?" he asked in a voice that was still every bit as tight as it had been upon our arrival.

"No one is beyond suspicion," Colin answered as he always did. "I should very much like to speak with you about *your* thoughts. To see if there is anyone who gives *you* pause."

"Oh, there is," he answered at once, his eyes holding steady on some finite point behind the bar. "Edward feckin' 'Oneycutt." He growled the name.

"Ah, come on, Doyle . . ." Mr. Chesterton started to say before Colin shot a hand out to silence him.

"I should very much like to speak with you about Edward Honeycutt then," Colin said, "as yours is an opinion that matters to me."

Doyle slid a scowl at Colin and I feared he had pushed too hard, but not a minute later the young man downed his third shot and swung around on his seat, heading for a back table. "A'right then, let's talk."

The look of surprise on Colin's face nearly made me laugh. Even so, he had the foresight to snatch the bottle of whiskey from the bar before he started for the table. "Put this on my tab," he called back to Mr. Chesterton. Constable Brendle and I trailed along after he told his two associates, Mr. Whitsett and Mr. Masri, to stay where they were by the bar.

"Not 'im." Doyle gestured toward Constable Brendle with his chin as we arrived at the table. He sat slumped in his chair with his legs stretched out as though he were there to enjoy a drink with some friends.

"I am the constable in Dalwich. You do not get to exclude me."

Doyle O'Dowd grabbed the bottle from Colin and poured himself a shot before sneering up at the officer. "I do when ya got a personal interest in all this. We both know you 'ad a go with me sister. She tol' me all about it. So piss off."

The constable's face beneath his dark ginger hair had gone ghostly pale and his lips were tugged back in a line so thin they appeared almost blue. "It's been over a year since I went with your sister."

"Why?" Doyle's face went rigid. "Weren't she good enough fer ya?"

"Perhaps you wouldn't mind waiting by the bar?" Colin cut in with an easygoing manner that he suddenly seemed so able to produce.

I could sense the constable's displeasure and humiliation as he held himself rigidly beside me. And I thought I could feel something more, something simmering just beneath the surface, yet what it was I could not begin to say. He finally gave a single nod and stepped back from the table, turning on his heels and stalking away.

"Arse," Doyle mumbled as he downed another shot.

"Do you believe Constable Brendle a likely suspect in your sister's murder?" Colin asked as we both sat down.

"I think me jaw still bloody well 'urts," he snarled.

Colin rubbed his right hand and gave a sympathetic sort of shrug. "My hand doesn't feel very well either."

"How about I see if I can get a bit of ice for the two of you," I said as I pushed myself up and approached the tall, slim Annabelle White, who was wiping down a nearby table. She flushed when I asked her for the cloths and ice, and it struck me that she was still very much a girl in spite of the fact that she had a strong build and was taller than most of the men in the pub. What amused me the most, however, was the fact that she curtsied before running off to the kitchen as though I were a personage of nobility. I decided I would have to set her mind at ease on that point.

By the time I returned to the table Colin already had Doyle deeply engaged, though *not* in the topic I had been expecting. "I was skinny . . ." Colin was saying, ". . . and I didn't fit in with the other diplomats' boys. My fair coloring and blond hair also made me most unappreciated by the Indian children, so I learned to fend for myself." A rogue's grin slowly spread across his face as I slid back into my chair. "I began wrestling in school and managed to get fairly adept at it." He shrugged. "But the more weight I put on, the more muscle I built"—he shrugged again— "eventually I was ostracized anyway." His smile went stiff and a slight stitch marred his brow for a single instant before he suddenly struck the table with a fist, startling both me and Doyle O'Dowd. "And what about you?" he asked with renewed exuberance. "You are clearly not intimidated by any man."

"I 'ad ta learn ta take care a meself," he nodded. "I 'ad me mum and little sister ta look after and me mum wasn't good fer nothin' once she started drinkin'. I got the shite kicked outta me a lot, but eventually I got better." He laughed as he pushed his empty shot glass toward Colin. "I tried ta teach Mo ta take care a 'erself, but she weren't that kinda girl. She 'ad 'er own way a workin' around a snipe. Weren't many people could get one up on 'er. She were a good girl. She wouldn't 'urt no one."

"Tell me about Edward Honeycutt," Colin prodded as he re-filled Doyle's shot glass.

"A cur."

"Yet he seemed very fond of your sister. He told me himself he planned to marry her."

"That weren't with me blessin', that's fer sure," he snapped as he downed another shot.

"Why is that?"

"Because 'e weren't good enough for 'er," he said, his tone growing harsh again.

Colin gave a nod, but I could see he was wholly unsatisfied with the answer and knew he would return to the question at some point. "And do you really believe Edward Honeycutt capable of murder?"

" 'Ell ya," he answered at once. " 'E thinks 'e's better 'an 'is whole family. Too good ta be a farmer. Gonna run off ta London and be in business fer 'imself." He released a hard snort. "Mo was always goin' on about that. 'Ow they was gonna go ta London together." He scowled and reached for the bottle and poured himself another shot. " 'E weren't never gonna take 'er ta London. 'E weren't gonna marry 'er. She didn't fit the kinda life he's so feckin' busy chasin' for 'imself."

"But murder . . . ?" Colin pressed.

Doyle turned a foul eye on Colin and snarled. "She were carryin' 'is baby. Did anyone tell ya that? She tol' me so 'erself two weeks ago. I said she 'ad ta tell 'im—see wot that'd do ta 'is 'igh-flyin' plans. Find out whether 'e were gonna do right by 'er or not." He snorted as he reached for his shot glass again. "Well, I'm bettin' she got 'er answer."

Colin opened his mouth to say something, though I could not begin to imagine what it was going to be, but before he could so much as launch a single sound from his throat Edward Honeycutt stepped out of the kitchen with a rag in each hand, both wrapped around its own fist-sized chunk of ice. He was looking toward the bar, either checking to be sure Doyle wasn't around or to find Annabelle White to give her the compresses, when Doyle O'Dowd abruptly leapt from the table with the ferocity and resolve of an attacking predator. Before I could make any attempt to get out of the way I was knocked over backward, my head thudding against the floor. There was an immediate upwelling of shouts as I quickly struggled to push myself back to my feet, my head throbbing from its cruel impact. But before I could steady myself enough to start heading toward the bedlam so suddenly unfolding near the kitchen door, the unmistakable crack of a gunshot roared through the pub.

# CHAPTER 12

The trajectory of a bullet is often a capricious and astonishing journey that can follow the laws of physics with regrettable accuracy, but then also appear to defy them as well. An unintended object, say a bit of metal on a suspender or a piece of jewelry, or perhaps the clavicle, humerus, or any of the numerous ribs in a chest, or even an unlucky bystander or animal who happens along the way, can all deflect the intended path of a fired bullet. Certainly the elements, such as wind and hail, can cause a bullet to go astray. It is beyond fundamental to make the argument that poor eyesight, an unsteady hand, or nerves themselves can detract a bullet from whence it was meant to lodge. But above all else, I believe it is the ephemeral brush of fate that most controls events: *Le fortune del destino*—"the fortunes of destiny." As it is, so it is. How else can it be possible to endure the gossamer-thin line between success and ruin? Well-being and frailty? Survival and death?

I was sitting by myself in the main hall of the Dalwich police station, such as it was. Really little more than one large room with worn plank-board flooring and a tall, sorrowful counter that looked well maligned and stretched half the width of the space, which was only about twenty-five feet across. There was a tight, narrow staircase tucked in a back corner that led to a loft that served as an open office for Constable Brendle, and right beside the staircase was a single barred cell. It seemed curiously placed given that it stood just inside the front doors, but it looked large enough to hold five men at one time, though I doubted it had ever seen more than one or two. In a town of five thousand it simply didn't seem possible.

I had been left here for two reasons. First, because I had been outside the fray when the gun was discharged, and second, because my head had persisted in pounding to the point that I had thought for an instant that maybe, just maybe, that lone bullet had found its way into the back of my skull. It had not, of course. Thankfully.

"This *weren't* me fault," the low, castigated voice rumbled from behind the nearby bars.

Not only did my head still feel like it had recently been cleaved, but the bench I was sitting on only added to my discomfort. I could verify that it had never been intended for any length of repose. "Shut up," I growled back.

"I'm jest sayin' . . ."

"I heard you," I snapped. "Not . . . another . . . word . . ."

Doyle O'Dowd held his tongue as he shifted on the floor of the cell where he was seated. He did, however, let loose a sigh that scrabbled up my spine as though it had razor claws at the ends of its feet. In truth, I could not honestly say whether I was suffering more from the crack to my skull or the shearing of my nerves. Whichever the case, I was profoundly relieved when the front door finally swung open and Colin entered with a breezy look upon his face and a clear vial in one hand containing a small amount of white powder.

"*Mr. Pendragon!*" Doyle O'Dowd sprang to his feet before I could even attempt to offer Colin any semblance of a smile. " 'Ow's 'e doin'? It weren't me fault, ya know. I didn't touch that ruddy gun."

"If you *please*, Mr. O'Dowd . . ." I heard myself whimper.

"Hush up, Doyle," Colin answered simply, and I knew right then that everyone must be fine. "I'll attend to you in a minute."

Without another word he grabbed my arm and pulled me up, ushering me behind the tall counter where he sat me down again on a small wooden crate. "How are you doing?" he whispered as he knelt beside me.

"My head is pounding . . ." I muttered, rubbing at my brow.

"I've brought you something from the doctor," he announced with a pleased expression, holding up the small vial with the white powder.

I blanched, fearing it to be laudanum with its ten percent component of opium. "You know I can't . . ."

Colin's brow folded down as a pout creased his lips. "Don't you trust me? Haven't I always looked out for you?"

"Of course . . ." I answered quickly, wishing I were not having this conversation while my head throbbed with such tenacity.

He leaned forward and pecked my forehead, and even through the agony I still had the wherewithal to note that Doyle O'Dowd could not see us. "I'll always take care of you . . ." he mumbled as he pulled a scrap of paper out of his vest pocket, unfolding it and carefully reading the notes he'd scratched on it in his blocky handwriting. "It's salicylic acid. It's made from the bark of some willow tree. No opium. I made certain of it." He gave me a tender smile. "You see? The doctor says it'll relieve your headache posthaste." He stood up and emptied the powder into a glass sitting atop the counter before filling it half full with water from a nearby carafe.

"I could use somethin' ta drink . . ." I heard Doyle O'Dowd call from the other side of the room.

"It's not your turn yet," Colin responded without malice as he started swishing the solution around in the glass. I could tell he was quite pleased with himself as he stooped down beside me again. "Now drink it all," he instructed. "I don't care how it tastes." I took it from him and tipped it down my throat, surprised to find that it had little flavor at all beyond a benign sort of chalkiness. "There you go," he beamed. He twisted around and grabbed a blanket and pillow tucked into the back of the counter, no doubt intended for an offender locked in the cell overnight, and sniffed at both of them. "These'll do," he decided as he spread the blanket out onto the floor near my feet and set the pillow at one end. "Now, lie down."

"What?!" I stared at him and my head did not thank me for the effort. "I'm not going to . . ." But I couldn't even finish my protest before he hustled me off the small crate and down onto the blanket.

"I know it's not the most comfortable, but the doctor says you need to lie down for a bit after taking that tree bark."

"I don't want to . . ." I started to object, the thought of reclining on this floor curdling my higher sensibilities, never mind that I had sought respite in far worse places in my youth, but Colin was not having it.

"Be a good patient or I shall send for Mrs. Behmoth. You'll do her bidding or pay the consequences," he chuckled.

I did not laugh as I allowed him to coax me onto my back. "What about everyone else? How are the constable and his men? And Mr. Chesterton?" I felt sickly and invalid and was wildly dismayed that he was making me do this.

"Everyone will be fine." He leaned over and planted another silent kiss on my forehead. "Now rest," he ordered. "I mean it."

I shut my eyes to suit him but knew I would never fall asleep. It was impossible given how offended I felt about the very thought of reclining on this floor. So I listened to the sound of him rustling about as he got up, followed by the forlorn chatter of Doyle O'Dowd as Colin clearly crossed out from behind the counter. I would concentrate on their conversation, I told myself, until I could not bear it anymore and then I would get up and pronounce myself better whether it was true or not, which seemed entirely unlikely. And yet, inconceivably, the next thing I became aware of was Colin tugging at my sleeve and whispering into my ear.

"Ethan . . ." His voice sounded a lifetime away. "Wake up, love."

I opened my eyes and found him hovering just above me, his handsome face and sparkling blue eyes filling my field of vision. It made me feel profoundly happy, though for an instant I wondered where the hell I was and how the bed I was in could be so bloody uncomfortable . . . before it all came rushing back at me in a hairsbreadth. "Did I fall asleep?" I heard myself mutter, my voice thick with slumber as he helped me up to a sitting position.

"You did." He brushed my hair back with his fingers. "How are you feeling?"

I blinked and yawned, and as I looked back at him I realized that my headache had receded to little more than a distant scratch. "Better," I answered. "Much better. What was it you gave me?"

Colin fumbled for the scrap of paper in one pocket after another but came up empty-handed. "Something acid, I think."

I chuckled. How could I expect *him* to remember such a thing? He helped me to a stool behind the counter and climbed onto the one next to me, allowing me the first opportunity to notice that the sole jail cell was now empty. "Where is Doyle? How long was I asleep?!" My eyes flashed to the windows set in the front door and I was relieved to find sunlight still streaming in through them.

Now it was Colin's turn to chuckle. "You've been asleep for almost an hour." His face sobered up again. "I released Doyle, so he'll be headed off to the coroner's office in Arundel to view his sister's body and make arrangements for her burial."

"You released Doyle? What did the constable say about that? How *is* the constable?!" I blurted out, suddenly realizing that I wasn't even sure who had been injured or how badly.

"What do you remember?" Colin prodded, and I wondered if he wasn't testing me at some doctor's behest.

"I remember Edward Honeycutt coming out of the kitchen with the compresses I'd requested in his hands, and then that balmy Doyle O'Dowd launched himself at Edward like a ruddy projectile. I don't even know how I got knocked over. And then I heard a gun go off. Who the hell fired a gun?!"

"Who knocked you over?"

"I don't know. I don't care. It doesn't matter."

Colin looked uneasy. "It wasn't me, was it? You don't think it was me, do you?"

Colin's crystalline eyes clouded as his brow furrowed with the gravitas of his words. "I'm sure it wasn't you," I answered, though I wasn't sure at all. "I probably did it to myself trying to hurry after you and Doyle. Now, stop fretting and tell me what happened."

"Right." He hopped off the stool and strode around to the front of the counter as though he were addressing a court, digging a crown out of his pocket and twirling it reassuringly between his fingers. "Constable Brendle was the first to reach the fray between Edward Honeycutt and the incorrigible Doyle O'Dowd. His two associates were directly on his heels." He glanced at me. "What are their names again?"

"Graham Whitsett and Ahmet Masri," I said without hesitation, and wondered again if he was testing me before deciding that he likely was not.

"Yes," he nodded, the coin picking up speed. "Well, it seems Mr. Whitsett decided, in his inscrutable naïveté, that someone, or perhaps all of us, was in mortal danger from Doyle's fists, and so made a regrettable grab for the constable's gun. Most unfortunate of all, however, was that he set the gun off before he'd fully yanked it free from its holster at the constable's waist, sending a bullet into the constable's femur. Extraordinarily, while the bullet did fracture his bone, it then ricocheted out the other side of his leg in an upward trajectory where it embedded itself in Mr. Masri's forearm." He tossed the coin up and seized it out of the air, dropping it back into his pocket in one smooth move. "It's a veritable miracle the bullet took the path it did, causing neither lasting, permanent, nor lethal damage to anyone. Although Mr. Whitsett's days as an associate constable may well be coming to a close."

I shook my head and knew my face was painted with a look of utter disbelief. "Well, that is indeed a relief. It could have been a catastrophe. How did Doyle end up here in the cell?"

"I shoved him in there to get him out of the way until he could calm himself down, which is exactly what happened." He leaned against the counter and studied me. "We're to have dinner with him tonight. There is still much to discuss now that he'll be of clearer mind. Thankfully, the one truly lasting effect of that bullet." He eyed me closely. "Do you feel well enough to go back to the monastery? We achieved little there this morning and I should like to get back to our investigation if you're up to it."

"Of course." I pushed myself to my feet and gave him the brightest smile I could forage. "I'll not be the cause of slowing you down."

"You never are." He suddenly leaned across the counter and kissed me, my eyes flying to the door where, of course, no one was.

"You mustn't do that," I could not help myself from saying.

"I know." He turned and started for the door. "Let's be off then. There is something I have not shared with you about the abbot that I am hoping could lead us to the very heart of his murder."

"You've been keeping secrets from me?"

"I wanted to be sure," he answered as we started back toward the Pig and Pint. "When we examined his body yesterday morning I noticed a series of long, thin cuts on his right hand. But there wasn't a spot of blood on any of them."

"Perhaps they didn't go deep enough?"

"There are only three layers of skin," he reminded me, "they were well deep enough."

"So what does it mean?"

"I have sent a telegram to Acting Inspector Evans asking him to enquire amongst his Yard experts about the flow of blood after the heart stops since we have no access to reference materials out here. I also reminded our good acting inspector he owes me updates on that blasted Charlotte Hutton and whether they've had any movement from the Swiss authorities. It sets me off every time I think of that vile woman. And there hasn't been a word from my father yet. I was hoping perhaps he might have had some luck with those damned pretentious bloody Swiss by now. . . ."

"Colin," I interrupted, "you cannot attend to everything at once. You have to remain focused on the murders of Abbot Tufton and Miss O'Dowd just now."

"Yes, yes . . ." He let out an exasperated sigh as he rubbed a thumb across his brow. "I know. . . ."

"Besides, I can answer your question about blood flow," I said proudly. "The instant the heart seizes, the blood stops flow-ing. There is nothing else to pump it through the body. Gravity simply takes over. It begins pooling at once. It'll flow out an open wound at the bottom of the body, but otherwise . . ." I shrugged.

A small smile slowly settled back onto his face. "Aren't you the clever one? Just don't tell me how you know that," he added. "But it does mean that those tiny cuts on the abbot's hand were postmortem, which is precisely what I had suspected. And that means he was holding on to some papers at the time of his death, and whoever killed him took them."

"Papers? Papers about what?"

"That is indeed the question," he answered simply.

"Well, that is most unfortunate since nothing is easier to destroy than paper."

"Perhaps so." He gazed at me as his wisp of a smile slowly turned up more broadly at one corner of his mouth. "But I have an idea how we might reproduce it."

# CHAPTER 13

Colin had already arranged a way back to Whitmore Abbey so I wouldn't have to walk, which suited me nicely even though I felt quite back to myself again. I would have to find out the name of the pain mixture he had given to me. It had left no residual dopiness in my brain, just as the doctor had told Colin, and no opiates, for which I was most grateful.

"... I weren't never gonna get the farm," Annabelle White was explaining to Colin as she drove Raleigh Chesterton's wagon, speaking far more than I'd ever heard her do before, "which was fine with me 'cause those hogs smell like shite." She immediately cringed at her choice of word, going crimson with embarrassment and quickly averting her gaze. "I'm sorry . . ." she mumbled.

"For what?" Colin asked obliviously. "Do go on."

"Well . . . so . . . me mum and da decided I could come work fer Mr. Chesterton. That were almost five years ago. And that's how I got ta know Mo. God bless 'er," she hastily added.

"I would suppose the two of you became fast friends . . ." Colin said in his breezy manner that informed me he was not idly chatting the young woman up.

"We was closer than sisters. I got six a them, so I know."

"Six?!" he said with some surprise, though I thought I also

detected the hint of envy in his voice of having been an only child. "Are you about the same age Miss O'Dowd was?"

"She were three years older, so she always looked after me. Made sure I were taken care of and didn't get no guff from anybody."

"And who looked after *her*?"

"Oh"—she gave an admiring laugh and waved at hand at Colin—"she didn't need nobody lookin' after 'er. She could take care a 'erself." It was the second time we had heard such a statement about the unfortunate Miss O'Dowd, and just as before, as soon as the words left Miss White's mouth her spine stiffened and her face went slack. "What am I sayin'? Oh, poor Mo. You must think I'm daft."

"I think no such thing," Colin reassured her. "I found Miss O'Dowd to be every bit the self-assured woman you're describing. Both Mr. Pruitt and I saw her easily handling a few of the more besotted chaps at the Pig and Pint with skill and confidence."

"Weren't nobody could get the best a 'er in there." She allowed a wistful bit of a grin. "And those blokes was always messin' with 'er and beggin' 'er ta go out with 'em . . ." She shook her head and her smile slightly widened. "She jest played 'em right back. Made 'em look like the fools they are with that big smile a 'ers so that they didn't even know she was makin' fun of 'em." She shook her head again and her smile dropped entirely. "I'm gonna miss 'er. I'm gonna miss 'er terribly."

Colin flicked his gaze to me and I could see the discomfort in his eyes. "Of course you are." I spoke up. "A friend like that . . . practically a sister . . . you'll remember her always. That is her greatest legacy to you."

Miss White nodded and we all fell silent for a few minutes as the open wagon jostled along the ruts of the earthen roadway, the muffled clomping of the horses' hooves and the jangling of their harnesses the only sounds beyond the chattering of birds in amongst the treetops. I could feel Colin's restlessness on the seat beside me, so I was not surprised when he finally spoke up as we came out of the wooded area and caught a glimpse of the compact bell tower atop the chapel at Whitmore Abbey.

"Is there anyone at all that you know of who was unhappy with Miss O'Dowd? Someone whom she had perhaps angered recently?"

"I don't know nobody like that. Not a soul. Everyone loved Mo. She 'ad the biggest 'eart of anyone I ever met." She shook her head and gazed off, hastily wiping the heel of a hand across her cheeks.

"Did she ever have occasion to come out here to the monastery?" he asked as we continued to draw closer.

"Nah." She shook her head. "I've only been out 'ere once or twice meself. These monks . . . they don't like 'avin' women around."

"Did she perhaps come out and pick up some of the ale for Mr. Chesterton once in a while?"

Annabelle White turned to Colin with a curious, almost bewildered expression on her face. "I don't believe them monks would 'ave a mind ta do any business with a woman."

"Yes . . ." Colin nodded. "I'm sure you're right."

Miss White pulled the wagon around at Whitmore's front entrance, in the center of the complex's U-shape, and brought it to a halt. "You've gotta find out who did this. The bastard needs ta hang fer it."

"Indeed I shall," he answered tightly. "I should like to ask just one more thing of you. Please try to recollect if there was anyone Miss O'Dowd had spoken about recently, even in a mocking or humorous way, who had been persistent in asking her to see him. Someone who might have been smitten with her whom she didn't feel the same way about."

" 'Alf the men that come in there were sweet on 'er, but she were only taken with Edward 'Oneycutt. She were true ta 'im."

"I understand," Colin replied, though he still did not climb out of the wagon. "And what do you think of young Mr. Honeycutt?"

"Oh . . ." she muttered under her breath as her eyes darted down and she folded her hands, still clutching the reins, onto her lap. " 'E's nice," she said with the trace of a shrug.

"Nice?" Colin repeated, the word sounding abhorrent when he said it.

" 'E treated 'er good. They was plannin' on gettin' married and movin' ta London. She was jest waitin' ta tell Raleigh 'cause she knew he was gonna be bloody well brassed off."

"Mr. Chesterton? Why would he be mad?"

" 'E can't run that place by 'imself. Edward does all 'is books, and Mo took care a everything in the pub and looked after the rooms upstairs too. I try ta 'elp"—she scrunched up her face and looked off toward the monastery—"but I ain't as good as Mo was." She gave another soft sort of shrug. "It don't bother me, though."

"I'm sure Mr. Chesterton relies on you very much," I quickly put in, intending to bolster this poor girl's timidity and not even convincing myself.

Colin cocked an eyebrow at me, which I attempted to ignore, before leaning toward Miss White, and asking, "Did Miss O'Dowd tell you that she was with child?"

Miss White's pale skin flushed pink beneath her deep auburn hair and I knew this most certainly had been the cause of her reticence toward Edward Honeycutt. "Yes," she answered almost without voice. "We told each other everything."

"And did she seem happy about it?" he pressed.

Her blush deepened as she gave a shy nod. "Yes."

"And Edward Honeycutt . . . ?"

She shrugged a single shoulder, her eyes having fallen to the ground. "I really couldn't say."

"Very well . . ." Colin said as he finally stood up. "You have been most kind to bring us here and allow me to pepper you with so many questions."

"I'll do anything ta 'elp you catch 'oo did this," she answered right back, and this time her gaze was firm and steady as she jerked the reins and headed back toward Dalwich.

"It hardly seems like there can be any correlation between Miss O'Dowd's murder and that of Abbot Tufton," I said as we walked toward the monastery's main door astride the small chapel. "So how is it that they both had their tongues removed?"

"A sound question, but one you have the answer to already," he parried back without further explanation.

We got all the way to the doors before I shot out a hand to keep him from opening them. "Would you care to expound on that sentence?"

A thin smile tugged at his lips, which immediately exasperated me. "The removal of Miss O'Dowd's tongue was an afterthought," he explained patiently. "Done in haste after she had been murdered to make the crime look like something it was not. That was nothing more than a feeble attempt to distract the constable from the truth."

"And how can you be so sure?"

"Think about what you saw, Ethan. The way the tongue was removed from Miss O'Dowd's mouth was ragged and careless with more than a third of it left behind. Yet in the case of the abbot, it was carefully, almost surgically, done. Straight, deliberate, with all but a nub of it sheared away. There was great intent in what happened to that monk, while with Miss O'Dowd, I am certain it was meant only to deceive."

I nodded as I recalled the gored remains of the tongues inside their mouths. It had been just as Colin described and I felt foolish for not having also understood that critical difference.

"Try not to look so chagrined," he said as he plucked my hand aside and pulled the main doors open. "We have other important conversations to hold just now and I need you at your best. Your poor, battered cranium notwithstanding."

"Don't bother yourself over me," I insisted. "I'm perfectly fine and you have this case to contend with."

He nodded absently as we walked through the hushed hallway that ran alongside the chapel to the point where the corridor cut to the right toward the monks' cells. Rather than continuing along that passage, however, Colin took a sudden left and pushed his way into the monastery's library. Filled to brimming with every manner of books, manuscripts, and stacks of papers, I wondered if there was truly any order to this room. Brother Bursnell came toward us at once, a pleasant smile on his boyish face, and I decided he could likely lay his hands on whatever was needed.

"Mr. Pendragon . . . Mr. Pruitt . . ." He shook our hands and flashed his perfect teeth, which looked whiter than they had any right to be. It made me wonder if he never ate. "To what do I owe the pleasure of a second visit?"

"You flatter us." Colin smiled back. "There are many who find such an interview less than a pleasure."

"Ah . . ." He nodded as he led us back to the old rectangular table in the center of the room. "So it's to be more questioning, is it?"

"It is ever thus during an investigation, I'm afraid," Colin half-heartedly explained as we all sat down. "You mentioned a catalog yesterday that you keep of your abbot's writings. I should very much like to see the sorts of things he was working on over the last six months of his life."

"Certainly." Brother Bursnell stood up with a thoughtful nod of his tawny head. "I'm quite certain Abbot Tufton would be well pleased to learn that laypeople were interested in his musings. If you will pardon me a moment . . ." he said as he retreated to a far corner of the library, not showing an ounce of hesitation just as I had presumed. "I keep all of the abbot's papers together," he called back to us, "regardless of the subject. Six months you say?"

"That should be a good start," Colin responded.

"And what is it we're looking for?" I asked quietly.

Colin shook his head as his eyebrows creased. "I haven't the slightest notion. I am hoping we will recognize it should we happen to stumble across it."

"Comforting," I muttered as Brother Bursnell came out from behind the bookcase at the back with a pile of papers held in the crux of his arm.

"Our dear abbot was quite prolific when the spirit moved him," he said with an admiring chuckle, laying the documents on the table in front of us and stepping back. "How about I get us some tea? Brother Green is bound to be puttering about the kitchen and would be happy to oblige us."

"A commendable idea," Colin answered as he began to paw

through the papers. "And do you also have the abbot's personal Bible? It seems to be missing from his cell."

"I do not. You should check with Brother Silsbury, I believe he has all of Abbot Tufton's personal effects."

"Very well. Thank you."

Brother Bursnell tipped his head again, making me wonder if he hadn't been a man of service at some point early in his life, and left us to fetch the tea. Before I could even start to ask Colin whether he had noticed the same oddity, he shoved the entire pile of papers toward me. "Start poking through these, will you?" he asked as he stood up.

"What?! Why? What will you be doing?"

"I should like to check the shelves where these came from myself to make sure this ever-so-charming brother hasn't over-looked something."

"Overlooked?"

He gave a quick shrug. "Unintentionally or otherwise," he said as he slid off the chair and started for the back of the stacks.

"What if he returns while you're snooping about?" I hissed after him.

"Good thought. Stir the papers about so it looks like we've been going through them and then go watch the hallway."

"I don't like this," I bothered to say, but it made no difference, nor had I thought it would, as Colin disappeared into the row Brother Bursnell had come from only a few moments before. In spite of my fluttering nerves, I shifted the singular pile of papers into several, spreading the whole of them out as though we had already gotten busy, before rising and stealing to the door. I pressed my ear on it and listened for a second, hoping someone did not shove against it while I was doing so, and when I heard nary a sound I eased it open just far enough to be able to peer down the hallway toward the kitchen.

The only thing I could hear was the rustling of Colin from within the stacks far behind me. It felt disconcerting and I wished there were a bit of coming and going along the corridor so that I might be able to blend into it if I had to quickly call out to Colin.

But there was only that unearthly silence, which propelled my mind to the next thought: How long would it take to brew a pot of tea?

Given that it was late in the afternoon it seemed likely that Brother Green would already have water simmering, making the entire preparation truncated at best. The realization ramped up my heartbeat as I quickly stole a look behind myself as though I might actually find Colin standing there, his foraging completed so we could set ourselves properly to the task at hand. But such was not the case. Instead, when I turned back to affix an eye at the tiny crack I'd allowed, there came a great cacophonous crash from somewhere behind me, followed by a bellowed, "*Dammit to bloody hell!*"

"Colin . . . !" I groaned, booting the door shut and leaning against it a moment, the galloping of my heart in my ears overwhelming every other sound for an instant. I did not say anything else as I struggled to catch my breath and steady my pulse before spinning back and drawing the door open a sliver, only to find Brother Bursnell carefully backing out of the kitchen with a tray full of tea things cradled in his arms. "He's coming!" I blurted too loud to be considered discreet as I shoved the door closed again. "Get over here."

"Look busy," he commanded from somewhere in the back.

Dutifully, but only because I could think of nothing better to do, I slid into the seat I'd initially been in and shuffled through a stack of loose papers, adopting a studied visage I hoped would be construed as thoughtful. Colin came out from around the far corner with an assortment of papers in his hands just as the door swung open and Brother Bursnell entered. I burst from my seat, placing myself between the monk and where Colin was striding up from, and announced with far too much force, "Do let me help you!" I snatched the teapot and held it while Brother Bursnell slid the plain, round tray onto the center of the table a safe distance from the manuscripts and paperwork.

"Most kind, Mr. Pruitt." He smiled.

I glanced around to find Colin stalking back and forth down the row between the stacks, his nose buried in the paperwork he was holding, making it appear that he was simply pacing. "You know," he said with a child's innocence, "I don't think these papers belong to your abbot at all. They have the initials *R.F.M.* on the bottom of the pages."

"Do they . . . ?" Brother Bursnell tilted his head as he moved over to where Colin had halted, peering over his shoulder. "So they do. Those belong to Brother Morrison." He gave a crooked smile. "It would seem I have not been paying proper attention of late. My apologies." He accepted the pages from Colin and headed to the rear of the library, precisely where Colin had just been rooting about, as Colin finally returned to the table.

"What was that all about?!" I whispered.

"It was the best I could do with what little warning you gave me," he protested as he poured tea for the three of us. "I didn't find anything of use anyway."

"Oh dear . . ." Brother Bursnell's voice drifted up to us. "It looks like I've made something of a shambles back here. I have several of the brothers' writings quite out of order." Colin tossed me a sheepish shrug as Brother Bursnell released a heavy sigh and wandered back to the table with an undeniable weariness. "It seems I've not been able to concentrate at all well this week. I shall review everything back there and let you know if I find any further papers belonging to our abbot over the last six months."

I spoke up. "It is well understandable."

Colin gave a gentle smile. "I'm sure we have plenty to keep us busy right here." He sipped at his tea as he began rummaging through several of the manuscripts, quickly scanning page after page before moving on to the next in the pile.

I followed suit, but given that there was little focus to our efforts, I rapidly found myself mired in teachings about ethics, patience, forgiveness, humility, charity, and the other tenets that drive religions. If there truly was something of value to be found here, I could not begin to see it. The abbot seemed a thoughtful and considered man in his writings, but there was nothing here that caught my eye in the least. Indeed, it seemed everything I was reading could be preached from a pulpit on any given Sunday.

Colin spoke up, interrupting my tedious review. "I am assuming . . . given some of what your abbot has written here, that he traveled to Egypt?" I looked up from the monotonous material I'd been flipping through with some envy at what Colin had obviously found.

"He did," Brother Bursnell answered as he refilled our tea. "He went about four years ago for six months. I suppose you could call it a sort of sabbatical. He traveled with two monks from Italy, one of whom is said to be very close to the Holy Father."

Colin's eyebrows arced skyward. "Interesting. Was there any particular reason for the sojourn?"

"As I am sure you are aware there have been many extraordinary archaeological findings coming out of Egypt over the last fifty years. The church is very keen on these discoveries given that the faithful are forever seeking proof for their beliefs." He gave a dry sort of chuckle. "Something of a dichotomy given that faith is, of course, predicated upon . . . well . . . *faith!*"

"Yes, of course . . ." Colin answered distractedly as he pawed through the pages he'd been reviewing. "Your abbot makes several mentions of Egypt here. It would seem to have made quite an impression on him."

"How could such a country not?" Brother Bursnell agreed. "A very strange and curious place. A desert of ancient ruins and pyramids that go back so many thousands of years. Even the camel is one of God's more curious beasts. It is not a place that I myself should ever like to see," he added.

"Not interested in that which is unique?" Colin prodded with an impish twinkle. But if Brother Bursnell had any intention of commenting he did not get the chance as the door abruptly popped open and Brother Green poked his soft, round face in, lit up with its usual glowing smile.

"Do you gentlemen need any more water?"

"You mustn't fuss over us," Colin answered, returning a grin. There was something infectious about Brother Green's depth of warmth given his unlikely height and broad circumference. He looked like a man who could intimidate with his size alone, yet his demeanor was as gentle and gracious as the humblest of servants.

"Fussing over you is my pleasure," came the immediate reply, sounding wholly genuine. "And you are welcome to stay for dinner tonight as well. Brother Rodney and I are making corned beef and cabbage. Shall I set a place for the two of you?"

"No, thank you. . . ." Colin waved him off gently. "We must get back to Dalwich soon. I'm afraid we've another matter that requires our attention before this evening is through."

"Well, you will be missed," Brother Green said with his usual exuberance, though I hardly thought that likely.

"There is something that I wonder if you might do for us?" Colin added quite unexpectedly.

"Of course."

"Could you arrange for us to speak with your newest member? Brother . . ." Colin turned to me, his face blank.

"Nathan," I dutifully supplied.

"That will be easy," Brother Green beamed. "He's just come in from the fields with Brother Duncan. I'm sure he's in the balneary washing up. It is difficult work they do out there, bless their hearts. Much too much for a man like myself," he added with a chuckle as he patted his ample belly. "Come into the refectory when you've finished here and I'll fetch Brother Nathan for you. You are welcome to speak with him there." His broad, smiling face puckered slightly, his eyes revealing a trace of disappointment. "Are you sure I cannot convince you to stay for supper?"

"Perhaps another time," Colin answered in a tone that assured me how unlikely that would be, though it didn't seem Brother Green caught it. "For now we shall briefly trouble Brother Nathan and be on our way."

"Of course," Brother Green nodded, his ever-present smile once again in place as he ducked back out the door.

"Such a kind man," Colin noted as he turned to Brother Bursnell. "Everyone has been accommodating," he hastened to add, "but there is something distinct about him."

"Brother Green came rather late to the calling," Brother Bursnell said as he began straightening the papers we had already gone through. "He grew up in Liverpool and was apparently something of a hellion in his youth. It seems to have made him more grateful now that he has devoted himself to God."

"How long has he been here?"

"Ten years. Almost from our founding. He is a bedrock for many of the other brothers."

"I can imagine that would be so," Colin remarked with a flickered grin as he slid the remaining documents back to the young, fresh-faced monk. "I cannot help but notice gaps in the abbot's writings. He appears to be quite regimented in his daily musings and yet there are days here and there where there seems to be nothing. Or in this instance"—he snatched up two sheets of paper and held them out—"this first page is starting to detail a story about Saint Catherine's Monastery in Egypt, yet on the page that follows he is talking solely about forgiveness and there appears to be no correlation with the preceding page. It's as if"—he flipped both papers over and glanced at their empty backs—"well . . . as if there is a page missing."

Brother Bursnell frowned as he leaned in and studied the two pages. "Perhaps someone has borrowed a portion of this manuscript. It's quite common. The purpose of keeping these writings is to let the other brothers study the ministries of our abbot. And those of the other senior members, of course," he seemed oddly compelled to add.

"Do you not keep a record of who takes what? It would seem rather arbitrary—these missing pages."

The monk gave an amused laugh, his light blue eyes as filled with merriment as surprise. "Really, now, Mr. Pendragon, we number but thirty-three. Do you suppose such things could not be easily found amongst the brothers should the need arise? And I am sure you don't mean to suggest that one of us, devotees to the church, might actually pilfer pages?" He gave a chuckle, but it sounded vaguely arid and harsh.

Colin tilted his head slightly and crooked a single eyebrow, giving a thin smile that I thought was meant to be reassuring but looked nothing of the sort to me. "Well, it doesn't seem you have any way of knowing if they were." He stood up and glanced back down at hastily reassembled piles of papers. "Did your abbot bring any writings back from his time in Egypt?"

Brother Bursnell's face had gone quite sober, though whether it was because he had taken offense at Colin's words or because Colin had actually given him something to ponder, I couldn't tell. "Yes," he answered crisply. "He brought several journals back with him. Would you like for me to retrieve one of them?"

"Very much."

The monk nodded and headed to the back of the library again.

"Could you try not to look so pleased with yourself," I whispered to Colin.

He leaned right over by my ear. "I am rather pleased with myself. We might finally be on to something here. Saint Catherine's Monastery in Egypt . . ." he said quite pointedly, as though that should mean something to me.

"I can't lay my fingers on them at this precise moment, Mr. Pendragon," Brother Bursnell called from the back. "Things are quite a jumble back here and it has undoubtedly gotten mislaid."

"That could be *your* fault," I reminded Colin under my breath.

"No need to concern yourself with it then," Colin called back after tossing me an amused look. "Perhaps you'll be able to locate it for us by tomorrow."

"I shall do my best," he answered as he poked his head out from around the shelving, his face betraying his obvious chagrin.

"Then we have troubled you enough for one day," Colin announced as he gestured for me to follow. "We shall leave you be and find Brother Green. You have, as always, been most generous with your time."

Brother Bursnell offered a fleeting grin but said nothing further as we let ourselves out and walked the short distance down the hallway toward the refectory.

"Since when do you give a whit about Egypt?" I muttered quietly.

"Since the abbot went to visit Saint Catherine's Monastery," he said as though the answer was as obvious as the sunlight itself. Nevertheless, it meant nothing to me and I wondered how it could mean something to him. "The *Codex Sinaiticus...*" he prodded, but it only sounded like another form of influenza to me and I had not known of any such illness to have come out of the African continent. "You haven't heard of it?! I'm rather stunned..." he admitted as he plastered on an obligatory smile and barreled into the dining hall. "*Brother Green!*" he called out.

"Mr. Pendragon and Mr. Pruitt!" came the warm response as Brother Green stood up from the farther table where he'd been sitting next to a rail-thin, young monk. The young novitiate had short dark blond hair slicked back and was wearing the telltale scruff of one too young trying too hard to produce a man's beard. "Permit me to introduce Brother Nathan. I'm afraid he's a bit disheveled yet as he's just returned from his day's work as I told you."

"I washed up some," the young man defended himself as he ran a quick hand through his damp hair.

"It will take more than a touch of untidiness to turn us away," Colin assured with a chuckle. "We are grateful for your willingness to give us a spot of your time. I promise we shall leave you to your evening's routine as quickly as possible."

"You mustn't worry about that," Brother Green answered for the young monk. "Brother Nathan is at your service. So I will leave you gentlemen be." True to his word, he ambled over to the side door that led to the kitchen and was gone.

"He is truly one of the most pleasant-natured men I have ever met," Colin said as he ushered Brother Nathan to a seat. "Is everyone here like him?"

To my amazement, the young monk actually took Colin's bait. "Mostly, though some of the older brothers can be prickly at times. Not that I blame them, mind you," he quickly added. "They have been devout for most of their lives and I've been here less than a year. I know I must tax their patience."

"Why would a faithful young monk such as yourself try their patience?" Colin pressed. "I should think they would be pleased for the freshness of a new devotee."

"Freshness?" He stared at us with confusion. "The order does not seek freshness in their ranks. They are following tenets that go back nearly two thousand years. There is no freshness, sir, only the word of God. And that precedes even time itself."

"Yes, of course," Colin mumbled, and I could tell he was surprised by the voracity of the young man's answer. "I meant no offense."

"None taken, sir," he answered right back.

Colin managed to rouse up an awkward sort of smile before finally proceeding. "Might I enquire as to the impatience you feel from the senior monks here?"

"It's really nothing of any matter," he said with a confidence that seemed to belie his youth. "We are rather like a small family and with any small family there are bound to be disagreements now and then. I came from Kinnoull Monastery in Perth, Scotland, and we had no such discord there, but then there were over a hundred and fifty of us at the time. If there had been discord, I doubt I'd have heard about it anyway." He gave an easy grin that made me quite like this self-assured young man.

"Discord?" Colin repeated casually, the fingers of his right hand tapping on his knee, alerting me to the fact that he was obviously aching to snatch a coin from his pocket and begin twirling it around.

"Yes, the usual sorts of disagreements from like-minded individuals. There can be great passion in debates, and I think it fair to say that these brothers are most certainly men of passion."

"Men of passion . . . ?!" Colin parroted with notable disbelief.

"Most certainly. Our entire adult lives are dedicated to God. Would you not consider that choice the very summit of passion?"

Colin turned to me with such an expression of incredulity that I was almost unable to suppress the laugh that begged to leap from my throat. "Your point is well-made," he conceded as he glanced back at the young man. "And what sorts of debates do the good monks of Whitmore Abbey have? Has there ever been one that brought you any level of concern?"

"Never. No matter the flare of temperaments or harshness of words, at the end of every evening we lower our heads as one community and pledge our lives, hearts, and souls to God. We are but vessels for His word and struggle only in our desire to better understand what He would have us know."

It took Colin a moment to respond. "Of course . . ." he finally said with a nod that I supposed was meant to cover his clear astonishment at having so thoroughly lost control of this conversation. "I wonder if we might trouble you to allow us access to your abbot's cell one more time."

"Oh . . ." Brother Nathan's expression instantly showed his disappointment. "The priest padlocked it and I certainly don't have a key. You might ask Brother Green."

"Thank you," Colin said as he stood up, once again offering something of a mirthless grin. "We appreciate your time and shan't trouble you a moment longer."

"As you wish." The young man gave a quick nod as he too stood up. "Shall I see you out then?"

"No, I think we shall take your advice and speak to Brother Green."

"Very well," Brother Nathan said as he padded back to the door and let himself out with the same remarkable silence these men seemed so practiced at.

"Well . . ." I heaved a sigh. "At least he's the first of these monks to admit there's been even the slightest amount of friction here."

"Indeed . . ." Colin muttered as he headed over to the kitchen door, "it seems this day may prove to be a watershed." Which instantly put me back in mind of the *Codex Sinaiticus* he had mentioned earlier. While I knew a codex to be a collection of ancient manuscripts, most often of scriptural texts, I had no notion of what a *Sinaiticus* was. And yet, before I could ask for even the most banal of explanations, he pushed open the door and called out for Brother Green. *"Might Mr. Pruitt and I trouble you one more time?"*

"It's no trouble at all," Brother Green stated patiently as he strolled back from the kitchen, his manner as genuine as ever. "Have you changed your mind about staying for dinner?"

Colin's eyebrows elevated and his smile warmed markedly. "You do make it hard to decline, but I am afraid we simply cannot stay tonight. I was actually wondering whether you might be able to let us into the abbot's cell for one more quick inspection. It is vital that we not overlook anything."

For the first time I watched Brother Green's face crumple as though his imminent failure was a distinct cause for humiliation. "I'm afraid Brother Morrison has the only key. Father Demetris gave it to him before he returned to Chichester. I would take you to Brother Morrison right now, but I know he's in vespers with most of the others and it would be so inopportune to disturb them. Perhaps you can wait until tomorrow?"

Colin's face went still, his own disappointment nearly as evident as Brother Green's. "Of course," he said. "Then permit me one last question."

"Anything at all." Brother Green practically beamed again.

"We have heard mention of several heated debates amongst the senior members of the abbey over the past year. Have there been any recently that elicited any sort for concern on your part?"

"Oh no," Brother Green chuckled, his broad face and ample belly jiggling at the very thought. "There's never been anything like that." He leaned forward as though about to impart a great secret. "As I am sure you can imagine, one of the hardest attributes of being a monk is the depth of our solitude, even as we live together in this community. Some of the brothers tend to forget diplomacy and end up being far more confrontational than they mean." He chuckled again. "But there's never any offense meant or taken. It is nothing more than friendly discourse, often with a dollop of ardor."

"And are you one of those fiery monks?" Colin asked.

"I've been known to have my say," he muttered unconvincingly, "but it is our most senior members who, rightfully, carry the heaviest responsibility for having their convictions deliberated."

"Of course . . ." Colin nodded. "Well, I'd say it's time we left you to your dinner preparations."

We thanked Brother Green and as I followed Colin out I took note of the sudden bounce in his step. While I too found it interesting that these men did not always agree, I hardly felt uplifted to learn that the elder monks debated their passions now and again. "You seem awfully pleased," I grumbled as we stepped outside.

"I'm beginning to feel there is much to be pleased about."

"Debating monks and some monastery in Egypt I'm rebuked for never having heard about?" I complained. "It all means nothing to me."

Colin glanced back at me with an amused grin. "Then allow me to tell you a most extraordinary story about a monastery at the foot of Mount Sinai while we walk back to Dalwich," he enticed.

# CHAPTER 14

We arrived at the boardinghouse where Constable Brendle resided with remarkable speed, a feat I attributed to the fact that we'd had much to discuss on our way. What pleased me the most was learning that *Sinaiticus* referred to the foot of Mount Sinai where the codex bearing its name had first been found, hidden away in the same Saint Catherine's Monastery where the abbot had gone several years before. And while I had not yet received answers to all of my questions, Colin had nevertheless begun to educate me on the astonishing facts surrounding the ancient monastery in Egypt and how it could conceivably correlate with the abbot's murder and mutilation. All of which left me flooded with mixed feelings when we managed to reach the constable's flat long before I was ready to do so.

"We will take up this topic again later," I warned as we climbed the stairs to the constable's rooms.

"How I wish you had access to The British Museum library just now," he answered back. "There is so much I can only strain to remember, and I think we would be in good stead if you could root about the reference materials for us just now."

"I would like nothing more at this moment," I agreed as he

rapped on the door. It pleased me that he valued my ability to sleuth amongst the stacks, but it also frustrated me as well since I would have no such opportunity.

To my surprise it was the towering, lanky Graham Whitsett who finally pulled open the door. The poor man looked pale and full of remorse and he was unable to offer so much as the ghost of a smile as he bade us enter. "Please . . ." was all he said in a wearied and demoralized tone.

"It's good to see you, Mr. Whitsett," I responded with as much bravado as the situation dared warrant. "I'm sure Constable Brendle is grateful for your assistance."

"I . . ." he started to say, but he seemed unable to articulate anything but his unequivocal regret and did not finish his thought.

"How is the patient doing this evening?" Colin asked as we moved into a small seating area that was devoid of personal touches yet managed to be quite homey just the same. There was a sofa and single chair arranged before a fireplace that was puttering more than anything else, and a small bedroom and water closet was off to one side. While the space was diminutive, it was also immaculate, attesting to the fact that either the good constable was a man of cleanliness and organization, or the proprietress of the establishment took extraordinary care of her boarders.

"He's . . ." Poor Mr. Whitsett was apparently quite unable to alight on any fully formed thoughts.

"*Why don't you come back here and ask for yourself?*" a voice thick with opiates called out from the other room.

"Now there's a good sign." Colin smiled as he led the three of us back to the bedroom. "I guess it safe to say you've now truly been indoctrinated into the constabulary profession."

Constable Brendle groaned. "I could have done without such an initiation."

"I am so sorry, Lachlan . . ." Mr. Whitsett mewled from behind me.

"Now, Graham, we've been over this—"

"I've an idea," Colin interrupted, swinging around and casting his gaze at Mr. Whitsett through a veil of false enthusiasm.

"I'm betting you've been fussing over the constable since we brought him back here. How about you get yourself some dinner and Mr. Pruitt and I will keep an eye on him for a while."

"Oh . . . I don't know. . . ."

"Go," the constable insisted with a heavy sigh. "I'm only going to sleep. You can come back tomorrow and see to me then."

"If you think it best . . ." Mr. Whitsett answered, though it was clear that *he* did not.

"Without question," Constable Brendle replied with surprising vigor and I could only imagine how Mr. Whitsett's mood had affected him.

Mr. Whitsett seemed to catch the tone and gave a nod that contained something of a grimace before he snatched up his bowler, shoved it onto his head, and bid us all a hasty farewell. The instant the door clicked shut behind him the room felt relieved of its burden, though the unfortunate constable looked not one whit better. His auburn hair was matted and tangled on the pillow, which only further set off the grayish tone of his skin. Though his eyes were mostly open, they looked unable to properly focus with his lids drooping listlessly, assuring me that he was indeed under the influence of either laudanum or some other comparable opiate. His right leg was elevated atop a multitude of pillows, and there was a large bandage covering his thigh from knee to groin.

"You look ever the worse for wear," Colin announced with a sympathetic smile.

"I am grateful it was not worse," the constable answered. "The doctor tells me the bone will knit and I shall have little more than the scars left by the bullet as mementos. And"—a wry grin ghosted across his face—"apparently the endless guilt of Mr. Whitsett as well."

We both chuckled. "Is there anything we can do to make you more comfortable?"

"You can find the man who killed Abbot Tufton and Maureen O'Dowd. I believe the laudanum will do the rest for me."

"You must watch out for that. . . ." I blurted without thinking. "What I mean is . . . it *absolutely* has its place in medicine. . . ." I tried to backtrack as artfully as I could even as Colin's gaze slid toward me, an eyebrow arced skyward.

"Yes." Colin offered a thin smile. "Do try not to make an addict of yourself." I grit my teeth, but the constable only chuckled. "And in the meantime you might find it notable that I am not in the least convinced that the same perpetrator is responsible for both of these murders."

"What?!" Constable Brendle jerked his head back, earning himself a wince for the effort. "You cannot mean to suggest . . ." He left the rest of his thought unspoken, but his gaze was more alert than it had been since our arrival.

"I will explain my current state of mind, but I wonder if you would allow me a bit of information first?"

The constable flipped his gaze between Colin and me as if trying to gauge whether there was some hidden intent on Colin's part between his momentarily withholding information and his sudden interest in plying him with questions. Which of course, there was. "What is it you would like to know?" he finally asked.

"You mentioned that you were one of Miss O'Dowd's indiscretions over the last few years. I believe that was the word you used—*indiscretion.*" The way Colin repeated the word made it clear that he keenly remembered it to be precisely what Constable Brendle had said.

"It's true."

"Did you know Miss O'Dowd to have had many such indiscretions?"

"Oh . . ." He heaved a wearied sigh and shook his head slightly. "You mustn't judge Miss O'Dowd. She had an enormous heart and took great joy in her life. And hers was not always an easy one."

"You misunderstand," Colin corrected at once. "I seek to make no judgments against Miss O'Dowd. I am hardly in any position to do so," he added with something of a rogue's grin. "I am only looking to assemble the facts around Miss O'Dowd's life as you know them so I may discern the truth of how she came to such an end. Everything from who she was to how she behaved, as

any one of these characteristics could prove to be the critical ele-
ment that culminated in her murder."

Constable Brendle let out yet another laden sigh as he stared
up at the ceiling for a minute, reminding me of how taxing our
visit had to be on him. But there was little room for subtlety if
we were to bring a swift end to the poor woman's murder. "Miss
O'Dowd was the type of woman who did as she pleased," he finally
answered in a voice that remained hesitant and thin through the
haze of the narcotics he was taking. "She was tied to no one before she and Edward Honeycutt began to court. That was when
she ended our dalliance. So yes, I believe she had her share of
assignations, but they were only the flirtations of a carefree
young woman."

"Were you angry when she put an end to your affair?"

"Angry?" His eyes flicked back to Colin with a curious
frown. "Whyever should I have been angry? We shared each
other's company from time to time. Nothing more. There was
nothing for me to be angry about."

"Then you did not wish to have your affections be taken
more seriously? Certainly communications between men and
women can be so confounding at times."

"She and I had no such quarrel. We were friends. Nothing
more. And sometimes we kept each other from being lonely."
He gave a modest shrug. "When she told me that she and Edward
had begun seeing each other, I was genuinely happy for her."

"And were there others at the time she broke it off with you?"

"Others?"

"Other men helping her stave off her loneliness?" Colin
pressed, and I felt myself squirm at his artlessness.

Constable Brendle flushed slightly and diverted his eyes, his
fatigue evident. "I didn't have any such conversations with Miss
O'Dowd of that nature," he mumbled.

I reached out and discreetly touched Colin's arm and he
snapped his gaze to me, his eyes as filled with determination as if
we were seated across from a suspect in a Scotland Yard interro-
gation room. "I think it's time for us to let the constable get some

rest." I spoke quietly as I knew the young constable would protest, which is exactly what he started to do.

"No, no . . ." Colin cut him off, a hint of disappointment nestling in behind his eyes just the same. "Mr. Pruitt is right. We have badgered you enough for one night. You must rest so you can take up your mantle again as quickly as possible."

"I cannot thank you gentlemen enough," he answered wearily, his eyes desperately seeking to drift shut. "I don't know what I would do if the two of you weren't here."

"We are pleased to be of service," Colin said with a quick smile.

"Is there anything we can do before we go?" I asked.

"Would you send up my landlady please?" he muttered. "She has promised to look in on me and be the keeper of my medicines. I'm afraid my leg has begun to set up quite a row."

"We shall fetch her at once," I soothed. "Do try to get some rest."

"We'll check back with you tomorrow and fill you in on our proceedings," Colin assured him.

"I would insist upon it," he said in a tone void of any insistence. "And you must tell me why you don't suppose these murders to be done by the same hand. I would demand to hear it now," he managed to add even as his eyes finally closed, "but I'm afraid I wouldn't remember what you'd told me. . . ." He chuckled hollowly.

"I shall," Colin agreed as we began to back out of the small room, "I shall."

Only after we eased the front door closed did I turn a scowl on Colin. "You cannot pepper him with so many questions and such thinly veiled accusations when he is in such a poor current state."

Colin scowled right back at me. "And what better time can you presume to rend the truth from a man than when he's swimming under the wave of opiates? Given the nature of how Miss O'Dowd's murder was obviously meant to appear an imitation of the abbot's, then who better to perpetrate such a replication than the man who investigated the first? It is imperative to remove him from suspicion."

"And have you done so?" I conceded.

He glanced over his shoulder at me with an incredulous look as we descended to the first floor to find the constable's landlady. "Not in the least," he replied flatly.

# CHAPTER 15

It appeared, as with any pub in the whole of the British Isles, that Saturday night was the most popular time at the Pig and Pint. If the residents of Dalwich totaled five thousand, Raleigh Chesterton's establishment felt crowded enough to be hosting the vast majority of them. Colin, Doyle O'Dowd, and I were sitting at a table at the very back of the pub and there were enough people hovering about in clustered groups with schooners of ale that even the floor space was at a distinct premium. And given the high-spirited volume and revelry of the throngs of people, we were finding it necessary to speak at an elevated level in order to be heard.

"I appreciate ya buyin' me dinner after wot 'appened," the young man said with a sloppy grin as he knocked back a slug of ale.

"I assure you that we all want the same conclusion," Colin stated simply.

"Do either of ya 'ave a younger sister?" he asked.

"Neither of us," Colin answered, leaving me both relieved and saddened that he had not mentioned my infant sister, Lily, whom I had lost so very long ago.

"Then ya can't really know what it's like," he stated emphatically. "Mo was too trustin' of ever'body. I was always tellin' 'er 'ow most people ain't worth a fig and she shouldn't give a ruddy shite about any of 'em, but she wouldn't listen ta me. She thought she was clever and could take care a 'erself, but she couldn't. And ya know what?" He stared at us keenly, his dark brown eyes almost black in the flickering gaslight. "That's all I got left ta remember now. I shoulda made 'er come ta Mountfield so's I could keep a watch on 'er. Maybe married 'er off ta one a me miner blokes." He took another pull of ale and dragged a sleeve across his lips. " 'At's what I shoulda done."

"Do you really believe you could have forced her to leave Dalwich?" I asked, eager to assuage his guilt just as I had so desperately needed someone to do for me after my mother's final rampage had left the entirety of my family dead.

He gave me a stiff shrug and stared off into the mass of people chattering and milling about, for whom this was just another Saturday eve. "I'd 'ave liked ta try," he muttered after a minute.

I sipped at my soda water as I had not wanted to drink alcohol after having hurt my head, then downed a bit more of the willow bark powder Colin had gotten from the doctor to soothe my returning pain. For his part, Colin was nursing an ale with far less flourish than Doyle, which seemed not to make the least bit of difference to the young man as he waved our barmaid over to order his third pint. She was a pretty woman of middle years named Molly who had a soft, cherubic figure that assured her much notice amongst the men. Mr. Chesterton had told us she only worked Friday and Saturday nights, but I wondered if that wasn't about to change given the death of Miss O'Dowd.

"That Molly seems quite taken with you," Colin remarked after she had left to fetch his order. "Has she been working with your sister for long?"

"Few years. But she's got five young kids, which is sayin' somethin' since 'er 'usband is at sea most a the year," he answered cheekily.

"Oh . . ." Colin shook his head and chuckled. "I must be mistaken then."

"You ain't," Doyle answered with a proud sniff. "We 'ave it off every couple a months when I'm around. She gets lonely, ya know? So I do wot I can," he laughed. "It's jest a spot a fun. It don't mean nothin'."

"And your sister . . . ?" Colin asked quite suddenly, seemingly apropos of nothing. I cringed as I held my breath and waited to see whether Doyle was going to launch himself across the table at Colin.

True to form, Doyle's brow caved in. "Wot?"

"What did your sister do when she got lonely?" Colin pressed with sublime innocence.

"Wot kinda balmy question is that?"

"It is nothing of the kind!" Colin defended. "I am trying to ascertain the murderer of your sister, Doyle. In order to do so, I must learn everything I can about her in spite of your determination to continuously paint her with the brush of a vestal virgin. And while Edward Honeycutt appears to be the only man she was truly in love with, you seem prepared to disembowel him with your bare hands. Now why don't you start telling me the same truth about your sister that you are so willing to share about Molly."

"Eh . . . ?" We all three turned to find Molly standing there, her brown hair curled up in a frazzled bun as she slammed another pint in front of Doyle. "Wot's 'at you're sharin' 'bout me?" she asked, her hackles raised as she stabbed her fists onto her hips.

"It weren't nothin'." Doyle waved her off. "I'm tellin' 'em about your feckin' kids."

She scowled at him as her name was hollered from somewhere off in the mêlée behind her. "That better be all you tell 'em. I ain't the one done nothin' here. I loved Mo. So don't you be sharin' shite about me." She poked Doyle's shoulder with a finger before disappearing back into the crowd.

He snickered. "She's full a sport, 'at one."

"I really don't care about her," Colin said, his voice going flat as his gaze bore into the side of Doyle's face.

I could tell by the shadow that crossed behind Doyle's eyes that he not only understood what Colin was driving at, but didn't particularly appreciate it, either. "Mo were me only family, ya know," he pointed out needlessly.

"Which is precisely why you need to start talking to us. Telling us the truth. Justice is the only vengeance you can bring to her death now."

Doyle O'Dowd heaved a pained sigh and took a long pull of his ale before sweeping a hand through his wavy black hair. "She 'ad a big 'eart, ya know? She liked people. She liked ta 'ave a good time and laugh. Ain't nothin' wrong with that. Nothin' at all." He gazed off a moment and I wondered if he was reconsidering the validity of his words. "After our mum brought us 'ere ta Dalwich, it weren't easy for Mo. She were barely more than a toddler, and our mum liked the inside of a whiskey bottle a 'ell of a lot more than she liked either one a us. After a couple a years I knew I 'ad ta get a job or we was gonna starve ta death. 'At's when I went ta Mountfield ta work at the mines. I did odd jobs fer a while, but soon's I was old enough they gave me a pick and sent me inside." He shook his head as though trying to jostle the memories free. " 'At's all I know. 'Cept leavin' Mo behind with our mum. . . ." His brow furrowed. "Didn't take 'er long ta start gettin' into trouble."

"What kind of trouble?"

"Why's 'at matter?"

"It could matter a great deal," Colin insisted.

Doyle glared off with an expression of pique, his lips pressed tightly together even as his eyebrows crumpled further. I thought it good fortune that Molly arrived at our table at just that moment with a dinner plate in each hand and a third balanced on her left forearm. "I got two fish and chips for the London chaps," she announced as she set the plates in front of Colin and me. "And one shepherd's pie for the cheeky bugger from the ruddy mines," she said as she swept the third plate from her arm and slid it in front of Doyle. "Now mind yer manners," she said with a snort before heading away.

"Ya see 'ow it is with 'er?" Doyle said with great seriousness as he stared down at the perfectly bronzed swirl of potatoes atop his pie. "She pokes and teases and shakes her arse ta get me eye. And she gets it too. 'Cause 'at's wot she wants. Someone ta pay 'er a bit a mind. Make 'er feel like she's worth somethin' once in a while. And 'at's 'ow it was with Mo. Our mum didn't give two figs about us, so I went down inta the mines and Mo got 'erself inta trouble with some a the young blokes." He dug into his dish, scooping out a massive forkful and stabbing it into his mouth with enough vigor to ensure we understood that he wouldn't be fielding any more questions at the moment.

"She started doin' some drinkin' of 'er own," he continued when he was ready. "And why wouldn't she when our mum made such a sport of it?!" he grumbled. "But Mo got it wrong. She thought all them sods she was flirtin' with really cared about 'er. Ya know?" He took another bite of the dense mixture of beef, vegetables, and potato while we waited for him to start up again. I was certain I knew where this story was leading and found I could only poke at my fish and chips, though Colin didn't seem the least disturbed as he splashed on another layer of vinegar and tackled what remained on his plate.

"You *know* wot them arses cared about," Doyle said after another minute. "It weren't long before she were carryin' a baby and couldn't even be sure who the wretched thing belonged to."

"Your sister has a child?" Colin sputtered.

"She lost it!" he snapped back. "Thank the Lord," he muttered as he quickly crossed himself, his fork bobbing through the air as he did so. "Our mum never knew, but Mo told me 'cause she 'ad ta tell someone." He shook his head and slid the rest of his meal away, sinking back into his ale. "I tried ta tell 'er these guttersnipes didn't give two bloody shites about 'er, but she wouldn't listen ta me. She said they made 'er feel special." He snorted derisively as he shoved his mug toward the end of the table next to his plate. "*Molly!*" he hollered to little effect across the din of the bar.

Colin poured the whole of his nearly untouched beer into Doyle's glass and slid it over to him. "I'm not much in the mood tonight," he explained.

"Not in the mood?" Doyle laughed. "I ain't never 'eard a such a thing." He snatched up the mug and took a slug with a cat's smile. "I do hate waste," he said with a snort.

"I should think," Colin spoke carefully as he pushed his plate away, "that given everything you've told us there must have been at least a few people in Dalwich who didn't approve of your sister's activities."

Doyle's mouth curled acidly. "Who are any a them ta think the less a 'er? She were a good girl. She were—"

"I don't need to be convinced," Colin interrupted. "I've already told you that I found her charming. What I'm trying to discover is who may *not* have thought her equally so? A spurned lover . . . ?" He eyed Doyle cautiously. "The wife of a spurned lover . . . ?"

"I don't know about any a that," Doyle snarled.

"Then let me ask you something you *do* know about." Colin continued to watch Doyle closely. "Edward Honeycutt tells us he was ready to make your sister his wife. Indeed, he appears quite distressed by her death. So why exactly is it that you find him so loathsome?"

Doyle's spine stiffened. "Ya think me sister couldn't a done better than the pissant son a some dairy farmer wot looks down on 'er? 'E thought 'e could 'ave 'er around whenever 'e wanted and when 'e got tired 'e'd jest push 'er away like an empty plate. I'd come back 'ere ta visit and she'd be all long faced and moonin' over the sod. Made me bloody brassed off. But every time 'e'd glance 'er way again, she'd go runnin'." His face screwed up with displeasure. "She always went back." His eyes appeared to almost blacken as he added, "And I know wot 'is da thought of 'er. I know wot 'e said about 'er."

"So what?! She wasn't going to marry his father. She was betrothed to Edward."

"Wot's a difference?" he sneered.

"Are you saying you're the same man your father was?" Colin pressed. "Because I can tell you that I am certainly very different from the man my father sought to raise."

Doyle glared at Colin as though he thought himself on the verge of being tricked. "I don't remember me da'," he answered sourly, "so I really couldn't say. But if that old shite farmer 'ad anythin' ta do with Mo's death, I'll kill 'is whole bleedin' family."

"I'll keep that in mind," Colin scowled, "should any of them turn up dead."

Doyle's frown deepened. "I told ya what ya wanted ta know, so you had best get the bastard responsible right quick. I ain't sittin' around waitin' while you lot pussy around like a bunch a slags."

Colin's expression fouled as he sat back and folded his arms across his chest, making me dread what he might be about to say. "We will ensure..." I quickly started talking before Colin could, "...that your sister's murderer faces the full wrath and judgment of the law. And if that doesn't suit you, then I would suggest you beware lest you end up facing the same fate yourself."

"*Pish,*" Doyle waved me off. "Let 'em come down inta the mines and find me."

"If I don't solve this case by week's end, you are free to do as you please," Colin put in from out of nowhere, his demeanor clipped and impatient.

"Week's end? Today's Saturday," Doyle said, his manner utterly wary. "Wot's week's end?"

"Friday," Colin responded coolly. "The end of the week is Friday. By next Saturday Mr. Pruitt and I shall be on a train back to London. So tell me, was there anyone your sister complained to you about recently? Anyone she professed to being bothered by?"

"Nah." He waved us off and slugged back more of his beer. "Mo didn't tell me shite like that. She knew I'd a torn anyone apart wot badgered 'er. Includin' that 'Oneycutt boy." He leaned forward and stabbed a finger at Colin. "You be sure an' look at 'im real close. I bet 'e weren't so 'appy about Mo 'avin' 'is baby wot with 'is plans ta start some new life in London and all. I still ain't convinced 'e were really gonna take 'er anyhow. It's easy ta say now that she's gone. And 'is ruddy da' ain't one whit better."

"We are looking at everyone," Colin reassured with noticeable impatience. "If you should remember anything your sister might have told you recently, I would ask that you let me know. I will not disappoint you, Doyle, but I will caution you to work *with* me, not against me."

Doyle finished his ale and wiped his lips with a sleeve as he shoved his chair back. "I won't even be near ya. I've gotta get back ta Mountfield or I'll lose me job." He stood up and leaned over us, his lithe body more menacing than it had any right to be. "But I'll be back at yer week's end and you'd best be a man a yer word." He snatched up his cap and faded into the crowd before either of us could devise a reply.

"Week's end?!" I said to Colin with my own scowl. "How the hell did you come up with that?"

"Things are beginning to take form," he responded quickly, his eyes flashing with enthusiasm. "It is a small town where everyone seems very much to have been about one another's business. I feel quite confident that Miss O'Dowd's killer will not be able to evade us for long."

"Can I get you gentlemen anythin' more?"

I looked up to find Annabelle White standing over our table rather than Molly, her mood still somber, yet far better controlled than it had been the night before. "I think we have had enough for one night," I answered with a faint smile, pleased to see that she could rummage the same in return.

"Might I pester you with a quick question or two?" Colin spoke up.

She glanced around herself and it was plain to see that she was checking for Mr. Chesterton's whereabouts. "I s'pose I've got a minute. . . ."

"What do you make of Doyle O'Dowd?"

A sideways grin blossomed across her face. " 'E's a good man. Loved 'is sister. Ya can't let 'is bite turn yer 'ead. 'E don't mean nothin' by it. 'E's jest scrappy. That's the way things 'ave been for 'im and Mo."

"Do you think he disapproved of his sister's behavior around the men in here?"

" 'E 'ad no room ta talk," she snapped, making me suspect that she'd fallen prey to Doyle's attentions herself at some point.

A thin smile flickered across Colin's lips and I knew he'd seen it too. "I see. And was there anyone in particular here, besides Edward Honeycutt of course, who was paying particular interest to Miss O'Dowd?"

"Nah"—she shrugged easily and quickly looked around again— " 'alf the men in 'ere were droolin' on Mo, married or not. Plenty a good men too. Forrest James, the son a the dressmaker, was always tryin' ta 'ave at 'er, and Mr. Whitsett 'ad been pesterin' me lately 'bout why she wouldn't spend some time with 'im." She suddenly leaned forward and dropped her voice. "I shouldn't be sayin' this, but even our good constable kept comp'ny with Mo awhile back."

"Yes"—Colin gave her an amused smile—"he did mention that to us."

She straightened up and gave a little shrug. "Well, it weren't no matter 'cause it was Edward finally stole 'er 'eart."

"*Git yer arse back ta work, Annabelle!*" Raleigh Chesterton hollered from across the pub, his voice managing to carry above the din.

" 'Scuse me," she said, her expression instantly mortified as she tipped us an awkward nod before scurrying off.

"No wonder Constable Brendle so readily admitted his liaison with Miss O'Dowd," I remarked as I watched Miss White disappear into the crowd. "It would seem to be one of the town's poorest kept secrets."

"Indeed it would," Colin agreed, a note of curiosity edging into his voice.

I looked back at him, aware of some consideration percolating behind his eyes, and was suddenly reminded of his assurance to Doyle. "I don't see how you expect to solve Maureen O'Dowd's murder by week's end. . . ." I said. "And what of Abbot Tufton? It feels like we've learned almost nothing. Those monks live in such a tight community I don't see how we'll ever get them to confide in us. And I'm quite certain that not one of them has, for one moment, conceived of the possibility that one of *them* might actually have killed their abbot. And now that you've said it to them"—I shook my head—"I'm afraid you've only made them trust you less."

He dismissed my concern with a blunt wave of a hand. "It doesn't matter. We are on the precipice of discovering the abbot's killer," he insisted. "We just need to get access to the abbot's cell again tomorrow and that disorganized monk in the library. . . . What's his name?"

"Brother Bursnell."

He nodded as though it sounded familiar, which I rather doubted. "Yes . . . him . . . he needs to find the abbot's journals from Egypt." He abruptly leaned toward me, his eyes aflame once again. "As I told you before, the *Codex Sinaiticus* was discovered some fifty years ago at Saint Catherine's Monastery, and it stunned the world's religions. Most specifically the Christian faith these monks practice. The documents, the oldest *ever* found, revealed that over thirty thousand errors, deletions, and changes had been made to the original biblical texts since the time of their initial writing. Profound changes!" He stood up and stared back at me. "Imagine how it would feel to have devoted your entire life to the study and contemplation of writings that turned out to have been manipulated *tens of thousands of times* to meet whatever requirements suited the scribe at the time." He gave a shrug and shook his head once, one of his eyebrows slowly drifting skyward. "Now, don't you find it just a touch curious that the abbot from Whitmore Abbey should have traveled to that very place just a few years ago with two emissaries of the Pope?"

"But it *was* a few years ago," I reminded. "Why might that make a difference now?"

Colin smiled and I knew he had a ready answer. "Because of Margaret and Agnes Smith," he said, and their names did clatter about my head with some familiarity. "The two sisters who have just returned from that very same monastery with yet another set of astonishing documents. The *Codex Syriacus,* they're calling it."

"Oh . . . !" I was struck at once by the familiarity of the name. "I have read something about that. But I don't recall what those writings signify?"

"They threaten to convulse the very foundations of Christianity itself," he said. "So, how do you suppose those monks feel now?"

# CHAPTER 16

The scream pierced my dream with the suddenness of an alpine avalanche. I do not recollect to where my subconscious had ranged at the point in my slumber when I was thusly struck. For wherever I had roamed I was returned to my body—to the bed in that minuscule room in Dalwich, Colin curled at my side, his upper arm draped haphazardly across my waist—with the speed of a North Atlantic squall. And when the second scream instantly followed, every bit as tormented and distraught as the first, my eyes flew open and I felt Colin burst from the bed. That was when I heard the unmistakable sound of a body collapsing to the floor. It took another moment before I became aware of footsteps pounding up the stairs to undoubtedly head our way.

I bolted up to a sitting position and found Colin coiled beside the bed panting like a feral dog, not so much as a thread covering him. My eyes swung to the left, seemingly of their own volition, and it was then that the full turn of events finally became obvious to me. For there, sprawled across the threshold to the room, was the young chambermaid, Dora.

"Cover yourself," I hissed at Colin, though what difference it made now I could not have explained.

With one motion he reached over, seized the blanket from the bed, and wrapped it around his waist, leaving only the thin muslin sheet to maintain my own bit of decency.

"What the bloody *hell!*" Raleigh Chesterton gasped as he steadied himself with a hand on the doorjamb even as his gaze ranged between Dora, already beginning to awaken from her collapse, Colin, and me. His eyes narrowed as he knelt down and assisted the young woman back to her feet, allowing her to lean against him as though she were gravely injured. "What's this then?" he growled with menace.

"I knocked . . ." Dora was the first of us to speak up, her voice weak and tremulous. ". . . but no one answered. I thought the room was empty, so I opened the door. . . ." Her gaze dropped to the floor as if she herself had been violated and I was certain that was precisely how she felt.

"Mr. Pruitt was not well last night," Colin explained sharply. "You will remember that he hurt his head during the mêlée yesterday when the constable and Mr. Masri were shot. I did not want to leave him alone lest his condition should worsen."

Mr. Chesterton's glare hardened. "Is that so?" He flicked his eyes between his chambermaid and me, clearly trying to measure Colin's words. "And how you feelin' this mornin'?"

"Fine," I blurted through my mortification. "Better," I corrected, and I could feel my face burning with shame.

"Uh-huh. So you jest let this one climb inta bed next ta you 'cause you weren't feelin' good? That's what yer tellin' me?"

I was all set to agree, to make him believe the sense in our having done exactly that, when Dora managed to find her voice one last time.

"That one ain't wearin' nothin'," she burbled, pointing a finger toward Colin as though she suddenly needed to defend the commotion she had caused. "He jumped up and—" She clasped a hand to her mouth and wriggled free of Mr. Chesterton's grip, taking off down the hallway with only the sound of her wailing voice drifting back.

"Well, that's just bloody ripe," Mr. Chesterton seethed. "Not under my roof ya don't. Pack yer things and get the hell out.

And be glad I don't report ya to the constable, ya buggery poofs."

"We are here at your constable's request to solve the murder of Miss O'Dowd," Colin fired back brusquely.

"Not anymore you ain't. The constable can take care of it himself. We've no need for people like you. Ya got twenty minutes," he added, withdrawing from the room with a snarl but leaving the door conspicuously open.

A thousand thoughts rampaged through my head in an instant. We had been so foolish. What had we been thinking to tempt fate in such a way? I feared that Mr. Chesterton or Dora would spread word of what they had seen and wondered what would happen to us as a result. Even if they did not tell the constable, we could be forced to flee the whole of Dalwich without explanation, leaving both murders unresolved. However would Colin explain that to his father or Bishop Fencourt?

I swallowed back all of this as Colin kicked the door shut and roundly cursed. I very much wanted to do the same, but my stomach had leapt into my throat and it felt like all I could do to continue breathing.

"So bloody *stupid* . . . !" he howled as he tore off the blanket and began pulling on his clothes. I had no idea whether he was referring to himself, me, the two of us, or the chambermaid Dora, and did not really wish to know.

I crawled out of the bed and began to dress, noticing for the first time that the day was gray and drizzling. That, I realized, was why we had not awoken at an appropriate hour. There had been no sun to poke at our eyelids or bird arias to prick our ears, and so we had slept far too comfortably, as though in our own home, and it had undone us completely.

# CHAPTER 17

———◦———

Constable Lachlan Brendle managed to summon a smile for us even though he was obviously in considerable discomfort. His injured leg was now swathed in a thick, clumsy metal brace and remained elevated atop a handful of pillows. But it was his sodden hairline, the beads of perspiration on his upper lip, and the glaze in his eyes that fully revealed the current state of his well-being. Whatever opiates he'd been prescribed were clearly not having the impact they should. Nevertheless, I admit to a bit of gratitude for his altered state as I knew it would be unlikely that he would discern the bleak mood that trailed Colin and me as we entered his room.

"Gentlemen . . ." he managed through the midst of his haze. "I am pleased that you've not forgotten me." He gave a lethargic sort of chuckle as we sat down next to his bed, and Graham Whitsett, once again in attendance to assuage his unnecessary guilt, folded his towering form into a chair near the bedroom's door. It was apparent that Mr. Whitsett meant to tend to the constable until he achieved a full recovery. And given the constable's current state of total incapacitation I knew he had to be grateful. "Tell me . . ." His voice was reedy and ever so slightly slurred. "Have you solved all of my cases yet?"

"You flatter us," Colin responded glibly, though there was not a trace of lightheartedness in his tone. Even now our trunk and two valises stood in the entryway of the constable's apartment, though Mr. Whitsett had not bothered to ask why we had brought them. Our options were few and the decision we'd been forced to make had left us both utterly glum. "I am afraid there is much work yet to be done," he added, but said nothing more.

"I insist you tell how you know Miss O'Dowd's murderer to be different from the man who killed the abbot at Whitmore Abbey. You played coy with me yesterday."

"How could you be sure of such a thing?" Mr. Whitsett piped up from the door.

Colin half-turned and offered him the ghost of a smile and I knew he had forgotten the lanky man was even there. "The mutilation of Miss O'Dowd's tongue was sloppy and careless. Clearly done for no greater purpose than to convince us that the murders were linked. If you will recall, the removal of the abbot's tongue was quite purposeful and diligently accomplished, which would seem to speak to the very heart of his murder."

"Oh . . ." Mr. Whitsett said with notable awkwardness, as though he should have discerned the obviousness of what Colin had seen even though none of the rest of us had.

"So where does that leave us?" Constable Brendle asked.

Colin sighed and brushed a hand through his hair, and I could see the frustration on his face even as he struggled to find a suitable answer. While little had actually changed between Colin's boasting to Doyle O'Dowd last evening that he would have his sister's murder solved by week's end, in truth, everything had changed. For myself, I could not stop wondering what had gone wrong with Colin and me in the creation of our minds and hearts. Why were we cursed to be intolerable?

My eyes drifted from the constable's bed to the table beside it that held a small brown bottle with a tincture of opiate. How I yearned for it. If I were closer to it, if I could have swept it off the tabletop without anyone noticing, I fear I might have done so. How peaceful would its thick obliteration have felt. Its release. From everything.

The intensity of my desire for that brittle escape shook me to my core. So many years had passed since I'd been wooed by such thoughts, yet here I was feeling like I could fall backward in the breadth of a heartbeat. I stabbed a hand into my trouser pocket and pulled out a half crown and slipped it to Colin. "Here," I said. "We're not at the monastery now."

He gazed down at the large silver planchet with Victoria's staid profile upon it and an appreciative smile slowly bloomed across his face. "Ah . . ." he murmured. He held the coin a moment, feeling its heft and warmth, before tossing it up slightly and catching it between his thumb and forefinger and quickly tumbling it over the fingers of his right hand. The familiarity of it comforted me at once just as I had known it would. "I was scolded by the monks for my impropriety," Colin explained to the constable with a silly grin. "It seems they are disapproving of money as a whole, let alone flashing it about. Which is something of a conundrum given the inability of most people to survive well without it."

"Not to mention that you would be hard-pressed to find an organization with more of it than their own parent church," the constable smirked.

"Nevertheless," Colin said, "the brothers at Whitmore seem quite content to make do with as little as possible. A noble effort if somewhat vexing when it comes to my own careless habits." He chuckled as he continued to sweep the half crown through its circuitous rotations. "But you asked where we stand on these cases," he remarked thoughtfully, his countenance stiffening even as his right hand continued its easy movements, "and I will indeed share, though I must first ask your kind associate here"—he gestured back toward Mr. Whitsett and I knew he had forgotten his name—"if he will permit us a few moments of privacy with you."

"Privacy?!" Mr. Whitsett's brow furrowed, surprise and embarrassment fighting for equal attention upon his face. "Have I done something to earn your distrust or disfavor? Surely you know the misfortune against Constable Brendle was an error. I remain mortified . . ."

"Now, Graham . . ." the constable started to say.

"Please . . ." Colin nodded toward the slender giant of a man, and I could tell by the apprehension in his gaze that he intended to confide what had transpired this morning to the constable. And so, for the second time in as many minutes, for a single instant I tried to conceive if there wasn't *some way* I might be able to get my hands on that blessed little bottle of opiate beside the constable's bed. "You have earned no such disapproval on my account," Colin reassured the man. "There are other items beyond these cases that I must apprise your constable of and I would ask your indulgence in appreciating their sensitivity."

Poor Mr. Whitsett continued to look startled as his jaw began to twitch before his voice caught up. "I . . . yes . . . yes, of course." He gave a stiff nod and quickly stepped from the room, pulling the door shut behind him.

"I'm afraid my accident has left him quite on edge," Constable Brendle said by way of explanation, though none was needed.

"It is understandable," Colin muttered idly, his mind clearly elsewhere as he seized the coin he'd been rolling between his fingers and dropped it into his vest pocket. "But I'm afraid we have something of a far more personal nature to discuss with you just now."

"Personal?"

"Something happened this morning that may be brought to your attention in your official capacity, and I need to know your feelings on the matter before Mr. Pruitt and I can continue to assist you."

Constable Brendle's brow folded down and his eyes looked more lucid than they had since our arrival. "Whatever are you referring to?"

Colin cleared his throat and scowled back, his nerves well contained within the frown he adopted. "While Mr. Pruitt and I took two rooms at Mr. Chesterton's dubious inn, when his potty little chambermaid burst into one of them this morning it was to find the two of us quite asleep in its bed. You remember that Mr. Pruitt hurt his head yesterday. I stayed with him last night merely to ensure the soundness of his recuperation. All innocence and propriety, mind you . . . ." He sniffed defiantly, though I noticed that his gaze had drifted from the constable's face. "Nevertheless, she set up a row and fainted in the doorway as though she had walked in on the doings of the ruddy Marquis de Sade himself. Scurrilous assumptions were made and Mr. Chesterton demanded we quit his establishment at once. Which we have most assuredly done. Even now our things are at your door waiting for transport out to the monastery where we shall be forced to stay for the rest of our time here," he added with poorly concealed distaste.

"I'm not sure I understand. . . ." The constable flipped his gaze from Colin to me, and when his eyes fell on mine I found I could not help but look away. If the medicines he was floating upon were diminishing his ability to sort out the implications, I had no intention of enlightening him further nor, I knew, would Colin.

"You understand perfectly," Colin insisted. "If Mr. Chesterton or his chambermaid seeks to file a complaint against us, I need to know what you're going to do."

"Do?!" Constable Brendle managed to summon up something of a chuckle. "I'm afraid I am quite incapacitated at the moment, and what with Mr. Whitsett on temporary leave and Mr. Masri nursing his own injury from the same blasted bullet, unless another murder is committed, the constabulary of this town is unable to *do* much of anything." His eyes clouded for a moment. "Besides, all innocence and propriety, you said. Whyever would something need to be done?" He let out a huff and then hastily focused on Colin again. "And should there actually *be* another murder, Mr. Pendragon, I would be very much in your debt for any additional assistance the two of you could offer. Otherwise I would have to send to Arundel for help, and that lot are quite full of themselves. I find it enough that we must share their coroner."

"We remain at your service then," Colin answered at once, the whole of his demeanor loosening for the first time since we had been awoken this morning.

I took a last glance back at the little brown bottle beside the constable's bed and hoped there was enough left to keep him thusly inebriated for some time to come lest he should have a sudden change of heart when allowed to drift free of its spell.

"Do you suppose we might trouble you to borrow your nursemaid Mr. Whitsett long enough to have him take us and our belongings out to the monastery?" Colin asked with a fleeting smile.

"I wish you would." The constable returned a soft laugh. "I think I should like to sleep without him looming over me all the time as though I were about to expire."

"Then we shall leave you be for today."

"Good and well," Constable Brendle managed as he tried to stifle a yawn, "but I would ask that you come back whenever there is an update."

"And so we shall." Colin gave a succinct nod as he stood. "This remains your investigation to which we are only assisting."

"You are too generous, Mr. Pendragon."

"No more so than is fitting."

I followed Colin to the door as he flung it open and called out for Mr. Whitsett, who had gone no farther than the far side of the short hallway, his lumbering form leaning against the wall as though he was just waiting to be summoned at any moment.

"Mr. Pendragon . . . ?" Constable Brendle's thin voice beckoned from behind us.

"Constable?"

"I do apologize at your being relegated to the monastery. If there were anything I could do . . ."

"Please." Colin smiled. "You have already done far more than you can imagine." And with that said we corralled Mr. Whitsett and our belongings and headed back to Whitmore Abbey—this time to stay.

# CHAPTER 18

In spite of the havoc he had caused, not to mention the grievous injuries to Constable Brendle and Mr. Masri, Graham Whitsett was proving to be a man of integrity and substance. Whether or not he would be allowed to continue to assist the constabulary in the future would be for a magistrate to decide, but his conscience was clearly a driving force in his life. Not only had he agreed to deliver Colin and me to Whitmore Abbey, but he had not so much as grimaced when Colin requested a detour to the telegraph office. The first missive Colin sent off was to Father Demetris to notify him that we were taking him up on his offer of staying at the monastery, though Colin certainly did not elucidate on the reason for our change of heart. The second communication went out to Maurice Evans of Scotland Yard advising him of our change of venue, though it seemed more an excuse for Colin to harangue the poor acting inspector for what he called the "glacial pace" at which the Yard was moving with regard to the whereabouts of Mrs. Hutton. And in spite of the fact that he still had not heard anything back from his father about the Swiss authorities, I noticed that Colin sent no further needling to him.

"Your constable will be out and about again in no time." Colin was reassuring Mr. Whitsett as we jostled along the rutted, dirt path that led to the monastery. In spite of his towering height, the man behaved with a gentleness that belied his stature. It was his marked slimness and the manner in which he persisted in slouching that kept him from being perceived as daunting at first glance, although that impression would be undone the moment he began to speak anyway.

"I appreciate your kind words," he answered in that shy, hesitant way of his. "It is truly a miracle that worse did not happen. I should never have lived with myself . . ." he said before falling silent.

"You mustn't imagine any such thing," I encouraged despite the fact that it had to be nearly impossible not to. "It was all an accident done with the greatest of intentions."

"Yes, of course," he muttered, though he did not seem particularly assuaged by my assertion as he artfully brought the carriage around at the front of the monastery. "Do you need me to wait for you?" he asked, but I could tell he was anxious to get back to the constable.

This time it was Colin's turn to look pained, which I would have found amusing if he had not begun to tug our trunk off the back of the carriage. It was a sobering sight as the reality of what it meant nestled into my stomach. "That won't be necessary as we shall be staying here now," Colin answered. "But perhaps you will be kind enough to offer us another ride back the next time we're in Dalwich? Might we say tomorrow?"

"You can count on me. You know where I shall be." Mr. Whitsett managed a discomfited sort of smile.

I grabbed the valises from the seat next to me and hopped out of the carriage, intending to make an offer of remuneration for the man's time, when I was interrupted by the sound of Brother Morrison's deep, sonorous voice coming from behind me. "What's this . . . ?" he called out from the main doorway as Colin dragged our trunk toward him. "What have you got there?"

"Our belongings," Colin informed him in a tone that was arguably a touch less affable than it could have been. "We are accepting Father Demetris's offer to stay here. It will allow Mr. Pruitt and me a better opportunity to get this case resolved with all due haste so we can leave you gentlemen to your peace, which, understandably, is what you wish."

"I'll not deny it," the elderly monk sniffed, stepping back from the door even as he held it open for us.

I waved Mr. Whitsett off and followed Brother Morrison and Colin into the monastery's entrance hall, toting our valises. As always, the monastery was eerily quiet the moment I stepped inside, and I lamented yet again the fact that our own recklessness had caused us to end up here. Had we learned nothing from Oscar Wilde's recent sentence of two years hard labor? One flouted the laws of morality at one's own risk. It was a disheartening fact to be thusly judged, but in spite of myself, I felt ashamed.

"Leave your things there." Brother Morrison gestured to a space by the main doors as he headed for Abbot Tufton's former office, favoring his right leg as always. "I'll have Brother Hollings move them to a couple of cells in the newer quarter. They may not be of the standard you are accustomed to, but they have cots with mattresses on them, which is far more than I can say for the majority of our rooms."

"You needn't worry about us," Colin answered simply. "I expect our work here to be completed before we so much as require a change of linens."

Brother Morrison lowered himself into the throne-like chair behind the elaborate desk and eyed Colin warily with a marked absence of warmth. "If you should require a change of linens, you shall have to do so yourself. This is not a public house."

"So we have seen."

"There are three toilets in a small outer building near the infirmary, and should you wish to wash yourselves you may do so in the balneary at the far end of the dormitory. I will see that you are given one towel each, but you'll not get another."

"Of course." Colin's nose wrinkled slightly, though he managed to keep his evident distaste to a minimum.

"We appreciate your hospitality," I hastened to add. "I know all of the brothers here are anxious to see this terrible crime resolved and the killer brought to justice."

Brother Morrison turned his gaze on me and I found it unsettling, almost accusatory. "The only justice that matters to me and the men who live here is God's justice. And that will be wrought for all eternity no matter what the two of you do." He leaned back in the huge chair. "*Never avenge yourselves,*" he recited slowly, "*but leave it to the wrath of God, for it is written, 'Vengeance is mine, I will repay, sayeth the Lord.'*"

"The book of Romans," Colin said.

Brother Morrison's face shifted with something akin to disbelief. "Well done, sir. And just how is it you plan on spending your time here? The brothers and I keep a strict schedule and the church teaches it is imperative that we maintain it. We are here at the service of the Lord, not the whims of others. I know Abbot Tufton would agree with me were he with us now."

One of Colin's eyebrows drifted skyward and for a moment I feared what he might be about to say since the monk's words sounded disingenuous given that his abbot *wasn't* here to agree. "Your concern is understood," Colin replied with the flick of a tight smile. "As I assured Father Demetris when he first delivered us here, our intent is not to cause disruption, but to allay it. So, at the moment, what I would like most of all is to inspect your abbot's cell once again and to speak with Brother Silsbury."

Brother Morrison furrowed his brow, making his imperious demeanor seem ever more so. "If I could excise that cell, I would do so. It is like a malignancy that infects everything around it. No one is likely to ever consent to stay there again, and at times I'm quite certain the brothers only pass by it from the far side of the hallway."

"Then you will be pleased to know that we can help with that," Colin announced pointedly, shifting a quick look in my direction that unnerved me when I noticed a dark sort of determination behind his gaze. "Mr. Pruitt will stay in that very cell," he said. "He will easily be able to dispel the anxiety around it within a night or two. And I suspect it should prove useful to our investigation as well. So I believe we will all gain."

"Is that so . . . ?" The elderly monk turned to me with a look as filled with skepticism as it was surprise.

For myself, it felt as though my heart had leapt into my throat and begun careening out of control like a star shooting across the night sky. *Me?!* I was aghast. Wherever had this idea come from? *His* idea . . . *his* scheme. So why was *I* the one who had to do the penance? "Of course," I heard myself answer benignly.

"Very well. Then I shall have Brother Hollings and Brother Nathan remove the furnishings and set up a more proper bed."

"You mustn't," Colin said at once. "That defeats the entire purpose. Leave it as it is. If you start moving items in and out you will only play into the uneasiness surrounding that cell. You absolutely must leave it be, Brother Morrison. I'm afraid Mr. Pruitt insists."

News of my determination to reside in that murderous place without the slightest modification was no less stunning to me than it obviously was to Brother Morrison. He turned to me again, his broad, heavily lined face and dubious gaze searching for an answer I'm certain he believed I was not willing to give. "Indeed," I muttered with as much insistence as I could muster. I was beginning to suspect what Colin was up to, though it hardly made me more appreciative of the fact of the matter: that I would be staying in the room, more accurately sleeping in the very bed, where a man was murdered.

"There you have it," Colin nodded with an abundance of self-satisfaction.

Brother Morrison seemed to carefully consider the whole of the idea before finally concurring with the faintest dip of his head. "Then I presume we can forego a visit there now?" he asked after a moment.

"Without question." Colin allowed a thin smile to breeze across his lips. "Has anyone else been in the abbot's cell since we saw it last Thursday?"

"Of course not," Brother Morrison answered impatiently, his brow collapsing down on itself yet again. "Have I not made myself clear? The brothers go to great lengths to keep their distance. And besides which, it has been kept locked since the morning of the murder and I have the only key."

"Very well." Colin stood up and nodded to me. "Then we

shall be off to speak with Brother Silsbury. I assume he is most likely to be found in the infirmary?"

Brother Morrison stared at us, not moving from the chair. "It is a safe supposition. But I will remind you once again to be respectful of the schedules the brothers keep."

"You have my word," Colin said without a moment's pause.

Even so, as I pulled the door closed behind us I was certain I caught a good deal of doubt on the aged monk's face. Had I not been otherwise preoccupied, I would have pointed it out to Colin, urged him to be more patient and sympathetic of these pious men, but I did indeed have far more personal concerns on the top of my mind. So instead, as soon as the door settled itself back in its jamb I spun on Colin, and fairly hissed, "*What the bloody hell?!*" I could not stop myself, or more honestly, I did not *care* to stop myself.

"What?" he looked at me without a wisp of guile.

"Why am *I* the one who has to stay in that godforsaken cell? If you're so anxious to inspect it again, then *you* stay there." The clicking of our heels echoed loudly along the empty corridor as we made our way toward the back door, reminding me that I needed to keep my voice down or risk being easily overheard. "I cannot *believe* you would volunteer me for such a ghoulish duty. Am I truly just your footman? Here to do your bidding whenever something unpleasant comes along?"

He reared back and stared at me as though I had just accused him of committing these murders himself. "Is that what you think?!" He turned stiffly and started walking again, pushing his way out the door and onto the gravel path that led to the infirmary beyond. "There will be great attention paid to the abbot's cell when you retire tonight. Your comings and goings will almost certainly be noted with every squeak of your door and every step that you take. I need to be able to move about freely the next couple of nights. I cannot be stymied in my movements or it will take me very much longer to solve this case. So while they are concentrated on you, all aflutter over your daring and pluck for sitting in that cell, I shall be pawing through their library, and the abbot's former office, and anywhere else I feel the need to invade." He stopped just outside the infirmary door and glared back at me. "Or would you like to reverse the roles and I will happily get some rest in that blasted cell—a *room,* mind you, nothing more than a *room*—while you go poking about this stifling place?"

His eyes were ablaze with a mixture of anger and offense even as I began to wonder how it was that I had gotten myself so far afield. "I . . ." My mind emptied itself quite completely, leaving me with my mouth agape and my face flooding with rising heat. "I shall inspect every inch of the cell and all of the furnishings thoroughly," I managed after a second.

"Yes." His tone was clipped. "If it wouldn't be too much trouble, I should like to see if you can pull any rubbings off the tabletop. Perhaps we will yet discern what was on the papers that were pulled from his hand after his death." He turned and yanked open the door, barreling inside, before I could summon an appropriately eager response. "*Hello!*" he called out as I followed him inside, my spirits flagging at my obtuseness. "Are you here, Brother Silsbury?"

"Who's there?" A voice echoed from somewhere off to our right, where I remembered the monk's office to be.

"It is Colin Pendragon and Ethan Pruitt."

"Yes, yes." The tall, broad-shouldered monk came bustling out of his small office with a stoic sort of reticence already marring his face. "Good day to you both."

"I hope we're not interrupting your work . . ." Colin said, which was decidedly peculiar given that the infirmary was, as before, empty.

"Not at all." Brother Silsbury waved him off as he pulled three chairs into a loose circle on the near side of the room. "I've just been doing some studying. There is always time enough for that. Now, what can I do for you?" He lowered himself into one of the chairs.

"I understand that you collected the abbot's personal effects and have stored them away for safekeeping."

"Personal effects, is it?" He leaned back and watched us with a deliberate sort of gaze. "I think you will find this a rather short conversation given what little the men here are allowed."

"I am not referring to his clothing or bedding," Colin explained.

"Just as well as I had his nightshirt and bed linens burned. There was no use to it anymore."

"Of course," Colin acknowledged with little interest. "What I am actually curious about are his personal effects. His writings, his Bible, anything he might have kept with him in his cell."

"I see." Brother Silsbury nodded once, crossing his arms over his chest and studying Colin through half-lidded eyes that made me think him oddly leery. "His public papers have already been given to Brother Bursnell for access in the library. I would suggest you start there."

Colin offered a smile that I presumed was meant to be gracious but looked more calculated and cunning to me. "An outstanding idea that we have already availed ourselves of twice before. Brother Bursnell has been generous with his time and the documentation that he has, but it is the items that are *not* there that most prick my attentions at this point. For instance, he mentioned journals the abbot kept from his sabbatical to Egypt a few years ago. . . ."

"Oh yes . . . Brother Bursnell has all of the abbot's journals. Abbot Tufton gave his permission to store his writings in the library some time ago. The things I'm holding are the few personal items that were in his cell at the time of his . . . death. I will be sending them up to his sister in Dorchester. She is his only surviving kin."

"Of course," Colin nodded. "But before you do, I should very much like to view those items, though I must admit to disappointment at hearing that you are not also storing the abbot's journals from Egypt. Unfortunately, they seem to have gone missing."

"Missing?!" Brother Silsbury leveled a disbelieving gaze upon Colin that seemed to question his soundness of mind. "I can assure you they are not missing. All of his journals are right here at Whitmore Abbey, where they belong. One of the brothers is obviously studying them. I can assure you that things do not go missing here, Mr. Pendragon. This is a monastery, not a prison."

"Ah . . ." Colin's eyes went wide and doughy, and for a moment I thought surely I was going to laugh. "But, of course. I did not mean to infer anything unseemly, only that the whereabouts of those particular writings are currently unknown. Just the same, I should still very much like to view the other items he kept in his cell." His smile softened into something more earnest as he added, "If you would be so kind."

Brother Silsbury shrugged slightly, as though he were considering the possibility in spite of the odds being against us. "It would be most unorthodox to have you pawing through the abbot's personal belongings when neither I nor any of the other senior brothers here have yet had an opportunity to review them ourselves." He allowed a tight-lipped bit of a smile to pull across his mouth as he continued to look at Colin and me. "We are but human," he added with an arid chuckle, "and sometimes even the ramblings of a monk can seem disquieting to the uninitiated."

"Disquieting, is it?" Colin repeated, nearly leaping on the word. "How very unexpected. And do you have reason to believe such musings might be in your abbot's papers?"

The monk's brow knit ferociously, though he was too young to have any but the faintest lines etched upon his forehead. "Do you mean to mock me, Mr. Pendragon? To find mirth in my desire to protect the memory and character of a man I admired and served for over ten years?"

Colin's demeanor sobered at once. "Brother Silsbury, the only thing I mean to do is find the person responsible for the death of your abbot. To that end, I would very much like to see the papers and books he was keeping in his cell at the time he was killed. You seem disinclined to allow me such access and I find that fact rather"—he paused and I found myself cringing, certain I knew what he was about to say—"disquieting," he uttered just as I had known he would.

Brother Silsbury popped out of his seat and pounded back to his office, his cassock billowing around his ankles in a display of ill temper as he disappeared without a word. I wanted to caution

Colin that perhaps he was pushing too hard, being too insensitive, but felt I had riled him enough already so chose instead to hold my tongue. To my surprise, I was rewarded with a quick, mischievous smirk just before the perturbed monk returned to the main room with an armful of loose papers and several books.

"Your efforts on behalf of our beloved abbot are an answer to prayer. . . ." The monk spoke with the requisite solemnity in spite of the fact that I could detect a rash of disapproval in his voice. "Which is why I am consenting to your rifling through his things before any of us have had an opportunity to." He carefully laid the pile of documents onto the closest empty bed to where we were standing. "I know you can appreciate how expeditiously we all hope you will be able to complete your time here. I feel certain you are as anxious to return to London as we are to have you do so."

"I could not agree more," Colin said with a rare flash of impeccable honesty as he stood up.

Brother Silsbury remained standing between Colin and the items on the bed, effectively blocking his view. "Just let me request one small favor," he added, a smile dusting across his face that was devoid of both warmth and genuine sincerity. "Please do not discuss the contents of these papers with anyone outside of this monastery unless you have first conferred with me, Brother Morrison, Brother Wright, or Brother Clayworth."

Colin snapped a like smile upon his lips and I knew he would agree to whatever was necessary to see those papers, whether he actually remembered who the latter two monks were or not. "Without question," he blustered. Which proved enough to get Brother Silsbury to stand aside.

"Your understanding is greatly appreciated," Brother Silsbury replied quite grimly, remaining just a step past Colin's shoulder as he began to slowly sift through the loose pages. "We take our responsibilities to one another very seriously. I rather suppose that might be evident given the nature of our lifelong vows."

"Does anyone ever quit?" Colin asked glibly, his attention now fully absorbed with the papers before him.

"*Quit?!*" The poor man looked startled. "This is not a fraternal club, Mr. Pendragon. One does not join or resign on a whim. It is a calling from God."

Colin glanced back at the aggrieved man and gave a succinct nod. "I am aware of that. I only wish to know whether a monk has ever left the monastery for a fresh"—he paused for a second before tipping his head slightly and fording ahead—"calling?"

Brother Silsbury exhaled with a note of irritation. "There are always a few men who will suffer a crisis of faith, but none of them were ever serving here at Whitmore Abbey."

"Very well." Colin flashed a distracted smile as he returned to the papers that he had quite handily splayed out across the bottom of the bed. "Do you mind if I avail myself of Mr. Pruitt's assistance?"

"As you will," the monk answered as he finally took a few steps back.

I did not wait for Brother Silsbury to reconsider but immediately stepped over to Colin as smoothly as I could. "What would you have me look for?"

"The usual," he muttered as he slid the bulk of the papers toward me, saving a thinner section for himself along with a Bible and a small book that was clearly some sort of journal. "Anything that raises your hackles."

I knew precisely what he meant. How many times had I searched through books, files, documents, manifests, inventories, registries, and catalogs over the years, looking for that unnameable something that scratches the unconscious and raises an inkling of suspicion? "Of course," was all I said, eager to wend my way back into his better graces.

"Then I shall leave the two of you to your rummaging." Brother Silsbury took another hesitant step backward. "I presume I am safe in the knowledge that you will neither mar nor remove anything?"

Colin lifted an eyebrow skyward but did not glance back at the man. "I am wounded that you would even feel the need to ask such a thing."

"Yes"—Brother Silsbury gave a stilted chuckle that sounded as though it had been dragged across gravel—"there it is then. I shall be in my office if you require anything further from me. Just let me know when you are finished." It took another moment before he finally turned and stalked back to his office, his long legs carrying him quickly across the room. As before, his cassock rustled around his ankles as he moved, making me marvel that the youngest members were so fleet-footed while those more senior seemed very much the opposite.

"Well, this seems a positive step," I said softly, even though we were alone, "no matter how tentatively given."

"I only wish I could find the abbot's Egyptian journals. A thing missing is always of the greatest interest to me. This"—he held up a handful of papers and let them sift through his fingers—"is unlikely to reveal much of anything."

I leaned forward and grabbed a small wad of pages and yanked them away from him. "You aren't helping by doing that. Besides, I will certainly do my best to see what I can lift from the table in the abbot's cell tonight." I snatched up the abbot's Bible and shoved it at him. "Why don't you study this? You were asking about it before. Perhaps he will have underlined some passages about Egypt." I had meant only to be facetious as I turned back to the pages I had grabbed, eager to find anything that might propel this case forward, but Colin dutifully began flipping through the book before a wearied sigh escaped his lips.

"Ach . . ." he mumbled. "There are an endless amount of passages underlined as though every page is brimming with inordinate value."

"He was an abbot in a monastery. What else would you expect to find?"

"Still"—he continued randomly flipping pages as a frown deeply furrowed his forehead—"how am I supposed to discern the essential from the pedestrian if there are so many bits and pieces called out? Didn't he realize that nothing truly has value if everything is deemed crucial?!"

I wanted to chuckle at his frustration even as I found myself sorting through endless lists of supplies such as candles of every size imaginable, communion wafers, and incense in a variety of fragrances. There was a listing of garments: cassocks, scapulars, cowls, tunics, undergarments, shoes, and sandals, which assured me how meticulously the clothing was monitored for each of the monks. Likewise the catalog of Bibles—one to a man—and the blankets, paper, pens, rosary beads, one pillow, one prayer rug, and on it went, the earthly belongings of each monk listed out with the precision of the military to ensure no monk was treated differently and that each of them made do with nothing more than that which was absolutely fundamentally necessary.

A second set of documents revealed a record of supplies requested for the infirmary by Brother Silsbury himself. There were also requests from Brother Green for foodstuffs and two four-quart cooking pots, which someone had crossed out. Brother Bursnell had submitted an inventory of supplies needed for the upkeep of the library, including a new set of shelving with the specific dimensions of seven feet high and three feet wide, though thinking of the current confines of the library I wondered exactly where he intended to put it.

There was a brief missive from Brother Clayworth, but rather than ordering supplies for his ale production, he appeared to be making a curt demand for more assistance. *As we have discussed, I find myself insisting I be given more support,* he had written, *or I will not be responsible for the fall in our production and its effect upon our solvency.* How like a business the running of this monastery suddenly seemed. For some reason I found the whole of it rather disturbing. How was it that a commitment to spiritual obeisance could end up as elementary as any other business endeavor?

I found a letter that Brother Wright had drafted to Abbot Tufton not about provisions for the garden he tended out back, but about the state of his health. The frequency and severity of his headaches was clearly worsening, and the poor man sounded torn by his suffering: *Has the Lord set before me a test, or am I merely at the whim of a physical body that seeks to dismantle my will with ever greater frequency?* I could not help the feeling of impropriety that coursed through me as I read these private words, but even so I noticed that someone, most likely Abbot Tufton himself, had written a note along the border that said,

*Seek the answer within.* It was a response I could not help but find unsatisfying and was relieved that Brother Wright had not received it back.

"Oh . . . !" Colin said as a folded scrap of paper tumbled out of the Bible and fluttered to the floor. "I do hope it's a treasure map."

"Well, it's awfully small if it is."

Colin snapped it up and carefully unfolded it, his face pinching almost at once as he stared at it. " 'Strauss,' " he read aloud.

"What?"

"*Strauss,*" he said again as he looked over at me. "So are we to believe that the abbot was such a fan of Richard Strauss's compositions that he kept the man's name in his Bible?"

"There are people who believe music is the language of angels."

He looked at me with a faint smile. "Well said. Perhaps our abbot was such a man." He folded the scrap of paper and slid it back into the Bible. "Have you found anything of interest in the rest of that mess?"

"Nothing I can ascribe any real value to. It all seems decidedly commonplace. If Brother Silsbury is holding this for his personal review, I'm afraid he'll be wasting his time."

Colin cast a perfunctory glance around the whole of the clutter of papers. "Just leave it then. There's little else here for us this afternoon." I began to neaten the pile of pages into something more tenable when Colin reached out and caught my arm. "Don't."

"Whyever not?" I protested. "It hardly seems appropriate to leave it in such disarray."

"It is actually quite appropriate." He gave me a mischievous smile. "I should very much like to continue perusing the abbot's Bible for a while and clearly this cagey monk will not allow me to take it to my room." He gestured to the clutter of papers and the small journal lying atop the bed and gave a crooked smile. "I'm hoping this will keep him from noticing its absence for a while."

I shook my head. "I'm not at all convinced about that. . . ."

He shrugged his left shoulder. "I'm afraid it's the best I've got at the moment." Then he stuffed the compact book under his vest against his left side, resting on the waist of his pants. "Discreet?"

"If you keep your jacket open I suppose it will do."

"Thank you, Brother Silsbury!" Colin hastily called out as he headed for the door. "We appreciate your assistance as always. We shall let ourselves out. No need to trouble yourself any further with us."

"As you wish," Brother Silsbury called back with marked disinterest.

And then, chortling like two impish schoolboys, we burst out the door and hurried back to the monastery.

# CHAPTER 19

Mirth is a funny thing and I intend no pun in so stating. When one is the perpetrator of the amusement, then it is indeed a time of great hilarity and joy. But should the situation turn, as such a circumstance often does when someone is the brunt of the entertainment, then it can quickly become wholly regrettable. And so it was for Colin and me when Brother Silsbury came barreling down the monastery's main corridor not three minutes after we had reached it, his annoyance evident in the swiftly cracking sound of his approaching footsteps.

He bellowed at us to stop, which, of course, we did, and then he chastised us, for I can think of no better way to describe his tone and manner, for having pilfered the abbot's Bible. Yet what I found most peculiar was when Colin went to return the small book, he pulled it not from beneath the left side of his vest where I had seen him secrete it, but from the right side. As though it had somehow traversed around his waist while we had attempted to make our getaway.

Brother Silsbury scowled at us as he snatched the Bible back, leveling the sort of self-righteous sneer at Colin and me that I had not seen since suffering under the tutelage of some of the sterner schoolmasters at Easling and Temple. Colin looked uncharacteristically contrite and I could feel the heat of embarrassment coloring my cheeks. It all seemed to placate Brother Silsbury, who shook his head once, and muttered, "I am terribly disappointed," before crisply turning and returning back the way he had come, the small Bible clutched at his side as though it were a holy relic.

"Well, that was unexpectedly vigilant of him," Colin said as he turned and started toward the abbot's office, his attitude curiously upbeat.

"How mortifying," I tsked warily as I was increasingly becoming certain that he was up to something. "Caught like common thieves."

"There was nothing common about our thievery," he smirked as he plucked an identical Bible from beneath the left side of his vest. "For we still have what we need."

"What?" I stared down at the black leather-bound book no larger than the length of Colin's hand and marveled that it looked so similar to the one he'd just handed over to Brother Silsbury. "But the abbot's underlining of passages, the scrap of paper he had stuffed inside . . . Brother Silsbury will know what you've done."

"He said himself that neither he nor any of the other members of this pious community had yet had an opportunity to review the abbot's personal papers, including his Bible. If he is lying and recognizes that I have given him an imitation, then he will have to accuse us of doing so and thereby implicate his own lie. And if he *is* lying, I shall hound him until I find out why." He flipped the abbot's Bible over in his hand several times, the gold-colored edging on the pages creating a striking contrast of severity and substance against the slick black cover. "Outwardly it looks just the same as the one I gave him. They're all the same. It is the standard issue given to each man upon his arrival at Whitmore Abbey. I presumed the abbot's would be no different and, I was pleased to notice when he first showed us his items, I was correct."

"When did you pick up that other one?"

"When I was rummaging through the back shelves in the library yesterday afternoon while you were playing lookout. There is a pile of these back there, so I availed myself of one, presuming it might come in handy."

"And then you underlined a mass of random passages with the intent of switching it for the abbot's Bible?"

He gave an uneasy sort of shrug. "I didn't underline nearly enough. If Brother Silsbury *has* looked at the abbot's Bible in any detail, he will almost surely realize that something is amiss." He chuckled, clearly not in the least concerned.

"When did you do all of this?"

"Last night while you were asleep. My mind wouldn't settle down, so it gave me something to do. I suppose it's part of the reason I overslept this morning."

I felt myself cringe at the memory of this morning. "Well, why didn't you just switch the two Bibles while we were in the infirmary? Why was it necessary to have him chase us down like a couple of reprobates?"

"Because I wanted to see how honest that monk was being with us. Making such a fuss about allowing us to see the abbot's papers. Are we to believe he was penning all manner of indecent material in his cell that has to be carefully filtered before the true nature of this abbey might be known?" He laughed. "Rubbish. I don't trust that monk and I wanted to see how long it would take him to notice the book was gone, and whether he would dare accuse me of swapping it for another."

"It certainly didn't take him long to realize you'd taken it."

"No, it did not." One corner of his mouth turned upward. "Duly noted. And now we shall see if he has the bollocks to accuse me of switching books on him." His eyes went dark. "It will be extremely telling if he does."

Colin rapped on the door to the abbot's office and we let ourselves in at the behest of Brother Morrison. The senior monk did not bother to look even passingly interested in our return from visiting Brother Silsbury, though I imagined he would be inestimably outraged if he knew that Colin had the abbot's personal Bible tucked beneath his coat. Because of Brother Morrison's indifference to us, or perhaps in spite of it, Colin made a fast end to our stop there and we were quickly back outside and on our way for a long overdue visit to Brother Clayworth and his brewery.

The building within which the ale production took place was some distance beyond the monastery on the opposite side from where the infirmary was. It stood just at the brink of where the monastery's wheat and barley fields rolled out from. The brewhouse itself was actually nothing more than a large barn that, given its slightly tattered and sun-beaten appearance, looked far older than the monastery's main building. Though it appeared to be constructed of redwood, its boards were noticeably warped and discolored along the bottom quarter of the building, no doubt a product of the cyclical saturation and baking it endured as a result of fanatical weather.

The large doors that had once swung wide to receive or disembark great teams of horses pulling carriages and wagons were still extant, though one side had been boarded up along the seam of the doorjamb, which only added to the building's general sense of disrepair. The other door appeared to still be usable, though it was closed at the moment, leaving only a small, regular opening near the far left corner to allow us access inside. There were no windows other than the pass-through in the hay loft, as is usual in many barns, but the scent drifting from it was anything but customary. It reminded me of the yeasty tanginess of rising bread with neither the seductive notes of dill, rosemary, caraway, or other herbs and seeds added for flavor, nor any warm, enticing aroma being released as it slowly bakes to a golden brown. This scent was far more elemental, as though we might step inside to find a pond with a thick crust of algae or scum across its surface.

No such sight greeted us as we entered through the small door, however. Rather there was a massive copper pot at one end of the room, large enough to hold half-a-dozen grown men, with a handful of steel, cylindrical-shaped containers of equal or greater size leading from the enormous pot out across the center of the structure, and ten huge wooden casks lined up along the far wall. There was also a series of smaller wooden kegs and metal pots scattered across the open space, none taller than my own waist or rounder than a portly chap of diminutive height.

Three monks were set about various tasks that I could not immediately discern, and while I recognized fresh-faced Brother Nathan, who we'd been told normally toiled in the fields, I could not identify the other two. Not a moment later Brother Clayworth came loping toward us, his black cassock fluttering about his lean frame even as a smile broke across his heavily lined face. As was true the first time we saw him, his silvery-gray hair was poking up defiantly in a myriad of directions, making me wonder if he ever bothered to try and tame it. There was a flush to his cheeks and a slight rosiness across his nose, and though he was taller than Colin, he was still several inches shorter than me.

"Gentlemen!" He shook our hands and clapped Colin on the back as though the two of them were old chums. "I have been wondering how long it would take the two of you to get out here to the heart of our monastery."

"The heart, is it?!" Colin responded with a devilish grin. "I'd have thought that might be your chapel."

"Wise words," Brother Clayworth chuckled as he turned and led us through the large, open working space to a small office near the back that I was quite certain had once been an oversized stall. "The chapel is the *soul* of our community, but this is its beating heart." He laughed and there was fond pride in his voice. "If it wasn't for our little operation here, I'm afraid we'd all be living a mite bit simpler than we do. As would many of the charitable organizations in and around Dalwich." He gestured us to seats as he sat himself on a tall stool behind what looked like a drafting table. There were papers strewn across it and an ever-familiar Bible sitting at one corner.

"So, I gather you have been expecting us?" Colin said.

Brother Clayworth grinned, the lines on his face rearranging themselves with unmistakable pleasure. "Everybody is interested in what we do out here. We don't give tours, you know. Wouldn't be right. After all, this is a monastery first. We just happen to make ale."

"And how is it that's what you've come to do rather than selling produce or baked goods or stained glass or tending to honeybees?"

"Really, sir"—the monk laughed outright—"such pedestrian ideas. There is little money to be made in those endeavors. But this"—he swept his arm toward the vast outer area—"this serves us well and even allows us to donate extra funds to the local charities in Dalwich, Arundel, and a few other nearby towns. There is also an artistry to our brewing that I am very proud of. Have you had the opportunity to taste our newest dark ale? We've only just released it to Mr. Chesterton."

Colin shifted a look at me as one of his eyebrows rose. "We have not."

Brother Clayworth popped off his stool with extraordinary speed and rushed out of the office. "Wait here, gentlemen," he called back, "for you are in for a treat."

As soon as he disappeared around the corner Colin looked at me with an expression of amusement. "I never imagined we would be sampling ales on this case."

"Nor I. But do you really suppose any of this has anything to do with the murder of their abbot?"

"We cannot yet know that, can we?" he asked in his usual reasoned way. "We are but fact-finding, are we not?"

"Yes," I sighed. "Of course we are." I knew better. I could have answered my own questions myself if I'd been asked them. Had I not been at his side for the past dozen years hearing him repeat the same mantra over and over? I started to say as much when Brother Clayworth abruptly returned with three glass steins clutched in his two fists, all three nearly filled to their brims with a dark honey-colored liquid. "Here we are then," he announced as he passed two of them between us before lifting his own in a toast. "To our blessed abbot, John Tufton."

The monk raised his stein, as did Colin and I, and then we each took a hearty pull of the rich, dark beer. Bright carbonation tickled my throat, leaving a clean, crisp taste in my mouth that seemed to have the slightest hint of fruit to it. The ale was neither thick nor malty, but remained sprightly and almost delicate, which was entirely unexpected given its deep, cloudy appearance.

"Wheat beer, if I am not mistaken," Colin said, "with citrus?"

"Ah," Brother Clayworth beamed, "a refined palate. So few

appreciate the true nature of what we do here." He took another sip and looked quite pleased with himself.

"It seems like such an oddity to have monks brewing ale," I said. While I understood the fraternities of monks who produced wines, mostly in France and Italy, given the small amounts used during the communion ceremony, I still did not grasp the purpose of brewing ale other than inebriation. One could hardly continue making the argument for either hydration or nutrient value as had been the case during the Middle Ages.

"Monks have been brewing ales for hundreds of years," Brother Clayworth patiently explained as though he had done so many times before. "Notre-Dame de Saint-Remy abbey in Rochefort, France, has been at it since the late sixteenth century. The abbey Notre-Dame d'Orval in Belgium was in full production by 1628. So you see, there is really nothing odd about it. We seek only to provide a product of value and worth that can sustain us here and, as I said before, any profits we earn beyond our modest needs are donated. So I must refute your contention of any sort of curiosity here."

"You must excuse Mr. Pruitt," Colin spoke up with a cavalier grin tugging at his lips, "but he is a Protestant."

"Ah"—Brother Clayworth nodded as he took another swallow from his glass—"that does tend to clarify."

I rolled my eyes as Brother Clayworth snorted a laugh. Colin tipped his mug toward me and took a second taste of his ale with a satisfied grin, so I did the same, which led merry Brother Clayworth to follow suit. His mug was now better than half empty, and I noticed that the rosiness of his cheeks and nose had intensified in tandem with the receding of his beer. This was a man who not only enjoyed what he did but also very much appreciated the outcome of the labors he oversaw.

"Have you been running this brewery from the start?" Colin asked as he set his glass down on the drafting table.

"I have," he answered, his tone sounding like it was meant to be formal and succinct even though there was an undeniable notch of pride to it. "I served many years at the abbey in Westmalle, Belgium, and learned the craft there. They've been brewing their own ales for over sixty years." He lifted his mug and took only a small pull before setting it down again, this time next to Colin's, providing a stark contrast of what each had consumed. "I have tasted everything from the sweetest, smoothest ales to the harshest, most bitter concoctions, and most assuredly have missed nothing in between. Which is why we have enjoyed our modest success over the years." He offered a shy smile, but I could tell he was well pleased. "Would you like to see what we do?" His face lit up like that of a boy as he pushed himself off his stool.

"We would like nothing more," Colin replied with ease and genuine interest. "But I wonder if we might not trouble you with a few questions first?"

"Of course . . ." Brother Clayworth nodded as he settled back down while I took the opportunity to slip my beer onto the table. "You may ask anything at all. You needn't be shy. We all want to see the end to this deplorable murder. God shivered in His Heavens when such a thing was wrought against His pious abbot."

"It is heartening to hear you say such a thing, as I fear some of the monks would rather we be on our way," Colin noted.

Brother Clayworth flinched ever so slightly. "You must understand, it is not out of any lack of concern for what happened to our abbot. Any one of us will provide whatever assistance he can. It is just that this thing, this investigation of yours, it disrupts the very nature of our lives. You must understand that ours is solely a commitment to the obedience, worship, and glorification of God. Any time not spent in His honor is time misspent, and that includes the toiling we do to keep ourselves clothed and fed and housed. Which is why we are so methodical about returning to prayers throughout the day. To remind us. To keep our hearts and thoughts forever focused on God." He crossed himself with the fluidity of someone who has done it infinite times before.

"I did not mean to suggest otherwise," Colin said in a thin voice, looking vaguely chastised.

Brother Clayworth waved him off and gave yet another of his ready smiles. "You cannot truly believe that one of the men here had anything to do with Abbot Tufton's death, do you? Please tell me you cannot possibly conceive of such a thing."

Colin returned a thin smile, his lips drawn tight and his eyes blunted with something akin to sympathy, and I knew what his answer would be. "I am paid to conceive of every possibility, Brother Clayworth, including the unthinkable. Doing so is one of the reasons to which I owe my success. If I did not permit myself that freedom, then I'm afraid I would rarely solve a case."

The monk grimaced and shook his head, his mess of silvery hair springing about like an unruly mop. "I cannot abide that thought and look forward to having any such notions dispelled with all great haste." He crossed his fingers on his lap and looked at Colin with renewed determination. "What else can I answer for you?"

Colin nodded grimly and I felt the moral weight of this case pressing down upon my shoulders as though I were sitting in Colin's place, the monk's unwavering gaze boring into me, daring me to find a malignancy where none could be. "I appreciate the generosity of your assistance, most especially because of your conviction," Colin said with remarkable ease, "so I hope you will tell me with all candor—has there been any sort of dissension amongst the brothers of late? Arguments or fervent debates that have been left unsettled and perhaps been allowed to cause a pall of discord to nestle into the monastery?"

Brother Clayworth eyed Colin closely before allowing the wisp of a pained smile to blink across his face. "We are but men here, so I would be dishonest if I tried to tell you that no such disagreements have ever taken place. But it is a very long stride from an argument to murder."

"Arguments can get out of hand," Colin pressed. "People in the throes of their passions can do things they never intended. And once a deed is done, after the icy strike of reality bores into the center of a man's chest, then that is when I find they are capable of doing anything, *anything*, to hide their culpability."

The monk's eyes widened and his face went slack. "Is that what you suppose has happened? That our abbot was killed in an act of passionate disagreement?" He shook his head dourly. "Then what of his tongue? And who would have gone to his cell to have such a row in the middle of the night? It isn't done, Mr.

Pendragon. Our cells belong to each of us alone. It is the place for our solace and solitude. It simply is not done."

"I do not suppose anything yet, Brother Clayworth." Colin leaned back as though to move himself beyond the breathless thrust of the monk's rapidly fired retort. "Please do not presume anything from our idle chatter. I am only trying to address your questions when, in fact, it is *I* who should be asking them."

"Oh . . . !" Brother Clayworth flushed. "Of course . . ." A grin brushed his lips as he looked back at us. "I do apologize. It would seem I am the very example you were referring to getting caught up in my own zeal to the detriment of the discussion at hand. I shall behave myself." He reached out and took another drink from his mug with a self-conscious shrug.

"You are more than fine," Colin chuckled. "And these debates within the brotherhood," he nudged. "The ones so emblematic of us mere mortals"—he grinned and, to my surprise, so did the monk—"what do they concern?"

"Everything from the mundane to the heretical. Exactly what one would expect when you take thirty-three distinct personalities and force them to cohabit as closely as we are."

"Indulge me," Colin persisted, the tight smile on his face as near to an order as I had heard him use with these men.

Brother Clayworth sighed wearily, either missing the edge in Colin's request or simply indifferent to it. "There was something of a heated conversation a few months ago about the thin variety of options in our diet. Some of the younger men miss their dear mothers' skills, and I can only tell you that poor Brother Green was cut nearly to the quick by the criticism. He and Brother Rodney work very hard to keep us well fed despite the paucity of selection." He grunted and shook his head. "It can be easy to forget, when the belly growls, that we are here to feed our souls, not our stomachs."

"And the heretical?"

He gazed off into the vastness of the barn behind us, though I could not imagine in which direction his thoughts might be turning. "If I tell you that the church is a living organism, do you have a notion of what I mean?"

"That it is not staid," Colin replied at once. "That it is responsive both to modernity and the needs of its flock."

The monk nodded, clearly pleased by the answer. "You are not far removed from the crux of it," he said, "though I am sure you understand that the church cannot possibly respond to frivolous or deviant alterations to doctrine simply because it happens to be the fashion of the moment. I fear we would have moral anarchy were that to be the case." He smiled, but there was an obvious sorrow behind his eyes. "God's tenets have not changed since the founding of Christianity anyway. There are no new recognized Scriptures or tablets or angelic voices to inform us, leaving the church with only the precepts that have been handed down for millennia from which to cobble and instill its truths. So you see, the church *must* be alive in order to remain relevant and viable as one age gives way to the next."

"You are referring to the ecumenical councils?" Colin asked.

"Precisely." Brother Clayworth beamed, apparently not used to having a layperson understand the labyrinth of doublespeak it sounded to me that he was using. "There have been twenty such councils of cardinals led, as always, by the Pope, with the last one having been closed just twenty-five years ago."

"Vatican Council," Colin said as he rubbed his smooth chin awkwardly, and I could tell he was yearning to be spinning a coin between his fingers.

"It is the only context in which the church can reasonably be expected to move forward in any profound way. Yet when rumors begin to surface . . . when the spectre of unverified writings suddenly rear up like a two-headed viper . . . some men expect the church to respond with the dexterity and finesse of a graceful dancer."

Colin's eyebrows vaulted upward. "You are talking about the two codices, aren't you? The ones found in that monastery in Egypt."

Brother Clayworth flinched and averted his gaze as though Colin had roundly cursed him. "There is disagreement about them in the Holy See, there is disagreement amongst scholars, there is disagreement here. Some seek to embrace them as a whole, others question whether they have any relevance at all." He glanced back at us and gave a pained sort of grimace. "Many of our brothers simply do not know *what* to think, for it takes a quiet heart to truly hear the word of God."

Colin's lips curled minutely and I could tell that he was well pleased. "I would be surprised if there was not some dissension amongst the group of you given the extent of it everywhere else. The *Codex Sinaiticus* alone revealed enormous amounts of inaccuracies and corrections made to the Scriptures in the first centuries after their initial writing, and now the *Codex Syriacus* would appear about to do the same thing all over again."

Brother Clayworth looked solemn. "They are saying that verses were added to the four gospels that alter what was originally written about the Resurrection of Christ. It would appear to strike at the very heart of our faith." He pursed his lips and let his eyes drift off. "I have not seen copies of it myself. I cannot profess to know, but I am sure of what I know in my heart."

Colin flashed an earnest smile. "Then I envy you your assurance. But tell me, have the brothers of Whitmore Abbey reached any sort of consensus amongst themselves?"

The monk frowned. "I'm afraid one cannot resolve the disparities of faithfulness and conviction easily. There is an endless chasm of passion whenever there is discourse around the will of God. It is as it was meant to be. God does not intend for us to follow like sheep, but rather to listen with our hearts and make our choices from there."

"And the Bible?"

He nodded as he let a soft grin settle onto his face. "It is our roadmap. Our template for living. It gives us the answers to so many of our questions."

"And the two codices?"

"Were I able to answer that," Brother Clayworth began, his dark eyes sparkling with mischief, "then I do not suppose I would be living here in the humble confines of this monastery."

Colin tipped his head smartly in an acknowledgment of the monk's artful sentiment and pushed ahead in what I thought to be a most incongruous way. "This ale you produce, am I to understand that you distribute it to the pubs and taverns solely through Mr. Chesterton?"

"Now there is a question I can answer." He leaned back on his stool with an affable smile. "That is correct. Mr. Chesterton comes out here once or twice a month and purchases all of our ale, then distributes it for a modest fee. We've been working with him from the beginning, almost thirteen years now, but it's only the last year or so that he's been able to provide us with proper accountings. Not that we didn't trust him, mind you," he quickly added, "but I don't believe he was up to the task. I know I am not."

"What changed?" he asked, though we knew what the answer would be.

"He's got a bright lad working for him now. I've even had him review our books several times as well. I may have a head for ale, but I can't bear staring at numbers." He gave a chortle.

Colin joined the monk's chuckle, but I could tell the wheels of his brain were spinning. "You are referring to Edward Honeycutt?"

Brother Clayworth nodded and I could tell he was impressed that Colin already knew that. "They told me you are a famous investigator in London, Mr. Pendragon, and now I see why."

"You flatter me," Colin said, but I knew it pleased him just the same. "We have been staying at the Pig and Pint and have had several occasions to speak with both Mr. Chesterton and young Mr. Honeycutt. They both seem decent sorts." He spoke simply and I could not help but wonder if the assessment of Mr. Chesterton had not caught in his throat.

"I can certainly vouch for Mr. Chesterton. He has done well by us and even though he has his rough edges"—Brother Clayworth grinned—"he seems to be a good man."

"Indeed," Colin answered, and now I could see that his eyes had gone cold. "But enough idle chatter . . ." he was saying. "We would appreciate that tour you mentioned."

"It will be my pleasure." Brother Clayworth fairly glowed with enthusiasm as he popped right off his stool. "Permit me just a moment and I shall usher you through each step of the process."

The monk gathered up what was left of our ales and hurried from the small room, allowing me just enough time to lean toward Colin and whisper, "It seems you are correct about those Egyptian manuscripts. Perhaps they truly have caused some friction amongst these men?"

"Perhaps"—he nodded with the slip of a shrug—"or perhaps Edward Honeycutt has his fingers in too many places in an effort to free himself from Dalwich?"

"Do you think . . . ?!" I was startled by the suggestion, but before he could answer Brother Clayworth called for us.

Colin stood up and smiled at me, his cerulean eyes sparkling warmly. "You know me, at this point there is no one above suspicion." He started out of the small office before quickly stopping and glancing back at me. "Except . . . perhaps . . . for you," he added with a low chuckle.

# CHAPTER 20

Beer, or alcohol of any kind, has never held much interest to me. I can confess to having drunk to excess a time or two in my youth, but in matters of inebriation I must admit to having always preferred the nimble caress of opiates. At least until a dozen years ago when those same soothing opiates had finally overrun my life completely and threatened to extinguish it. Such is their ephemeral touch that I find I must remain vigilant against them to this very day. So I cannot profess to having had much interest when Brother Clayworth escorted us through the numerous stages of his brewery. Colin, however, was quite taken with the whole event.

While the monk gave ponderous explanations around the mashing, lautering, boiling, and cooling of the product, I could not get past the thick, malty smell hanging incessantly in the air. Colin peppered Brother Clayworth with innumerable questions and I pondered the importance of the two codices on this case, or whether the heart of both murders was going to be found in the only link that I could see between these two killings: Raleigh Chesterton and Edward Honeycutt. While I certainly had no consideration for Mr. Chesterton anymore, it pained me to think that Edward Honeycutt might be culpable. He had seemed so undone by Maureen O'Dowd's death. Yet I had borne witness to such acts of duplicity before. Far too many times.

At some point during Brother Clayworth's dissertation it all became more than I could bear, so I excused myself, having determined to pay a quick visit to Brother Bursnell in the library to see if I could ferret out anything further about the two codices. Colin could continue bantering on with this monk, but I was going to return to the matter at hand. My enthusiasm, however, turned quickly to frustration when I arrived at the library to find the doors closed and the lights extinguished.

The sound of distant chanting, a slow, tuneless sort of lament, drifted past my ears and I realized the monks had retreated to the chapel for their afternoon devotions. It made me wonder that Brother Clayworth had not joined them and I ruminated as to whether it was his passion for the brewery or simple negligence to comprehend the waning day that had caused him to be remiss. Whichever the case, I pushed through the library doors anyway and stood quite alone just inside, looking around at the mass of books, bound manuscripts, and piles of loose papers twined together with string, and knew that I would never find anything I sought without the knowledgeable aid of Brother Bursnell. For if there was any order to this place it was likely known to him alone.

Not wanting to return to the painstaking minutiae of ale brewing, I set off and began wandering the central hallway of the monastery rather aimlessly. When I could stand its utter silence and shadowy oppressiveness no more, I headed out the rear door and went around to the side of the main building to where I remembered Brother Wright oversaw the vegetable garden. Even though I knew no one would be there, I was relieved to be outside in the fresh air to catch the last of the faltering day. The only unfortunate consequence was that it abruptly reminded me of how I was to spend my night tonight—alone, in the cell of a murdered monk, the result of our own blatant foolishness at the Pig and Pint. And still, I could not imagine what we had been thinking.

The last wisps of the sun had just folded beneath the horizon when I heard Colin calling for me. I came back around the side of the monastery and found him by the back door. "And where have you been off to?" he asked as he ushered me inside.

"Nowhere useful, I'm afraid."

He shook his head with a sigh. "Have I taught you nothing?"

Before I realized where we were going he led me to the refectory where all of the monks were assembling for supper. The two of us took the same places we'd sat in during our last visit, at the end of the second of the long tables, and as soon as everyone had settled in, the lot of us bowed our heads while a handful of monks hastily prattled off invocations, most of which were in Latin. Of the ones I could understand I heard blessings for our food, our lives, and our souls, but none of them mentioned the solving of their abbot's murder. At least not in English. I wondered if they prayed for justice.

Brother Rodney brought in a large tureen filled with some sort of stew and set it on our table before going back and bringing out an identical tureen for the farther table. It consisted of carrots, potatoes, and shredded beef in a thick, tomato-laden sauce. To my mind the best part, however, was the half-dozen loaves of freshly baked bread that were disbursed about the tables, still warm from the oven. It made a perfect implement to swipe out the bottom of my bowl, which I eagerly did as there were clearly no second helpings to be had. Brother Green clearly knew precisely what was needed and made no more. I thought it rather a form of artistry.

The meal passed with little conversation, just as had been the case the first time we'd been here. There were pockets of murmuring here and there, but nothing of any consequence that I could tell and most certainly nothing that united the two tables in any singular matter.

"Brother Morrison tells me you will be staying with us now," Brother Silsbury said as the meal drew to its conclusion. His voice was measured so that I could not discern what he might actually think of the idea, nor could I tell whether he was still angry that Colin had tried to take the abbot's Bible. I could only imagine what he would do if he discovered that even now Colin had the abbot's actual Bible tucked in his waistband at the small of his back.

"Indeed we shall," Colin answered smoothly. And if he had any concerns about his subterfuge I could not see it.

"Let us pray that it will allow you to bring a swift end to this business then," Brother Wright said. "Our dear abbot deserves such a resolution and it will do us all good to have this wound healed."

"Come, come . . ." Brother Morrison chimed in, his voice, as always, scratchy and dour, ". . . you are being sentimental. Resolution will take place only through the judgment of the Lord. His will is righteous and final, and no man can claim such a victory over that which is evil. I should think we all must know that by now."

"Now, Robert," Brother Clayworth chided softly. "God does not forbid the meting of a little justice of our own. An eye for an eye, don't you know."

Brother Morrison's craggy face rearranged itself to one of obvious disapproval. "You are taking liberties with the text."

"Stop quibbling," Brother Silsbury cut them both off. "There is no denying the breadth and reach of God's will."

"Amen." Brother Morrison nodded before languidly crossing himself.

"Have you any idea how long you will need to stay?" Brother Silsbury asked as he turned to Colin, and I knew this was what these men most wanted to know. How long would it take before we solved this murder or gave up trying?

"I think we should be done by this week's end," Colin answered with the thinnest of smiles flashing across his face. "That should suffice."

Brother Morrison spoke up again. "I have had a telegram this afternoon. Father Demetris informs me that he will be returning here at the behest of the bishop tomorrow morning. So it seems we will have no shortage of visitors this week." It sounded to me as though he said the word *visitors* very much like he would have said *annoyances*.

"We must make Brother Green aware," Brother Clayworth said as he turned and murmured to young Brother Hollings beside him. The solemn young man got up at once and padded over to the other table, where he leaned in by Brother Green's hefty shoulders and whispered in his ear as though imparting a state secret.

A moment later Brother Rodney once again came through the doorway from the kitchen, this time cradling a huge wooden bowl filled with apples. He set it down at the farther table as he took his seat, but almost at once Brother Green swept it up and brought it over to the table where we were seated. "Our guests should have the first choice," he said with his usual charitable grin. "And won't it be wonderful to have Father Demetris back with us again?!"

"There, you see, Robert"—Brother Clayworth gave a sly smile to Brother Morrison as he passed the bowl of apples to Brother Wright without bothering to take one himself—"here is someone perfectly happy to entertain another guest."

"Now you're just being contrary, Brother Clayworth," Brother Wright scolded as he turned back to Colin. "Can you tell us how your questioning is going, Mr. Pendragon?"

Colin looked up from the apple he'd just taken a bite of and was wearing the most curious expression. There was an unmistakable glimmer in his eyes and one corner of his lips was ever so slightly curled upward. Yet it was only after I noticed his left eyebrow slowly arching toward the ceiling that I sucked in a breath and girded myself for his answer.

"I'm so very pleased that you have asked," he said too easily. "Everyone here has been most accommodating, though I have had a devil of a time trying to get my hands on some of the abbot's papers." His use of that vernacular made me frown as I knew he had chosen it with great purpose. But my belly sank even further when he quite suddenly rose to his feet. *"Excuse me . . ."* he called out across the room in his strong, bellowing voice. *"Could the one of you who has borrowed the abbot's journals from his sabbatical to Egypt please raise his hand. I am most anxious to get a look at them and promise to return them just as quickly as you please."* A sea of wide eyes and blank faces stared back at him, and I was certain that no one had ever made such a spectacle of himself in this refectory before. "*Nobody?!*" he pressed with great angelic innocence. "My, my ..." He settled his gaze on Brother Bursnell at the far table, still maintaining the same pristine expression to match his carefree tone. "Perhaps they have been misplaced then?"

From where I was sitting it looked like Brother Bursnell flushed quite roundly as he continued to stare back at Colin. "I shall make it my priority to search the library first thing tomorrow morning," he answered in a halting voice.

"There you have it," Colin said as he resumed his seat and turned back to Brother Wright again, "everyone has been most accommodating."

If Brother Morrison spent the majority of his time looking displeased, he looked ever more so now. "Really," he grumbled as he stood up, leaving his half-eaten apple on his plate. "This is not some workhouse. We do not bawl across the room at one another."

"You must forgive me," Colin said at once as he stood up and nodded to the elderly monk. "I meant no offense—only to make use of this singular gathering of your brotherhood."

Brother Morrison studied Colin a moment, his face pinched with his irritation, before giving a curt nod and heading out of the refectory, Brothers Silsbury and Hollings immediately falling in line behind him.

"I think you like to rattle him." Brother Clayworth eyed Colin with a faint grin as he drained his mug of ale.

"I do no such thing," Colin protested unconvincingly, which, though it only further amused Brother Clayworth, had quite the opposite effect on Brother Wright. Yet it was Brother Bursnell who caught my eye as he took his leave, for he cast such an indignant scowl our direction, the likes of which I had never before seen upon his face, that I was left wondering whatever to make of it.

# CHAPTER 21

⇒⊶⊷⇐

The silence was crushing.

Once dinner had been dispatched, some of the monks had shared a bit of communal time in the refectory, though it had been exceedingly polite and remarkably subdued. I could not discern whether this was a function of Colin and me being there or if it was indeed status quo, but I thought it somehow unnerving if it truly was a result of the latter. This spot of socialization did not last long and was highlighted by Brother Wright's recounting of the loathsome weed whose central root had seemed to be fastened somewhere around the earth's core, and Brother Green's harrowing run-in with a quart jug of milk that had been delivered with a hairline crack near its lip that he'd been forced to find a substitute carafe for to ensure that no harm would come to anyone from the rapacious container.

Throughout it all I smiled and nodded and clucked my tongue at all the appropriate places, yet I could not help but wonder that these men did not seem to conceive of the stress and injustices that bombarded and shaped the lives of the people beyond their monastery's walls. I had found it disheartening. But when Brother Morrison returned some thirty minutes later with neither Brother Silsbury nor Brother Hollings in his wake, I would have relived the entirety of the banal conversation rather than face what I knew was coming next.

Brother Morrison had dismissed the men with the finality of a headmaster before beckoning to Colin and me to follow him so he could escort us down the dimly lit hallway to our cells for the night. And that was precisely how it felt to me as we plodded along behind him. Favoring his right side as always, I found myself hoping he would need to stop a moment to regain his breath or relieve the discomfort of his left leg, but he did neither thing. Instead, we drew inextricably closer to the miniscule cubby where I was going to have to spend the night. The place where a man was brutally murdered five days before. To sleep upon the very bed where the victim had breathed his last breath.

Each step made my stomach twist and my heart thunder, my own body taunting me with the knowledge that I was not at all ready for this moment. When Brother Morrison stopped in front of the abbot's cell, my cell now, I secretly begged for him to say that my sacrifice was no longer necessary, but he only reached out and unlatched the padlock from the door, holding it in his stout palm like an unpleasant thing. Perhaps to him it was, given that there were no other locked doors within the monastery. I cannot say I had even a trace of sympathy for him.

He pushed the door open and just as before, the tiny room was cloaked in absolute darkness. Only the lantern Brother Morrison was carrying in his other hand was able to allow the barest hint of light to creep into the cell. It was as though we were staring into an infinite chasm whose dimensions could only be guessed at. Just sitting there—quietly, calmly—waiting to swallow me whole as soon as the door swung shut again.

Brother Morrison shuffled in ahead of me and struck a match that he seemed to produce from out of nowhere, and in another moment had two candles lit, one on the table and the other atop the stand where the bowl had been on our last visit here. Colin snatched up our valises from the hallway just outside the tiny room and set them on the bed. Brother Morrison explained that he'd had Brother Hollings leave them there before he'd taken our trunk to the room where Colin would be staying as it was, apparently, marginally larger. That news set my mood even further on edge.

Solemn good nights were quickly dispensed, driven by the indifference of the elderly monk, and though I wanted to catch Colin's eye to make sure he realized how miserable I was, I somehow failed to do so. In the next instant the two of them were back in the hallway, Brother Morrison pulling the door shut behind him, not even bothering to toss me a final glance. And then I heard the sound of the latch clicking firmly into place, and in that moment I thought I might actually begin to weep.

I stood there, frozen, just inside the door. The cot upon which the abbot's body had fallen on my right, the tall square stand holding a white tapered candle that persisted in flickering despite the lack of any semblance of a draft on my left. Not ten feet in front of me stood the tiny round table with its single chair and the room's only other candle doing what it could to dispel the night's shadows, which was precious little.

I could not tell you if I stayed like that for one minute or twenty. All I know is that before I moved a faint sound had begun to reach my ears. I knew at once what it was—chanting. But this was different from anything I had heard here before as it was both discordant and disjointed. I listened for a while, wincing at the inharmonious sounds as they drifted past in differing tones, timbres, beats, and volume, before finally understanding why. The monks were in their own cells, each hymn a singular expression of that man's devotion. They probably did not pay one another the slightest heed, so concentrated were they on their own efforts.

Gradually, without even being aware of it, I found that I had begun to calm down. My breathing had deepened and my heart had resumed its normal cadence, and I decided it was the result of those murmuring chants in spite of their jaggedness. They had lulled me with the depth of their soulfulness. So finally, at last, I was able to steal across the miniscule space and settle into the straight-backed chair tucked up under the table. It turned out to be a fortuitous choice on my part as not a handful of minutes later the songs began to blink out, one after the other, some fading away while others abruptly ceased, until there was only one lone voice, sweet and pure, that continued to float through the tiny cell just a few minutes longer before it too was finally gone.

And that was when the silence descended upon me for the second time like some fanged beast that had been hiding just beyond my view in the blackness of a forest. It immobilized me again and I found myself straining to hear anything . . . anything at all: the shuffling of a boot on the wooden hallway floor, a far-away throat being cleared of nighttime irritants, or even the stifled yawn of someone settling into bed. But there was nothing. It was as though I had become the last man alive in the blink of an instant. There was only me and the tortured spirit of the abbot who had been slaughtered not four feet from where I was now sitting.

I dug out my watch and turned it toward the candlelight until I could see that it was just past nine o'clock. Had I been of a mind to retire to that cot, which I most surely was not, it would have been the earliest I had gone to bed without being ill since childhood. Yet it mattered not in the least as I had no intention of lying down at all this night. If I got drowsy enough I had already determined to do no more than rest my head on the table and snatch whatever sort of fleeting nap I could get that way. It was all I could bear to allow myself. Colin simply *had* to solve this murder without delay or I was bound to end up very much the worse for it.

The candle on the table in front of me burned steadily, casting its glow across my folded hands where they rested atop the table. I could picture myself sitting like that, rigid and utterly on edge, before forcing myself to rearrange my position as I quite suddenly had the eeriest vision of the abbot having done much the same thing on many a night. He would have had either his Bible or a sheaf of writing papers laid out before him, but I otherwise felt unnervingly akin to him in that moment.

I considered going outside to use the toilet, though I did not have the need, and then decided to save that expedition until I could not stand being here an instant longer. That time would inevitably come somewhere in the smallest hours of this night. I knew that as certainly as I trusted the ceaseless movement of my watch's sweep hand. As though to prove the point to myself, I quickly rewound my watch before dropping it back into my vest pocket. I would not look at it again, I vowed, until I was desperate. By then, I tried to convince myself with much great optimism, the night was bound to be nearly over.

The sound of my own steady breathing was my only companionship. Not even the faint rhythm of a single monk's slumbered breathing wafted through the walls of the cell and I could not fathom how that was possible. Surely one or two of the more elderly monks had to be snorting in their sleep by now. It felt entirely unnatural that there could be a silence this complete; but no matter how hard I tried to cajole myself, it nettled at the back of my mind like a portent.

I remained sitting in that chair contemplating nothing and everything, when the slightest shiver of sound whispered past my ears. It was nothing, I told myself, beyond the seeds sown by an overactive and highly charged imagination. And then I heard it again. It was soft and furtive, like the *tick-tick* of a teeny mouse as it steals into the kitchen to check for unattended crumbs and, indeed, for an instant I was convinced that my cell had been invaded by just such a fiend. But when I seized the candle and hastily swept it across the space, I found no remnants of any such vermin. So when I heard the sound for the third time I knew with great certainty that it had to have come from the hall.

My outstretched arm froze in midair, the candle wavering ever so gently as it tried to cast its paltry glow as far as the door. Nothing would please me more than to state that I stood up and prepared to confront whomever . . . whatever . . . was coming to my cell, but I did not. Rather I sat there like that, arm at attention, candle fluttering listlessly, and attempted to dispel visions of the floating spectre of the abbot himself, his hair askew, his body oozing blood from its dozens of stab wounds and his mouth gaping open in agony to reveal the gory void where his tongue should have been. The very thought of the apparition clutched at my throat before I could scoff at it, so that by the time the doorknob began to twist with ghostly stealth, I was sure I would have collapsed to the floor if I had been standing.

"Ethan . . ." Colin whispered with the delicacy of a gentle breeze. Who else had I expected it to be? Hadn't I always known at the back of my mind that it would be him? How could I still be so ridiculously foolish at this stage of my life? "What are you doing?" he asked in a voice as quiet as a shadow as he slowly, carefully eased the door shut behind him.

I could only imagine how I looked to him. "Nothing," I murmured casually as I finally lowered my arm.

"How is your work coming on the table?" he asked as though I were a carpenter who'd been sent to sand and refinish the sad little overused piece of furniture I was sitting in front of.

"What?" My mind was still attempting to right itself.

He stared at me, tilting his head to one side like an endearing puppy who is trying to ascertain what its master is saying. "Have you taken a rubbing of the tabletop yet?" he asked with the obviousness it deserved before wrinkling his brow and stepping toward me. "Are you all right?"

I heard myself release a stifled sort of chortle that I, nevertheless, managed to accomplish without making much noise. "I am staying in a room the size of a thumbnail where less than a week ago a very pious man was murdered and mutilated. So, no, I do not think I am very all right at all."

Colin may have cracked the thinnest smile, it was too bloody dim to tell for sure, but when he spoke in his hushed whisper, his voice remained even and smooth. "Come here."

I did not particularly feel like doing his bidding, but I got up and moved to him anyway. I cannot say for certain what I thought he was going to do or say, but I must profess to being surprised when he pulled me to him. "Everything is going to be just fine, you know," he whispered into my ear.

"Easy enough to say when you're not the one staying in this room," I responded just a touch more petulantly than I had intended.

For some reason he seemed to find that amusing. "Where would I be without you?"

"Staying in this cursed old cell yourself," I groused back.

That apparently amused him even more as he squeezed me to him and in spite of my mood and the events of this morning, I let him. "Don't lose faith in me. I know I will be able to make an end to these killings quickly. I can feel the momentum starting to take shape . . . the answers to these riddles are drawing ever closer." He looked at me with an eager smile. "Before you know it we will be on our way back home where we belong."

I stepped back from him and crossed my arms over my chest as I watched the flickering candlelight play across his broad, handsome face. "Good," I grumbled. "Because this place has just about got me missing Mrs. Behmoth."

We both chuckled as he moved toward the door again, sending my mood back down as if over a precipice. "Wish me luck," he said, his face alight with a devilish grin. "While you're tracing the top of that table I shall be off to the library to see if Brother Bursnell is trying to deceive us."

"Be careful," I warned, though I doubted he would earn much more than a furrowed brow if he were caught snooping around. Which was about as likely, I had to admit to myself with a measure of chagrin, as the ghostly specter of Abbot Tufton coming back to his cell to terrorize me.

"I'll be fine," he said under his breath. "We shall have the end of this tragic case before you know it." And then he was gone. And as I stood there a minute, the darkness and silence quickly reasserting their presence, I prayed that he was right.

# CHAPTER 22

Constable Brendle looked markedly heartier as we stood at the end of his bed, traces of morning light streaming in through the nearby window and helping to liven his color. He was sitting fully upright for the first time since the accident, and the genuine smile on his face was a welcome sight. Tall, slender Mr. Whitsett was beaming from his usual position behind us, and this particular morning also found his compatriot, the swarthy Mr. Masri, on hand. His left arm was wrapped in a bandage up to the elbow and lay nestled in a cloth sling. Beyond the obviousness of his injury, however, Mr. Masri looked notably well, making the relief of all three men almost palpable.

"I have either gotten used to the pain," the constable was telling us with a lopsided grin on his handsome young face, "or it has settled into something of a dull ache. Either way, I am feeling inestimably better today. I should like to think that I will be able to unfetter my arse from this wretched bed in a matter of days, not weeks."

"Take it easy, Lachlan." Mr. Whitsett stepped forward and tutted. "You know you mustn't rush yourself. You heard what the doctor said."

Constable Brendle waved him off. "That man would have me on my back for the better part of a month, and you can be sure I'll not follow such archaic advice as that."

"But I've already told you I will attend to anything that might require your attention, and Mr. Masri is sure to come as often as he can, so you mustn't rush yourself needlessly."

"Now, Graham . . ." The constable's voice softened as he gazed back at Mr. Whitsett, whose face held a mixture of pity and regret. "Even though you are on leave while this accident gets sorted out by that lot from Arundel, that doesn't mean you need to spend all your time fussing over me. I'm sure they'll have everything settled with all due haste and then we will need you back to work. It isn't right having those boys loping around our village. It will be up to you to maintain the proper constabulary order until Ahmet and I can join you again." He gave a dry sort of chuckle. "And while I cannot speak for Ahmet, I can tell you that I do not intend to lie about here for very long."

"I certainly won't be staying home a moment longer than I must," Mr. Masri piped up with a smile. "My missus is already complaining that I'm getting underfoot. Why'd ya think I'm here right now?!" he added with a laugh.

"And I thought it was because you were fretting about me," the constable put in with a laugh of his own.

Mr. Masri waved him off with a wide grin. "You're fifteen years younger than me, you can fret about yourself."

I glanced back at Graham Whitsett and found that, while he too was wearing a smile, there was no humor behind his eyes. They looked distant and wounded and full of regret, and I realized that all of this bantering was at his expense. It was not meant to be but was thusly so just the same.

"I'm sure the both of you will be well recovered in due course," Colin said, and I was glad for Mr. Whitsett's sake that he had done so. "But I wonder if we might not turn our attentions to the graver matters at hand before one of your provisional constables decides to insert himself into these cases."

"An excellent point," Constable Brendle answered at once,

his face donning resolute seriousness, which made the spectacle of addressing him in bed feel suddenly ludicrous. "What is it you have for us today?"

"What I have is a further need to question Mr. Chesterton. And as you are aware, Constable, I believe it unlikely that he will wish to cooperate with me." Colin cleared his throat and though he held his eyes steady I could tell that he was girding himself against this most uncomfortable conversation. "I was hoping you could have him sent for and that we might perhaps speak with him together."

The constable nodded without hesitation, his face remaining thoughtful and somber, though I was certain I could sense a tick of delight in his manner, pleased, no doubt, to be involved in the case again. "I think that an exemplary idea," he said. "Mr. Whitsett, will you please be so kind as to request Mr. Chesterton's presence at once."

"Me?"

"Well, I do think you are the fittest of us. Do you have a better suggestion?"

Mr. Whitsett flipped a baffled sort of look between the four of us before finally allowing the slimmest shrug of his shoulders. "I suppose you have a point." He took a few steps back, though it was clear he really did not wish to leave. It seemed almost as if he thought we might actually solve the case in his brief absence, or that perhaps none of us would supply the care to the constable that he alone could provide. Nevertheless, after a moment more he said, "I'll bring him right back." And then he turned and bolted from the room.

"Did you remember about the autopsy?" Mr. Masri asked of the constable as we heard the front door open and shut. "You said you wanted to show Mr. Pendragon and Mr. Pruitt the telegram. . . ."

"Yes, of course," Constable Brendle mumbled, and it was clear he had not remembered at all. He reached over and snatched a folded piece of paper from the stand beside his bed and held it out for Colin. "It's from the coroner's office in Arundel. Preliminary findings from the autopsy they performed on Miss O'Dowd over the weekend. I think you will find it rather curious."

"Indeed . . . ?" Colin said as he accepted the single sheet and quickly perused it. "Indeed . . ." he said again, his brow cascading down on itself. He looked at the constable and then turned his gaze to me. "It confirms her death by asphyxiation. They have managed to pull a partial handprint at the front of the throat. But it goes on to say that there are no additional signs of physical assault against her person. Most curious given the disheveled state of her clothing." I could see in his eyes that while the information was unexpected, he was nonetheless already beginning to consider a myriad of possible explanations. "And they have confirmed that she was with child," he added grimly as he handed the telegram to me.

I read the three short lines swiftly and tried to surmise what it all could mean. It seemed that either the perpetrator had been interrupted before he could see his intentions through, or that the tableau was a hoax meant to divert us from the truth of what had actually led to the young woman's murder.

"Whatever do you make of it, Mr. Pendragon?" The constable interrupted my scattered thoughts.

"I would be foolish to make anything of it just yet," he answered carefully, "and I would caution you against doing the same."

Constable Brendle looked startled by Colin's response before quickly seeming to collect his faculties and nodding his agreement. "Most certainly," he acknowledged with great solemnity. He leaned across his side table again and this time grabbed the small bottle of medicine sitting there. "May I ask . . ." he said after taking a small sip from the bottle and returning it to its place, ". . . what is it that you wish to discuss with Mr. Chesterton?"

"I should like to hear about his visits to the monastery to purchase their ale. I assume you are aware that Mr. Chesterton is the only person who is permitted by the monks to distribute it?"

"That fact is quite well-known, but it never occurred to me that it might have any relevance to either of these murders."

Colin's face tightened almost imperceptibly. "We cannot know what is relevant or irrelevant until every question has been answered."

"But surely you cannot suspect Mr. Chesterton of having something to do with either of these murders? Not only is he a man of some years, but it's a fact that he thought of Miss O'Dowd very much as his own daughter."

"Mr. Chesterton may be older than any of us here," Colin spoke decisively and with a noticeable thinness of patience, "but there are men his age and older who would not think twice about inflicting themselves on an unwilling woman, biological inclination or not. That is a simple fact, Constable, that you would do well to remember."

"It's true." Mr. Masri spoke up. "When I was a bobby out in Cardiff we hunted a man who was preying on young girls. Turns out he was almost sixty. Somebody's great-grandfather." He shook his head. "They hung the bastard."

"Rightfully so," Constable Brendle added with a marked note of contrition sneaking into his voice. "Forgive me, Mr. Pendragon, I do not mean to question how you are conducting your investigation." He gave a small shrug. "You clearly have many years of experience on me and I can only tell you that it leaves me somewhat ill at ease over that which I do not yet know."

I had to refrain from chuckling as I watched Colin's face curdle ever so slightly. "I am hardly an elder statesman, but you would do well to keep an open mind until the perpetrator has been apprehended. I should think that would have been one of the first tenets of any training you received. You did receive training?" he pressed, and this time it was Mr. Masri, not me, who actually let out a guffaw.

To his credit, Constable Brendle also managed a chuckle, though I knew Colin's intent to be amusing had been secondary. "Perhaps we had best leave that line of questioning until after Mr. Chesterton's appearance." The constable blushed. "Can you tell us of anything you've learned about the unfortunate abbot at Whitmore Abbey?"

"What I have learned is that young Master Honeycutt was known to have assisted the monks in balancing their ledgers."

"Edward?!"

"Indeed." And I could see that Colin had taken the measure

of how his unexpected news had caught both Constable Brendle and Mr. Masri.

"The monks told you this?"

Colin flicked a tight smile at the poor, youthful constable. "And who else might I deem to accept such information from?"

Constable Brendle blinked as though stung until Colin deigned to crack a wider smile, at which point the two lawmen did the same with obvious relief. "It pains me to hear you say it's possible that Edward Honeycutt could be caught up in any of this. He seems to hold such promise." The constable tightened his expression as though speaking of someone a good deal younger than himself.

"It is a *possibility*," Colin agreed with a stiff nod of his head, "but once again I would caution against drawing any sort of conclusions until we have greater knowledge of the facts. Do not forget that just as you must be cautious of discounting someone for their age, you need also to guard against casting aspersions simply because of opportunity. There can certainly be truth to both suppositions, but only after the full weight of circumstance, motive, and capacity have been fully scrutinized."

"Yes, yes, of course." The constable grimaced as though having been admonished. "I really must blame my senselessness on these ruddy opiates. They have absolutely turned my judgment to mush."

Colin flashed a brief smile. "It's all well and good as long as they are also doing the same to your pain," he said, but I suspected he really thought the opiates were making little difference in the constable's thinking.

In the next instant we heard the sound of the front door open and close from the other room. "*I'm back with Mr. Chesterton!*" Mr. Whitsett called out like a school-aged boy as he came gliding into the room, his tall, lean form in diametrical opposition to Mr. Chesterton's far shorter and stouter one.

Mr. Chesterton's jowl-laden face sank the moment he spied us. "Ya didn't tell me *these* two was gonna be here," he growled, making the number sound like the worst sort of slight.

"They are here at my insistence," Constable Brendle answered at once. "You will treat them with the respect that you accord to me."

"I ain't respectin' a couple a feckin' poofs," he shot back under his breath.

My heart leapt to my throat and I dared not look at anyone.

"And I believe that is called slander," Colin responded calmly. "A crime punishable by imprisonment."

"I will not have you speaking to these men in such a way in my own home," the constable barked at Mr. Chesterton. "You will answer their questions with the deference you show to me or you *will* spend the night in a cell where you can consider your words more carefully."

Raleigh Chesterton's look of contempt revealed his precise thoughts as he crossed his arms over his chest and grunted his assent without casting the slightest glance at either Colin or me. It was all the invitation Colin needed, though I remained relieved that neither Mr. Whitsett nor Mr. Masri had yet to say anything nor take so much as a furtive step away from us.

"How many years have you been collecting and distributing the monks' ale?" Colin proceeded with the simplicity of a trifling conversation over dinner.

Mr. Chesterton kept his watery eyes glued on Constable Brendle, his broad face unyielding in its determination. "What's it been, Constable? Eleven . . . ? Twelve years . . . ?"

"I suppose. Something like that."

"Is it really necessary for me ta discuss every little thing I do with these two when you already know all about me?" He tilted his head toward Colin without budging his gaze. "I take a shite nearly every day, ya wanna know about that too?"

"*Mr. Chesterton!*" the constable warned again, but I thought it came out rather flat and toothless.

Colin waved him off. "How often do you go up there to take delivery?"

"Once or twice a month," he sniffed. "Less in the winter."

"And did you usually take Edward Honeycutt with you?"

His face became ever more surly, though I would not have thought that possible, as he slid his eyes to Colin for the first time. "What's yer interest in that lad?" He shifted his gaze back to Constable Brendle as his veiled accusation hung there. "It ain't right. . . ."

"Answer the question, Mr. Chesterton," Constable Brendle warned yet again. "Answer it as if I had asked you myself. I shall *not* tell you again."

Raleigh Chesterton's face contorted with his displeasure. "Yeah, I brought him. Them kegs are too big fer me ta handle on me own. And them monks ain't much use. Most of 'em make *me* look lively." He cracked a slight, one-sided smile at his own joke, but there was little merriment behind his eyes. "Edward Honeycutt's a good lad, Constable. Ya know it like ya know yer own men here," he said, gesturing to Mr. Whitsett and Mr. Masri, who had thankfully remained as stoic as statues. "Don't let these dandies turn yer head against him," he sneered, and the way he said it made me feel abhorred.

"No one is altering the way they look at anyone, Mr. Chesterton," the constable answered tightly. "We are collecting facts and nothing more." It was heartening to hear him parrot back Colin's own words even though it seemed to have no effect in mollifying Mr. Chesterton.

"And how long has Edward been doing your ledgers?" Colin pressed with his usual determination.

"'Bout a year, I suppose."

"Do you review young Mr. Honeycutt's work?"

Mr. Chesterton's eyes flicked over to Colin with a disapproving scowl and then shifted immediately back to Constable Brendle. "What for? That's what he gets paid ta do. If I gotta do 'em myself, then I sure as hell don't need him."

"And who's idea was it that he should start assisting with the monks' ledgers?" Colin continued as if the answers being hurtled back were as pleasant as a teatime repast.

"You'd have ta ask them."

"Did Maureen O'Dowd ever tell you that she planned to marry Edward Honeycutt and move to London with him?"

Something feral seemed to pass behind Mr. Chesterton's eyes as he took a moment before answering. "I knew," he finally admitted. "She didn't think I knew, but I did. She told anybody who'd listen. Weren't no secret in that."

"Do you think it plausible that Mr. Honeycutt and Miss O'Dowd were ever really going to be able to move to London on the salary they were each earning at your fine establishment?"

Raleigh Chesterton puckered his face having clearly caught the scorn in Colin's words. "Why the feck would I pay a bit a mind ta what them two was talkin' about doin'?"

"That seems curious," Colin muttered with feigned innocence. "They would appear to have represented a good portion of your staff. Wouldn't losing the two of them require your finding suitable replacements? That could hardly be an easy task in such a small town as Dalwich."

"I got plenty a help. You're a bloody arse."

"*Mr. Chesterton!*" the constable scolded, sounding undeniably fatigued by his continuing endeavor to get the older man to behave.

A taut grin drifted across Colin's face an instant before he breached the subject I knew he'd been eager to address from the start. "Mr. Chesterton, did you know that Miss O'Dowd was pregnant?"

For the first time since his arrival Mr. Chesterton's face was shot full of surprise as his eyes flicked over to Colin. "She what . . . ?" His mouth gaped open as his arms fell to his sides. I heard a stunned breath exhaled and thought at first that it was Mr. Chesterton, but as his jaw remained slack I realized it had come from either Mr. Masri or Mr. Whitsett, who were standing behind me. "Bloody hell . . ." Raleigh Chesterton finally muttered with a shake of his head. "Does Edward know?" And this time he asked Colin directly with neither disparagement nor distaste.

"He does," Colin answered. "Are you surprised that neither of them told you . . . ?"

"Huh . . . ? Surprised . . . ?" It took a second before the scowl slowly re-formed on his forehead. "Nah . . ." His voice had grown cold again. "They don't have ta tell me shite." But I was certain he felt otherwise.

"Did you ever hear Edward profess any desire to have a family?"

"Well, who doesn't?" he snapped carelessly, which I thought curious given his own state of childlessness.

"Do you suppose Edward is ready to do so now?"

"And how the bleedin' hell would I know that...?" he hurled back, his shock at learning of Miss O'Dowd's pregnancy clearly overshadowed by Colin's persistent line of questioning. "I ain't his ruddy parent. The bloke works for me. That's all."

"I know you were close to Miss O'Dowd, and I can see the same is true between you and young Mr. Honeycutt. You mustn't take offense. I'm only trying to ascertain if either of them had confided anything to you that might prove to have value to this case. You mustn't get upset."

"I ain't upset."

"Of course not," Colin answered in the face of the man's truculent scowl. "I can see that."

"Them two was daft about each other. Anybody with half a brain knew it. If ya think Edward had anything ta do with her murder, then you're a bigger shite than I already pegged ya for."

"In the face of great passion there are often found the scars of terrible tragedy." Colin spoke slowly, as much for the constable and his men, I was certain, as for Mr. Chesterton. "It is usually wrought from the seeds of jealousy, or perceived betrayal, or the sudden cooling of affections by one of the pair. Mr. Pruitt and I have beheld such travesties in too many cases over the years. It is foolish to rule out such a possibility no matter the seeming absurdity of the notion. And that is why I seek to understand whether your Mr. Honeycutt may have been feeling the pressure of his decision to marry and move to London when the fact of impending fatherhood had so suddenly become a part of that equation. Given that he had no prospects for employment, you must admit that it adds up to a very profound burden, wouldn't you say?"

Raleigh Chesterton glared at Colin a minute before finally settling on the only answer I assumed he could come up with. "You're a feckin' wanker."

"When is the last time you and Mr. Honeycutt were up at the

monastery?" Colin moved right ahead as though Mr. Chesterton had not said a word.

"Last Thursday."

"The day after the abbot's murder."

"If you say so."

"Did you speak to any of the monks about the murder when you were out there?"

"Well, a course. Brother Clayworth was natterin' on like a bloomin' scullery maid."

"And did he tell you and Edward Honeycutt exactly how his abbot had been murdered?"

"He didn't have ta." Mr. Chesterton sniffed with an odd sort of pride. "The constable had already told me about it the night before when he came ta me tavern for a drink."

Colin glanced over at Constable Brendle and I caught the fair-skinned young man noticeably flush. "Did he mention the bit about the severed tongue?"

"It was foolish of me," the constable said with embarrassment. "Be assured that I shall never make such an error again."

Colin swept his eyes over to Mr. Chesterton even as he waved a dismissive hand toward Constable Brendle. "And did you tell Edward Honeycutt?"

"I s'pose I did," came the irritable reply. "What of it?"

"What indeed . . . ?" Colin responded, giving the first warm smile since Mr. Chesterton's arrival. But if Colin meant to impugn Edward Honeycutt, I found it impossible to concur.

# CHAPTER 23

"I always thought the lad would do right by his family," Graham Whitsett was saying as he guided the horse and landau carriage toward the Honeycutt farm just outside of Dalwich, "but I can see how you would have suspicions given his access to the monastery and the work you say he was doing on their ledgers. If that abbot discovered Edward pilfering their accounts so he and Miss O'Dowd could go to London . . ." He let out a low whistle as though the obviousness of his words required any further demarcation.

For once I wished it had been raining so we could raise the coach's roof and shut the overly eager Mr. Whitsett out from where he sat in front of and above us. He was nice enough, yet his accidental shooting of the constable and Mr. Masri had propelled him into an orbit of almost giddy earnestness that I could not help but find grating. I understood that he was only attempting to make amends for his terrible mistake, but it made little difference and I wished he would seek some solace in a touch of introspection.

A quick shift of my eyes revealed Colin's expression to still be filled with the same somber intensity that had flooded over him while we'd been in Constable Brendle's rooms. Given his near silence on this journey to the Honeycutt farm I knew he was busy reflecting upon one possibility after another and was anxious to see where his thoughts might be leading him. Did he believe as Mr. Whitsett was stating, or was there someone else upon whom his greatest suspicions lie?

"Have you been able to learn anything else about that poor abbot's murder now that you've been staying at the monastery?" Mr. Whitsett continued to prattle on, turning around in his seat as he was wont to do, his gangly arms and bony shoulders accentuating the unusual length of his frame.

"Not yet," Colin answered dismissively.

"You mustn't lose faith," Mr. Whitsett called back over his shoulder.

Colin jerked his head up as he stared at the back of Mr. Whitsett. "What?"

"Faith . . ." Mr. Whitsett repeated, tossing us a hopeful look. "You cannot lose faith."

Colin glanced at me as one of his eyebrows arced toward the open sky. "You may rest assured, Mr. Whitsett, that a shortage of faith in my abilities is never the issue." Mr. Whitsett laughed, but then he had no way of knowing that Colin was being entirely serious.

I, on the other hand, found myself continuing to struggle with grave uncertainties around the abbot's murder. Not only had Colin's prowling about the monastery's library for almost three hours the night before revealed nothing, but I had suffered a similar lack of success myself during my deplorable time spent in the abbot's cell. And I had been meticulous in my efforts. Colin had barely taken his leave of me in that spectre-laden cell before I'd finally managed to corral my better nature and set about the duty I was tasked.

Tearing copious sheets of paper from my notebook, I laid them out across the small table and began to color over each sheet with broad strokes from the pencil I kept in my valise. I took special care over every ridge, dent, and bump on the tabletop, hoping to lift a few words of value from within the murky gray scribbles I was creating in an ever-widening arc. And I did

find some. There was part of a Psalm that I recognized and a bit
of some biblical quote that I did not, as well as various words, or
pieces of words, that seemed to have no correlation to one another whatsoever. Even Colin had looked at my endeavors in the
morning light with less than his usual enthusiasm before tucking
it all into his coat pocket. Which left it impossible for me to feel
the same level of faith that Colin insisted he maintained, and therefore I could only offer an uneasy smile as Mr. Whitsett brayed at
what he thought was meant to be a joke.

"May I ask you a personal question, Mr. Whitsett?" Colin
spoke again as we finally turned onto the long dirt drive up to the
Honeycutt house.

"Anything at all."

"Are you married?"

"Married . . . ?" He released a leaden sigh. "I was," he said after
a moment. "My wife died almost four years ago now. She was a
delicate girl, my Ava. Couldn't carry a child nearly long enough.
The last one"—he tilted his head slightly and gazed ahead as we
continued to jostle along the ruts in the drive—"she got sick and
there wasn't anything anyone could do about it. I lost her and
the baby. Would've been a son too . . ." He shook his head as his
voice drifted to silence.

"I'm sorry to hear that," Colin said, and I suddenly felt guilty
for the impatience I had been feeling against this poor man.

Mr. Whitsett settled a warm grin back onto his face as he
turned to look at us. "Well, I'm happy to say that I've been squir-
ing the sweetest girl for the last bunch of months. She lives in
Arundel with her parents, so I only get to see her on the occasional weekends. Her father is an advocate for the courts there.
That's how I met her, through him. He's a kind and whip-smart
man who likes the fact that I help keep order here in Dalwich."
His pride was well evident. "But his daughter is like a porcelain
doll. Tiny and fragile . . ." He outright laughed. "I know we
make the most unusual pair when I'm escorting her about, me
nearly as tall as the trees and her no bigger than a flower, but I
don't care. Neither one of us cares." He gave a contented shrug
as he swung his eyes forward. "I may ask her to marry me one of

these days and then I'll be able to answer *yes* if you ever ask me that question again."

"I shall hope to hear of your nuptials quite soon then." Colin smiled. "And Mr. Masri . . . ? How long has he been married?"

"As long as I've known him," came the answer. "He has a handsome wife. A great, full-bodied woman. But they do get to arguing sometimes. I suppose that's what suits them." He shrugged as the Honeycutt home came into view, its modest size and unadorned façade leaving it to look like the clapboard box it was with its simple black pitched roof atop.

"Mr. Whitsett . . . ?" Colin's voice quite abruptly turned curiously provocative. "In the time between your wife's death and your fine courtship with the young woman from Arundel, did you ever have occasion for a shag or two with Miss O'Dowd?"

Because Mr. Whitsett was facing away from us I did not hesitate to drop my jaw and roll my eyes before expelling a disbelieving breath. And while I felt Colin's eyes boring into the side of my face, I did not dare look at him as I knew he would justify the bluntness of his question until the end of eternity.

"No, sir," Mr. Whitsett answered after a moment, and I suspected that he too had been quite caught unawares. "I thought she was a lovely girl, funny and all, but I didn't look at her that way."

"And Mr. Masri?"

"He's married."

"So you've mentioned," Colin muttered drolly. "But did he ever have it off with Miss O'Dowd and perhaps brag about it to you?"

"Well, she *was* more his type . . ." came the thoughtful reply, ". . . since he likes his women rounder and all, but he never said any such thing to me. Not that he would have, mind you."

"And what about your constable?" Colin pressed ahead, and now I knew he was testing Mr. Whitsett.

"Constable Brendle is a fine and honorable man," came the answer as he eased the coach to a stop near the short fence that encircled the Honeycutts' home. "That's all I know."

"Of course," Colin muttered as the two of us climbed down

from the open cab. "You know that he's already admitted such an indiscretion to us himself. Does that change the extent of your feelings toward him?"

"Not in the least. That's his business to tell you, not mine."

Colin smiled with satisfaction, his azure eyes catching the midday sun with a sparkle. "Then you have just proven your own honor as well, Mr. Whitsett." He nodded and stepped away from the carriage before just as quickly halting and turning back around. "Our thanks to you for this ride, and you needn't wait on us. We shall make our own way back to Whitmore Abbey."

"Are you sure?" he asked, and I would have said that he sounded almost crestfallen. "I think the constable might be happy to a have little time to himself," he admitted with a shy sort of smile.

"Quite," Colin called back as he headed for the front door that, even now, was being pulled open. "We've bothered you more than enough for one day."

I turned to find Colin smiling beatifically at a lovely girl in her middle teens with waves of dark brown hair cascading below her shoulders and warm honey-brown eyes. She was dressed simply in a white dress that was gathered just below the bodice, accentuating a lush figure that made me suspect she would be married before very much longer. Tied over the bottom part of the dress was an apron cinched around her waist that was smudged with flour and something faintly yellow, butter I presumed, attesting to the fact that she, and probably all of the girls in the Honeycutt household, were expected to earn their keep, just as we already knew the boys did. While the young woman did not smile back at Colin, neither was her face closed or disapproving. "Yes . . . ?" she asked as her eyes flicked to me and then the carriage with Mr. Whitsett that was just now disappearing from view.

"Colin Pendragon and Ethan Pruitt," Colin announced with bountiful pleasure. "And you are?" I knew he hadn't the slightest recollection of most of the Honeycutt children's names, but I was willing to bet this was the second oldest daughter, Francine.

"Francine," she answered even as I was thinking it, her eyes narrowing the tiniest bit. "You're those ones was talkin' to Edward, aren't ya?"

"Indeed, we are," Colin answered, his smile remaining indelibly intact as he tipped his head ever so slightly. "And I'm afraid we have come to bother him with just a few more questions. Is he at home?"

"'Oo is it?" a woman's voice hollered from somewhere behind the girl, and I was certain it had to be Mrs. Honeycutt.

"Them blokes was askin' about Edward a few days ago," Francine shouted back over her shoulder without bothering to fully turn her head away from us. "They say they wanna talk ta 'im again."

"Well, let 'em in. We ain't got nothin' ta 'ide." The girl immediately did as bade, swinging the door wide and stepping back even as her mother came pounding down the stairs. "Gentlemen," she said with the same sort of taut smile she'd displayed on our first visit, which seemed to belie her statement of a moment ago. "Come in and settle yerselves. Frannie, go tell Ben ta fetch Edward. 'E's round back tendin' to the layin 'ens." As Francine scurried down the hall toward the back of the house, Mrs. Honeycutt showed us to a tidy, if compact, front room to the right of the entrance that was filled with well-worn furniture and an old stone fireplace that had years of char scorched across its face. The meticulousness of the room was most impressive given that I remembered the Honeycutts to be raising nine children. "Clare . . ." Mrs. Honeycutt called back toward the stairs, "fetch some tea and biscuits fer our guests."

"You mustn't go to any trouble," Colin said at once as she gestured us to the cornflower-blue slope-backed couch with its cloth button tufting. It had obviously been a fine piece of furniture at one time, though its fabric was now thin in spots and its stuffing had shifted over the years, leaving me to land rather harshly when I hit the cushion.

"'Tis no trouble." She waved us off, her deep brown hair held up with a confluence of pins atop her head. Despite a figure that showed the effects of having borne so many children, I pegged her to be no more than a handful of years older than me, and it was still easy to see where her daughter had gotten her comely looks from. "Is there some trouble?" she asked after she settled herself down on a chair across from us, her face clearly revealing her concern.

"Not at all," Colin assured with a warm, patient smile. "We are merely looking for a bit of additional information. Your Edward seems to be a fine lad," he added, but it wasn't as filled with the reassurance of his first statement. "You really mustn't worry yourself."

"I'm afraid 'tis a mother's job ta worry," she replied with the same tight smile, and her words instantly sliced through me as thoughts of my own mother stormed my mind.

A young woman with a tall, bony frame, almost boyish in figure, swept into the room with a tea tray full of mismatched cups and saucers and a plate of shortbread biscuits with an ample jar of jam. "Eddie's comin'," she announced as she set the tray down on the heavily scarred table between the couch and the chair where Mrs. Honeycutt sat.

"All right, darlin'," Mrs. Honeycutt said as she scooted forward and quickly poured three cups of tea. "This is me daughter Clare," she muttered, pushing two of the cups toward us along with a nicked ceramic creamer and a small pewter sugar bowl. "She's a good girl," she added, though I had no idea why.

Clare Honeycutt gave us an odd, off-balanced curtsy as if we were nobility and then bowed her head, casting her gaze to the floor. "'At's fine." Her mother tipped her a tender grin before waving her out of the room. "Now go on and git back ta yer chores."

The girl scuttled out of the room in a curious way that made me realize she was simple in her manner. It had to be a particularly grave disappointment given that she was their eldest daughter. Nevertheless, Mrs. Honeycutt made no mention of it, which I admired, and a moment later young, handsome Edward Honeycutt entered the room, wiping his hands on a rag.

"Mr. Pendragon . . . Mr. Pruitt . . ." he said with a note of surprise, making it clear his younger brother had told him nothing of why he was being summoned.

"Young Master Honeycutt." Colin stood up with a smile, holding out a hand.

"Right . . ." Mrs. Honeycutt stated with finality as she too got up and headed over to the door where her son remained. "I'll leave ya to it then. Good ta see ya again . . ." she added to Colin and me, but there was little real conviction in her voice and I understood why.

"Our regards to your husband," Colin called after her, but she did not respond and I doubted George Honeycutt would give a whit to know that we'd returned.

"Have you learned anything?" Edward Honeycutt asked as soon as his mother disappeared, before he even came fully into the room.

Colin sat down again and I followed suit. "I try to make it a habit to learn something new every day," he answered cheekily.

Edward perched on the seat across from us where his mother had just been, his face a mask of soberness and concern. "I meant about Mo," he corrected as though Colin might actually have misunderstood him.

"Of course." Colin sat back for an instant before reaching out and picking up his teacup again. "What I have learned is that there are ever more questions surrounding both Miss O'Dowd's death and that of the abbot at the monastery."

"The abbot?!" He looked genuinely caught off guard. "Whatever does the abbot's death have to do with Maureen?"

"An excellent question. Now, I know you accompanied Mr. Chesterton on his visits to the monastery once or twice a month, but when was the last time the two of you visited there together?"

Edward glanced between the two of us as though checking for signs of the correct answer and I wondered if he feared stating the wrong thing. "Last Wednesday. The day after the murder. We didn't know very much about it until we got there. At least I didn't." I found it a curious answer as I could not tell whether he was concerned about speaking on behalf of Raleigh Chesterton or if he meant to leave some unspoken possibility ajar.

"And who told you about what had happened when you arrived there?" Colin asked without his usual bravado since we knew all of these answers already.

Edward glanced down and seemed to come to some momentary decision before looking back up and locking his eyes on Colin. "Brother Clayworth, the elderly monk who runs the brewery. He was quite chattery as a matter of fact. But then he usually is."

"Meaning . . . ?" Colin prodded, and I knew what he was looking to have Edward admit.

"He drinks," the lad said pointedly. "It was before nine in the morning and I could tell he'd already been into his ale. Because of my work at the Pig and Pint I know the look a man's eyes get when he's downed some spirits." He broke off his gaze with a shake of his head. "I'm sorry, I don't mean to disparage him. I'm sure he is a good man. A fine monk. He has always been kind to me. But he does know how to drink just the same."

"Yes," Colin nodded slowly, "so I have noticed." He set his teacup down and slid two fingers into his vest pocket, digging out a single crown and sending it gliding across the back of his right hand. "Brother Clayworth tells us you've done some work for him," he continued, his tone as nonchalant as the rhythm of the coin in his hand.

"I help him with his accounts about once a month. There is little to it, but the poor monk seems ill-suited for it. I'm happy to oblige as it gives me practice and a bit more coin."

"And if I were to review those ledgers . . ." Colin maintained his blasé air as the coin continued its leisurely stroll betwixt his fingers. ". . . is there any chance that I might stumble upon any sort of impropriety?"

While I was taken aback by the directness of his question, Edward Honeycutt was even more so. The poor young man looked so startled that he actually recoiled as though Colin had taken a swipe at him. "Impropriety?!" he repeated with dismay. "Have I shown my character to be no better than that of a common thief, Mr. Pendragon? And against a brotherhood of monks no less?" Anger began to rise within his eyes as he held his gaze on Colin.

"Review their ledgers. In fact, I *insist* you do so. Then see if it is fitting for you to suggest such a thing."

A smile slowly spread across Colin's face as he kept his gaze equally fixed upon Edward Honeycutt, the coin in his hand having picked up a modicum of speed. "Your offense is very winning and yet we shall, of course, review the monk's ledgers for ourselves. I promise it shall lift my heart to prove your indignation well-founded. Yet I am sure you can imagine that in my line of work I too often find the greatest umbrage concealing the most egregious crimes. So let me ask you something I must confess to have been pondering a great deal of late. How did you propose to move yourself, Miss O'Dowd, and your unborn child to London without so much as a prospect of finding a job?"

"I have saved the money I earn from my father and Mr. Chesterton without fail," came the answer in a hard, forthright manner. "And Mo did what she could with what she earned as well. But it was easier for me since I still live here. Mo had to pay for a room in Dalwich. It wasn't much, but it still cost her every month."

"Were you ready to become a father, Edward? How was that going to fit in with your plans?"

The young man rubbed a hand across his forehead before glancing toward the open doorway, and it suddenly occurred to me that he had never told anyone in his family about his plans or the baby. "I wasn't happy at first. I can admit that"—he glared at Colin and me—"but Mo was so thrilled that I couldn't help but get caught in her joy. It was just going to be the three of us—making a new start. Our own family . . ." He shook his head and his shoulders slumped forward. "I loved her," he added softly, all of the former harshness that had been steeling him abruptly replaced by a welling of pain that seemed to stretch the depth of his lifetime. For the second time in speaking with this young man I found myself swallowing back a lump that was forming in the crux of my throat and threatening to unravel the decorum that I so resolutely clung to.

"Forgive me." Colin slid the coin back into his vest pocket

and reached for his tea again. "It is not my intention to upset you. I only mean to discover the truth, just as I'm sure you wish me to."

"With all my heart," he announced firmly, the veil of rigidity hooding his eyes again in an instant.

Colin took a brief sip of his tea as though we were enjoying the most banal social visit. "When you went to the monastery the morning after the murder, did you notice anything unusual?"

"Unusual?" Edward frowned at the absurdity of the question and I could not blame him. "Everything was off. The whole place was in turmoil. We had no sooner turned onto their drive when we spotted the constable's carriage out front of the main building and it looked like just about every monk who lived there was milling about as if they had nothing to do. Which is *never* the way of it out there."

"So we have seen. And did you find Brother Clayworth straight-away?"

"We did. We carried on about our business because we had no reason not to. Headed straight out to the brewery where Brother Clayworth was waiting for us same as always." He glanced down and then right back up again. "As I said, he had already been into his ale."

"What about Mr. Chesterton? Did he say anything to you before you reached Brother Clayworth?"

He gave a weak shrug. "I guess he was wondering what was up, same as me."

"And then Brother Clayworth told you what had happened? *How* it had happened?"

"Right off. Before I could even get down from the wagon he was telling us about the stabbing and how they cut the abbot's tongue right out of his head."

"I see . . ." Colin nodded as he stood up and looked toward me. "I do wish that were not the case," he added as he turned and started for the door.

"What . . . ?" Edward got up and trailed along behind us. "What are you saying? What do you wish were not the case?"

"We shall report back to you once we have had a look at those ledgers," he replied evenly. "I look forward to confirming your integrity."

"But, Mr. Pendragon . . ." Edward Honeycutt began to protest even though Colin had already made it as far as the front door. "Mr. Pruitt . . . ?! "

I glanced back to find his gaze leveled on me, as if I had a wisp of control over Colin or any insight into his mind. "You must trust Mr. Pendragon to find the truth of these cases," I said, unable to think of anything more reassuring, "no matter where that truth may lie." And then I too made a hasty retreat, determined to bombard Colin with questions until I, at least, understood what he was up to.

# CHAPTER 24

My head ached and my eyes insisted on displaying their fatigue by continuously welling up as if I were the victim of my own emotions. I dabbed at them with the handkerchief Colin had loaned to me before glancing sideways to make sure Brother Clayworth was still asleep. To my relief he remained just so, his chin hung forward until it nearly touched his chest and his breathing coming in a deep, rhythmic flow. I began to feel it likely that I could drive a team of mules through the open brewery without disturbing him in the least, though whether it was a function of his age or the nipping he'd undoubtedly been doing throughout the day, I could not say.

I rubbed my thumbs on my forehead just above my eyebrows in an attempt to lessen the pain, but it had little immediate impact. What I was really most exasperated about was where Colin had gotten off to. He had started out beside me in Brother Clayworth's awkward little office in the corner of the converted barn pretending to be paying attention, albeit poorly, to the multitude of ledgers the kindly monk had laid out for our perusal. But the review of such figures is simply not his forte, so long before the other monks had returned from their afternoon prayers, Colin had gotten up and blithely wandered away. Only Brother Clayworth had remained to keep me company, dismissing the need to attend one afternoon's prayers for the sake of the work Colin wished me to get done. In point of fact, however, I suspected the monk merely yearned for nothing more than a bit of sleep.

I had presumed that Colin would at least *pretend* to return to the work at hand once the small cadre of monks who toiled here began to filter back, but he did not. And so I had persevered alone to the accompaniment of the smells and sounds of ale production, along with the soft, muted snoring of Brother Clayworth. The whole of it had conspired to leave me in the condition I now found myself deeply mired in: cranky, achy, and leaking about the eyes like a sodden oaf.

"Have you found any signs of potted revelry with a coterie of local slags on hand?"

I froze at the sound of Colin's whispered voice, terrified that Brother Clayworth might have heard, but when I quickly slid my eyes sideways it was to discover that the good monk had heard nothing more than the inner mumblings of his dreams. "Are you now trying to get us expelled from this monastery?" I hissed, my current mood charging aggressively forth. "Or perhaps you mean to have us banned from the whole of Dalwich altogether?!"

He seemed to consider that possibility before a roguish smile eased itself onto his face. "You cannot think I mean to vanquish myself when I am moving ever closer to the solution of this case. But I can see I have left you to this tedium too long. You mustn't be cross." He moved closer to me so he could peer over my shoulder at the ledger I had open before me. "*Have* you found anything of any use? Any discrepancy that Edward Honeycutt did not properly account for?"

I let out a disgusted snort. "These books are flawlessly kept and do not contain even a modicum of questionable input. I would let Edward Honeycutt keep *our* ledgers. And speaking of which"—I turned my head to scowl at him and was rewarded by a renewal of the incessant pounding—"you still have not told me why you were needling Edward back at their house. What game is it you're playing against him?"

"Game?!" He looked back at me with arch surprise as if I had just offended the whole of his character. "Since when do you know me to be a man who plays games?" He leaned forward and whispered into my nearest ear. "I find him to be too contrite. I wish to unnerve him some. After all, beyond the monks themselves, only he and Mr. Chesterton had the details of the abbot's death before Miss O'Dowd's body was found. Somebody wanted us to believe the two murders linked. Someone who knew about the abbot's tongue having been severed."

"Oh . . ." I shook my head and let my wearied body slump forward. "I simply cannot believe that Edward Honeycutt could have had anything to do with Miss O'Dowd's murder. It's too awful."

"Now, Ethan . . ." he started to say, but the sound of the elderly monk beginning to stir on my other side instantly brought Colin upright and condemned him to silence.

"Gentlemen . . ." Brother Clayworth rubbed his eyes and rolled his head slightly, easing the cricks that had obviously settled there during his protracted slumber. "I must have dozed off a moment," he mumbled.

"I'm afraid it was more than a moment," I responded, letting my own exhaustion get the best of me.

"We have had time enough to finish with your ledgers and be summoned by the newly returned Father Demetris," Colin cut in smoothly.

"Summoned . . . ?" I cast a glance at Colin to see whether we had truly been requested by the priest or if he was simply making an excuse.

"I ran into him fresh from the train station while I was exploring the grounds and he asked that we join him in the abbot's former office."

"Off you go then," Brother Clayworth said as he pulled himself back to his feet. "Never mind about these things, I'll put them away. You don't want to keep the bishop's emissary waiting." He gave us a broad grin.

I was only too happy to follow Colin out of the brewery and away from a task that I could see held no use for us. If Edward

Honeycutt was pilfering money, it most certainly was not from the monks. I dreaded the possibility that Colin might want me to go through Raleigh Chesterton's books next, provided Constable Brendle could convince Mr. Chesterton to give us a look at them. The very thought of it was enough to keep me silent on the topic lest the idea had not already occurred to him. "Where did you get off to anyway?" I asked instead as we walked back to the main monastery building. The edge of annoyance that persisted in my voice was slowly becoming easier to control as the fresh air immediately began to soothe the pounding in my head.

"You know I don't have the patience for that sort of thing. And you're so much better at it than I am."

"Better at straining my eyes and sorting through numbers? Hardly a compliment," I groused.

He chuckled, but then I had known he would. "I shall make it up to you," he said quite simply.

The sound of our boots clacking along the empty monastery hallway was the only company we had as we made our way back to the abbot's office. For some reason I felt as though we were about to be censured and could not quite understand why. There was no doubt that the priest had been sent to see how we were progressing and that, I supposed, was where my unease lay. For it seemed to me we had little to show for our efforts, which nettled me as I checked Colin's expression and found a look of pure nonchalance.

"*Gentlemen!*" Father Demetris said as he pulled the door open, his welcoming smile adding to my apprehension. "Please come in." He stepped aside and waved us to the same chairs in front of the ornate desk. "It is heartening to see you both again, and I cannot tell you how pleased I am that you have decided to stay right here for the remainder of your enquiry. It can only help you succeed in solving this case all the more readily."

"Precisely our intention," Colin answered easily. "And how was your journey back?"

"Uneventful. Which suits me. I must confess that I still do not find speeding along behind a steam locomotive to be a natural event in the least. And now the press is all abuzz about those horseless carriages. I do not understand it. I do not understand it at all."

"The automobile." Colin grinned eagerly. "How I would like to get my hands on one."

Father Demetris gave a mock shiver as he let loose a chuckle. "I'll take a horse any day."

"But the automobile is so much cleaner than a horse and far less temperamental."

"They may be cleaner, but I'll not agree that they're less temperamental. In any event, I much prefer God's creatures to man-made contraptions. But tell me, Mr. Pendragon, how has your investigation progressed into the abbot's death?"

"We have learned a great deal." Colin flashed a tight grin. "But I will admit to having many critical questions that still remain unanswered. And then there are some potentially useful documents that seem to have quite disappeared."

A quizzical expression settled upon Father Demetris's face. "What documents? I have been quite clear with the brotherhood that it is the bishop's wish that every assistance should be accorded you. Have they not done so?"

"The monks have been appreciably generous with their time and information," Colin tossed back, "but we've had a devil of a time getting our hands on some of the abbot's personal papers. Brother Silsbury was even rather stingy in letting us review the abbot's Bible." Colin reached into his coat and pulled out the small, leather-bound book. "I finally had to resort to *borrowing* it for a bit without his knowledge," he added with a lopsided grin.

The priest shook his head with a twinge of embarrassment, though I decided his look also included a fair amount of astonishment at Colin's audacity. "Well, I do apologize for that. You have my permission to keep the abbot's Bible for as long as you deem necessary."

"Thank you." Colin gave a perfunctory nod as he shoved it back into his pocket and I knew he would have found a way to keep it no matter what the priest had determined. "But what flusters me the most," he continued, "is the fact that no one can seem to lay their hands on the abbot's journals from his sabbatical to Egypt."

"Egypt?!" Father Demetris leaned forward with a look of surprise. "But that was years ago. Whatever do you want to see that for?"

"Why did he go?" Colin pressed, ignoring the priest's question.

"I really couldn't say. That would have been something he took up with the bishop, not me."

"But you're the bishop's confidante, are you not?" And I was stunned to hear Colin appealing to the man's ego as he would to any common man.

"I have become so, yes. But that trip was years ago."

"Three years ago," Colin clarified. "Just over three and a half to be precise. Were you not with the bishop long before then?" Colin abruptly raised a hand and waved the priest off perfunctorily. "Perhaps he simply thought you ill-suited for whatever the matter was. You needn't concern yourself about it. I shall have my father check with Bishop Fencourt directly."

Father Demetris ran a hand through his deep brown hair and released a sigh as he sat back in his chair once again. His weary eyes revealed the obvious turmoil raging within his mind as I continued to marvel at Colin's ability to manipulate the ego of such a pious man. The two of us remained silent as the priest appeared to be weighing his words carefully before he finally chose to speak up once more. "You needn't trouble yourself or your father, Mr. Pendragon. I will tell you what you wish to know, though I believe you will find it has no bearing on his murder. It is my understanding that Abbot Tufton went to Egypt because he was suffering a sort of crisis of faith. He went there to study and learn, and to search for answers to the questions that had been clouding his mind. I am happy to inform you that at the conclusion of his journey to the Middle East he came right back here to Whitmore Abbey, where he resumed his position for the remainder of his life." He smiled. "But then you already know that."

"And the questions he was searching for answers to..."

Colin mused as he leaned back, and I watched his hand reach for his vest pocket to release a crown before it abruptly stopped, left hanging impotently in midair. He shifted his eyes to me and I knew he was adrift, so I grabbed the nub of pencil I always carried in my coat pocket and handed it over to him. His eyes wandered down rather vacantly before he slowly started to flip it through his fingers, though with far less dexterity then he would have done with a coin. "And those questions . . ." he began again, his hand picking up a bit of speed with that nub of pencil, ". . . were they about the *Codex Sinaiticus* and *Syriacus*? Perhaps even the release of the Gospel of Peter that, if memory serves me, was published just prior to the abbot's sojourn?"

Father Demetris pinched the bridge of his nose and rubbed at his eyes. "I see you have done your research," he muttered in a way that made it clear he had not meant it as a compliment.

"It is why your bishop brought me here," Colin replied plainly.

"Doubters and men of science have been trying to disprove the authenticity of the Bible since its inception." Father Demetris dropped his hand and spoke in a slow, grave cadence that seemed to bear out the weight of the topic for him. "Always to no avail. It has been as impossible to refute as it has been to validate. Such is the definition of faith." He gave a small shrug and heaved a prolonged sigh. "And then that German man found the *Codex Sinaiticus* about sixty years ago."

"Constantin von Tischendorf," Colin supplied without hesitation, startling even me.

"Yes . . . yes . . ." Father Demetris nodded solemnly, and I could see that the topic weighed heavily on him. "When the codex was released five years ago it set the whole of the Christian, Jewish, and Muslim faiths into a most precarious position. Think of it—here was half of the Old Testament and the *whole* of the New Testament written over fifteen hundred years ago. The oldest versions known to exist. And they were *filled* with changes. The hand of man revising the original words of God. There were thousands of them. . . ."

"More than *thirty* thousand," Colin bothered to state.

Father Demetris heaved yet another sigh as his shoulders

slumped forward. "Yes, so many changes made to a text we had been preaching as sacrosanct. And for the first time we had proof that the books of the Bible that had been handed down to us from ancient times were neither historically accurate nor reliable."

"And the Gospel of Peter . . . ?" Colin asked.

"That is not a recognized biblical text."

"Meaning you discount its more fantastical accounting of the Resurrection?" Colin pressed.

"Out of hand," he answered at once.

"And the discovery of the *Codex Syriacus* in the same monastery several years ago . . . ? Have you seen the photographs the sisters took of it?"

"I have not," Father Demetris answered, looking neither pleased nor impressed.

"They are saying these are the original versions of the first four books of the New Testament," Colin pressed with almost an embarrassment of enthusiasm. "And there is no mention of Jesus visiting his disciples after the Resurrection. It seems now that all first-person accounts were added to the manuscripts more than a century later, including the last twelve verses of Mark, which are entirely missing from the original."

Father Demetris's face pinched as his eyes settled on the two of us. "These writings . . . these documents . . . whatever they are and however they fit into the whole of God's design, I cannot say. But in the end, they are the reason the church must point to the canon of faith to defend itself against such attacks. It is the surety that resides only in a man's heart and soul that matters. That is the tenet that guides each one of us."

"Your conviction is powerful"—Colin nodded as he handed the stub of pencil back over to me—"but as I am a man mired in the conundrum that cost your abbot his life, I would still very much like to see what he wrote in his journals while in Egypt. Brother Bursnell has promised to do a thorough search of the library for us, but he has yet to produce so much as a single sheet of paper."

"I shall speak with him," Father Demetris assured, though with far less veracity than he had displayed a moment ago.

Colin stood up. "Then I think we can ask no more of you for now." He went to the door and grabbed the knob, but before opening it he glanced back, and asked, "Did you ever have occasion to speak to the abbot about his sojourn to Egypt?"

"Not directly. But John Tufton remained a querying man throughout his life. It is what made him such a fine and devout leader for the brotherhood here at Whitmore Abbey."

A contented smile settled upon Colin's face as he nodded ever so slightly. "You have done his memory a great service," he said. And while I could not discern what had pleased him so suddenly, I was happy to note it as I followed him back out into the utter silence of the monastery's central hallway.

# CHAPTER 25

Dinner that night, such as it was, was dispatched with its usual banality. It consisted of roast chicken cut up into small, unrecognizable pieces so that each monk received a like, if diminutive, portion, boiled greens with just a touch of pork tossed in for flavor, and cubed potatoes that had been pan-fried with rosemary. The whole of it tasted adequate.

Conversation during the meal had been typically sparse. Father Demetris, Colin, and I had briefly remained in the refectory afterward to share some benign conversation with the senior monks, Brothers Morrison, Silsbury, Clayworth, and the oft-ailing Brother Wright. But our chatter had been idle and I knew Colin was only waiting for the moment when the monks would announce it was time to retire for the evening.

Brother Bursnell had been invited to join our brief exchange but had begged off, insisting he was going to return to the library to have one last go at finding the abbot's missing Egyptian journals. I noticed Colin studying the young monk as he scurried out of the refectory and could easily sense Colin's growing distrust of the man. And sure enough, a short time later when we were all filing back to our cells for the night, we passed the library only to find it dark and silent. If Brother Bursnell really had come back to initiate a final search, it had not lasted the length of a quarter hour.

For whatever reason I did not feel as oppressed when delivered to the abbot's cell. I suppose it seemed less intimidating since it was my second night doing so. I was already warming up to the notion of getting a decent sleep tonight when Colin quickly leaned over and whispered that he would be by later.

"Whatever for?" I mumbled back under my breath.

"We have work to do," he answered with a measure of disbelief as though I was balmy to have asked such a question.

"What?" Brother Morrison turned around and barked. He was closest to us given the way he had to hobble as a result of the lameness on his left side.

"Just telling Mr. Pruitt to have a blessed evening." Colin flashed a complacent smile, which made me want to cringe.

"Then perhaps we are having a beneficial effect on you after all," Brother Clayworth chuckled softly.

I forced myself to look amused but was relieved to be able to make a hasty exit by ducking into the tiny cell. As I leaned against the door a minute, the sound of clicking boots retreating down the hallway assured me that the lot of them had departed. I simply could not allow myself to feel comfortable around these monks. I dared not trust them—for one of them had almost certainly murdered their abbot—and I knew I would be wholly reviled were these monks ever to learn how Colin and I lived.

Heaving a sigh to banish such thoughts, I took the small candle I'd been given and lit both the slender taper on the stand next to the pitcher of fresh water and the far stouter one on the table, which is where I planted myself. For a short while after I settled in I heard the same soft sounds of disharmonious chanting drift from the cells near me and found it somehow comforting as I sat there wondering how I might fill my time. With no better idea coming to mind, I finally fetched up a few more sheets of paper and a fresh pencil, and began rubbing at the tabletop again, concentrating on the places where I had found the incomplete markings the night before.

As I dragged the side of the lead in great sweeping arcs, I found myself feeling strangely intrusive, much as I had the previous night, as though I were trying to peer into the abbot's private thoughts by attempting to get the tabletop to reveal his secrets. But just as before, I found myself having little real luck. I dredged up the bit of Psalm I recognized—*"lamp to my feet and a light to my path"*—and even though it was undeniably familiar to me, I could not supply the rest of the verse. Why I had not picked up one of the multitude of Bibles around the monastery I could not fathom. As there are some hundred and fifty Psalms, I must admit that it seemed like an exercise in futility. And even if I did manage to locate it, there was little reason to believe that it would impart so much as a hint of value with respect to the abbot's murder.

I turned myself back to the rubbing and quickly found the last name, *Strauss,* again. It was obviously the match for the bit of folded paper Colin had found in the abbot's Bible. I would have to check with him when he returned to see if he still had that scrap of paper on him. If nothing else it would prove to be notable if they were the same, though I was still perplexed at the abbot's evident interest in Richard Strauss's music. I had always found it engaging, but it was certainly not canonical.

This time I was also able to tease out the name *Mona,* which I had not discovered on my first attempt, but as there was nothing written on either side of it I was left to ponder who this woman might be; a sister or cousin seemed most likely. The word *sin* came into view, just as it had the night before, hardly a cause for interest or curiosity. I would have been rather surprised *not* to find it written somewhere on here. But nothing else I could coax from the table made a whit of sense whatsoever. They were clearly partial bits: *icus, ne, ith, w, bar,* and *mew.* While the last two were, in fact, actual words, they both seemed unexpected, if not inappropriate, to be written by the abbot of a monastery.

Sometime shortly after unearthing these same fragments for the second time, my eyelids betrayed me and I sank to the tabletop without realizing I had done so. It was only after the faintest click of a door settling into place abruptly sheared through my brain that I bolted up and found myself staring at a hulking shadow hovering just inside the cell. The tapered candle on the washstand had sputtered out at some point, leaving me to blink repeatedly in an effort to try and get my eyes to adjust to the faint darkness. It was just as my heart began to ratchet up that Colin took a small step forward into the thin light of the table's candle.

"Were you asleep?"

"No," I heard myself lie inexplicably without a second thought. "I was just tired of waiting for you." At least that part was true.

"I hope I didn't frighten you."

"I wasn't frightened," I lied again.

He chuckled as he sat down on the cot. "Ever the brave one." He reached over and grabbed the sheets of paper I'd been working on. "I had to give these good, pious gentlemen time to fall asleep," he bothered to explain as he studied the pages, one after another. "Did you find anything new?"

"A woman's name." I stifled a yawn. "Mona. Do you remember anyone mentioning the abbot having a sister named Mona?" He gave me a disbelieving smirk and I knew the question was absurd. I doubted he even remembered the abbot's name. "None of it makes any sense nor seems to have the slightest relevance to the murder," I groused as I rubbed my eyes.

"Really?" he asked simply, and the underlying tone in his voice assured me that I had missed something. "Do you not recognize the partial bit of that Psalm?"

"I know I've heard it before, but I certainly couldn't tell you what the rest of it was," I answered, trying not to let my disappointment show as I began to realize that he could recall the whole of it.

"*Thy word is a lamp to my feet and a light to my path,*" he recited smoothly. "*I have sworn an oath and confirmed it, to observe thy righteous ordinances.*"

"And just how the hell do you remember that?!" I blasted back perhaps a little too harshly.

He chuckled quietly. "I didn't. I had to look it up in the abbot's Bible." But even this admission forced me to grit my teeth as it meant Colin had taken the time and effort to find this single quote while I had dismissed the effort out of hand. "The dear man had underlined it," he confessed with a lopsided grin.

I shook my head, though his declaration did allow me to feel marginally better. "I still don't see what it has to do with anything," I repeated. "And why was the abbot so obsessed with Richard Strauss?" I pointed to the rubbing of the composer's name. "Does this match that little sliver of paper you found in Abbot Tufton's Bible?"

Colin's grin widened as his dimples bloomed on his face. This had to be good, I realized. Very good. "I have to admit that I was wondering the same thing," he said as he dug a hand into his vest pocket and pulled out the neatly folded scrap of paper. As he opened it and handed it to me, I could see at once that it was *not* the same instance of Strauss's name that I had been able to reveal from the tabletop.

"I don't get it," I grumbled. "What the bloody hell was his interest in Richard Strauss?!"

Colin stared at me, the flickering of the candle on the table amplifying the merriment just behind his gaze. "Your error is in your presumption."

"What?"

"It isn't *Richard* Strauss that he was so balmy over. It was *David Friedrich* Strauss."

And before the name had fully left Colin's mouth, it all made sense. "The theologian . . ." I muttered.

"And writer," he corrected. "Scandalized the whole of Europe with the publication of his book, *The Life of Jesus, Critically Examined*. He was the *first* to point out that the books of the Bible had been hand copied for greater than a thousand years, and seldom by professional scribes. The poor bastard was roundly chastised for making the case that the books of the Bible are *filled* with inconsistencies."

"But why would Abbot Tufton have anything to do with David Strauss's assertions? The man was vilified."

"Why indeed?" Colin leveled his gaze on me, the single candle's light casting shadows across his eyes, making them look almost black. "What unusual thing do we already know about the abbot?"

"That he had a crisis of faith a few years ago and traveled to Egypt to assuage it," I answered back resolutely, the warmth of Colin's smile confirming that I had struck at the very heart of what he was alluding to.

"And what else did you manage to tease up with your rubbings of his table?"

"A bit of Scripture and some useless, random words—"

"Look at what you just did," he cut me off. "Look at the placement of those fragments and tell me you don't notice any sort of pattern," he urged as he held the sheets of paper up for me.

"Pattern?" I stared at the mess of it all and tried to make sense of it.

SIN  ICUS          NE  ITH

STRAUSS

W   MONA          BAR  MEW

"Well, I certainly recognize David Strauss's last name now, and there is no mistaking the word *sin* . . ."

"Allow me." Colin tossed me a patient look as he dropped the pages back onto his lap and snatched the pencil from the tabletop. "You will curse yourself when you see the first three," he warned as he began to rewrite the fragments of words onto a fresh sheet of paper.

And only after he had done so, in the exact order and configuration that I had found them, did he begin to fill in the blanks. Even from where I was sitting I immediately began to see actual, sensible words beginning to take shape from out of the splinters I had culled. And he was right. By the time he finished the first line, I was aggravated for not having spotted it myself. The only saving grace was that I had no awareness of the bottom line. If it was meant to make sense to me, it still did not.

"Now, then . . ." He held the paper up and looked at it a moment before passing it back to me, sliding my pencil back onto the table by my elbow with great satisfaction. "Does that help at all?" He grinned roguishly.

I stared at the paper and wondered how he had seen these things when I had found only gibberish. Even the sound of his whispered snicker could not assail against my astonishment.

## *SIN***AIT***ICUS* **AGNES SM***ITH*

## *STRAUSS*

## **WHITE** *MON***A***STERY BARTHOLO***M***EW*

"What is the White Monastery?" I asked after a minute. "And who the devil is Bartholomew?"

"The White Monastery is also in Egypt and is where the ancient testament of Bartholomew was found just a handful of years ago. It includes a story of Jesus, post-Resurrection, going to Hell and rescuing all of those who had fallen from God's grace. While it, like the Gospel of Peter I mentioned to Father Demetris earlier, is not a recognized biblical text, it is still quite incendiary nonetheless." Colin's face sobered. "For a man who supposedly fought his demons in Egypt nearly four years ago, it would appear Abbot Tufton was still very much conflicted."

"And the Psalm . . ." I muttered, finally recognizing the connection there, ". . . it's referring to God's words, the Bible, and the need to commit to following them. Words we now know were manipulated innumerable times since their original writing."

Colin nodded grimly. "Well done. I would say that all of this conspires to inform us that the poor abbot was well adrift, and it seems to me that someone here must have found that fact untenable."

"But *murder?!*" I heard the skepticism in my voice and winced at my own naïveté. Did I not know firsthand of killings that had been committed for lesser reasons? And those that appeared to have been carried out for no reason at all?

"Somebody cut out the man's tongue. They meant him to be silenced in every possible way," Colin explained as calmly as if he were instructing how to unlatch a door. "That deed alone provides us a great deal of insight into the mindset of the man who did this."

"Yes"—I slumped forward and rubbed my brow—" . . . yes, of course."

"Now, we have work we must accomplish tonight," he said as he pushed himself off the cot. "I trust you had a good nap while you were waiting for me," he added, one side of his mouth curling into a thin smile.

"I suppose I did," I admitted. "What are we going to do?"

"I am going to pillage my way through the abbot's office," he said, "before availing myself of the library yet again and rooting through their trash. Which is why I need you to go out to the infirmary and take another look at the abbot's papers. Now that we know the sort of thing we're searching for, I need to make certain we haven't missed anything."

I raised an eyebrow as I stared back at him through the shimmer of the fat, fluttering candle. "Wouldn't it be simpler to just ask Father Demetris to get those papers for us? He seems perfectly willing to get us whatever we ask for."

Colin nodded reticently and once again I knew there was something I was missing. "My concern is that Father Demetris will have no knowledge if Brother Silsbury decides to hold back an item or three. I would rather you steal a look at the papers without them first being sorted through by anyone."

I knew he was right, but it still left me uneasy. "It seems somehow wrong to suspect a Benedictine monk of such a deception," I said, realizing how absurd the statement sounded the moment I said it.

"And it will seem even more so when I accuse one of them of murder," he pointed out, completing the obvious conceit that I had already realized. "Now, give me five minutes before you head out," he hissed as he moved the few steps to the door. "And for heaven's sake be careful." He turned and grabbed the door-knob, opening the door just enough to slide out into the hallway before tossing me a quick shrug of his eyebrows and disappearing with the same faint click that had preceded his entry.

I remained at the table, listening intently for the sound of his footfalls sneaking off down the hallway, but heard nothing. Had we been schoolboys I might have thought he was waiting just outside the door to give me a proper scare, but under the circumstances I knew he was setting an example of stealth I would be expected to emulate. At least I would be alone in the infirmary since Brother Silsbury would have long since retired for the night. That fact was likely the reason Colin was sending me out there while he remained within the monastery itself. Never mind that I'd actually had far more experience skulking about when I was a youth than he ever did.

Unable to rein in my eagerness another moment, I finally stood up and removed both my jacket and vest, and slid one of my suspenders down an arm. If I was spotted by anyone, I decided it would look most natural if it appeared I was merely on my way to the loo. I yanked off my boots and pressed an ear to the door, listening carefully before gradually easing the door open just a crack. Just as I had known would be the case, Colin was not coiled up to spring at me, nor was anyone else. Even so, it felt strangely relieving to find the shadowed hallway very much empty.

I moved out of my cell as quietly as a church mouse, taking care to ensure the door didn't make any but the tiniest sound as it settled back into place. For an instant I wished I could have brought the fat taper from the table with me but, of course, knew that would never do. I would be far from discreet stealing across the backyard to the infirmary with a candle pitched out in front of me.

After letting my eyes adjust for a moment, I found that even in the relative blackness of the hallway I was still able to find my way to the monastery's rear exit at the juncture where the corridor turned toward the library, refectory, and the abbot's office. For an instant I imagined I could hear Colin slipping the bolt on the abbot's door and edging inside, but I decided that was impossible. For if I were a church mouse, he would be nothing more than a shift in the room's ambient temperature, a feat that exasperated me given his ability to otherwise disrupt a gathering of people whenever it suited him.

I delicately pushed my way outside and eased the door back into its jamb with the utmost patience. There was nary a click as it nestled into place, bringing a satisfied grin to my face. I could do this, I told myself resolutely, before taking two steps forward and nearly collapsing to the ground as the gravel beneath my stockings gouged into the delicate pads of my feet. A howl surged up through my throat that I managed to cage before it could escape into the chilled night air. My ingenuity within the monastery was leaving me ill prepared to walk outside, and yet I wasn't about to slink back to my cell for my shoes. I didn't want to be doing this in the first place—I certainly wasn't about to do it twice.

The moon had yet to make an appearance and the stars were spotty at best, informing me that a contingent of clouds was accumulating overhead and would block out whatever light I had hoped to use to guide my way. Just the same, I could not let it deter me. Staring into the darkness that surrounded me, I realized that I could just make out the wooden structure of the infirmary. It wasn't far, but neither was it close.

Girding myself with a silent warning to the soles of my feet, I started forward again, hobbling like an elderly man until I could stumble off the stone path and onto the strip of grass astride it. While there were twigs, bits of bark, and scraps of hard-shelled pods scattered about, it was far less unyielding than the pebbled path, and before I knew it I was sidling up to the small infirmary building itself.

The steady rhythm of cicadas was the only sound that accompanied me as I made my way around the right side of the building where I remembered the main door was located. A lone owl hooted overhead, followed by a great flapping of wings, but though I glanced up at the obsidian sky I could not see so much as a shadow swoop across my vision.

With everyone asleep I knew I would have this little building to myself, yet I vowed that I would behave as if someone were coming lest Brother Silsbury should unexpectedly have any reason to make a visit and happen upon me rooting through Abbot Tufton's things. There would be no suitable explanation for my actions, and even Father Demetris would have a hard time defending me to the monks.

I seized the door handle, anxious to get out of the damp night air, swinging the door hurriedly to move inside, and instantly froze, quickly catching the arcing door with the palm of my hand even before I could step over the threshold. The infirmary's main room was dark and still just as I had expected, but on the far left side where I knew Brother Silsbury's office to be, there was a faint glow of candlelight and the even fainter murmur of voices. I was so startled I remained immobile for what felt the longest time, holding the door open with my right hand while looming in the doorway like an unbidden statue. Yet in truth I probably stood there no longer than an instant as I immediately realized that if anyone else were on their way to join whatever furtive meeting was taking place here they would come upon me hovering where I had no business being.

Without another thought I crept inside, allowing the door to close behind me with the greatest care. I was hardly surprised to feel my heart hammering and my breath coming in tight, shallow bursts, and as I stood there like that, I tried to figure out what it was I should do next.

"... prattling about ..."

"... the sheer audacity ..."

"... God have mercy on us all ..."

Fragments. I could hear nothing more than fragments. And I couldn't even be sure how many voices there were or who was speaking.

"You mustn't get yourself rattled so ..." someone muttered

in a slow, languid sort of way as I moved forward, now grateful to have nothing more on my feet than stockings. "*Many are the afflictions of the righteous: but the Lord delivereth him out of them all.*"

"Don't preach to me," a second voice snapped.

I thought I heard a low, sly chortle but could not be certain, so I crept farther into the room, crouching low against the wall lest anyone should come in and see me. There was a wooden table with a set of drawers near the open doorway to Brother Silsbury's office, so I nestled behind it. It was enough to protect me if someone came out of the office, but if anyone entered the room from the main door behind me I would be found incongruously crouched here. I'd have a hell of a time trying to explain myself. I glanced around the area but saw no better place to secrete myself unless I went behind one of the handful of beds. That would ruin my proximity to Brother Silsbury's office, however, leaving me too far away to make my efforts worthwhile, so I decided to take my chances and stay where I was. My heart instantly took great zeal in taunting me over my gamble, thundering with an alacrity that threatened to burst my chest at any moment.

"Do calm yourself." It was the same languorous voice I'd heard a moment ago. It sounded familiar, though I could not readily place it.

"If you say that to me one more time I shall pitch you out into the night right onto your besotted head," the surly voice hissed back.

But this time the second man's words were enough to make me wonder if perhaps it was Brother Clayworth I was hearing, speaking in his listless, ale-infused way? I had to find out. Sucking in a stilted breath through the aridness of my mouth, I slowly slid forward just far enough until I could peer around the piece of furniture I had all but attached myself to.

The room within was a mire of shadows, interrupted only by one tall, thick candle on the desk and two small lanterns seated on the floor. That explained why I hadn't noticed any reflected light when I'd passed the few windows dotting the side of the infirmary building. I peered into the gray darkness and could make out two men sitting in chairs across from each another as though facing off. Narrowing my eyes as I stared into the flickering gloom, my heart scampering in my ears, I was finally able to discern Brother Silsbury and Brother Clayworth. Brother Silsbury was hunched over slightly with one hand dug into his short dark brown hair wearing a great agitated frown, while Brother Clayworth looked quite the opposite, lolling back, his head tipped slightly to one side as though he were on the verge of falling asleep.

"I cannot tell whether the ale is any good if I do not taste it," Brother Clayworth bothered to explain, releasing a soft chuckle that appeared to belie his own defense.

"Is that what you tell yourself?" Brother Silsbury shot back without looking at him.

"Brothers. . . ." a third voice cut in from somewhere behind Brother Silsbury where I could not see, causing me to cringe backward. "The only thing we are accomplishing with this bickering is setting my head to pounding." The voice was surly and short-tempered, and given what he had said I wondered if it might be Brother Wright.

"And what would be your suggestion?" Brother Silsbury groused, turning and glaring behind himself.

"We should speak with Father Demetris," came the unseen monk's answer. And before I knew what was happening a black figure moved out of the darkness from behind Brother Silsbury and stopped in the middle of the small office between the other two monks. I could tell at once by the tall, lean form that I had been correct, it was indeed Brother Wright. When he began to speak again he turned his head, glancing from one brother to the other, and I could make out his distinctive jawline beard etched upon his chin. "We cannot have our shame disgorged in front of those two men. It is unseemly."

"'Vengeance is mine, I will repay, sayeth the Lord. . . .'" Brother Clayworth murmured.

"*Good Christ, Clayworth!*" And to my horror Brother Silsbury leapt up and seized the older monk by the collar before Brother Wright reached out and heaved the two of them apart.

"*Get hold of yourselves, dammit,*" Brother Wright barked. "Do we not have enough happening here without the two of you fighting like reprobates?! There will be no protections if we cannot unify as we are meant to do." His voice came out rapid and harsh. "Now gather your wits, both of you." He turned on Brother Clayworth as Brother Silsbury slumped back into his seat. "I suggest you get yourself some sleep and start showing a little bloody self-control."

"I have self-control . . ." came the lazy reply, which only seemed to further confirm Brother Wright's point.

"You will if I have to have Brother Nathan follow you about to make certain of it," Brother Wright sallied back without a hint of jest.

"That sniveling little prig!" Brother Clayworth groused, for the first time sounding very much put-upon. "He's always watching me as it is. Why do I get all the novices?"

"Because you *need* watching," Brother Wright snapped. "Now, come on," he said, bending low and snatching up one of the lanterns. "There's nothing more to be done tonight."

And before I could so much as draw a breath the hem of a black cassock swept past within a foot of my face. I did not move, cursing my heart for rattling my frame as I was sure it was doing, and not a moment later Brother Clayworth brushed by and I would have sworn that the hem of his robe touched the side of my leg. Only after I heard the front door behind me open and slam shut did I slowly ease myself back behind the piece of furniture I'd so thoroughly wrapped myself around. While I could no longer see into the office, I had not heard Brother Silsbury move and decided he must still be sitting in his chair.

I remained where I was for a minute, trying desperately to calm myself, all the while listening for any sounds of Brother Silsbury moving about. But nothing came. And when my muscles began to protest from being thusly crouched, I finally decided to get out of there. Perhaps Brother Silsbury meant to spend the whole of the night here anyway.

With painstaking care I slid back toward the exit, once more grateful for the stockings on my feet. This time I wouldn't complain when the stones on the path bit into the bottoms of my feet. I would not complain at all.

# CHAPTER 26

I dunked my head under the running water and held it there for a moment, trying to rinse the tendrils of sleep from my mind. Sleep had been elusive in the early hours of the night after I'd returned to my cell, so once it came it did not loosen its grip readily. I had wanted to sneak over and speak with Colin as soon as I'd returned from the infirmary, but I feared our being overheard or spied upon and knew I was better served to wait until morning. Still, I had been left quite unsettled for the greater part of the night as I wondered what Colin would make of the hushed conversation I had stumbled upon.

With cold water rushing over my head I could only yearn to have been able to slide into a proper bath to start my day, but there were no bathtubs here. Instead there were only the two long, metal troughs running along opposite walls with spigots interspersed down their lengths. The monks appeared to be content to disrobe to a single cloth wrapped around their waists before washing themselves with their hands and large cakes of common-use soap. Since I was given no such waist cloth to wrap around myself I settled for remaining in my underdrawers, which felt entirely unsatisfactory.

I lifted my head and swiped at my face with a small rag before hurriedly brushing my hair into place with my fingers. Even though there were only two other monks in the rather large bathing space, neither of whom I recognized, I did not like the lack of privacy as I struggled to make myself presentable. The whole of it reminded me of my time at the Easling and Temple Senior Academy. I had not liked it there, either.

One of the monks slipped his cassock on, dropping the little waist cloth to the floor after the cassock was fully fastened in place. He stooped to pick it up and left the balneary without a word as I began to soap my upper body. It was all such personal business that I nearly had to fight a blush as I attended to my cleaning, my eyes riveted on the wall in front of me as though that might make me less exposed to the other man in the room.

Even with all of my intensified concentrations I still sensed a moment later when someone else came into the balneary. This new monk's movements struck me as being hesitant, almost clandestine, and I could not help being piqued by them. If the other monk and I were trying to be discreet, this new entrant seemed to be aiming for invisibility.

In spite of my efforts to mind my own business, I quickly slid my eyes sideways even as I leaned back over the trough to wash the soap from my chest and underarms, and recognized the new entrant as young Brother Hollings. His tall, lanky form with his shoulders arched forward to effectively dispel several inches of his height could not be mistaken for anyone else. For an instant I thought perhaps I should call a greeting to him. Yet standing as I was, half naked and fully out of place, I seized my tongue and kept to my own concerns. When I spied him slinking to the end of the opposite trough in the far corner, I was glad I had held my tongue.

As I dried my upper body I allowed my eyes to dart back to where Brother Hollings was and found him with his cassock still fully on, though he had unfastened the collar several inches. I caught sight of a small patch of something black curling up from his opened neckline before realizing that it had to be an undershirt since a ginger-haired young man would most certainly not be sprouting dark hair across his chest. Undoubtedly the black shirt beneath his cassock was standard issue for these somber monks since it was still quite cold on most days. Brother Hollings rolled his sleeves up to the elbows and I noticed that his arms were as smooth and hairless as his face, leaving me to wonder how old he actually was and whether he'd truly been allowed to settle his own mind about committing himself to this life.

Whether it was the sight of Brother Hollings's extraordinary modesty or merely the fact that I had suddenly begun to feel overly exposed, I felt compelled to reach over and pull my under-shirt over my head, and was instantly relieved that I had done so. The other monk in the balneary smoothly repeated the process I had glimpsed earlier of slipping his cassock on before stepping out of his waist cloth with utmost discretion. He swooped it up and was gone in a breath, leaving me and Brother Hollings alone, though we could hardly have been farther apart.

I was actually considering the idea of speaking with the young monk again when a small scuffle in the hallway caught my attention. I turned fully away from the trough to find the cause of the ruckus only to see Colin bound into the room in just his trousers and boots, an undershirt clutched in one hand and a hearty smile alighting his face.

"There you are!" he said as though we had not seen each other in days. "I checked your cell on my way here and found it empty. I was beginning to wonder if you never made it back last night." He chuckled as he came over to me and, before I knew what he was doing, reached out and squeezed my nearest hand.

"Hey!" I hissed, yanking away from him as I shot my eyes over to the corner where Brother Hollings was, surprised to dis-cover that he was gone.

"What's the matter?" Colin asked, his smile fading.

"Brother Hollings . . ." I mumbled, glancing around and seeing that we were, in fact, quite alone. "He was just here. I didn't want . . ." But I knew I didn't need to finish the sentence. "Sorry."

"I suspect that poor boy ran off the minute he heard me coming. He was here when I came in yesterday as well and did the same thing. I would swear he wears more clothing when washing than our Victoria does when she attends church."

"Why are you so jittery this morning," he asked as he turned toward the trough and twisted the spigot on.

"Need I remind you how we were compromised just two days ago," I answered under my breath. "Have you forgotten that?"

"We were sleeping," he muttered dismissively as he started washing his face. "Perfectly civil."

I looked up at the ceiling and exhaled an exasperated breath. "It didn't feel very civil when we were being thrown onto the street with our belongings. And look at you prancing about the monastery this morning in just your trousers. Have you no prudence?"

"Prudence?" He stood up and stared at me, his face dripping water onto his chest. "This place is full of men. Nothing but men. What is imprudent about anything I am doing in that circumstance?"

"They're not men," I shot back before I'd truly considered what I was about to say. "They are monks."

Colin let out an abrupt laugh. "Well, I suppose you have a point, but I'll bet more than a few of them would be deeply offended by your statement." He turned back to the trough and dunked his head fully under the spigot.

I pulled my shirt on and wondered how I had gotten so sideways in trying to explain what I meant. It had seemed to make sense as it was coming out of my mouth, but once released it sounded as foolish as the incessant humiliation that continued to nettle me since our expulsion from the Pig and Pint. Why did I even care what Raleigh Chesterton thought of Colin or me? I could not say, yet I knew that I did.

"Did you have any success last night? Did you find anything of interest?" Colin asked as he stood up and toweled his tawny hair before running his fingers through it just as I had done with my own.

"I never had a chance to get the papers," I stated simply, knowing he would be surprised at this perceived failure on my part. I allowed a tiny grin. "Because I stumbled upon a late-night conversation in the infirmary between Brothers Silsbury, Clayworth, and Wright. All very clandestine," I added, dropping my voice.

"And . . ." he prodded with his typical impatience.

I was on the verge of sharing what little I had managed to overhear when Brother Rodney drifted into the room, his small frame moving with the stealth of a breeze. "Good morning, Brother Rodney," I called out to make sure Colin realized we were no longer alone.

"Gentlemen," he answered in a near squeak, and I realized that I had never heard him speak before. Brother Green had always done the talking whenever we were with the two of them. It felt strangely relieving to know that Brother Rodney actually had a voice.

"Put your undershirt on," I muttered to Colin as Brother Rodney turned away from us, remaining as far away as he could just as Brother Hollings had done before he'd simply decided to flee. "You're embarrassing everyone."

Colin rolled his eyes but did as I asked before snatching up his towel. "Why don't we finish getting dressed and meet at the entry by the chapel. We need to return to Dalwich and discuss a few things with the constable. I should think a brisk walk will do well to calm you down some. And on our way you must tell me the rest of what you overheard last night."

"Of course." I nodded with some chagrin as I grabbed my own small towel and we headed for the door. "Good day to you, Brother Rodney," I called back to the diminutive man, noticing that he too had only gone as far as loosening the collar of his cassock. That so many of these monks were clearly so painfully reserved once again reminded me of the boys at Easling and Temple. I wondered if it was our presence alone that put them so on edge or if it was just the way of it. "I am afraid," I murmured to Colin as we walked back down the hallway, "that what I heard last night amounts to nothing. Those men seemed far more concerned about our being here than who has killed their abbot."

"Which means we have set them on edge and I am quite content to have done so." We stopped by the door to my cell. "We are drawing ever closer to the perpetrator, Ethan. That meeting you happened upon proves it. We have set this monastery on edge and it is only a matter of degrees now before we force the killer into the abyss."

I nodded as I pushed into my cell and quickly finished dressing, a feat I was able to accomplish with minimal fuss, though my hair was not nearly as cooperative as my truncated wardrobe. All the while I hoped that Colin was correct even as I wondered how he could feel so certain. I threw on my vest and jacket and headed for the vestibule, having deigned myself presentable enough, given that there were no mirrors anywhere to ensure it.

I was still buttoning up my vest as I came barreling around the last corner just past the chapel doors and nearly collided with Father Demetris, who was hovering just outside of the abbot's office. "Right on time . . ." Colin beamed as I managed to pull myself up short. "It is nice to be able to rely on some things in this world," he added.

"Indeed it is," Father Demetris agreed as he threw the office door open. "Such is the way of the Lord." And now it was his turn to beam as he ushered us in. "Sit down, sit down," he bade us, seating himself behind the large desk as usual. "I wanted you to know that I have already spoken with Brother Bursnell this morning and he tells me he did a thorough check of the library and has been unable to find any of Abbot Tufton's Egyptian journals. He confessed to being at it until far past vespers last night, so you can rest assured that he has done everything he can. I'm afraid they have been mislaid, although perhaps Abbot Tufton removed them at some point himself." Father Demetris looked to be considering that possibility for the first time as a thoughtful scowl colored his face. "They did belong to him, after all. And it's certainly not as if one of the other men would have coveted them. Everything in the library is for the use of all of the monks. There would be no call for such an action." He leaned forward in what felt like an effort to make sure we were following his logic. "It hardly merits saying that I would never expect a man capable of stealing to have taken the vows required of living in a monastery."

"And yet . . ." Colin spoke up and I knew precisely what he was about to say. "It does still remain most probable that the man capable of murdering your Abbot Tufton made those same vows and resides here even now." He flashed a pained sort of smile before waving his hand through the air as though to dismiss the entire sordid conceit. "Let us assume, for a moment, that the abbot did take his journals back. Wherever do you suppose he would have put them? There was certainly nothing to be found in his cell."

"Where . . . ?" Father Demetris tilted his head and stared at us blankly, and I could tell he remained quite disturbed by Colin's assertion of a moment ago. "Well, I'm sure I wouldn't know," he managed after a moment.

Colin nodded perfunctorily before pressing ahead. "Then let me ask you one other thing. Do the monks here practice any sort of mortification as a show of their penance?"

Father Demetris's eyes went wide as though the very suggestion was somehow offensive or shocking. "We are *not* living in the Middle Ages, Mr. Pendragon. The church has not condoned such archaic forms of self-torture in hundreds of years."

"My apologies," Colin said, allowing a tight grin to fleet across his face, yet as always there appeared to be little honest regret in his tone. "I needed to avail myself of the loo last night and heard someone crying in his cell as I traversed the hallway. The sound was quite muffled and impossible to discern from which cell it came, but it did put me in mind of such past disciplines and I felt obligated to verify whether those activities were still practiced."

"I can assure you they are not."

"Just a moment of sorrow for one of the brothers then," Colin answered blithely as the slightest hint of a grin tugged at one corner of his mouth. "Otherwise it would seem to me that such a practice would appear to suggest a guilty conscience, wouldn't you say? For one reason or another," he added as though it was an after-thought, which I knew it almost certainly wasn't.

"All very good and well," Father Demetris said as he settled back into his chair again, "but I am afraid you are off the mark. Far more likely that one of the brothers merely became over-whelmed with the Holy Spirit during his prayers. God's love is a powerful force."

"Indeed." Colin flashed that same tight smile again as he stood up. "And now you must excuse Mr. Pruitt and me for a few hours as we have a bit of unfinished business to conclude in Dalwich."

"Is it about that poor young woman who was murdered?"

Colin nodded grimly as he started for the door. "That it is."

"God grant you whatever you need to triumph," the priest called after us.

"He already has," Colin answered cryptically as we walked out and pulled the door shut.

"You sound quite sure of yourself," I noted as we headed for the front doors.

"Yes, I suppose you could say that . . ." he muttered distract-edly, his face having grown restive.

"I must confess I haven't necessarily felt that to be true."

Colin shoved his way out the door and I found myself hurry-ing to keep up with him in spite of the fact that my legs are longer. If I was having doubts about the certainty of his state-ment, the pace of his stride assured me that he was not. "I passed the library several times last night," he abruptly blurted out, "and never once saw Brother Bursnell in there searching for anything. So either he is lying to Father Demetris, or Father Demetris is lying to us."

"Lying?! They're clerics. . . ." But I stopped myself from fin-ishing that thought, well aware of how foolish I would sound. "What about Maureen O'Dowd? You said we were on our way to *conclude* that case?"

Colin shot a hasty glance my direction without the slightest hesitation in his stride. "Father Demetris has just now put me in mind of something that has been rumbling about my brain for the last several days."

"He has? Whatever would that be?"

"Coveting and pilfering," he said bleakly as we charged down the uneven path toward Dalwich.

# CHAPTER 27

⸻⸻•⸻⸻

Constable Lachlan Brendle looked almost like a man renewed. The color was returning to his cheeks and his eyes looked clearer than they had since he'd been shot three days before. I eyed the small medicine bottle next to his bed and was pleased to find it slightly more than half full, a testament to the clarity behind his eyes. He was once again fully upright in his bed, though he had informed us with a heavy sigh that the doctor insisted he not attempt to get out of it for another three weeks. His cheeks and jaw were freshly shaved, removing the auburn shadow he had been cultivating, and his hair had been carefully parted down the middle and slicked back on both sides. He looked rather like a young magistrate who chose to dispense justice from the comfort of his bed.

Colin and I had pulled chairs alongside the constable's bed, and Mr. Masri was seated across the room near the door in the spot usually occupied by Mr. Whitsett. As before, Mr. Whitsett had been sent to the Pig and Pint to fetch Raleigh Chesterton, but this time he'd also been requested to bring Edward Honeycutt and Annabelle White. There was no doubt that Mr. Chesterton would be livid at this decimation of his lunchtime staff, but I knew it made little difference to Colin, who was focused on collecting his suspects.

"But surely you must have *something* concrete you can share . . ." Constable Brendle was practically begging, the flush in his cheeks and the determination behind his eyes a further attestation to his rapidly improving health.

Colin chuckled quietly as he dug out a crown and sent it scurrying between his fingers. "It isn't as though I am hiding something from you," he said, the lie coming as smoothly as the gossamer threads from a spider. "While I will confess to being a man who keeps his own counsel, Mr. Pruitt being something of an exception," he added, gesturing at me with a distracted wave of his free hand that spoke to the fact that I too was often kept in the dark, "it is also not my habit to neglect cooperating with the proper authorities." A thin-lipped grin fleeted across his face and I wondered how he could say such a thing without being struck by lightning or at the very least blushing. Indeed, if the present circumstances had not been so grim, I believe I would have laughed out loud myself. As it was, I held my tongue while imagining the dreadful shade of plum that Constable Varcoe would turn were he still alive to hear Colin's self-assessment.

"I didn't mean to suggest such a thing," the constable backpedaled exactly as Colin had intended. "I was only hoping for an insight into the way you work, Mr. Pendragon. There is so much my men and I can learn from you and I would hate to squander such an opportunity."

"Oh . . ." A faint grin raised the corners of Colin's mouth as the coin he was spinning through his fingers halted for an instant. "You flatter me," he said with noticeable pleasure before he started the coin on its rotation again.

"Mr. Pendragon has greater than ten years on you, Constable." I finally spoke up, perfectly content to prick Colin's ego a touch lest it should derail him. "There is much to be said about the significance of pure experience."

Colin's eyebrows ticked a lack of amusement, just as I had known they would. "Yes. . . ." he muttered.

264 / *Gregory Harris*

"Some things simply cannot be taught," I added.

No sooner had the words left my mouth than I heard the front door open and close in the other room. The footfalls of multiple shoes clattering upon the floorboards grew closer, though no one could be heard to be speaking. Lanky, awkward Annabelle White was the first to enter the room, all angles and shuffling feet, followed by Edward Honeycutt wearing an expression somewhere between discomfort and distress. Mr. Chesterton entered a whole moment later, Mr. Whitsett coaxing him with a steady hand on his back, which the older man seemed quite displeased about.

"Oh, bloody hell . . ." Raleigh Chesterton pulled up short in the doorway as he spotted Colin and me. "Are these two gonna be here every time you send for me?" Mr. Whitsett tried to prod Mr. Chesterton into the room, but his efforts were soundly rebuffed. "I got nothin' more ta say ta them. I told ya that the last time." I presumed he was speaking to Constable Brendle, but this time his eyes did not leave Colin and me for an instant.

"I'll not have this conversation with you again, Raleigh," the constable answered at once, his eyes flashing darkly. And if I had not already known that he was feeling better I could most certainly see it now. "You will find yourself a chair, sit down, and be civil, or you will end up in a cell for impeding this investigation until I can get a magistrate from Arundel to release you. And in my present condition you can be sure it will take some measure of time for me to accomplish that!"

Raleigh Chesterton gave a deep-throated snort as he grabbed one of the wooden chairs Mr. Masri had dragged in from the other room and pulled it opposite to where Colin and I were seated. "I ain't the one belongs behind bars . . ." he groused as he heaved himself into the chair, folding his arms across his chest like a petulant child.

"If you please . . ." Constable Brendle said to the others, waving a hand toward the remaining chairs stationed around the room for Annabelle White, Edward Honeycutt, and Mr. Whitsett, leaving Mr. Masri seated back by the entrance to the room, his left arm dangling within the muslin sling fastened around his neck like an injured bird. Everyone looked confused and uneasy with the notable exception of Mr. Chesterton, who appeared to be nothing less than incensed. "Now, Mr. Pendragon has requested to speak with the lot of you about the murder of Maureen O'Dowd. Please know that he does so with the full support and authority of my office, and I *will* expect each of you to behave accordingly. And I hold myself to this same standard since, as you are all aware, I had a brief liaison with Miss O'Dowd some time back and therefore do not presume to hold myself above the very law I seek to enforce." He flicked his eyes between everyone in the room before landing on Raleigh Chesterton.

"So what . . ." he snapped back corrosively, "she courted her share a men. What does that have ta do with anything?"

"She *loved* me," Edward Honeycutt flung back, sounding almost pitiful, leaving me to wonder if he was trying to convince us or himself. "I'm the one she was going to marry and move to London with. We were going to raise our baby there . . ." The young man's voice caught.

"Remind me again . . ." Colin said at once before anyone else could interject, " . . . how exactly were you planning on making your way in the city with little money and no prospects for a job?"

"I told you, we were saving everything we could. We had been doing so for the better part of a year. We already had enough to get us there and a room for a couple of months if we chose carefully. I saved nearly every farthing I earned at the Pig and Pint, and from what Brother Clayworth gave me for looking after his books. Did you check the accounts? Did you see that I never stole a thing?!"

"As a matter of fact"—Colin flashed a brief smile—"Mr. Pruitt did indeed check the brewery's accounts and you are correct. He found everything quite in order."

"Exactly as I told you," Edward pronounced with satisfaction as he glanced around the room at each of us, an air of defensiveness alighting his voice. "I said it all along. Mo couldn't save as much because she had to pay Mr. Chesterton for her room. . . ."

"Well, a course she did," Raleigh Chesterton cut in sourly. "I ain't runnin' no damn workhouse. I paid 'er fair for her work and she paid me fair for her room. It's jest business. Ain't nothin' to it but that."

Colin slid his eyes toward Mr. Chesterton and I found myself suddenly holding my breath. "Didn't you also give a room to Miss O'Dowd and her mother when they first arrived years ago?"

"I didn't *give 'em* shite. Her mother paid me from her wages for their rooms, and when she drank more than she worked I gave Mo 'er job and *she* paid me. All neat as ya please. Jest like it's supposed ta be."

"Did Miss O'Dowd's mother ever pay you with something other than money?"

"Wot?!" Mr. Chesterton narrowed his eyes and glared back at Colin corrosively.

"Did you ever allow her to exchange favors for their board?" he clarified ever so glibly as he stood up and started sauntering around the periphery of the room as though we were discussing laying hens. "You know . . ." he pressed easily, ". . . trade a shag for a bit off here and there . . ."

"I didn't have ta," Raleigh Chesterton answered, his gaze going hard as one corner of his mouth turned up malignantly. "She were happy ta 'ave a go at it now and again fer nothin' at all. 'At's the way nature intended it," he added with a snarl.

I heard Annabelle White suck in a mortified breath and hoped she did not recognize the inference Mr. Chesterton was clearly sallying at Colin and me. It made me wonder why Colin had insisted on her being here? I couldn't imagine that she might be involved in the murder of her friend. If anything, she seemed quite undone by Miss O'Dowd's death—and yet I had been fooled by such perceived sentiments before.

"And what of Maureen O'Dowd . . . ?" Colin was forging ahead before I realized what he was implying. "Did you ever presume to try and initiate the same sort of arrangement with her that you had done with her mother?"

"*How dare you!*" Raleigh Chesterton roared even as I noticed Edward Honeycutt stiffen in his chair. "I loved that girl like me own daughter. Only a right bastard like you would dare ta suggest such a vile thing." He pushed himself to his feet, the bulk of his round frame clearly meant to be an implied threat in spite of his advanced age.

"Do sit down, Mr. Chesterton," Colin sniffed without so much as a hint of concern in his tone. And to my surprise, Mr. Chesterton did as bidden. "I am merely asking the most obvious of questions," Colin explained. "Your outrage is duly noted." He spoke as though the topic was tiresome, his arms clasped behind his back as he continued to slowly pace from one end of the room to the other. Only Constable Brendle, from his central position on the bed, was able to follow Colin's course without having to turn his head. "What about you, Miss White?" Colin abruptly paused near Annabelle White so that his body momentarily blocked her view of Mr. Chesterton. "Had you ever known Mr. Chesterton to have sought favors from your friend Miss O'Dowd?"

"No, sir," she answered at once, her voice higher pitched than I remembered it normally being and carrying a slight quiver.

"And you . . . ?" Colin pursued, placing his hand on the back of her chair and leaning over her as though the two of them were enjoying an intimate conversation. "Has your Mr. Chesterton ever made such a suggestion to you?"

She looked terrified as she stared back into Colin's face hanging scandalously close to her own, her bright brown eyes appearing almost ready to pop free of her head. "Never . . ." she gasped.

"*I ain't sittin' for this shite!*" Raleigh Chesterton howled as he sprang back to his feet again. "I ain't the one that's flouncin' around with 'is own ruddy kind." He spun on the constable with rage in his eyes, his round face and shining pate burning to a deep crimson. "You can throw me in a cell fer as long as ya like, but I ain't listenin' to another feckin' minute a this rot."

"You might want to rethink your logic, Mr. Chesterton," Colin piped up before anyone else dared utter a word. "Because if you insist on being imprisoned, I will simply have these proceedings moved to the constabulary office, where you will be forced to listen and respond from inside a cell." It was a patently absurd bluff on Colin's part as the constable was not fit to be moved under any circumstances, and yet it was enough to give Mr. Chesterton pause. He appeared to momentarily deliberate Colin's words before slowly lowering himself back into his seat with a churlish snarl. "All right then," Colin said as he turned to face Edward Honeycutt. "You were obviously the person closest to Miss O'Dowd, and I will apologize now for anything I am about to say that might offend you. You must understand that I only mean to discover the identity of the fiend who took her from you."

The young man nodded silently but did not look back at Colin. "I know," he mumbled under his breath, and it immediately renewed my sense of pity for him. The poor thing seemed such a sorrowful lad that I scarcely knew what to make of him anymore.

"You are aware that your fiancée had something of a reputation at one time?" Colin started in again, his voice sounding rather perfunctory.

"That was in the past," Edward Honeycutt shot back, his eyes remaining downcast.

"What about you? Were you true to her?"

The young man's eyes finally shot up as he glared at Colin. "I already told you I was. Ask anyone."

"Miss White . . . ?" Colin called out at once, never taking his eyes from Edward Honeycutt. "Did you ever witness the fine Mr. Honeycutt here trying to fiddle about with another girl after you knew him to be serious with Miss O'Dowd?" And having asked the question, he slowly turned back toward Annabelle White. "Perhaps with you . . . ?"

Her pallid face seemed to grow even whiter as she stared back at Colin, her eyes locked on his as though he held her in a trance. "No, sir . . ." she answered as though from somewhere far away. "No, sir," she repeated, and then her eyes flicked down and I wondered if perhaps that fact had disappointed her.

"Very well." Colin allowed a mirthless bit of grin to pull his lips taut as he began to circle back to the side of the room where I was seated, passing Mr. Masri and Mr. Whitsett as he came. "We have all heard Constable Brendle admit to a brief liaison with Miss O'Dowd before she began to be squired by Mr. Honeycutt . . ." Colin nodded to the constable as he came up behind the chair next to mine and stood there, leaning against it as though he had suddenly become too wearied to stand on his own. "What about you, Mr. Whitsett? Or you, Mr. Masri? Do either of you have any such similar confessions to make?"

"No sir," Mr. Whitsett said just as he'd done the first time Colin had asked him that question. "I was very fond of Miss O'Dowd, but she wasn't suited to me."

"And what about you, Mr. Masri?" Colin slid his gaze to the olive-complected man.

"I am a married man," he answered simply, his eyes as black as the thick hair that covered the top of his head. "I have two children. Why would I do such a thing?"

Colin chuckled. It was low and brief, but none of us missed it, and I felt embarrassed for Mr. Masri for either being so naïve or for imagining Colin to be so. "If I must tell you *why* you would do such a thing, then I fear your children must be of an immaculate nature," he teased. "But let us leave that improbability for a moment and turn our attentions to what we *know* rather than what we do *not* know. For it is there that we shall finally be able to uncover the facts of this case."

Colin straightened up and moved away from the chair, taking a slight step sideways so that he was standing right behind me. It was not something he did often, drawing me to the center of attention, and for the first time I had an inkling of what it must feel like to have him tightening the noose around someone's neck. As an uneasy chill abruptly careened down my spine I found that I did not like it.

"I must start by requesting your indulgence," Colin was saying. "Most especially from you, Miss White, for I know some of this will be distressing for you to hear. Please know I do not undertake it lightly. Be assured that you are here for a reason."

As I stared across the small room at her I thought she looked close to apoplectic, her ashen face giving her the appearance of being faint, and I feared she might topple over at any moment. She did not respond to Colin, but her eyes slowly drifted to the floor as her angular shoulders sank inward.

"We know that Miss O'Dowd was last seen working at the Pig and Pint on Thursday last, finishing her shift at . . ." Colin turned his gaze on Raleigh Chesterton. "What time *did* she complete her duties on Thursday, Mr. Chesterton?"

The cantankerous old man flicked his gaze over to Colin for an instant, immediately sliding it back to the constable before deigning to answer. "'Bout midnight, I suppose," he grumbled. "Same as usual."

"Were you still there, Mr. Honeycutt?" Colin shifted his focus quickly.

"No, I'd gone home a couple hours earlier. I usually help my father on Friday mornings with his deliveries."

"But you didn't this past Friday. Your brother David did. Why was that?"

"I wasn't feeling well."

"A fortuitous illness," Colin remarked pointedly as he wandered over to the window beside the constable's bed. "How much worse it would have been had you been there when her body was discovered."

Edward Honeycutt closed his eyes and I presumed he was either trying to keep that vision from invading his mind or to still it from having already done so. In either case, he did not otherwise move, which made me aware of the steely rigidity that had gripped Mr. Chesterton from his place next to young Edward.

"Did you see Miss O'Dowd leave with anyone, Miss White?" Colin continued.

"No, sir." She shook her head and I could sense her jumpiness as though it had a texture of its own.

"And you, Mr. Chesterton . . . ? Did you notice Miss O'Dowd with anyone at the end of her shift?"

"I'd already gone up ta bed," he answered dismissively. "I

THE DALWICH DESECRATION / 271

don't watch over all a them tossers what works for me . . ." But I could see his sentiment suddenly stick in his throat, and for the first time he looked ashamed for what he had said.

"Well, we certainly know that *someone* saw her after her shift ended that night, because at some point she was accosted and murdered." Colin turned to Constable Brendle with a frown. "What time did you receive word from David Honeycutt that he and his father had discovered the body?"

"Five thirty that morning. I had only just gotten up and hadn't even gotten my tea on yet. The poor boy was pounding on my door like a madman. I knew something was wrong before I even answered it."

"And did you head right back with David Honeycutt?"

"No . . ." The constable shook his head, a slight crease marring his youthful forehead. "We stopped on the way to collect Mr. Whitsett. I knew I would need his assistance."

"Why Mr. Whitsett and not Mr. Masri?"

Constable Brendle seemed to color slightly as his eyes shifted to his men. "Well, Mr. Masri is married and has children. I didn't relish waking the whole of his household with such distressing news. Graham . . . Mr. Whitsett . . . has no such ties, so I decided I would collect Mr. Masri after Mr. Whitsett and I had a chance to take a look at the scene."

"Would you call that standard protocol then?" Colin asked with the assurance of someone who already knows the answer.

"Standard . . . ?" The constable faltered momentarily, blinking his eyes as though unsure exactly how to respond. "I can hardly say there is such a thing as standard protocol in the occurrence of a murder in Dalwich. Other than these two cases there has only ever been one other killing during my tenure here, and given that it was a crime of passion, the perpetrator never even left the scene of his undoing."

"I see." Colin nodded as he started to meander toward Mr. Whitsett and Mr. Masri. "Tell me, Mr. Whitsett, what did you find when you arrived at the place David Honeycutt brought you to?" He paused in the vacant space between the two junior constables.

The tall, lanky man swung his eyes down and seemed to fold into himself. "I would really rather not," he murmured in the ghost of a voice.

"But you must," Colin pressed him. "You were the first to arrive at the scene with the constable, and when he left to fetch Mr. Masri, you alone were left to protect the integrity of the site. Which means you spent more time viewing it than any of us. Surely it has left an indelible impression on you that the rest of us cannot possibly attest to."

Mr. Whitsett, in spite of his towering height and thin, bony shoulders, looked nearly as diminutive in that moment as Constable Brendle reclining in his bed. "She was lying in the grass just off the north side of the road," he said, his voice barely above a whisper and his tone as reluctant as his demeanor. "She looked like she was staring into the woods as if she were searching for something . . . or someone . . . but her face was a terrible color. Not natural . . ." He let his voice trail off.

"Did you surmise that she had been strangled?" Colin asked, and I heard Annabelle White try to stifle a sudden intake of breath, which made Colin turn toward her. "I'm sorry, Miss White," he said, and I knew he meant it. "You must be strong and bear with us." He glanced back to Mr. Whitsett. "If you please . . ." he prodded.

Graham Whitsett tilted his head the tiniest bit and appeared to give something of a shrug. "I don't know what I thought."

"Did Constable Brendle make any supposition?"

Again he appeared to hesitate. "I don't know. I don't remember. I suppose he might have."

"Is it your intention to maintain your position as a junior constable, Mr. Whitsett?" And the incongruity of Colin's question struck me as much as it did Mr. Whitsett, who finally looked up and met his gaze.

"Yes, sir."

"Then I would suggest you pay closer attention to such things."

Colin flashed the whisper of a hollow grin at him before plunging immediately ahead. "What else *did* you notice?"

"Her bodice was open," he mumbled.

"Yes . . ." Colin shook his head as he crossed back around behind Raleigh Chesterton. "Was it open like she had been readying herself for bed perhaps?" And I had to stop myself from scowling as we all knew the answer to that question.

"No, sir," came Mr. Whitsett's hushed reply. "It was ripped."

"Ripped," Colin repeated, and it sounded almost cruel. "Is that what you found upon your arrival, Mr. Masri?"

The Middle Eastern man seemed to start under Colin's question, appearing to be inconceivably miserable at having been singled out. "Yes . . . No . . . Yes . . ." he sputtered all at once. "Constable Brendle told me it had been ripped open to her waist, but by the time I got there Mr. Whitsett had already placed his coat over the poor girl, so I did not see it myself."

"Yes . . ." Colin flinched at the remembrance of the scene having been thusly sullied. "Tell me again why you did that, Mr. Whitsett?"

"It was improper," he answered at once. "Miss O'Dowd deserved better than that. You wouldn't leave your sister to lie like that . . ."

"If I had a sister," Colin shot back at once, "I would leave her exactly as her killer had left her so I could conduct a proper investigation, which would allow me to hunt the bastard down and cut his bits off with all due haste." He flicked his gaze to Annabelle White. "My apologies, Miss White." The room remained silent as he slowly moved the few steps needed until he was standing just behind Edward Honeycutt. "How about you, Constable Brendle? Did you take note of anything in particular when you first saw the body?"

"I did." His eyes held Colin's, his face hard, and I realized that he knew, as I now did, exactly where this was heading. "Her skirts had been shoved up in the front and she did not appear to be wearing any undergarments."

"You must forgive the unseemliness of this question, Miss

White, but did you know your friend to be a woman who did not avail herself of bloomers?"

"No, sir," she said, her eyes darting about the room without settling anywhere before finally landing on the floor by the constable's bed once more. "She were always proper."

"Do you remember seeing the same thing, Mr. Masri?" Colin continued as though the conversation was almost mundane.

"Well . . ." His eyes fluttered about the room as though he was searching for the right answer. "By the time Constable Brendle got me and took me back to the scene, she was already covered by Mr. Whitsett's coat. I didn't see how she'd been left until after you and Mr. Pruitt arrived."

"Yes," Colin grumbled. "Really, Mr. Whitsett, you were most detrimental to the solving of this crime with your puttering about."

"It just wasn't right," he defended himself morosely. "It wasn't proper."

"Miss White . . ." Colin took the last few steps over to Annabelle White, placing himself directly between Edward Honeycutt and the young woman. "Did Miss O'Dowd complain to you about anyone being a nuisance to her over the last month or two?"

Her eyes fluttered briefly, but she did not meet Colin's gaze. "I do remember her mentionin' that someone had been botherin' her for a while, but she weren't really troubled by it and said she could take care of it herself. I think she didn't want ta get Edward upset." She glanced up at Colin as she heaved a little shrug.

"Did she tell you who it was?"

"No, sir."

"But you did tell me on Saturday night that someone had been pestering you with questions about Miss O'Dowd lately. Lamenting that she wouldn't spend time with him when she had been known to be rather free with her affections with others before."

"Yes . . ." she whispered.

"Who was that again?" he asked as if this was a name he would be likely to forget.

Annabelle White sat quietly for a long moment, and I began to wonder if perhaps she had said the name and I'd missed it. But in a tone barely above a whisper I finally heard her murmur, "Mr. Whitsett."

Colin swept Miss White off her chair and walked her to the door, doing so with such suddenness and force that she wouldn't have been able to keep up with him if his hand hadn't been hovering at the small of her back. "You have been extremely helpful," he said as he ushered her into the front room, muttering something to her that I did not catch before I heard the door open and shut. A moment later he appeared back in the bedroom doorway, resting up against the doorjamb. "Mr. Whitsett . . . ?"

The man shook his head and heaved a confused shrug. "Maybe I did fancy her some. There's no dishonor in that. But I didn't know she was betrothed to Mr. Honeycutt . . ." Once again he let his voice trail off as though he had said enough.

Now it was Colin's turn to heave a sigh. "That *is* curious, Mr. Whitsett, because you have told me repeatedly that Miss O'Dowd was not the kind of woman who held any interest for you. Did I misunderstand your meaning?"

"I . . ." He scowled and glanced about the room, his demeanor beginning to edge toward something watchful and alert. "I said it to avoid just this sort of ridiculousness. You should be asking Edward here how deep his jealousies ran." He glared at the young man. "Maybe you didn't like the way she flitted around that pub, all smiles and cheek for any man." Edward Honeycutt stared back at him blankly, his jaw unhinging as he seemed to be trying to fathom how to answer. "Lachlan . . ." Mr. Whitsett abruptly turned to the constable, who only stared back without the hint of a reaction. "Ahmet . . . *you know me* . . ." His words came out harsh as he turned his gaze on Mr. Masri.

"What *I* know," Colin interrupted before Mr. Masri could form a response, "is that other than the monks at Whitmore Abbey, on the night Miss O'Dowd was murdered the only people who knew that the abbot's tongue had been cut from his head are the men in this room." He waved a dismissive hand as he began to walk back over to Edward Honeycutt. "And I think we can all agree that the monks had nothing to do with Miss O'Dowd's murder." No one made a sound.

"You meant for this crime to appear to have been perpetrated by the same man who killed Abbot Tufton," Colin continued as he walked around to the far side of Edward Honeycutt and stopped. "But just in case, you arranged her body as though she had been violated, which, we know from the coroner's report, she was not." Colin peered across Edward Honeycutt at Mr. Whitsett. "What a godsend it must have seemed when Constable Brendle fetched you first and then left you alone at the scene with her body. The scene you had so carefully set up that you were then able to completely foul by pulling her bodice closed, fixing her skirts, and laying your blasted coat atop her to supposedly protect her modesty. If there had been any evidence to be gathered, you utterly soiled it, knowing that yours would have been the only evidence left behind anyway. And then you could not apologize enough for not having followed appropriate protocol. Happy to hide behind your inexperience."

"This is preposterous!" Mr. Whitsett babbled, half-rising from his chair, his eyes darting between Constable Brendle and Mr. Masri as though trying to gauge whether they were being swayed by Colin's words.

"How noble you have looked staying right by your constable's side since the accident, seeming to be assuaging your guilt when, in truth, I rather think you shot him on purpose to ensure you were kept at the center of every step of this investigation. . . ."

"*That's a bloody lie!*" He was standing now. "I would *never* hurt Lachlan. You're wrong. You have no proof."

Colin gave a mirthless smile, his lips pulling tight. "And in that you are woefully mistaken. For I shall look forward to proving that your handprint matches the one left round the neck of Miss O'Dowd." He took a step toward Mr. Whitsett. "Did you decide her refusal not in earnest?" he snarled. "That you had a right to press your attentions where they were not wanted . . . ?"

And before Colin could take another step forward Edward

Honeycutt launched himself across the room, landing on Graham Whitsett with a battering of fists and garbled screams. Mr. Masri, his left arm encapsulated in its sling, and Constable Brendle, confined to his bed, could be of no use, so it was left to Colin to cross the room after a long minute, a minute in which I knew he had purposefully hesitated, and yank Edward Honeycutt off the cowering scarecrow of a man.

*"Get him off of me!"* Mr. Whitsett screeched, sliding himself across the floor on his backside until he'd shoved himself into one corner of the room, his face bleeding and his nose a battered pulp. "It wasn't me . . ." he protested, his voice cracking with fear and desperation, ". . . it was her. She wanted me to pay her for favors so she could get money for London. And then she tried to toss me instead. Started screaming and clawing at me . . ." His gaze flew around the room, his forehead slick with sweat and his lips pulled back as though with rictus. "I was just defending myself . . ." he howled. "I swear it . . ."

"Of course . . ." Colin spoke icily. "I can see how a man might throttle a woman half his size in self-defense. How utterly heroic."

Edward Honeycutt released a primal wail as he thrashed about in Colin's grip, and it was enough to finally cease Graham Whitsett's pitiful excuses, leaving the contemptible man to hunker back on the floor and shut his mouth.

It was Raleigh Chesterton who moved then, standing up and seizing Edward Honeycutt in a bear's grip, the pitiable young man sagging against him as he began to weep. The two of them remained like that a moment, Mr. Chesterton stoic and hard, before he finally pulled Edward from the room taking care not to pass anywhere near Mr. Whitsett. As the two of them left, Mr. Masri instinctively pushed himself to his feet, his face a reflection of aggrieved sorrow, and went over to Mr. Whitsett. Moving with awkward, rudimentary motions, Mr. Masri managed to haul Mr. Whitsett's arms behind his back, one after the other, and fasten handcuffs around his wrists. I was struck by the fact that Mr. Whitsett put up no fuss, and as he cowered in that corner, trussed like the criminal he was, it occurred to me that he was the most pitiable soul of all.

When I slid my eyes back to Constable Brendle, an impotent hostage in his own bed throughout this ordeal, it was to find him staring toward the side of the room, away from all of us, his gaze blank and unwavering, unable to face the scene laid bare before his eyes.

# CHAPTER 28

In spite of Colin's success earlier in the day, by nightfall he had become perceptibly uncommunicative and moody. Yet another awkward dinner with the monks had passed. Brother Green remained the most hospitable of the assembled men, with the other monks bringing little added warmth or camaraderie in their dealings with us.

Nothing more profound than the state of the crops in the fields and predictions around the severity of the storm that had been brewing since late in the afternoon along the western horizon were bandied about the dining tables. Throughout the mundanity we shared meager portions of roast chicken, asparagus, and corn rolls. Father Demetris had been right on our first day here, the food was simple, but it was good.

During the meal I had glanced around at the disparate monks and tried to conceive of Colin's assertion that one of these devout men had slain their abbot. The multiple knife wounds . . . the excised tongue . . . I did not know how it could be. So it was with some measure of relief that the meal finally ended, taking with it my macabre musings.

As we all began to shuffle out of the refectory, Father Demetris asked Colin and me to return to Abbot Tufton's office with him, informing us that two telegrams addressed to Colin had been sent up from Dalwich just before supper. That news was the only thing to even partially rouse Colin from the somber temperament that had been descending upon him since our return. If he had some notion as to what they might be concerning he did not let on, leaving the three of us to pad the short distance from the refectory to the abbot's office in the usual silence.

"Please sit down . . ." Father Demetris invited as we stepped inside. "I've got them both right here," he muttered as he fumbled through a sheaf of papers piled on one corner of the desk. He appeared well settled in even though he had only been back at the monastery for a day. "Ah . . ." He pulled an opened envelope from the pile and passed it over to Colin, which drew an immediate frown that I noticed the priest did not miss. "This first one was actually addressed to me. There are, however, a few lines meant for you," he explained as he sat down and immediately began thumbing back through the pile in search of the second telegram.

"So I see . . ." Colin pulled a single sheet from the envelope and shifted his gaze to me. "It's from Bishop Fencourt."

"He is enquiring after my safe arrival in the first line, but it is the next several lines that I knew you would want to see," the priest babbled as he finally extracted a second envelope, a sealed envelope, with a flourish and a sigh.

CONFIRM FOR YOUNG PENDRAGON THAT ABBOT'S SABBATICAL TO EGYPT WAS INDEED A DEVOTIONAL CRISIS. STOP. HIS FAITH WAS SORELY TESTED BY RECENT DISCOVERIES AND REMAINED SO UNTIL HIS DEATH. STOP. AM IN RECEIPT OF RECENT LETTER WHERE HE ASKED TO RESIGN FROM WHITMORE. STOP. CITES DISSENSION. STOP. QUOTES PROVERBS 3:5. STOP.

Colin lowered the sheet of paper and stared across at Father Demetris, the frown he had already adopted creasing deeper into his forehead. "What does Proverbs 3:5 say?" he asked, though I was certain he was loath to do so.

Father Demetris allowed the hint of a grin to whisk across his face as he snatched up a Bible from the corner of the desk. "To tell you the truth, I had to look it up myself," he admitted as he quickly flipped through the pages of the book. " '*Trust in the Lord with all thine heart; and lean not unto thine own understanding.*' " He looked back at us as he set the Bible down, his face a mixture of confusion and distress. "Whatever do you think Abbot Tufton could have meant by it?"

Colin's forehead knit ever deeper as he glared at the wall behind the priest. "I wish I knew . . ." he mumbled, managing to look as agitated as he did mystified. "And the other telegram . . . ?" he asked in more of a bark than a question.

"Right here . . ." Father Demetris said as he handed over the second telegram.

Colin tore one end of the envelope off and tipped out a single sheet of paper that he slowly read. His face remained ever stoic, and yet I could see by the gentle loosening of his brow that he found this news far less aggravating. It took a long moment before he finally handed the page to me, standing up as he did so. "Thank you for your time tonight, Father," he said quite suddenly, speaking with renewed vigor. "Let us meet first thing in the morning and see what the new day has to offer us." He turned to me with a curt nod that could not hide the obvious exhilaration that had so abruptly nestled in behind his eyes. "Come then, Mr. Pruitt."

I glanced down at the telegram and read it quickly as I stood up. It was from Acting Inspector Evans of Scotland Yard. The telegram contained only two short lines, but I understood at once what had so profoundly changed Colin's mood.

SWISS HAVE AGREED TO FREEZE HUTTON ACCOUNTS. STOP. IS THERE ANYONE YOUR FATHER CANNOT SWAY? STOP.

Charlotte Hutton. The only person I knew who had outmaneuvered Colin, cleverly leading us down a trail until, in the end, she had disappeared as neatly as an apparition.

"Tomorrow morning then . . ." Father Demetris was saying.

"Quite so," Colin tossed over his shoulder as he rushed me out into the empty hall and pulled the door shut behind us. "As if we did not have incentive enough to solve this case," he hissed, herding me along like a wayward sheep, "now I feel like we have run out of time."

"We cannot leave here until we've seen the end of this terrible business. These monks . . . Bishop Fencourt . . . *your father* are all counting on you."

A ready scowl creased his forehead in an instant. "Yes," he snapped, "I am well aware of that and am *not* proposing to simply leave. But I will solve this case come morning. I have tended this virtuous garden long enough and have only to coax the infected flower open. And that is what I shall do." We paused as we arrived at the door to my cell . . . Abbot Tufton's cell . . . and he looked at me keenly. "This is the last night you shall have to sleep in that horrid little space. I give you my word."

"I've gotten rather used to it," I shrugged glibly.

He easily saw through my deceit. "Nevertheless"—he leaned forward slightly—"tomorrow night you will have my cold feet to contend with once again."

"Maurice Evans is right, you know," I said before Colin could turn away. "It seems there is nothing your father is unable to accomplish."

The ghost of a smile fleeted across his face. "Yes . . . well . . . he did set a rather high standard when I was growing up."

"And you are every bit the man he is," I reminded. "Which you will prove once again when you bring an end to this dreadful case, whether it is tomorrow or not," I could not help but add.

"Doubt." He gave me a stiff smile before turning and starting away. "I shall accept that challenge," he said as he headed off for his cell.

"Colin . . ." I called in a hushed voice, forcing him to stop and glance back at me. "Get some sleep tonight."

He waved me off with a taut grimace that I supposed was meant to be a smile. "There will be time enough for that tomorrow night," he mumbled as he started off again. And with that sentence he spoke to my deepest fear. For now I was certain that he had no idea how he was going to entice this case to unfurl.

# CHAPTER 29

The night was fitful for me. I worried about Colin, imagining him pacing throughout the night in his cell, trying to decipher an outcome that I myself had no inkling of. For a time I had tried to take his advice and rummage back through the facts, the things we had been told, the things we had learned, but I could discern no murderer amongst these holy men. And as that thought pressed in on me, I had known I would get no sleep tonight.

I had thought Colin might come back to my cell once he was certain the monks had settled in for the night to test his thoughts or suppositions upon me, but he never did. So sometime deep in the heart of the night I finally gave up my vigil and forced myself to lie down on the cot in the tiny room, remaining fully dressed, and pretended that I was going to fall asleep. I would tell you that I never managed to do so except for the fact that at some point I was awakened by the slightest rattling of the door in its jamb. The noise had been minute and clandestine, but it caused me to bolt upright on the accursed cot nonetheless, my ears attuned like those of a night hunting owl, but it had been nothing. No other whispered murmur of any type followed, though I do not believe I was able to catch even the merest slumber after that.

At the first sounds of the monks beginning to move around I

was up and in the balneary trying to wash the night's troubles from my heart and mind, but other than the cleansing of my body, I seemed to have little success. My head felt as dopey as if I had spent the night in the embrace of an opiate. No amount of cold water splashed into my face made the slimmest difference. So after dousing the whole of my head under the spigot I finally gave up and decided to return to my cell and finish dressing.

I could hear the monks' distant chanting drifting from the chapel as I headed back to my cell, its dirge-like quality continuing to sound both reverential and haunting to me. It only served to further unnerve me. I quickened my pace and was glad to arrive at my cell so I could diminish the brunt of their voices behind the closed door. For once I was grateful there were no mirrors about as I was certain I must look the sight, red-eyed and wearied. There was only so much I was going to be able to do to vanquish my exhaustion, leaving me to worry ever the more about Colin.

"Now, that is a fine monastic specimen." The words hit me the moment I shoved the cell's door open. Colin was seated at the small table at the back of the cell and had the tapers already lit, including a third one that he had obviously brought himself. He looked well sorted and wore the hint of a grin as his icy blue eyes slipped across my face. "Although I will admit you look a touch worse for the wear this morning."

I kicked the door shut behind me as I shrugged into a fresh shirt. "I didn't sleep well," I mumbled, glancing over at him as I slumped down onto the bed to pull on my boots. "But you don't seem to have suffered the same fate."

He waved a dismissive hand at me. "Sleep is overrated," he announced as he stood up and pulled my vest and coat from the back of the chair and began tossing them to me in order. "This morning shall prove to be the defining moment for the men of this monastery. I fear we are going to tremble it down to its foundations." He pursed his lips and came out from behind the table. "It is an unenviable task that lies before us, but one that must not be avoided. If you had slumbered without recourse last night I should have to wonder at the state of your heart."

"Yes . . ." was all I could muster in response as the awareness that he had actually suffered the same sort of night as me began to penetrate my murky brain. He was, I now realized, operating solely under the force of his determination to see this case brought to its inexorable conclusion. And it was providing him with a drive that I had to admire. "Have you solved this murder then?"

"Solved it?" He tilted his head slightly before taking the few steps to the door. "Let us just say that I know enough to be nettlesome and I suspect enough to be lethal."

"Are you going to tell me?"

"Indeed." He nodded as a smile ghosted across his lips. "Just as soon as we have gathered together the fine brothers of this monastery."

I was about to protest, to insist he take me into his confidence, but before I could do so he pulled a small cloth from the waistband of his pants, its corners appearing to have been folded in upon themselves many times over. He handed it to me and I realized at once that it was not a cloth at all but one of his cummerbunds that had been rolled up and pressed flat. "What is this . . . ?" I mumbled as I squeezed the contents, noting their pliability and yet quite unable to discern precisely what was nestled inside.

"What does it feel like?" he asked as a cockeyed grin slowly bloomed onto his face.

I unrolled the cummerbund partway and was immediately struck by the pungent scent that rushed up at me, caustic and harsh. There was no need for me to unwrap it further as I knew at once what it was. "Where . . . ?" I started to say before he interrupted me.

"I need you to secrete that from everyone until I ask you to hand it to me." His eyes crackled with exhilaration and I finally understood the nature of his mood this morning.

"Did you . . . ?" But the rest of my question halted in my throat as Colin reached over and flung the door open.

"Let us be on our way and have this unfortunate business resolved," he muttered, all signs of his earlier grin vanquished from his face.

I carefully folded the cummerbund again and slid it beneath my suspenders at the small of my back so no one would see it until Colin deemed it time. I tugged on the back of my coat to ensure there was no telltale bulge and then hurried after him, my heart thundering heavily, and I only hoped that we were ready for this final joust.

"Father Demetris . . ." I heard Colin call as the priest rounded the corner from the chapel with a bevy of monks at his heels.

"Mr. Pendragon . . ." He glanced behind Colin and gave me a quick smile. "Mr. Pruitt . . . God's blessings on you both this morning."

"And the same to you, Father," Colin replied at once, though the tautness in his voice was unmistakable to me. "Might I trouble you and some of the brothers to join us for a meeting in the refectory? Much progress has been made on the abbot's murder and I should very much like to discuss it with those of you who have been most helpful."

"Of course." Father Demetris managed to summon up something that faintly resembled a smile, but like Colin, there was no joy behind it. "Who do you wish to address?"

Colin stepped forward as the monks filed past on the way to their daily obligations. "Most certainly these good men right here," he said, gesturing toward Brothers Silsbury and Wright, before pointing across the hallway at Brother Bursnell, who was just on the verge of ducking into his library. "And perhaps Brother Clayworth and Brother Green . . . ?" Colin's smile turned warmer when he said the last monk's name, though I was instantly disheartened to hear that he would need that congenial man to take part in this final parley. "Good morning, Brother Hollings . . ." Colin called to the young man, clouting his back as though they were aged comrades, but the gesture only earned him a grimace for his efforts. "You will join us, won't you?" he asked before turning to find Brother Morrison ambling toward us in the young monk's wake. "And, of course, Brother Morrison."

"Of course Brother Morrison what . . . ?" the elderly monk repeated, his visage as unyielding as ever.

"Mr. Pendragon and Mr. Pruitt have asked that a few of us gather in the refectory for a short discussion," Father Demetris answered before Colin could do so.

"I really must get out to the brewery," Brother Clayworth reminded, giving an uncharacteristic scowl. "Those young neophytes don't know what they're doing without me to keep an eye on them."

"I give you my word that I shan't take more time than is absolutely necessary," Colin responded. Still, it was evident Brother Clayworth was not happy about being thusly restrained from his duties, and I wondered if his demeanor was at all attributable to the fact that he had likely not gotten any fire into his belly yet this morning.

"Fine, fine," he mumbled, turning and following Brother Bursnell into the refectory.

"Then I should think we have a quorum," Colin announced grimly as he too pushed through the door.

"A quorum?!" Father Demetris turned to me, the look on his face as confused as it appeared uneasy.

"It's just an expression," I said with the fragment of a shrug, though in truth I had no idea what Colin's intentions were.

The priest and I went inside to find the seven monks assembled around the nearer table with Colin strolling casually across the front of the room, his arms held firmly behind his back. Father Demetris took his place at the head of the table and I sat at the opposite end, closest to the door. It was reminiscent of other cases where I was meant to create a physical barrier with my presence, though I had to remind myself that these were monks, seekers of religious devotion, not common miscreants looking to undermine the cogs of justice. So I forced myself to expel a determined breath as I sat back in my chair and waited for Colin to begin.

But it was Brother Silsbury who finally broke the uneasy silence. "You wished to speak with us?" he said with the thinnest underpinning of annoyance in his tone.

"Yes." Colin finally stopped moving and turned to face the monks as though just realizing that they were all quite suddenly assembled in front of him. "Indeed." A tight grin flashed across his face in an instant, his lips drawn tight and his eyes likewise pinched but noticeably watchful. "I have some questions I should like to pose to the lot of you, and thought this far more expedient than continuing to putter about one at a time."

"Oh, fie," Brother Morrison groused, the heavy lines pocking his face drawing tight with disapproval. "How much longer must we endure this?"

"Perhaps we can end this sorrowful business here and now," Colin shot back, and that got their attention just as he had meant for it to. "So, let me ask you, Brother Morrison, did you ever have occasion to discuss with Abbot Tufton the circumstances of his spiritual crisis?"

"Well, of course I did," the elderly monk huffed. "Most of us did at one time or another. That is the way of it in a monastery. When one of us bleeds we all suffer." He turned quickly and glared down the table to where Brother Hollings was seated. "Except for our youngest members," he corrected, pointing a finger at the ginger-haired young man who seemed quite content to try and go unnoticed. "Why in the Lord's heaven do you even have him here?"

"He found the abbot's body," Colin reminded with unaccountable patience. "There may well be pieces to this case that he still has not yet remembered." Colin smiled gamely at the young man but got no response whatsoever. If Brother Hollings had anything he wished to add to the conversation I knew it would take some doing for Colin to extricate it.

"We shall let Mr. Pendragon do as he sees fit," Father Demetris announced with the authority that had been granted him from Bishop Fencourt. "It is time that we have this done."

Colin gave the priest a slight nod as he moved his gaze to Brother Wright. The slender monk with the jawline beard had his thin brown hair swept back from his forehead and was holding himself with the rigidity of a man who does not suffer tensions well. It was a decidedly unfortunate truth considering there were so many tensions to be suffered.

"Are you feeling well today?" Colin asked.

"Well enough," Brother Wright responded.

"I am sorry for your affliction. I can remember my mother suffering such bouts when I was a boy. Sometimes they would last several days."

"They are a curse," Brother Wright answered stoically, and I could tell that he too did not like to be the center of attention for his monastic brothers.

"Is there anything particular to which you attribute the cause of your sufferings?" Colin pressed.

"Were I able to attribute a cause I would avoid it with my life. I should think that someone who has witnessed such sufferings firsthand might have discerned that answer for himself."

"Quite right," Colin agreed, allowing the wisp of a grin to brush across his lips once again. "I wonder if tension and strife do not play some role in your unease as even now your brow is beginning to bristle with your displeasure." Brother Wright did not respond, but I could see the furrowing of his forehead just as Colin had pointed out. "Has there indeed been particular tension and discord here at Whitmore Abbey of late?"

Brother Wright did not answer at once, his discomfort palpable, choosing instead to look as though he was pondering his answer, his brown eyes brooding and his thin lips pressed firmly. "We are a brotherhood . . ." he began after a minute, ". . . a family. As there is disharmony amongst any family, so it can be found here from time to time. Our devotion to God does not preclude the fact that we are but mortal men."

"So I have been told." Colin's response was quick and dismissive. "But is there anything of note that brings you specific distress?"

"Are you looking for me to admit something?" the monk snapped back, his brow now every bit as pinched as the rest of his face.

"Yes," Colin answered with marked simplicity. "I should like you to admit the truth." He flicked his gaze to Brother Silsbury, whose broad shoulders and powerful torso rose higher than any other monk's with the exception of the soft, round Brother Green. "You provided Brother Wright with the laudanum he required to endure his pain. Did you ever seek to ferret out the foundation of his enfeeblement?"

"I am not a physician," Brother Silsbury reminded in a tone more harsh than seemed necessary.

"I am well aware," Colin allowed with the flash of his own bit of curtness. "Yet the good brother here seems quite coiled, which, as I remember with my own mother's sufferings, is not good. So tell me, Brother Silsbury, is there any *particular* disharmony that picks at the binds of your brotherhood?"

"Really, Mr. Pendragon. You seem determined to find something untoward when no such crisis exists." To his credit, Brother Silsbury actually managed to force a slight snicker though no one else joined him.

"Then why were you so determined to keep me from the abbot's personal papers and Bible?"

"I showed them to you!" he fired back, the offense thick in his voice. "I gave you access to all of them the second time you came to the infirmary."

"And so you did." A gracious smile eased onto Colin's face for just a moment and I knew he was finally stroking the spine of what he had been after all along. "Yet you proscribed time limits and restrictions, and until Father Demetris returned and forced you to do so, you had no intention of letting me study the abbot's most personal papers at length. Instead you gave me some twaddle about needing to review them first yourself, which would defeat the purpose of my looking at them entirely if you chose to redact or omit pages." If Brother Silsbury intended to respond he was not given the chance as Colin quickly turned on Brother Clayworth, whose thin, well-lined face seemed to grow gaunter as Colin singled him out. "What have you to say, Brother Clayworth? You are one of the most senior members of this brotherhood. In fact, your running of the brewery provides the lifeblood from which this monastery runs. I cannot believe that you would be unaware of a powerful dissent amongst your fellow members."

"It was nothing at all as you seek to make it . . ." he blurted out before quickly ceasing and rubbing at his eyes.

"It . . . ?! " Colin seized the word, repeating it slowly, kicking the proverbial door wide that poor Brother Clayworth had inadvertently cracked open.

"Abbot Tufton struggled with doubt after the *Codex Sinaiticus* was found," Brother Clayworth answered, his voice slow and soft, his eyes pinned on his hands resting on the table in front of him. "So many thousands of changes to our Bible. A book we had thought sacrosanct. It was hard for many of us to accept. It is why Abbot Tufton went to Egypt in the first place." Brother Clayworth looked pained, his white hair framing the colorlessness of his face. "I think for myself the most shattering thing to learn was that the last twelve verses in the canon of Mark were not even part of the original text. They were added much later." He shook his head. "It changes so much of what we thought we knew about the Resurrection. . . ." He fell silent.

"I cannot sit for this," Brother Silsbury spoke up into the stillness. "These were private struggles of our abbot's and are most certainly not meant to be bandied about like some sort of fodder. Do you mean to condone this conversation?" He turned an outraged glare onto Father Demetris, who quickly averted his eyes, gesturing for Colin to continue nevertheless.

"Did you discuss your abbot's doubts with him?" Colin looked back at Brother Clayworth.

"Of course. As Brother Morrison has already told you, I am certain most of us here did." He nodded but still did not remove his gaze from his folded hands. "I reminded him of Proverbs 3:5—'*Trust in the Lord with all thine heart . . .*' "

" '. . . *and lean not unto thine own understanding,*' " Colin finished for him with a slight nod. "And it is my belief that your abbot very much wanted to follow that advice as that particular proverb was included in the last communication Abbot Tufton had with the bishop."

"Through God's grace I know Abbot Tufton had been healing spiritually," Brother Clayworth said, glancing around at his assembled brothers as though looking for agreement, of which I saw none. "And then those two women released those accursed photographs of the four excised gospels they had just found in that same blasted abbey in Egypt. . . ."

"The Smith sisters," Colin supplied. "Which appears to have reignited your abbot's questions . . . and doubts . . ."

"There are no *doubts* for a man of true faith," Brother Morrison rumbled into the conversation, his craggy face matching the finality with which he spoke. "If believing were easy, there would be no need for men like us."

"Are you suggesting your abbot was not a man of true faith?" Colin asked. But he got no further reply, and after a moment his lack of doing so began to invoke the response he seemed unwilling to give.

Obviously content with the inference of the protracted silence, Colin turned his attention toward Brother Bursnell. Even with his pleasing features and dark blond hair, he suddenly looked every bit as gaunt and strained as the rest of his colleagues. I wondered at the change in him since our first meeting in the library, but could do nothing to explain his evident hindrance to our investigation beyond the growing feeling that he was somehow involved in the abbot's murder. And if not, then he surely knew who was.

"I know you have had no success in learning the whereabouts of your abbot's Egyptian journals," Colin said with resignation. "It is a pity as they would seem the most likely place where he would have detailed his misgivings."

"It is not for lack of effort," came Brother Bursnell's cautious reply.

"Is that so?" Colin tipped his head to one side as though considering the younger monk's words with some measure of skepticism, as I well knew he was. "Because I was able to find them in only the second place I looked," he announced as he flicked his eyes to me and gave a single nod, the assembled monks instantly beginning to rustle and glance about at one another.

None of the men spoke as I stood up and reached beneath my coat, extracting the rolled cummerbund from its hiding place beneath my suspenders at the crux of my back. Colin had already reached me by the time I held the small package in my hands, so I turned it over to him and quickly retook my seat. As Colin made his way back to the front of the room I became aware of the lingering stares of Brother Clayworth and Brother Bursnell watching me. It felt almost as though I had betrayed them in some fashion, and I wondered at the depths of dissension within this group of men.

"This is what remains of your abbot's Egyptian journals," Colin was saying as he freed the small, blackened books from within the cummerbund. "I found them last night in the incinerator behind the infirmary. It would seem someone had a mind to destroy them," he added unnecessarily, the two books heavily charred with only small amounts of writing legible on the innermost pages. "And yet it is enough. Enough to see tortured musings about the many manuscripts found in Saint Catherine's Monastery, most especially the *Codex Sinaiticus.* He also makes mention of the non-biblical testaments brought back from the White Monastery in Egypt. Though they remain unrecognized by the church, they still clearly left him with needling doubts.

"All of it bore out the proof of Man's hand everywhere amongst the words that were said to belong to God. The thousands of changes, excisions, errors, and discrepancies that threatened the very foundation upon which you and your abbot have dedicated your lives. The abbot's writings make plain his torment not only for himself, but for all of you as well." He set the savaged books onto the table in front of Father Demetris and cast his eyes to Brother Bursnell again. "You did not look for these journals because you already knew they had been cast to the flames."

Brother Bursnell looked stricken, and though I had always thought him a handsome man I could see no traces of it now. "I did not know any such thing. They had been borrowed from the library and I had no reason to believe they would not come back in due course."

"Such a banal answer," Colin sniffed as he moved down to where Brother Hollings was sitting. The young man looked almost as if he was sleeping, his head bowed forward and his eyes clamped shut, with his straight ginger hair dangling about his face like a veil. But as I continued to stare at him I noticed that his lips were moving rapidly. At first I thought perhaps he was whispering something to Brother Green, who was seated beside him, but I quickly realized that he was, in fact, reciting a prayer.

"I am sorry that you have been drawn into all of this," Colin said as he reached the young monk, dropping a hand on his shoulder and causing him to jump slightly and instantly draw his head up, abruptly ending his prayer. As we all watched, Colin leaned forward and brought his lips nearly to Brother Hollings's ear. "May I ask you to do something for me that I know you will find distressing?" he asked barely above a whisper.

The poor lad blinked repeatedly and I felt unaccountably sorry for him. He looked pitiable as he sat there, not daring to glance up at Colin but rather holding his gaze on the tabletop in front of him as though his very existence depended on his doing so. "What . . . ?" And it was only because I could see his lips that I knew what he had said.

Colin's expression remained flat and unreadable, his voice steady. "Will you please lower your cassock to your waist? You needn't stand up."

Brother Hollings did not move and I was fairly certain that he must have ceased to breathe as well. Why Colin would ask such a thing of a young man we both knew to be inordinately shy I could not understand.

"What is he saying? What is the meaning of this?" Brother Morrison blasted from the far side of the table before turning to glare at Father Demetris. "I insist you put a stop to this nonsense immediately."

"This is the first step to setting your spirit free." Colin continued to coax Brother Hollings, as though Brother Morrison had not even spoken a word. "It is the only thing I shall require of you."

I was certain Brother Hollings would never consent to doing what Colin was asking, but to my amazement the young man quite suddenly reached up and, with quivering hands, undid his collar. It took less than a breath before he was lowering the top of the garment, and at first I could not understand what was being revealed beneath. Still, neither I nor any of the other monks averted our eyes and, in a minute, I saw that Brother Hollings was wearing a mid-sleeve, tight black undergarment woven of animal hair. A hair shirt. And in that moment I understood.

"Oh Christ." Brother Morrison pushed himself back from the table as though the garment itself might sully him in some way. "You bloody ass. You have the conviction of a toad. You are a disgrace to this abbey."

"Wait a minute . . ." Brother Silsbury interrupted, his eyes moving between Brother Morrison and Brother Hollings. "I don't understand. Where did you get that, Brother Hollings? Whoever told you to wear such a thing?"

It took only an instant for the young man's eyes to shift to Brother Morrison.

"*John Tufton was a goddamn heretic!*" the elderly monk roared, his face turning crimson with his fury. "There are *no* doubts for a man of true faith," he spat his earlier conviction again. "He would have polluted this entire brotherhood with his sacrilege. Brother Hollings did the Lord's work by removing that demon's tongue and throwing it to the Hell fires."

"Brother Hollings?!" Brother Silsbury lurched in his seat, turning to stare at the young man. "Oh, Rupert . . . no . . ."

"Brother Morrison said I was called to it," he answered in a single breath, stabbing his hands to his face and beginning to weep. "He said I must do whatever the Lord needed me to . . ." His voice was so rough with tears it was nearly impossible to hear what he was saying.

" '*If a man has a stubborn and rebellious son who will not obey the voice of his father,*' " Brother Morrison howled as he heaved himself to his feet, " '*then all the men of the city shall stone him to death with stones; so you shall purge the evil from your midst!*' Do any of you even recognize the word of God anymore?!"

"You have perverted His intent." Brother Silsbury rose to his feet, his cheeks flush and his face as pale as milk. "You have dishonored us all and ruptured the soul of this poor boy."

Brother Hollings cried out through his fingers and slid from the bench to the floor, his face slick with tears as a clutch of hysteria gripped him. I thought to go to him, to try and console him in some way, but what did I understand of the depths of his belief or the surety of his faith that had propelled him to follow the distorted convictions of his elder monk? So I was profoundly relieved when I watched large, ponderous Brother Green awkwardly lower himself to the floor and wrap his arms around the young man.

"God has forsaken the bloody lot of you," Brother Morrison was growling as he straightened his cassock, staring down at the quivering form of Brother Hollings with obvious distaste. "*The bloody lot of you!*" he repeated. And then he turned and began to move toward the exit as though what he had said should be enough.

"You incited a horrible, brutal murder." Colin spoke quietly as he stepped in front of the man.

"I have severed the head of the asp and left the tail to Hell," he spat.

"Brother Morrison . . . Robert . . ." Brother Clayworth stood up, his pallor gray and his eyes as flat as death. "You have lost your way, but God does not forsake you. . . ."

The elder monk spun on him with surprising deftness. "Do not presume to judge me," he sneered. "I am a soldier of the Lord. How could you understand that, you besotted wretch? How could any of you understand?"

He turned again and ambled from the room, and this time Colin did not try to stop him. We all remained as we were, the frantic sounds of Brother Hollings's wails smothered in the black fabric of Brother Green's cassock, the look on the older monk's face a mask of anguish and shock. Even so, he held on to the broken young man and I admired Brother Green's extraordinary devotion and strength.

"Were we in London I would summon the Yard," Colin said after a minute had passed, a decided lack of conviction in his voice. "I must confess to being at a loss here. . . ."

"They are the church's burden," Father Demetris answered at

once. "I will contact Bishop Fencourt. He will want to consult with the Apostolic Palace. The Holy See will guide us now. And they will warrant the salvation of our poor Brother Hollings."

Colin looked pained as he stared out at the tortured faces of the men gazing back at him—all but Brother Hollings. The young monk continued to weep in the consuming arms of Brother Green, who was still rocking him gently from their position on the floor.

Colin let a burdened sigh escape his lips before he began to speak, his voice sounding hesitant, with an unaccustomed hitch to it. "Should I agree to allow you to do as you say, you cannot permit Brother Morrison to leave his cell and"—he cleared his throat awkwardly, his eyes flicking about the room—"there is always the possibility he might try to harm himself . . . or Brother Hollings here . . ."

"I will stay with Brother Hollings as though he were a part of my own body." Brother Green spoke up at once. "We will remain together until the Holy Father's wishes are known, and then I will remain with him even so if he needs me to."

"And I will make certain that Brother Morrison remains in his cell until we receive word," Brother Silsbury consented, his gaze wearied. "He will not harm himself. To do so would be a sin against God."

Colin looked as though he were about to state the obvious before he seemed to think better of it, thankfully snapping his mouth shut and settling for a simple nod of his head.

"I shall watch over our poor Brother Morrison as well," Brother Clayworth put in. "It is the least I can offer to him now."

"As will I," Brother Wright added. "I know we will all be unified in our support and prayers for both of our brothers. We would have learned nothing if we could not offer one another solace at such a time as this."

"Then I shall not interfere," Colin said. "Mr. Pruitt and I will be gone by midday."

And so we were.

# CHAPTER 30

There is quite simply nothing like being at home and sleeping in one's own bed. And I felt that truth ever more so given that I had also been sleeping alone for the past several nights. While I cannot recall precisely when I became fully enamored with sharing a bed, I will admit that it suits me now, making a night on my own feel foreign and discomfiting. Not to mention that I had just been trying to slumber at the scene of a murder.

So it was a pleasure to open my eyes and stare into Colin's sleeping face not a handful of inches away from me, his right arm tucked under my neck and the other strewn across my side. In the next instant, however, I had the sudden realization that my neck was throbbing all along the length of where his arm was stashed beneath it, and that I could not feel my left leg whatsoever. "Colin . . ." I mumbled, the word coming out dry and cracked, alerting me to the fact that I had likely been sleeping with my mouth agape for the better part of the night. I dragged my right hand up to my chin to check whether a thread of drool might be crusting there and found that it was. What a sight I would be. "Colin . . ." I said again with far greater determination, and this time his brilliant blue eyes sprang open.

He started to smile at me before his face abruptly screwed up in a display of evident pain. "My arm . . ." he gasped, ". . . it feels like someone's stuck a thousand blasted needles into it."

"I can't feel my left leg at all."

We began to delicately extricate our jumble of limbs, nerve endings throughout both of our bodies screaming their wretched torment, when the sound of approaching footsteps caught my attention. "Mrs. Behmoth is coming," I yawned.

"Well, thankfully, unlike the chambermaid at the Pig and Pint, she isn't about to come barging in here," he said as he began to massage his sleeping arm, releasing a hiss of pain as he did so.

And, of course, I knew he was right. Even when our bedroom door quite suddenly burst open I still believed he was correct. And so he was. For it was not Mrs. Behmoth who stood in our doorway but Colin's father, Sir Atherton Rentcliff Pendragon.

"How can the two of you be lying about like a pair of jackanapes when you have wrought such havoc upon that poor monastery in Dalwich?" he demanded as he came ambling into the room and lowered himself onto the foot of our bed. All I could think was how grateful I was that he had not arrived one minute earlier. "What a sorrowful affair," he muttered, his eyes heavy with weariness as he ran a quick hand through his thick, steel-gray hair. "Nevertheless, Bishop Fencourt has already had a letter delivered to me this morning with his personal thanks to the two of you, however aggrieved the results of your investigation did prove to be." He shook his head and gazed back out toward the hallway, his thoughts clearly very far away.

"Umm . . . might I ask for a favor . . . ?" Colin spoke gently to his father, clutching the covers up around his throat. "Why don't you go back out to the sitting room and we'll join you there in a minute. Have Mrs. Behmoth bring up some tea if she hasn't done so already."

"It's already 'ere," she hollered from the front room. "But I sure as 'ell ain't bringin' it in there."

"What?!" Sir Atherton blinked and looked around the bedroom, seeming to spot the two of us in earnest for the first time. "Oh my . . ." He stood up from the bed and brushed at himself in a gesture that looked at once as embarrassed as it was apologetic. "Yes, yes . . ." he muttered as his eyes darted around the ceiling until he had backed all the way to the door. "I'll just wait out there," he said as though the thought had been entirely his own. "You boys take your time." And with that he dashed out and swung the door shut.

"God help me . . ." Colin mumbled as he threw the covers back and scampered across the room to grab our underclothes. "Almost fourteen years together and we get intruded upon twice in one week." He tossed my things to me. "I hope that never happens again as I long as I live."

We both dressed with all due haste, though Colin accomplished the feat far faster than I, sending him out the door first. "I shall get your tea ready," he called back over his shoulder before disappearing down the hall.

I did my best to move quickly but still took several minutes before I had adequately splashed the slumber from my brain and pulled myself together with sufficient care. By the time I got out to the study, Colin and his father were sipping their tea and idly chatting. As I entered the room I took note of the fact that while I was appropriately ready for the day, Colin looked rakishly disheveled with his shirt collar open and his tie lying impotently untethered. I crossed the room and gladly accepted the cup of tea that Colin held out to me. It tasted as comforting as being home felt. I dropped onto the settee next to Colin since his father always preferred to sit in Colin's chair, and returned the warm smile Sir Atherton was sending my direction.

"I trust you will forgive my frightful manners this morning," he said to me, as though he really needed to ask. "I must admit my mind was very much elsewhere. . . ."

"It's no matter," I answered, eager to be through with this line of conversation. "You mentioned a letter from the bishop . . . ?"

"Yes, yes. Very grateful for your work and the way you handled yourselves." He leaned forward and patted Colin's knee. "You see? You can be quite the charmer when you choose to be. You get that from me."

"It was a difficult case," Colin said over the rim of his teacup, "that was made harder by the fact that it happened in a monastery." He lowered his cup and stared at his father, one of his eyebrows stretched toward the ceiling. "A monastery . . . !" he repeated, ". . . filled with *monks!*"

His father stared back at Colin, his face a vision of absolute serenity. "Yes," he said after a moment, "I should think you'll find all monasteries are filled with monks."

"You aren't funny."

"I wasn't trying to be."

Colin leaned forward. "I don't think your bishop friend would be as amused if he knew the way Ethan and I live."

"What does that have to do with anything?" Sir Atherton looked from Colin to me, but I had nothing to offer.

"Are we not a disgrace?" Colin pressed. "A heretical blunder against his spiritual convictions?"

His father pinched his face and waved him off. "God does not blunder, boy. Now, stop being so disagreeable." He leaned forward and tossed a lump of sugar into Colin's teacup. "Now, then, the bishop specifically asked me to convey to you his gratitude for allowing the church to handle the outcome of the case in their own way. You see . . . ?!" He reached forward and slapped Colin's closest knee. "You've both done a fine thing." He beamed as he sat back in his chair. "So, tell me what happened. The bishop tells me you've left the monastery all at ends now."

Colin heaved a sigh. "I suppose we have at that," he agreed before beginning to recount the events that had transpired to his father, the fire in his eyes slowly stoking the deeper he got into the story. I did note, however, that he omitted the part about our humiliating eviction from the Pig and Pint. It reminded me once again that in spite of his bluster and assurance, Colin was really not so different from me at his core.

"After I found what was left of the abbot's Egyptian journals," he was explaining to his father, "I knew without a doubt that I had landed upon the reason for the abbot's murder. Then it became a simple matter of discerning which of the monks was most likely to have been so unforgivably aggrieved by their abbot's doubts and struggle."

His father shook his head with amazement. "An utter travesty . . ."

"It was the hair shirt that I'd glimpsed Brother Hollings wearing in the balneary one morning that first caught my eye. And when Father Demetris adamantly assured me that the church no longer condones mortification I knew something was terribly amiss with the young monk. Even so, he did not strike me as the type of person who would take matters into his own hands."

"But when did you come to realize the involvement of the elder monk?" his father pressed.

Colin gave a slight shrug as he sipped at his tea. "The young man attended to Father Morrison and followed him around like a lap dog. He seemed the most likely suspect to me, especially given his obvious rigidity around their way of life at the monastery." He took another quick swallow of tea before adding, "I think it rather a stroke of ingenuity for Brother Morrison to have made his little underling address the murder scene once they had removed the body. It kept anyone else from stumbling upon anything that might have piqued their suspicions. If that place were not so bloody awkward, I would have solved the case sooner."

Sir Atherton looked about to say something, but an abrupt pounding at our door downstairs halted his words.

"I thought I heard a carriage pulling up," Colin said as he burst off the settee and hurried to the window. "Ah! It would seem that the good Acting Inspector Maurice Evans has come to welcome us home." His eyes were ablaze with exhilaration as he turned back to his father and me. "No doubt he has come to fawn over you," he said to his father, "for your remarkable diplomatic success with the Swiss."

"Oh, don't let him make a fuss," Sir Atherton muttered with a discomfited shrug. "I didn't do it for him. . . ."

"It's yer Yarder bloke," Mrs. Behmoth hollered up the stairs. "But then ya already know that, 'cause I 'eard ya runnin' cross the room ta look out the bleedin' winda," she bothered to add as the sound of Maurice Evans making his way up the stairs accompanied her shouts. His unruly mop of dark brown hair bobbed into view just as she finished.

"Gentlemen! . . ." Mr. Evans called out cheerily as soon as he reached the landing. "Oh!" He stopped in the doorway the moment he spied Colin's father standing up. "Sir Atherton . . ." He flinched. "I hope I'm not interrupting anything."

"Not at all." Colin strode over to him and quickly drew him the rest of the way into the room. "Your timing is impeccable. I was just thinking about that wretched Charlotte Hutton. Now that we're back I should very much like to see what you have discovered. . . ."

"It's not what *we've* discovered," he hastily corrected as his hands fiddled nervously with the rim of his bowler. "It's Sir Atherton here we have to be grateful to."

"Now, now," Colin demurred as he led the acting inspector to a chair, "you mustn't flatter him or he'll be impossible to get back out the door."

Poor Maurice Evans looked quite mortified until Sir Atherton snickered, and shot back at Colin, "You're looking at your own future, boy." And then turned back to Mr. Evans, and added, "You're being far too generous. I've simply been around forever, which means that I know everyone. Sometimes it can prove useful."

"What you have done . . ." Mr. Evans said as though he were addressing Victoria herself, ". . . is given us a very good chance at flushing Mrs. Hutton out of hiding. I have even gotten the Assistant Commissioner to agree to fund a trip for your son and Mr. Pruitt to go to Zurich and see what will come of this freeze to her accounts. It could prove to be the fulcrum that changes the entire bearing of this case."

"*Extraordinary!*" Colin grinned.

"And it's all because of you, Sir Atherton," Mr. Evans pronounced with such overt gratitude that it made his face flush pink.

Sir Atherton allowed a slight smile to tickle one corner of his mouth as he gave me a quick wink. "If you say so. But I must be off now. I simply cannot stomach such treacly blandishments this early in the day." He started for the door, grabbing Colin's arm as he moved past. "You've made me proud," he said as the two of them headed for the landing. "You have *both* made me proud," he called back to me as they headed downstairs.

"Can I pour you some tea, Inspector Evans?" I asked as we both sat down again, me happily moving to my usual chair.

"Acting Inspector . . ." he corrected me.

"Yes, yes," I muttered glibly. "But I should think you won't mind if we hope they make it permanent. Has there been any word on the matter yet?"

He shook his head, his disappointment evident all across his face.

"Well, you mustn't lose faith."

Colin came sprinting back up the stairs even before I heard the door click shut below our feet. "Let us not discuss faith so soon after returning from that monastery," he quipped.

"I was just asking when the Yard plans to make Acting Inspector Evans's promotion permanent. It is such a mouthful."

Colin snatched up his teacup as he sauntered back over to the window. "I would happily put in a good word for you, but I'm not at all certain that might not do more harm than help."

"Not if you agree to work with us in Zurich. Losing Mrs. Hutton has been another black eye for the Yard. . . ."

But he didn't get to finish his thought as yet another sudden pounding on our door interrupted the morning.

"Aren't we just the bustling hive today?" Colin said as he peeked through the curtains onto the street below. And when he turned back to us I could see that he was eminently pleased.

"Who is it?" I asked.

"It would seem to be a servant, who has arrived in the carriage of the Endicott family."

"Lord Endicott?!" I repeated with the same sort of ludicrous awe I had just seen Mr. Evans use with Sir Atherton.

"More likely one of his spinster sisters," Colin answered as I heard Mrs. Behmoth pull the door open.

"There has been some bad business out at their house. I had

better let you be." Mr. Evans popped out of his seat and headed for the stairs.

"We shall come and see you later today," Colin promised, following him as far as the landing. "*Hello!*" Colin called downstairs. "Do send that chap up, Mrs. Behmoth."

"Thanks," she shot back. "I was wonderin' wot I was gonna do with 'im."

Maurice Evans chuckled as he started down the stairs, only to be replaced almost at once by a black-haired man with a broad, open face, high cheekbones, and a close-cropped beard and moustache who looked to be no more than thirty. He was a handsome man save for the look that was, even now, haunting his dark brown eyes.

"Colin Pendragon at your service." Colin shook the man's hand and led him into the room. "And this is my associate, Mr. Pruitt."

I stood up to greet the man and found myself staring directly into his eyes. Unlike me, however, this man was broadly built and well-muscled, attesting to the fact that he obviously did some sort of physical labor. He gave me a curt, tight-lipped smile as he shook my hand, displaying neither a hint of pleasure nor conviviality to it. The man's obsidian eyes did nothing more than rake my face in the most rudimentary way.

Colin settled our guest onto the settee while I poured him a fresh cup of tea, but he appeared decidedly uninterested in any of our niceties. It was only after I was able to steal a keener look at him that I realized his complexion was sallow and his eyes ringed with fatigue. He looked to be suffering from some notable strain or unease, and I suspected he had not slept properly for several days.

"What brings you to see us so early this day?" Colin asked with his usual enthusiasm whenever a potential client first presented themselves.

The man seemed startled by Colin's question and blinked several times before he answered. "I apologize if I have arrived at an improper time . . ." he started to say.

"Time is not improper," Colin explained blithely as he poured himself some more tea, "it is the things we humans do with it that constitutes its waste or relevance." The man's face remained somber and unyielding. If he found any solace in Colin's contrived assertion he did not show it. "Right," Colin muttered after a moment. "You were saying . . . ?"

The young man blinked again, casting a glance between Colin and me as though trying to remember exactly *what* he had been saying, before finally clearing his throat and beginning. "I have come from Layton Manor. I work for the Endicott sisters, Miss Adelaide and Miss Eugenia." He shifted on the settee with evident discomfort before drawing a quick hand across his forehead, though he was not perspiring in the least. "My name is Freddie Nettle. I assist with Miss Adelaide's care. She is infirm and has been so for the better part of a year now. I attend to her every need except those most private, which are taken care of by several nurses who rotate their shifts. But I am *always* there. I even sleep in the antechamber to her bedroom should she require my aid during the night. She relies on me and I have never let her down. . . ."

Colin flashed a brief smile as Mr. Nettle let his voice drift off into silence. "Well . . ." he spoke up when Mr. Nettle's stillness began to stretch oddly long, "Miss Endicott must be a very fortunate woman to have so devoted a man at her behest. I believe she is quite aged, is she not?"

He nodded, the first suggestion of engagement apparent behind his eyes since his arrival. "Just past her eighty-third year. But that is where it ends . . ." he continued, once again allowing his voice to simply trail off.

Colin set his teacup onto the side table between us and leaned forward, his eyebrows knitting with unmistakable curiosity. "Where *what* ends?"

Mr. Nettle dropped his gaze and wiped a hand across his forehead again, and this time I could see a glistening of film just along his hairline. "Three nights ago Miss Adelaide was unusually agitated, so Miss Eugenia had me take her up to bed early. I carried her up the three flights of stairs to her room, same as I do every night, and settled her in without issue. She kept making little mewling noises, but sometimes Miss Adelaide would do that. She did not otherwise speak very much anymore," he added with a shake of his head. "But I could always tell what she wanted. After more than a year with her . . ." He ticked off the slimmest shrug before falling silent again.

"Three nights ago . . . ?" Colin prodded with a conspicuous lack of patience.

"Yes . . ." He nodded, running the same hand across his forehead. "Once I had her settled in for the night I retired myself. I always stay to her schedule so that I'm available whenever she needs me. I wouldn't serve much purpose otherwise." He sucked in a breath and I could see what a labor this story was for him. "That night . . ." He halted again and this time his hand went up to his brow and stayed there, rubbing it for a moment in what I felt certain was an attempt to dislodge whatever memory was slinking about his mind. "It was late. The house was quiet. I know I had dozed off because I was awoken by the sound of Miss Adelaide screaming. She sounded loud and shrill and horrified. It wasn't like confusion or alarm, I tell you it was the sound of terror! I leapt up and ran into her room so quickly that I didn't even stop to grab a proper robe." Because his hand remained across his brow I did not immediately realize that he had begun to weep.

"Take your time, Mr. Nettle," I said.

He pulled a handkerchief from a vest pocket and hastily wiped at his eyes before continuing. "I found her standing by the window. *Standing!*" he repeated as though that should have some significance for us. "And it was the window all the way across the room from her bed."

"Could she not walk?" Colin asked.

"Not since I began working for her. That's why I was brought in. It was my duty to either push her in a wheeled chair or carry her, whichever she preferred. I had never known her to stand or walk on her own and yet, there she was," he muttered with dismay, clearly still unable to fathom the sight of it himself. "She was wearing such a look of fright. As if the devil himself had crept into her room." He closed his eyes and rubbed at them again, but I knew this was a vision he would not soon dispel. "I called to her . . . I wanted to rush across the room for fear she might lose her balance and hurt herself, but found I could not move. And then . . . and then . . ." his voice caught pitifully, ". . . she turned from me and cast herself from the window." As soon as the words left his lips he shrank into himself and wept, covering his face with his hands as if to keep us from seeing his humiliation.

"We are so sorry for your pain," I said at once.

"I must confess," Colin glanced over at me, "I had not heard that Miss Adelaide had died. Did you . . . ?" he added under his breath to me.

I scowled at him and gave him a quick shake of my head.

"Yes, of course . . ." Colin sniffed as he turned back to Mr. Nettle. "We are both very sorry for what you have endured, and yet I'm not at all sure what it is you are seeking from us?"

Mr. Nettle blew his nose and stuffed his handkerchief back into his pocket, finally looking back at the two of us, his eyes red and swollen with the tracks of his grief. "It's Miss Eugenia," he finally admitted. "She does not believe the story I have just told you. She has decided me guilty of murdering her sister and has already been to Scotland Yard to demand my arrest. But I have done nothing. Nothing at all. It has happened just as I have told you. Every word of it. And yet I will be condemned to spend the rest of my life in jail if you do not help me, Mr. Pendragon. They will listen to you. *Please.*"

Colin said nothing for a minute before turning to look at me, one eyebrow cocked toward the ceiling. "I have met Miss Adelaide many times over the years. And Miss Eugenia for that matter. Two very different sorts of women, though there is little question as to the reason for their shared spinsterhood." He turned back to Mr. Nettle as I cringed at his statement. "We shall come out to Layton this afternoon and speak with Miss Eugenia. And then"—he gave a brief smile—"we shall see."

But I was not fooled by Colin's ambivalence. I knew he would accept this case as surely as I knew that I believed Freddie Nettle and his unlikely tale.

# ACKNOWLEDGMENTS

The discoveries of Constantin von Tischendorf and Agnes and Margaret Smith are all true, as are the *Codex Sinaiticus* and *Codex Syriacus*. Each was responsible for an avalanche of controversy when initially discovered and I find them no less compelling today. Much has been written about these religious scholars and their provocative discoveries, and a search in your local library or a few moments online will reveal a host of material. None of it should startle or frighten as faith is as solid as the heart that carries it.

I owe much thanks to the folks at Kensington Publishing for their tireless efforts and support. In particular I must once again call out Kris Mills for another eye-catching cover and Paula Reedy and her team for keeping me honest. It is John Scognamiglio to whom I owe the deepest thanks, however. He keeps me on point and pushes me to try harder, dig deeper, and I cannot thank him enough for that—and for deciding to take a chance on me nearly four years ago now. I hope I have made him proud.

I must thank, as always, Diane, Karen, and Melissa, who generously read early drafts and give me notes—sometimes harsh but always helpful—for without their three very unique perspectives, I would never have a draft for John.

My thanks to Kathy Green for seeing something early on that made her want to work with me. I would still be shouting into the wind were it not for her.

My parents and family have supported me beyond my imaginings. I am humbled.

My dear friends, how fortunate am I to be loved and encouraged by such special people. And to every reader who has picked up one or more of these books and enjoyed it—I thank you for spending some time with me. These are just words on a page until you bring your imagination and curiosity to bear upon them. I thank you for that.